NOVELTIES & SOUVENIRS

collected short fiction

■ ■ ■

JOHN CROWLEY

Perennial

An Imprint of HarperCollins*Publishers*

FIRST EDITION

Designed by Elias Haslanger

Library of Congress Cataloging-in-Publication Data
Crowley, John.
   Novelties & souvenirs : collected short fiction / John Crowley.— 1st ed.
    p. cm.
   ISBN 0-380-73106-1 (trade pbk.)
   I. Title.

  PS3553.R597N58 2004
  813'.54—dc22

2003066350

04 05 06 07 08 ❖/RRD 10 9 8 7 6 5 4 3 2 1

Praise for the Work of John Crowley

The Translator

"Thrilling. . . . [Crowley] succeeds with what no prudent novel ought to attempt." —*New York Times*

Dæmonomania

"Haunting . . . gripping . . . astonishing." —*Washington Post Book World*

Love & Sleep

"A master of language, plot, and characterization, Crowley triumphs in this occult and hermetic tale, at once naturalistically persuasive and uncannily visionary." —Harold Bloom

Ægypt

"*Ægypt* is a must; it is a land of questions, more questions, and mysteries, because crafting mysteries is what John Crowley, an original moralist of the same giddy heights occupied by the likes of Thomas Mann and Robertson Davies, does best." —*San Francisco Chronicle*

Little, Big

"The kind of book around which cults are formed, and rightly so. There's magic here." —*Los Angeles Herald Examiner*

The Deep

"Crowley writes with style and wit, creates characters that live and breathe." —*New York Newsday*

Beasts

"Haunting, thought-provoking . . . extraordinarily touching." —*Booklist*

Engine Summer

"A strikingly original and involving book . . . with uncommon sensitivity and grace." —*Washington Post Book World*

Jerry Bauer

About the Author

JOHN CROWLEY lives in the hills above the Connecticut River in northern Massachusetts with his wife and twin daughters. He is the author of *Dæmonomania; Love & Sleep; Ægypt; Little, Big;* and, most recently, *The Translator*.

Also by John Crowley

CONTENTS

◻

AUTHOR'S NOTE

■

The stories in this volume were written over the course of twenty-five years, out of varied impulses, and intended for differing venues. After considering possible arrangements, I have decided to present them here in the order of their first publication, which in most, but not all, cases is the order in which they were composed.

NOVELTIES & SOUVENIRS

Antiquities

□ □ □

"THERE WAS, OF COURSE," Sir Geoffrey said, "the Inconstancy Plague in Cheshire. Short-lived, but a phenomenon I don't think we can quite discount."

It was quite late at the Travellers' Club, and Sir Geoffrey and I had been discussing (as we seemed often to do in those years of the Empire's greatest, yet somehow most tenuous, extent) some anomalous irruptions of the foreign and the odd into the home island's quiet life—small, unlooked-for effects which those centuries of adventure and acquisition had had on an essentially stay-at-home race. At least that was my thought. I was quite young.

"It's no good your saying 'of course' in that offhand tone," I said, attempting to catch the eye of Barnett, whom I felt as much as saw passing through the crepuscular haze of the smoking room. "I've no idea what the Inconstancy Plague was."

From within his evening dress Sir Geoffrey drew out a cigar case, which faintly resembled a row of cigars, as a mummy case resembles the human form within. He offered me one, and we lit them without haste; Sir Geoffrey started a small vortex in his brandy glass. I understood that these rituals were introductory—that, in other words, I would have my tale.

"It was in the later eighties," Sir Geoffrey said. "I can't remember now how I first came to hear of it, though I shouldn't be surprised if it was some flippant note in *Punch*. I paid no attention at first; the 'popular delusions and madness of crowds' sort of thing. I'd returned not long before from Ceylon, and was utterly, blankly oppressed by the weather. It was just starting autumn when I came ashore, and I spent the next four months more or less behind closed doors. The rain! The fog! How could I have forgotten? And the oddest thing was that no one else seemed to pay the slightest attention. My man used to draw the drapes every morning and say in the most cheerful voice, 'Another dismal wet one, eh, sir?' and I would positively turn my face to the wall."

He seemed to sense that he had been diverted by personal memories, and drew on his cigar as though it were the font of recall.

"What brought it to notice was a seemingly ordinary murder case. A farmer's wife in Winsford, married some decades, came one night into the Sheaf of Wheat, a public house, where her husband was lingering over a pint. From under her skirts she drew an old fowling piece. She made a remark which was later reported quite variously by the onlookers, and gave him both barrels. One misfired, but the other was quite sufficient. We learn that the husband, on seeing this about to happen, seemed to show neither surprise nor anguish, merely looking up and—well, awaiting his fate.

"At the inquest, the witnesses reported the murderess to have said, before she fired, 'I'm doing this in the name of all the others.' Or perhaps it was 'I'm doing this, Sam [his name], to save the others.' Or possibly, 'I've got to do this, Sam, to save you from that other.' The woman seemed to have gone quite mad. She gave the investigators an elaborate and horrifying story which they, unfortunately, didn't take down, being able to make no sense of it. The rational gist of it was that she had shot her husband for flagrant infidelities which she could bear no longer. When the magistrate asked witnesses if they knew of such infidelities—these things, in a small community, being notoriously difficult to hide—the men, as a body, claimed that they did not. After the trial, however, the women had dark and unspecific hints to make, how they could say much if they would, and so on. The murderess was adjudged unfit to stand trial, and hanged herself in Bedlam not long after.

"I don't know how familiar you are with that oppressive part of the world. In those years farming was a difficult enterprise at best, isolating, stultifyingly boring, unremunerative. Hired men were heavy drinkers. Prices were depressed. The women aged quickly, what with continual childbirth added to a load of work at least equal to their menfolk's. What I'm getting at is that it is, or was, a society the least of any conducive to adultery, amours, romance. And yet for some reason it appeared, after this murder pointed it up, so to speak, dramatically, that there was a veritable plague of inconstant husbands in northern Cheshire."

"It's difficult to imagine," I said, "what evidence there could be of such a thing."

"I had occasion to go to the county that autumn, just at the height of it all," Sir Geoffrey went on, caressing an ashtray with the tip of his cigar. "I'd at last got a grip on myself and begun to accept invitations again. A fellow I'd known in Alexandria, a commercial agent who'd done spectacularly well for himself, asked me up for the shooting."

"Odd place to go shooting."

"Odd fellow. Arriviste, to speak frankly. The hospitality was lavish; the house was a red-brick Cheshire faux-Gothic affair, if you know what I mean, and the impression it gave of desolation and melancholy was remarkable. And there was no shooting; poured rain all weekend. One sat about leafing through novels or playing Cairo whist—which is what we called bridge in those days—and staring out the windows. One evening, at a loss for entertainment, our host—Watt was his name, and . . ."

"What was his name?" I asked.

"Exactly. He'd become a student of mesmerism, or hypnotism as he preferred to call it, and suggested we might have a bit of fun probing our dark underminds. We all declined, but Watt was insistent, and at last suborned a hearty local type, old squirearchical family, and—this is important—an inveterate, dirt-under-the-nails farmer. His conversation revolved, chiefly, around turnips."

"Even his dark undermind's?"

"Ah. Here we come to it. This gentleman's wife was present at the gathering as well, and one couldn't help noticing the hangdog air he maintained around her, the shifty eyes, the nervous start he gave when she spoke to him from behind, and also a certain dreaminess, an abstraction, that would fall on him at odd moments."

"Worrying about his turnips, perhaps."

Sir Geoffrey quashed his cigar, rather reproachfully, as though it were my own flippancy. "The point is that this ruddy-faced, absolutely ordinary fellow *was cheating on his wife*. One read it as though it were written on his shirt front. His wife seemed quite as aware of it as any; her face was drawn tight as her reticule. She blanched when he agreed to go under, and tried to lead him away, but Watt insisted he be a sport, and at last she retired with a headache. I don't know what the man was thinking of when he agreed; had a bit too much brandy, I expect. At any rate, the lamps were lowered and the usual apparatus got out, the spinning disc and so on. The squire, to Watt's surprise, went under as though slain. We thought at first he had merely succumbed to the grape, but then Watt began to question him, and he to answer, languidly but clearly, name, age, and so on. I've no doubt Watt intended to have the man stand on his head, or turn his waistcoat back-to-front, or that sort of thing, but before any of that could begin, the man began to speak. To address someone. Someone female. Most extraordinary, the way he was transformed."

Sir Geoffrey, in the proper mood, shows a talent for mimicry and now he seemed to transform himself into the hypnotized squire. His eyes glazed and half-closed, his mouth went slack (though his mustache remained upright), and one hand was raised as though to ward off an importunate spirit.

" 'No,' says he. 'Leave me alone. Close those eyes—those eyes. Why? Why? Dress yourself, oh God . . . ' And here he seemed quite in torment. Watt should of course have awakened the poor fellow immediately, but he was fascinated, as I confess we all were.

" 'Who is it you speak to?' Watt asked.

" 'She,' says the squire. 'The foreign woman. The clawed woman. The cat.'

" 'What is her name?'

" 'Bastet.'

" 'How did she come here?'

"At this question the squire seemed to pause. Then he gave three answers: 'Through the earth. By default. On the *John Deering*.' This last answer astonished Watt, since, as he told me later, the *John Deering* was a cargo ship he had often dealt with, which made a regular Alexandria–Liverpool run.

" 'Where do you see her?' Watt asked.

" 'In the sheaves of wheat.' "

"He meant the pub, I suppose," I put in.

"I think not," Sir Geoffrey said darkly. "He went on about the sheaves of wheat. He grew more animated, though it was more difficult to understand his words. He began to make sounds—well, how shall I put it? His breathing became stertorous, his movements . . ."

"I think I see."

"Well, you can't, quite. Because it was one of the more remarkable things I have ever witnessed. The man was making physical love to someone he described as a cat, or a sheaf of wheat."

"The name he spoke," I said, "is an Egyptian one. A goddess associated with the cat."

"Precisely. It was midway through this ritual that Watt at last found himself, and gave an awakening command. The fellow seemed dazed, and was quite drenched with sweat; his hand shook when he took out his pocket-handkerchief to mop his face. He looked at once guilty and pleased, like—like—"

"The cat who ate the canary."

"You have a talent for simile. He looked around at the company, and asked shyly if he had embarrassed himself. I tell you, dear boy, we were hard-pressed to reassure him."

Unsummoned, Barnett materialized beside us with the air of one about to speak tragic and ineluctable prophecies. It is his usual face. He said only that it had begun to rain. I asked for a whiskey and soda. Sir Geoffrey seemed lost in thought during these transactions, and when he spoke again it was to muse: "Odd, isn't it," he said, "how naturally one thinks of cats as female, though we know quite well that they are distributed between two sexes. As far as I know, it is the same the world over. Whenever, for instance, a cat in a tale is transformed into a human, it is invariably a woman."

"The eyes," I said. "The movements—that certain sinuosity."

"The air of independence," Sir Geoffrey said. "False, of course. One's cat is quite dependent on one, though she seems not to think so."

"The capacity for ease."

"And spite."

"To return to our plague," I said, "I don't see how a single madwoman and a hypnotized squire amount to one."

"Oh, that was by no means the end of it. Throughout that autumn there was, relatively speaking, a flurry of divorce actions and breach-of-promise suits. A suicide left a note: 'I can't have her, and I can't live without her.' More than one farmer's wife, after years of dedication and many offspring, packed herself off to aged parents in Chester. And so on.

"Monday morning after the squire's humiliation I returned to town. As it happened, Monday was market day in the village and I was able to observe at first hand some effects of the plague. I saw husbands and wives sitting at far ends of wagon seats, unable to meet each other's eyes. Sudden arguments flaring without reason over the vegetables. I saw tears. I saw over and over the same hangdog, evasive, guilty look I described in our squire."

"Hardly conclusive."

"There is one further piece of evidence. The Roman Church has never quite eased its grip in that part of the world. It seems that about this time a number of R.C. wives clubbed together and sent a petition to their bishop, saying that the region was in need of an exorcism. Specifically, that their husbands were being tormented by a succubus. Or succubi—whether it was one or many was impossible to tell."

"I shouldn't wonder."

"What specially intrigued me," Sir Geoffrey went on, removing his eyeglass from between cheek and brow and polishing it absently, "is that in all this inconstancy only the men seemed to be accused; the women seemed solely aggrieved, rather than guilty, parties. Now if we take the squire's words as evidence, and not merely 'the stuff that dreams are made on,' we have the picture of a foreign, apparently Egyptian, woman—or possibly women— embarking at Liverpool and moving unnoticed amid Cheshire, seeking whom she may devour and seducing yeomen in their barns amid the fruits of the harvest. The notion was so striking that I got in touch with a chap I know at Lloyd's, and asked him about passenger lists for the *John Deering* over the last few years."

"And?"

"There were none. The ship had been in dry dock for two or three years previous. It had made one run, that spring, and then been mothballed. On that one run there were no passengers. The cargo from Alex consisted of the usual oil, dates, sago, rice, tobacco—and something called 'antiquities.' Since the nature of these was unspecified, the matter ended there. The Inconstancy Plague was short-lived; a letter from Watt the next spring made no mention of it, though he'd been avid for details—most of what I know comes from him and his gleanings of the Winsford *Trumpet,* or whatever it calls itself. I might never have come to any conclusion at all about the matter had it not been for a chance encounter in Cairo a year or so later.

"I was en route to the Sudan in the wake of the Khartoum disaster, and was bracing myself, so to speak, in the bar of Shepheard's. I struck up a conversation with an archaeologist fellow just off a dig around Memphis, and the talk turned naturally to Egyptian mysteries. The thing that continually astonished him, he said, was the absolute *thoroughness* of the ancient Egyptian mind. Once having decided a thing was ritualistically necessary, they admitted of no deviation in carrying it out.

"He instanced cats. We know in what high esteem the Egyptians held cats. If held in high esteem, they must be mummified after death; and so they were. All of them, or nearly all. Carried to their tombs with the bereaved family weeping behind, put away with favorite toys and food for the afterlife journey. Not long ago, he said, some *three hundred thousand* mummified cats were uncovered at Beni Hasan. An entire cat necropolis, unviolated for centuries.

"And then he told me something which gave me pause. More than pause. He said that, once uncovered, all those cats were disinterred and shipped to England. Every last one."

"Good Lord. Why?"

"I have no idea. They were not, after all, the Elgin Marbles. This seemed to have been the response when they arrived at Liverpool, because not a single museum or collector of antiquities displayed the slightest interest. The whole lot had to be sold off to pay a rather large shipping bill."

"Sold off? To whom, in God's name?"

"To a Cheshire agricultural firm. Who proceeded to chop up the lot and resell it. To the local farmers, my dear boy. To use as fertilizer."

Sir Geoffrey swirled his nearly untouched brandy and stared deeply into it, watching the legs it made on the side of the glass, as though he read secrets there. "Now the scientific mind may be able to believe," he said at last, "that three hundred thousand cats, aeons old, wrapped lovingly in winding cloths and put to rest with spices and with spells, may be exhumed from a distant land—and from a distant past as well—and minced into the loam of Cheshire, and it will all have no result but grain. I am not certain. Not certain at all."

The smoking room of the Travellers' Club was deserted now, except for the weary, unlaid ghost of Barnett. Above us on the wall the mounted heads of exotic animals were shadowed and nearly unnameable; one felt that they had just then thrust their coal-smoked and glass-eyed heads through the wall, seeking something, and that just the other side of the wall stood their vast and unimaginable bodies. Seeking what? The members, long dead as well, who had slain them and brought them to this?

"You've been in Egypt," Sir Geoffrey said.

"Briefly."

"I have always thought that Egyptian women were among the world's most beautiful."

"Certainly their eyes are stunning. With the veil, of course, one sees little else."

"I spoke specifically of those circumstances when they are without the veil. In all senses."

"Yes."

"Depilated, many of them." He spoke in a small, dreamy voice, as though he observed long-past scenes. "A thing I have always found—intriguing. To say the least." He sighed deeply; he tugged down his waistcoat, preparatory to rising; he replaced his eyeglass. He was himself again. "Do you suppose," he said, "that such a thing as a cab could be found at this hour? Well, let us see."

"By the way," I asked when we parted, "whatever came of the wives' petition for an exorcism?"

"I believe the bishop sent it on to Rome for consideration. The Vatican, you know, does not move hastily on these things. For all I know, it may still be pending."

Her Bounty to the Dead

□ □ □

WHEN PHILLIPPA DERWENT at last got through the various switchboards and operators, and a young voice said "Hello?" in a remote, uncertain way, it was as though she had tracked some shy beast to its secret lair, and for a moment she wished she hadn't embarked on this; she hated to be thought a busybody, and knew that sometimes she could act like one.

"This is Phillippa Derwent," she said, and paused a moment. When there was no response, she said, "Are you John Knowe? Amy Knowe was my . . ."

"Yes. Yes, of course. Aunt Phil. I'm sorry. It's been so long. . . ."

It had indeed been long—over twenty years—years which, Phillippa knew, would have passed far more slowly for her nephew, aged eleven when she had last seen him, than for herself. A certain amount of constrained catching up was thus the next duty. Her nephew's life, she had always supposed, had been filled with incident and probably not happy; her own, which seemed to her happy, hadn't been eventful. Her sister Amy had married a man she hadn't loved, for her son John's sake, she said: they had left New England—the last Phillippa had seen of them—and begun a series of removes farther and farther west. Amy's letters, not pleasant to read, had grown more and more infrequent, now reduced to a Christmas card with a distracted note written on the back. The stepfather had vanished; at any rate, he ceased to be mentioned. When their mother—with whom Phillippa had lived alone for many years—died, Amy hadn't come to the funeral.

Somewhere down the years Amy had written that John had entered a seminary, and when Phillippa saw mentioned in her local paper that a John Knowe had been appointed to the faculty of a Catholic girls' school in Westchester, the possibility that this might be her nephew, revolved eastward, grew slowly (for it was hard for her to think of him as other than a shy, large-eyed, and under-grown boy) to a certainty. For many reasons (mostly not the reasons she chose to give herself) she didn't call him; but when the lawyer's letter came informing her that Cousin Anne's will had at last been straightened out, she took it on herself to inform John of it. Foolish, she told herself, living so near and not reopening relations; if he wouldn't begin, she would.

"She had some property in Vermont," she told him. "Nothing very grand; but she's left some of it to you, or rather you've come into it by default or something. . . ."

"Not the old farm," he said, his voice far away.

"Oh no. No, Mother and I sold the farm years ago. No, a parcel of land—not too far north of the farm—and I thought perhaps you might like to see it. I was planning a trip up there in any case—the leaves ought to be just at their peak—and I thought . . ."

"I don't drive."

"Well, I do." She was growing faintly impatient. "There are

apparently some papers to sign at her lawyer's up there. It could all be taken care of."

"Well," he said, "it's very kind of you." There was a pause, and then he said: "I'm sorry about the farm."

Slight, darkly bearded, not in clerical dress, he stood on the steps of the college with an abstracted yet attentive air that struck her as familiar. Who was she reminded of? Of him, no doubt; him as a boy. For a while she studied him without getting out of the car or hailing him, feeling unaccountably swept into the past.

"John."

"Aunt Phil." He was as astonished as she was not. She felt embarrassed; she must appear a ghastly crone in comparison to his mental image. Yet he took her hand warmly, and after a moment's hesitation, kissed her cheek, tenderly almost. His large eyes were as she remembered them. For a moment a hard thickness started in her throat, and she looked at the sky as an excuse to turn away.

"I should warn you," she said, "I'm a weather jinx. I can go anywhere and a blue sky will turn black." And in fact, in the west, hard, white clouds were moving over, preceded by wind-twisted pale mare's tails—stormbringers, her mother always called them.

Parkways north: already along these most civilized of turnpikes the ivy had turned, burdening the still-green trees with garments of many colors. Since the twenties, when her father had bought the farm for their summers, she had made this journey many times, at first on dirt roads through then-rural Connecticut, later traveling under these arching bridges each one different, and now skating along superhighways that reached—it had once seemed impossible to her that they ever would—deeply into Vermont itself. At this season, she and Amy and their parents would have been traveling the other way, not toward but away from the farm, where they lived from May to October; going home, they always said, but to Phillippa at least it had always seemed the reverse: leaving the true home for the other, the workaday place, the exile.

"We sold it in 1953," she said in answer to his question. "The summer after you left this part of the world. It had become just a burden. Dad was dead, and you children weren't coming up anymore; Mother and I needed money to buy the house in Rye. We got a sudden offer at the end of the summer—a pretty good one— and sold. We were grateful. I guess."

"What was a pretty good offer then?"

"Five thousand. And another hundred or so for the furnishings; the buyer took most of those too."

"Five thousand." He shook his head.

"We paid two, in the twenties. And much of the acreage was gone by then."

"Nineteen fifty-three," he said softly, as though the date were something precious and fragile; and then nothing more, looking out the window, absorbed.

She had rather feared this, his remoteness, a probably inevitable constraint. She passed a remark about the weather—the trees were turning up their silvery undersides, as though raising hands in dismay, and the sky was growing increasingly fierce—and then asked about his work. It seemed to be the right question; talking about theology, about the politics of the soul, he became animated and amusing, almost chatty.

Phillippa's religion, or lack of it, was that of the woman in the Stevens poem, sitting on Sunday morning with her coffee and her cockatoo: *Why should she give her bounty to the dead?* And that about April . . .

There is not any haunt of prophecy,
Nor any old chimera of the grave,
Neither the golden underground, nor isle
Melodious, where spirits gat them home,
Nor visionary south, nor cloudy palm
Remote on heaven's bill, that has endured
As April's green endures. . . .

"Yes," he said, putting the tips of his fingers together, "heaven is a difficulty. It seems hardly worth all the effort to end up in a white robe singing praises; like an infinity of choir practice. Of course, there's to be an ineffable, indescribable bliss; but it's damn hard to imagine, isn't it?"

"I suppose really religious people sense it," Phillippa said, feeling odd to be defending heaven.

"I don't know. I think people who really believe it invest the ordinary things they love with the idea of heaven; so that when they say 'This is heavenly,' they really mean it." Phillippa noticed his shapely hands, mobile now where they had been meekly folded before. They too reminded her of someone; yet how could so changeful a thing as hands, so markable by time, retain a reminder of him as a boy?

"Mother—Amy—always said," he went on, "that she didn't care about heaven if she couldn't have around her all the people and places and times she loved most, in their characters—I mean not abstracted; not in white robes; not on clouds. I think I believe that. Heaven is where you are—or will be, or have been, there being no time in heaven—most happy."

Where for her, Phillippa wondered; and knew, without assenting to the possibility: the farm, in high summer, years ago. If that were so . . . But it wasn't. If there was one thing Phillippa knew, it was that happiness is something you lose, fast or slow. "I wouldn't think," she said, "your church would go along with those ideas."

He laughed, pleased. "No, well. All that is up in the air, now, you know. I'm something of a heresiarch anyway, really. In fact, I've recently worked up a new heresy, or refurbished an old one. Would you like to hear it?"

"If you can promise we won't be punished for it," Phillippa said. To the north, a vast, curdled darkness was advancing across their path. "I mean look at that sky."

"It goes like this," he said, crossing one sharp-kneed leg over the other. "I've decided that not all men have immortal souls. Immortality is what Adam and Eve forfeited in the garden. From then on it was dust to dust. What Jesus promised to those who believed in him was eternal life—the possibility of not dying eternally. So that the believer, if his faith and hope and charity are strong, *creates* his own immortality through Jesus—the first immortal man since Adam: the new Adam."

"What about the outer darkness, and the weeping and wailing and gnashing of teeth?"

"A metaphor for death. I think it's easier to explain those few references to fires and so on as metaphors for death than to explain all the many references to death as metaphors for eternal punishment. Jesus said, He who believes in me *shall not die;* that seems clearly to mean that everybody else will."

"No hell?"

"No. A great problem solved there. Those who don't care about salvation merely go under the ground, utterly extinguished, having failed to accomplish their immortality."

"Comforting."

"Isn't it. Also clears up the problems of infant damnation and the Good Pagan. More than that, though: it makes the choice harder. The choice for Jesus. When the alternative doesn't seem so terrible."

"In fact—I'm sorry—preferable. Eternal life doesn't appeal to me."

"Well, there you are. Perhaps it isn't an unalloyed good. Perhaps it's quite difficult—as difficult as any kind of life."

"Dear me."

"Maybe some have no choice. The God-possessed, the saintly." He had grown more still, more inward. She wondered if he were still joking. "In fact, I would think the population of heaven would be small."

Phillippa thought of medieval pictures of the court of heaven, the winged saints in rows intended to suggest great numbers but really absurdly few. But that wasn't the heaven he envisioned, was it? Where ripe fruit never falls. If it were to be a heaven composed of the things one loved most, it would have to include (as far as Phillippa was concerned) change of season, fall of leaves, days like this one, raddled with dark, flying clouds; the flame of swamp maples, going out; April's green. And yes, for there to be enough of it to go around, perhaps there would need to be only a few to divide it among; the rest of us, mortal, resigning it to them. She thought, suddenly, of an old convertible turning in at the stone gateposts of the long weedy drive leading up to the farm.

Who could that be? her mother said. *No one we know.*

The car, with orange leaves stuck beneath its windshield wipers, nosed into the drive tentatively, uncertainly.

Just turning around, perhaps, lost, Phillippa said. They sat together on the porch, for it was quite warm in the sun. It was so utterly still and blue that the leaves fell seemingly for no reason, skating with slow agility to the ground. Their clicking fall among the rest was sometimes audible: it was that still.

The car stopped halfway up the drive and a young man got out. He wore a wide fedora—every man did then—and smoked a long, straight pipe. He stood with his hands in the pockets of his pleated slacks, looking at the house, though not, it seemed, at them. When at last he began to walk toward them, he did so not purposefully, nor did he hail them; he might have been arriving at a deserted house, or a house of his own. When at last he did greet them, it was with a kind of lazy familiarity. He wasn't a Vermonter, by his voice.

He had been told, he said, in the village, that the ladies were thinking of selling. He was in the market for just such a place; a writer, he needed someplace quiet to work. Were they in fact selling? Might he see the place?

It had been that very week that Phillippa and her mother had come to see that another summer in this house wasn't possible. The people in the village had, apparently, come to the same conclusion; not surprising, really, but a little forward of them to put it up for sale without asking. Well, her look asked her mother, here he was: why not show him around?

It's kind of a rambling old place, she said as they went in through the straining screen door. He stood in the parlor, seeming less to see the place than to inhale its fragrance, of woodstoves and old furniture and cidery autumn air. *Wouldn't it be too big for you?*

Room to spread out, he said, smiling as though he didn't really care. She showed him the kitchen, deprecatingly; there was no inside plumbing but a pump; no toilets; no stove but this iron monster. It would need a lot of improvement.

I think I'd leave it as it is, he said complacently. *It suits me.*

But the winter, Mother said. *What would you do then?*

He shrugged happily. *Hibernate, maybe.* He touched the huge old sinks fondly. *Soapstone,* he said. *When I was a kid I thought these sinks were called soapstone because you washed in them.*

It was difficult to move him through the house. Whatever room he entered he seemed to want to stay in forever, looking around dreamily. Phillippa found she couldn't be impatient with him, because he was so obviously taken with what she so much loved. By the end of the tour she found herself rather wanting this stranger to have her house.

And in the end he did have it, over her mother's objections— she wanted to give it to the local real-estate broker, an old friend— and most of the furniture too, Victorian junk they had collected through twenty summers of auctions.

"Junk," John Knowe said. "It wouldn't be that now, would it?"

"No. Antiques. But of course we didn't know that then."

"The fat horsehair sofa. Grandpa's big desk in the den, with the brass paperweight, very heavy, and the letter opener like a sword. The old clock, with weights like pine cones . . ."

"You remember that?"

"Yes. Of course. All of it."

He said it simply, as though it were no feat; and so he would, Phillippa thought: not having seen it since he was eleven, his memories of it all must be very sharp, as though preserved in a clear amber unclouded by grown-up perceptions of use, worth, price, burdensomeness. The farm had not altered for him, grown problematic, in the end insupportable. She felt, unwanted, a pang of loss; for herself more than for him. A few fat raindrops exploded against the windshield, then no more.

Through Massachusetts the storm that they seemed to be driving fast toward, as toward a destination, had grown, changed shape continually; as though hung for a pageant, moving on wires, two and sometimes three ranks of clouds crossed the sky at different speeds, and spotlights of sun picked out now this, now another bit of golden hillside. When they crossed into Vermont, the wind began to press hard on the car, and great flights of leaves blew across the highway like the flights of starlings in the brown fields. Northwest the clouds were not distinct, they were a solid cloak of the deepest gray, fuzzy with unseen rain. "That's where we go," Phillippa said. "But at least here's Vermont." She knew it was foolish, but couldn't help saying, "Whenever I cross the border, I always think of the lines about *Breathes there the man with soul so dead, Who never to himself hath said . . .*"

"*This is my own, my native land.*" He said it without irony, as though just discovering it to be true. "The land of heart's desire."

She remembered a photograph Amy had sent once. John, perhaps thirteen, stood before a shabby stand of alders and nameless undergrowth. Through the thin growth a midwestern landscape could be seen, featureless. Caught in the twiggy undergrowth were bits of paper, trash, human residue. Amy had written on the back "John's 'woods,'" as though that were what John called them. Exile. Maybe hell was where you had been most unhappy. No: no hell in his heresy. "We'll see Ascutney soon," she said. "Or maybe not, in this weather."

"Outside the kitchen door," he said—and it took her a moment to realize he was still thinking of the farm—"there were raspberry bushes."

"Yes."

"Very thick; so thick it was hard to open the door. And a little stone porch."

"Just a flagstone step. It was large to you, maybe."

"Bees. And the smell of those bushes . . ."

You can pick quarts of them in the summer, she said. *The smell of them in the sun is terrific.*

Yes, he said, looking not at the brown November garden but at her. Inside, her mother and the movers walked back and forth, their footsteps hollow. *I'm sorry, really, to be taking it all from you.*

Don't be silly. His eyes, large, liquid, remote, were—were whatever is the opposite of silly. She felt no anger at him, and not envy; she did want him to have her house; only—for a wild moment—wanted desperately not to lose it either. She wanted to share it, share it all; she wanted . . . He went on looking at her, fixedly and unashamedly as a cat; and there came a flaw in time, a doubling of this moment, a shadow scene behind this scene, in which he asked her to come now, come to stay, stay now, stay always, yield it all to him and yet have it all. . . . As instantly as she perceived it, the flaw healed, and *No, no,* she said, blinking, turning back to the kitchen door, shaken, as though, unaware, she had found herself walking out on ice.

She remembered that moment now, a cold wave rising beneath her heart. Mount Ascutney rose up very suddenly, blackish and with storm clouds disturbed by its head as though it wore wild hair. The pale gash of the road seemed to plunge into it.

"You never went back," John Knowe said.

"No. Never. It would be very changed, I'm sure."

"Yes. No doubt."

Wind shoved them suddenly, violently. The road had become shiny as a ballroom floor, the day dark as night. No doubt, no doubt. John Knowe drew a long, straight pipe from his pocket and put it unlit in his mouth. "It looks like this is it," he said.

Rain coursed down the windshield as they rose up and shot down a rise with heartsickening speed, blind. She fumbled for the wiper button, peering into the silver nothing. Hail fell clattering, roaring; the wipers stuck. She braked, panicking, and they seemed to rise up smoothly off the road, accelerating, gliding toward the cloudy head of Ascutney—she could see it fast approaching. The brake, pressed down, had no effect in air—that was the thought she had—and a piece of mountain, a tall black rectangle of it, detached itself and flew out of the nothing to meet them, changing size swiftly.

You can come too, John Knowe said, and it was already not his voice. *You can come now.*

NO, and she twisted the wheel violently away from the black rectangle that would have engulfed them

and when she was helped from the car, rain washing the sticky blood from her hands and face, in the deep fearful calm of shock she saw not this car half crushed beneath, against the black stalled truck, but an old convertible, with autumn leaves caught beneath its wipers, turning carefully, lost yet found, into a weed-spined drive between stone gateposts; and heard, not the shriek of sirens and the shouts *He's dead, he's dead,* but the faint yet audible click of a falling leaf joining the others on the littered ground.

The Reason for the Visit

□ □ □

SHE WASN'T AS TALL as I had supposed she would be; I'd always imagined that she would tower over me. Certainly she has always been described as "tall," but just as certainly those people who are largest in our imagination can never be quite as large in the flesh (though I suppose that's not strictly speaking what she was in). The big, sculptured features and long hands, the seeming *distance* of all her parts from one another—hands from wrists, brow from mouth, chin from breastbone—were all as they would have been in one as greatly tall as I had always imagined her to be, but the whole was on a smaller scale, as though I saw her at a great distance, coming toward me.

"Good afternoon."

"Good afternoon."

I had the presence of mind to make a social gesture immediately, as I'm sure she would have done had I thus suddenly come to visit her, to forestall, for a moment, the inevitable discomfiture in store for us. I offered her a cup of tea, which she accepted; but when she followed me into the kitchen, already marveling at what she saw of my place (a perfectly ordinary New York apartment) I found I had only instant tea.

"It's better iced," I said, trying to make little of the weird tall jar of brown powder. I remember my father vainly trying to introduce iced tea to England in the hot summer of 1944. That is, I don't remember it; I was only two, and lived on Washington Square. I remember him telling the story. Be nice with a bit of rum in it, they said.

"Iced?" she said, her macaw's eyes wide. I explained about iced tea. I couldn't tell if the expression of fascinated surprise she wore was assumed, to fend off genuine shock, or was genuine shock. I saw her surprise when the little light went on in the refrigerator, and when I squeezed lemon juice into the tea from a plastic lemon. The plastic lemon she found enormously witty. For a moment I felt a profound and inappropriate pity for her. I made mayonnaise sandwiches with Pepperidge Farm bread. "What an extraordinary number of things you take out of jars and bottles," she said.

We had our tea. I expected that she—being the visitor—would be shy and at a loss, and that it would be up to me to explain, to explicate mysteries, to compare and contrast. It had seemed to be up to me to do that for other visitors; to Dr. Johnson, for instance, I'd explained about elevators (he wouldn't understand that the little room had moved upward; he continued to suppose that the scenery outside had been quickly shifted while we were enclosed within). And to Max Beerbohm I'd insisted that I would be considered well-dressed—even something of a dandy—wearing my old, yellowing tropical suit and a vulgarian's Hawaiian shirt. But those visitors were figments, really. This visit was hers, and she asked the questions, and I was shy.

She was always interested in the situations of others, in how they got on with their lives. I answered carefully, trying to gloss over what in my life would be utterly incomprehensible to her. She—so conscious that she lacked a university education—was astonished that I'd gone to a decent school and not got past reading Ovid, of which I remembered next to nothing, and that even so I was unusual for having at least attempted it. I didn't try to tell her that with all its holes my education was considered, in my circle, so extensive as to be positively esoteric. I didn't want to look like the fool I felt before her.

Taking cues from my answers, she began to invent a life for me, as everyone says she often did for people she'd just met. Only for me she had to invent a time, too, and a place. The plastic lemon and the instant tea—"not nasty at all, really," she said, but didn't drink much of it—gave her the idea that society was geared now to providing a simple and Bohemian life for contemplatives, removing the necessity for servants and complex social relations so that other impulses could flower. She even suggested that the light in the refrigerator was there so that an absentminded poet would realize he was looking into the larder and not the wardrobe as he stood fuddled with thought before it. It was a brilliant flight. I didn't try to describe to her how sadly wrong she was. I only enjoyed the vivid future she imagined from her standpoint in the past, a future that was of a piece with that past and that standpoint, and which would never happen; had never happened.

"Like your essay about flying in a plane over London."

"I see. How is that?"

"Where it's revealed at the end that you never took the flight, only imagined it."

"Oh. Was I quite right about the sensation of it?"

"Not quite, no."

"Oh, dear."

A silence fell, and she rolled a cigarette. The difference between imaginary visitors and real ones is that with imaginary visitors you can immediately start in on whatever it was that occasioned the visit, without preamble or confusion; the elevator occasioned Johnson, and when it had been explained to him, and he had rejected the explanation in favor of his own, then the visit was over. But she and I must face each other now in an uncomfortable silence, with a whole world around us to be explained, or ignored; we must choose. When she lay back, the wicker of the chaise longue groaned faintly. She thrust one lovely hand deep into the pocket of her old gray cardigan. Her bun was beginning to come down. I was interested that the sheen of silk stockings, so hypnotic a detail in photographs, is the same as the sheen of silk stockings in actuality; and then too utterly different. She began, speculatively, dreamily, almost to herself, to wonder about the reason for the visit.

Her theory—a very natural one—was that she had fled from her historical moment into her own Immortality, her own urn-burial. From some approaching madness, the febrile disintegration that always attended finishing one of her big books, she had escaped into the calm changelessness which that very book would in part earn for her. The country—this one; the time—this present; none of that mattered. "Not until the lamp is utterly shattered," she said, "and all pages everywhere sealed up in mildew—but then one would only cease to be, wouldn't one? Till then, simply changelessness. How deliciously restful. It's what one wanted, isn't it, what one had prepared for and sought after—what one had *invented* out of all the terrible longings and dissatisfactions, never knowing that this exactly was what one was inventing—and yet having no other reason, all along, but this. How pleasant and odd that it should be so. . . ."

And yet she wasn't restful. Her repose was the enormously active repose she shows in so many photographs, that quiet as of a momentarily still candle flame. I thought she was wrong. I knew she was wrong. Her luminous brave eyes looked over the spines of my books, but the ones she had every right to expect to find would not be there. This was the difficulty: I knew her, I knew her in some deeply intimate way; her books I knew much less well. I can't remember if I ever got to the lighthouse; if I had, I suppose I'd remember. What I'd read was the essays, and the little biographies, and Leonard's memoirs; the letters and diaries and ephemera. I was a friend of hers, not a fan of hers. Her immortality—this visit to me, anyway—lay not in the perfect urns she had placed in the one great columbarium but in her old mortality.

"Well, I really love your 'Lives of the Obscure,' " I said. "I read them over and over."

"Yes? Such fun to do."

"I think in some ways they're the best things you did."

"Not the novels?"

"Well, I'm not really—familiar with everything you wrote, I'm afraid."

"I see."

I suppose I blushed. She continued to look politely interested, enormously gracious, but it was an instant mask now, slipped on without a skipped beat, for terrible disappointment.

Oh, antique lost fine manners! No reason for me to feel like a graceless boor before her, to feel at a loss, measured by the height and breadth and depth of her calibrated sociability and found wanting. I know well enough that nothing is lost that isn't replaced by something new of equal value, however different; I know that my life is brimful of satisfactions unimaginable to her. But nostalgia—this pain I felt—has no interest in all that; it only and always suffers from irremediable loss, especially loss of what one has never quite had. Yes! I began to see the reason for this visit.

"The little seaside provincial library," I said, "where you found those memoirs and biographies. Empty; a few people nodding over the *Wesleyan Chronicle* as through the window comes the cry of the man selling pilchards on the cobbled street. Dully ordinary. But don't you see, that little library is gone now, and every other one like it. There is no such thing left alive in my world. Yet I see it; I feel it; I smell it. I touch the beeswaxed wood and hear pages turn. I am transported back to it as wholly in your brief, dismissive paragraphs as you were to the old parsonages and country lanes in those memoirs.

"You see, things have been changing so fast. I know, I know: you felt them to be changing with dizzying speed. Believe me, the pace has picked up. Unimaginably. The whole physical world, the man-made part anyway, seems to alter utterly every few years. So that *your* life, your place in time and its sensations, the constellation of feelings caused in you by the world, are the farthest-off now that I can completely grasp. They are a hair's breadth out of reach beyond my own; yet I seem to be able still to feel them wholly. But because the world changed so much more slowly in your growing-up, your sense of the past—your experience of sensations felt in the past—was longer than mine, your grasp reached farther. You could touch hands a hundred years away, not merely thirty or forty. And because, a hundred years before you, the wheel was turning so slowly, the physical facts of the world changing so imperceptibly—I mean a wood fire in 1820 made a vicarage parlor smell as the same room smelled in 1720, or 1620—those hands you

touched touched hands that could touch hands that were held in
the old, old changeless circle around the old, original fire."

She hadn't interrupted this headlong rush; had seemed to grow
remote. Her hands lay now in her lap, the long white hands.
Rosamond Lehmann said that when Virginia held up her hands
before the fire to warm them, they seemed almost transparent, as
though you could see the fine bones through the skin. But there
was no fire here.

We said no more. In a little while Leonard, apprehensive that
she might be overtiring herself, came to collect her.

And yet when she was gone, her scent lingered a long time in
the room, a scent chosen nearly at random in a shop in Jermyn
Street; a scent chosen for its lovely name, not its odor, which she
didn't like to trouble the clerk to demonstrate for her on the inside
of her wrist where the blue vein beat. Besides, she must reach
before it closed a shop nearby, if she could remember the street and
how exactly it intersected with this one, where pens were sold, and
where she would be able to make her demands more specific—
where, that is, she would have demands. Standing in Oxford Street,
oddly exhilarated by the first breath of incipient autumn which cut
through the London air like a new nib across coarse-grained paper,
she thought suddenly to telegraph Leonard to say that after all she
had decided to stay up in town and attend Lady Colefax's party;
she could imagine it, a lamplit conversation piece in a dark wood
frame, that vast drawing room and the self-possessed identical
young men in evening dress, hair and eyes black and smooth as
their satin lapels. But—she is aware now of the throng around her,
breaking around her as a stream breaks around a stone, with the
same murmurous apologies—that would mean facing the telegraph office, and the blank accusatory form, she never could make

herself clear in telegrams. No; she would return this same long evening to Rodmell as she had promised. It would still be light as she came up from the station; the roses that had hung in such heart-tugging profusion so late into the year over the wall of Monk's House dropping the last of their innumerable petals along the way she would walk to the doorway where lamplight shone. And tomorrow Vanessa and the boys would come and they would read the Sunday papers in the garden while Leonard weeded thoughtfully, and there would be letters to write, and a new book materializing "in that hour between tea and dinner, when so many things seem not only possible, but already accomplished." Victoria Station, then, the vast smoky space, and the bit of pasteboard, and the stale-smelling compartment perhaps empty.

She turned, orienting herself. As she did so, she sensed Time as an enormous conical spiral. She sensed it tightening as it rose, tightening toward some furious stasis of immediacy. Time is compressible; it was quite simple really, she could compress it to a point. She could compress it all into the tiniest of compasses—into a day, into an evening—no, into an hour, even into the turning of a head: the single half-turn of a single great-eyed head.

The Green Child

■ ■ ■

THIS STORY IS RECORDED by Ralph of Coggeshall and by William of Newburgh, both of whom say that it took place in their own time, about the middle of the twelfth century, in West Suffolk.

At a place called the Wolf-pits, a woman of the village came upon two children at the entrance to one of the pits, a girl and a younger boy. The Wolf-pits, though everyone knew about them, had never been explored, as they were considered dangerous and unlucky, and no one knew how deep they were or where they led. The two children stood blinking in the sunlight, their pale eyes blank as though they had just opened them on this world. They were quite small for what seemed their age, and their skin was green, the pale, luminous green of the verges of a twilight sky in summer.

The woman dropped the ball of wool she had been gathering, crossed herself, made other signs against the Evil Eye and the Good People; the children watched her, but made no response, as though they didn't understand these gestures to be directed at them. The woman, feeling that despite their green color, the color

THE GREEN CHILD 33

of fairies, they might be just lost children after all, approached them, asking their names and where they came from. They drew back from her, the boy attempting to run into the pit's mouth; the girl caught him, and held him back, and spoke words to him the woman couldn't understand. The boy shook his head and shouted, as though not believing what the girl told him; she pulled him again roughly away from the pit's entrance, and spoke sharply to him. The boy began to weep then, a storm of tears, and his sister—it seemed to the woman they must be brother and sister—held him tightly as though to smother his tears, all the while looking with her large pale eyes at the woman, for help, or from fear, or both.

Pity overcame the woman's wonder, and she came to them, telling them not to be afraid, asking if they were lost.

"Yes," the girl said, and her speech, though in form different from common human speech, was intelligible. "Yes. Lost."

The woman took them to her own house. The boy, still weeping, refused to enter it, but with her rough yet protective manner his sister drew him in. The darkness within seemed to calm them both, though the boy still whimpered. The woman offered them food, good bread, a bowl of milk, but they refused them with revulsion. The woman decided to get help and advice. Making gestures and speaking softly, she told them to stay, rest, she would be back soon; she put the food nearby in case they should want it, and hurried out to call her neighbors and the priest, wondering if when she returned the green children would not have disappeared, or her belongings, or the house itself.

She brought back with her a weaver known to be a fairy doctor, who could cure the stroke, and his wife, and several others whom she met, though not the priest, who was asleep; and they all went to see the green children, the village dogs barking behind them.

They were as she had left them, sitting on the bed, their arms around each other and their bare green feet hanging down. The fairy doctor lit a bit of blessed candle he had brought, but they didn't start at it; they only looked with silent trepidation, like shy wild things, at the faces peering in the door and window at them. In the darkness of the house they seemed to glow faintly, like honey.

"They won't eat," the woman said. "Give them beans," the fairy doctor said. "Beans are the fairy food."

They were fairies to this extent, at least; when the woman gave them beans, they devoured them hungrily, though they still refused all other food.

They would answer no questions about the place they had come from, or how they had come to the Wolf-pits; when asked if they could return to where they came from, they only wept, the boy loudly, the girl almost grudgingly, her face set and her fists clenched and the tears trembling on the lashes of her luminous eyes. But later, at twilight, when the people had all gone away, and the boy had fallen asleep exhausted by grief, the woman by kindly questions did learn their story, holding the girl's cool green hand in hers.

They came from a land below the earth, she said. There it is always twilight, "like this," she said, gesturing to include the dimness of the house, the crepuscular fast-darkening blue of the doorway and the window, perhaps also the birds sleepily speaking and the hush of evening wind in the leaves outside. It was cool there; the rushing cool breath the villagers had noticed coming even in high summer from the Wolf-pits was the exhalation of her country. Everyone there was the same hue as herself; she had been as much frightened, she said, by the woman's odd color as by the unbearable brilliance of the sun.

She and her brother were shepherd's children, and had gone in search of a lost lamb. They had got lost themselves, and after a long fearful time had heard, far off, a bell ringing. They had followed the sound of the bell, and had found the exit of the pit.

Would they go home again? the woman asked. No, they could not. Whatever is an exit from that country, the girl said, is not an entrance; she was sure of that, though why this should be so she couldn't explain. They couldn't go back that way again. Her brother, she said, wouldn't believe this; but it was so.

Night had come, and the woman again offered the girl the bowl of sweet milk. She took it now, with a kind of reverent fear, and as carefully as though it were mass-wine, she drank some. She gave the bowl back to the woman, wiping her mouth with the back of her hand, her face frightened yet resolute, as though she had drunk poison on purpose. The woman put her to sleep on the bed with her brother, and curled up herself on the floor. In the night she heard the boy more than once awake and cry; but the girl cried no more. Years later the woman would look back and try to remember if the girl had ever cried again; and did not remember that she ever had.

In the morning the priest came. He questioned the children closely. The boy hid himself behind his sister and was silent, but the girl, less tongue-tied now, told in her strange accents what she had told the woman the previous evening, shyly insisting this was the truth, though the priest tried subtly to trap her into an admission that they were of the devil, either minor demons themselves or figments created by the devil to lead mortals into error. They had no fear of his cross or of the saints' relics he had brought in a glass vial; yet the girl could not answer any questions he put to her about their Savior, the church, heaven or hell. At last the priest slapped his knees and rose, saying that he couldn't tell who or what they might be, but they must at least be baptized. And so they were.

The boy remained inconsolable. He would not eat any food but beans, which he gorged on ravenously, without seeming to gain nourishment from them; he spoke only to his sister, in words no one else understood. He wasted rapidly. His sister would let no one else nurse him, not the woman, especially not the fairy doctor, though it was clear the boy declined; soon he even ceased to weep. In the middle of one night, the girl woke the woman and, dry-eyed, told her that her brother was dead. After some thought and prayer, the priest determined that he might be buried on consecrated ground.

The girl continued to live with the woman, who was childless and a widow. She came to eat human food without difficulty, and in time lost most of her green color, though her eyes remained large and strangely golden, like a cat's, and she never grew to proper size, but remained always tiny, thin, and somewhat insubstantial. She helped the woman about the house; she herded the village sheep, she heard Mass on Sundays and holy days, she went to processions and festivals in the village. The priest, still alert for devilish signs, heard stories that she was wanton and had no modesty and that any boy who asked her in the right way might have her under the hedge; but she was perhaps not the only one in the village of whom that might be said.

The woman, grateful that she had stayed and had not sickened like her brother, ceased asking her about her far country and what went on there; but many others wanted to hear her story, and came from some distance away to question her. She received them all, sitting in the chimney corner in her best dress, and rehearsed the tale for them; and over time it grew a little longer. She said that the name of her country was St. Martin's Land, because St. Martin was its patron. The green people there were Christian, she said, and worshiped our Savior, but on Saturdays like the Jews. She said that at the border of her country was a wide river, and beyond that river was a bright country where she had always longed to travel but could never reach. When she talked of this bright land, her pale eyes sometimes grew tears. The woman, old now, hearing her tell these things, and remembering how before the priest she had been ignorant of religion, wondered if these stories were not substitutes for true memories of her far dark country, which she had lost over time as she had lost her twilight color.

Eventually, it is recorded, the green child married a man at Lenna, and there "survived many years." It's not recorded what sort of man he was, or what sort of wife she made; nor if there were children of this union, and, if so, whether the blood in them of the land their mother called St. Martin's Land made them different from other children. If there were children, and children of those children, so that in some way that green land elsewhere and also the distant bright country glimpsed across the wide river entered our plain human race, it must surely be so diluted now, so bound up and drowned in daylight and red blood, as not to be present in us at all.

William of Newburgh says these events took place in the reign of King Stephen, and that at first he didn't believe the story, but that later the general testimony compelled him to believe it to be true.

NOVELTY

□ □ □

I

HE FOUND, QUITE SUDDENLY and just as he took a stool mid-way down the bar, that he had been vouchsafed a theme. A notion about the nature of things that he had been turning over in his mind for some time had become, without his ever choosing it, the theme of a book. It had "fallen into place," as it's put, like the tumblers of a lock that a safecracker listens to, and—so he experienced it—with the same small, smooth sound.

The theme was the contrary pull men feel between Novelty and Security. Between boredom and adventure, between safety and dislocation, between the snug and the wild. Yes! Not only a grand human theme, but a truly *mammalian* theme, perhaps the only one. Curiosity killed the cat, we are warned, and warned with good reason, and yet we are curious. Cats could be a motif: cats asleep, taking their ease in that superlatively comfortable way they have—you feel drowsy and snug just watching them. Cats on the prowl, endlessly prying. Cats tiptoe-walking away from fearsome novelty, hair on fire and faces shocked. He chuckled, pleased with this, and lifted the glass that had been set before him. From the great window south light poured through the golden liquor, refracted delicately by ice.

The whole high front of the Seventh Saint Bar & Grill where he sat is of glass, floor to ceiling, a glass divided by vertical beams into a triptych and deeply tinted brown. During the day nothing of the dimly lit interior of the bar can be seen from the outside; walkers-by see only themselves, darkly; often they stop to adjust their clothing or their hair in what seems to them to be a mirror, or simply gaze at themselves in passing, momentarily but utterly absorbed, unaware that they are caught at it by watchers inside. (Or watcher, today, he being so far the bar's sole customer.) Seen from inside the bar, the avenue, the stores opposite, the street glimpsed going off at right angles, the trape-zoid of sky visible above the lower buildings, are altered by the tinted windows into an elsewhere, oddly peaceful, a desert or the interior of the sea. Sometimes when he has fallen asleep face upward in the sun, his dreams have taken on this quality of supernatural bright darkness.

Novelty. Security. *Novelty* wouldn't be a bad title. It had the grandness of abstraction, alerting the reader that large and thoughtful things were to be bodied forth. As yet he had no inkling of any incidents or characters that might occupy his theme; per-haps he never would. He could see though the book itself, he could feel its closed heft and see it opened, white pages comfortably large and shadowed gray by print; dense, numbered, full of meat. He sensed a narrative voice, speaking calmly and precisely, with im-mense assurance building, building; a voice too far off for him to hear, but speaking.

The door of the bar opened, showing him a momentary oblong of true daylight, blankly white. A woman entered. He couldn't see her face as she crossed to the bar in front of the window, but he could see, drawn with exactitude by the light behind her, her legs within a summery white dress. When young he had supposed, without giving it much thought, that women didn't realize that sun behind them revealed them in this way; now he supposes that of course they must, and thinks about it.

"Well, look who's here," said the bartender. "You off today?"

"I took off," she said, and as she took a seat between him and the window, he saw that she was known to him, that is, they had sat here in this relation before. "I couldn't stand it anymore. What's tall and cool and not too alcoholic?"

"How about a spritzer?"

"Okay."

He caught himself staring fixedly at her, trying to remember if they had spoken before, and she caught him, too, raising her eyes to him as she lifted the pale drink to her lips, large dark eyes with startling whites; and looked away again quickly.

Where was he again? Novelty, security. He felt the feet of his attention skate out from under him in opposite directions. Should he make a note? He felt for the smooth shape of his pen in his pocket. "Theme for a novel: The contrary pull . . ." No. If this notion were real, he needn't make a note. A notion on which a note had to be made would be stillborn anyway, his notebook was a parish register of such, born and dead on the same page. Let it live if it can.

But had he spoken to her before? What had he said?

II

When he was in college, a famous poet made a useful distinction for him. He had drunk enough in the poet's company to be compelled to describe to him a poem he was thinking of. It would be a monologue of sorts, the self-contemplation of a student on a summer afternoon who is reading *Euphues*. The poem itself would be a subtle series of euphuisms, translating the heat, the day, the student's concerns, into symmetrical posies; translating even his contempt and boredom with that famously foolish book into a euphuism.

The poet nodded his big head in a sympathetic, rhythmic way as this was explained to him, then told him that there are two kinds of poems. There is the kind you write; there is the kind you talk about in bars. Both kinds have value and both are poems; but it's fatal to confuse them.

In the Seventh Saint, many years later, it had struck him that the difference between himself and Shakespeare wasn't talent— not especially—but *nerve*. The capacity not to be frightened by his largest and most potent conceptions, to simply (simply!) sit down and execute them. The dreadful lassitude he felt when something really large and multifarious came suddenly clear to him, something *Lear*-sized yet sonnet-precise. If only they didn't rush on him whole, all at once, massive and perfect, leaving him frightened and nerveless at the prospect of articulating them word by scene by page. He would try to believe they were of the kind told in bars, not the kind to be written, though there was no way to be sure of this except to attempt the writing; he would raise a finger (the novelist in the bar mirror raising the obverse finger) and push forward his change. Wailing like a neglected ghost, the vast notion would beat its wings into the void.

Sometimes it would pursue him for days and years as he fled desperately. Sometimes he would turn to face it, and do battle. Once, twice, he had been victorious, objectively at least. Out of an immense concatenation of feeling, thought, word, and transcendent meaning had come his first novel, a slim, silent pageant of a book, tombstone for his slain conception. A publisher had taken it, gingerly; had slipped it quietly into the deep pool of spring releases, where it sank without a ripple, and where he supposes it lies still, its calm Bodoni gone long since green. A second, just as slim but more lurid, nightmarish even, about imaginary murders in an imaginary exotic locale, had been sold for a movie, though the movie had never been made. He felt guilt for the producer's failure (which perhaps the producer didn't feel), having known the book could not be filmed; he had made a large sum, enough to finance years of this kind of thing, on a book whose first printing was largely returned.

His editor now and then took him to an encouraging lunch, and talked about royalties, advances, and upcoming titles, letting him know that whatever doubts he had she considered him a member of the profession, and deserving of a share in its largesse and its gossip; at their last one, some months before, she had pressed him for a new book, something more easily graspable than his others. "A couple of chapters, and an outline," she said. "I could tell from that."

Well, he *was* sort of thinking of something, but it wasn't really shaping up, or rather it was shaping up rather like the others, into something indescribable at bottom. . . . "What it would be," he said timidly, "would be sort of a Catholic novel, about growing up Catholic," and she looked warily up at him over her Campari.

The first inkling of this notion had come to him the Christmas before, at his daughter's place in Vermont. On Christmas Eve, as indifferent evening took hold in the blue squares of the windows, he sat alone in the crepuscular kitchen, imbued with a profound sense of the identity of winter and twilight, of twilight and time, of time and memory, of his childhood and that church which on this night waited to celebrate the second greatest of its feasts. For a moment or an hour as he sat, become one with the blue of the snow and the silence, a congruity of star, cradle, winter, sacrament, self, it was as though he listened to a voice that had long been trying to catch his attention, to tell him, Yes, this was the subject long withheld from him, which he now knew, and must eventually act on.

He had managed, though, to avoid it. He only brought it out now to please his editor, at the same time aware that it wasn't what she had in mind at all. But he couldn't do better; he had really only the one subject, if subject was the word for it, this idea of a notion or a holy thing growing clear in the stream of time, being made manifest in unexpected ways to an assortment of people: the revelation itself wasn't important, it could be anything, almost. Beyond that he had only one interest, the seasons, which he could describe endlessly and with all the passion of a country-bred boy grown old in the city. He was coming to doubt (he said) whether these were sufficient to make any more novels out of, though he knew that writers of genius had made great ones out of less. He supposed really (he didn't say) that he wasn't a novelist at all, but a failed poet, like a failed priest, one who had perceived that in fact he had no vocation, had renounced his vows, and yet had found nothing at all else in the world worth doing when measured by the calling he didn't have, and went on through life fatally attracted to whatever of the sacerdotal he could find or invent in whatever occupation he fell into, plumbing or psychiatry or tending bar.

III

"Boring, boring, *boring*," said the woman down the bar from him. "I feel like taking off for good." Victor, the bartender, chin in his hand and elbow on the bar, looked at her with the remote sympathy of confessors and bartenders.

"Just take off," she said.

"So take off," Victor said. "Jeez, there's a whole world out there."

She made a small noise to indicate she doubted there was. Her brilliant eyes, roving over her prospects, fell on his where they were reflected in the bar mirror. She gazed at him but (he knew) didn't see him, for she was looking within. When she did shift focus and understand she was being regarded, she smiled briefly and glanced at his real person, then bent to her drink again. He summoned the bartender.

"Another, please, Victor."

"How's the writing coming?"

"Slowly. Very slowly. I just now thought of a new one, though."

"Izzat so."

It was so; but even as he said it, as the stirring stick he had just raised out of his glass dripped whiskey drop by drop back into it, the older notion, the notion he had been unable to describe at all adequately to his editor, which he had long since dropped or thought he had dropped, stirred within him. Stirred mightily, though he tried to shut doors on it; stirred, rising, and came forth suddenly in all the panoply with which he had forgotten it had come to be dressed, its facets glittering, windows opening on vistas, great draperies billowing. It seemed to have grown old in its seclusion but more potent, and fiercely reproachful of his neglect. Alarmed, he tried to shelter his tender new notion of Novelty and Security from its onrush, but even as he attempted this, the old notion seized upon the new, and as he watched helplessly, the two coupled in an utter ravishment and interlacement, made for each other, one thing now and more than twice as compelling as each had been before. "Jesus," he said aloud; and then looked up, wondering if he had been heard. Victor and the woman were tête-à-tête, talking urgently in undertones.

IV

"I know, I know," he'd said, raising a hand to forestall his editor's objection. "The Catholic Church is a joke. Especially the Catholic Church I grew up in . . ."

"Sometimes a grim joke."

"And it's been told a lot. The nuns, the weird rules, all that decayed scholastic guff. The prescriptions, and the proscriptions—especially the proscriptions, all so trivial when they weren't hurtful or just ludicrous. But that's not the way it's perceived. For a kid, for me, the church organized the whole world—not morally, either, or not especially, but in its whole nature. Even if the kid isn't particularly moved by thoughts of God and sin—I wasn't—there's still a lot of church left over, do you see? Because all the important things about the church were real things: objects, places, words, sights, smells, days. The liturgical calendar. The Eastern church must be even more so. For me, the church was mostly about the seasons: it kept them in order. The church was coextensive with the world."

"So the kid's point of view against—"

"No, no. What I would do, see, to get around this contradiction between the real church and this other church I seemed to experience physically and emotionally, is to reimagine the Catholic Church as another kind of church altogether, a very subtle and wise church, that understood all these feelings; a church that was really—secretly—*about* these things in fact, and not what it seemed to be about; and then pretend, in the book, that the church I grew up in was that church."

"You're going to invent a whole new religion?"

"Well, not exactly. It would just be a matter of shifting emphasis, somehow, turning a thing a hundred and eighty degrees . . ."

"Well, how? Do you mean 'books in the running brooks, sermons in stones,' that kind of thing? Pantheism?"

"No. No. The opposite. In that kind of religion the trees and the sky and the weather *stand for* God or some kind of supernatural unity. In my religion, God and all the rituals and sacraments would stand for the real world. The religion would be a means of perceiving the real world in a sacramental way. A Gnostic ascension. A secret at the heart of it. And the secret is—everything. Common reality. The day outside the church window."

"Hm."

"That's what it would really have been about from the beginning. And only seemed to be about these divine personages, and stuff, and these rules."

She nodded slowly in a way that showed she followed him but frankly saw no novel. He went on, wanting at least to say it all before he no longer saw it with this clarity. "The priests and nuns would know this was the case, the wisest of them, and would guide the worshipers—the ones they thought could grasp it—to see through the paradox, to see that it *is* a paradox: that only by

believing, wholly and deeply, in all of it could you see through it
one day to what is real—see through Christmas to the snow; see
through the fasting, and the saints' lives, and the sins, and Baby
Jesus walking through the snow every Christmas night ringing a
little bell—"

"What?"

"That was a story one nun told. That was a thing she said was
the case."

"Good heavens. Did she believe it?"

"Who knows? That's what I'm getting at."

She broke into her eggs Florentine with a delicate fork. The
two chapters, full of meat; the spinach of an outline. She was very
attractive in a coltish, aristocratic way, with a rosy flush on her
tanned cheeks that was just the flush his wife's cheeks had had. No
doubt still had; no doubt.

"Like Zen," he said desperately. "As though it were a kind of
Zen."

V

Well, he had known as well as she that it was no novel, no matter
that it importuned him, reminding him often of its deep truth to
his experience, and suggesting shyly how much fun it might be to
manipulate, what false histories he could invent that would
account for the church he imagined. But he had it now; now the
world began to turn beneath him firmly, both rotating and revolving; it was quite clear now.

The *theme* would not be religion at all, but this ancient conflict
between novelty and security. This theme would be embodied in
the contrasted adventures of a set of *characters,* a family of Catholic

believers modeled on his own. The *motion* of the book would be the sense of a holy thing ripening in the stream of time, that is, the seasons; and the *form* would be a false history or mirror-reversal of the world he had known and the church he had believed in.

Absurdly, his heart had begun to beat fast. Not years from now, not months, very soon, imaginably soon, he could begin. That there was still nothing concrete in what he envisioned didn't bother him, for he was sure this scheme was one that would generate concreteness spontaneously and easily. He had planted a banner amid his memories and imaginings, a banner to which they could all repair, to which they were repairing even now, primitive clans vivified by these colors, clamoring to be marshaled into troops by the captains of his art.

It would take a paragraph, a page, to eliminate, say, the Reformation, and thus make his church infinitely more aged, bloated, old in power, forgetful of dogmas long grown universal and ignorable, dogmas altered by subtle subversives into their opposites, by a brotherhood within the enormous bureaucracy of faith, a brotherhood animated by a holy irony and secret as the Rosicrucians. Or contrariwise: he could pretend that the Reformation had been more nearly a complete success than it was, leaving his Roman faith a small, inward-turning, Gnostic sect, poor and not grand, guiltless of the Inquisition; its pope itinerant or in shabby exile somewhere (Douai, or Alexandria, or Albany); through Appalachia a poor priest travels from church to church, riding the circuit in an old Studebaker as rusty black as his cassock, putting up at a plain frame house on the outskirts of town, a convent. The wainscoted parlor is the nuns' chapel, and the pantry is full of their canning; in autumn the broken stalks of corn wither in their kitchen garden. "Use it up, wear it out," says the proverb of their creed (and not that of splendid and orgulous Protestants), "make it do, do without": and they possess themselves in edge-worn and threadbare truth.

Yes! The little clapboard church in Kentucky where his family had worshiped, in the Depression, amid the bumptious Baptists. In the hastening dawn he had walked a mile to serve six o'clock mass there. In winter the stove's smell was incense; in summer it was the damp odor of morning coming through the lancet windows, opened a crack to reveal a band of blue-green day beneath the feet of the saints fragilely pictured there in imitation stained glass. The three or four old Polish women always present always took Communion, their extended tongues trembling and their veined closed eyelids trembling, too; and though when they rose crossing themselves they became only unsanctified old women again, he had for a moment glimpsed their clean pink souls. There were aged and untended rosebushes on the sloping lawn of the big gray house he had grown up in—his was by far the best off of any family in that little parish and when the roses bloomed in May the priest came and the familiar few they saw in church each week gathered, and the Virgin was crowned there, a Virgin pink and blue and white as the rose-burdened day, the best lace tablecloth beneath her, strange to see that domestic lace outdoors edge-curled by odorous breezes and walked on by bugs. He caught himself singing:

> O Mary, we crown thee with blossoms today
> Queen of the Angels
> Queen of the May

Of course he would lose by this scheme a thousand other sorts of memories just as dear, would lose the grand and the fatuous baroque, mitered bishops in jewel-encrusted copes and steel-rimmed eyeglasses; but the point was not nostalgia and self-indulgence after all, no, the opposite; in fact there ought to be some way of tearing the heart completely out of the old religion, or to conceive on it something so odd that no reader would ever confuse it with the original, except that it would be as concrete, its concreteness the same concreteness (which was the point . . .) And what then had been that religion's heart?

What if his Jesus hadn't saved mankind?

What if the Renaissance, besides uncovering the classical past, had discovered evidence—manuscripts, documentary proofs (incontrovertible, though only after terrible struggles)—that Jesus had in the end refused to die on the cross? Had run away; had abjured his Messiah-hood; and left his followers then to puzzle that out. It would not have been out of cowardice, exactly, though the new New Testaments would seem to say so, but (so the apologetic would come to run) out of a desire to share our human life completely, even our common unheroic fate. Because the true novelty, for God, would lie not in the redemption of men—an act he could perform with a millionth part of the creative effort he had expended in creating the world—but in being a human being entire, growing old and impotent to redeem anybody, including himself. Something like that had happened with the false messiah Sevi in the seventeenth century: his Messiah-hood spread quickly and widely through the whole Jewish world; then, at the last minute, threatened with death, he'd converted to Islam. His followers mostly fell away, but a few still believed, and their attempts to figure out how the Messiah could act in that strange way, redeem us by not redeeming us, yielded up the Hassidic sect, with its Kabbalah and its paradoxical parables, almost Zenlike; very much what he had in mind for his church.

"A man of sorrows, and acquainted with grief"—the greatest grief, far greater than a few moments' glorious pain on that Tree. Mary's idea of it was that in the end the Father was unable to permit the death of his only begotten son; the prophecy is Abraham and Isaac; she interceded for him, of course, her son, too, as she still intercedes for each of us. Perhaps he resented it. In any case he outlived her, and his own wife and son, too; lived on, a retired carpenter, in his daughter's house; and the rabble came before his door, and they mocked him, saying: *If thou art the Christ, take up thy cross.*

Weird! But, but—what made him chuckle and nearly smack his lips (in full boil now)—the thing would be, that his characters would pursue their different destinies *completely oblivious of all this oddity*, oblivious, that is, that it *is* odd; the narrative voice wouldn't notice it either; their Resurrection has always been this ambiguous one, this Refusal; their holy-card of Jesus in despised old age (after Murillo) has always marked the Sundays in their missals; their church is just the old, the homely, the stodgy great Security, Peter's rock, which his was. His priest would venture out (bored, restless) from that security into the strange and the dangerous, at first only wishing to be a true priest, then for their own sakes, for the adventure of understanding. A nun: starting from a wild embracing of all experience, anything goes, she passes later into quietness and, well, into habit. His wife would have to sit for that portrait, of course, of course; though she wouldn't sit still. The two meet after long separation, only to pass each other at the X-point, coming from different directions, headed for different heavens—a big scene there. A saint: but which one? He or she? Well, that had always been the question; neither, or both, or one seeing at last after the other's death his sainthood, and advocating it (in the glum Vatican, a Victorian pile in Albany, the distracted pope), a miracle awaited and given at last, unexpectedly, or not given, withheld—oh, hold on, he asked, stop a minute, slow down. He plucked out and lit a cigarette with care. He placed his glass more exactly in the center of its cardboard coaster and arranged his change in orbits around it.

Flight over. Cats, though. He would appropriate for his Jesus that story about Muhammad called from his couch, tearing off his sleeve rather than disturbing the cat that had fallen asleep on it. A parable. Did Jews keep cats then? Who knows.

Oh God how subtle he would have to be, how cunning. . . . No paragraph, no phrase even of the thousands the book must contain could strike a discordant note, be less than fully imagined, an entire novel's worth of thought would have to be expended on each one. His attention had only to lapse for a moment, between preposition and object, colophon and chapter heading, for dead spots to appear like gangrene that would rot the whole. Silkworms didn't work as finely or as patiently as he must, and yet boldness was all, the large stroke, the end contained in and prophesied by the beginning, the stains of his clouds infinitely various but all signifying sunrise. Unity in diversity, all that guff. An enormous weariness flew over him. The trouble with drink, he had long known, wasn't that it started up these large things but that it belittled the awful difficulties of their execution. He drank, and gazed out into the false golden day, where a passage of girl students in plaid uniforms was just then occurring, passing secret glances through the trick mirror of the window.

VI

"I'm such a chicken," the woman said to Victor. "The other day they were going around at work signing people up for the softball team. I really wanted to play. They said come on, come on, it's no big deal, it's not professional or anything . . ."

"Sure, just fun."

"I didn't dare."

"What's to dare? Just good exercise. Fresh air."

"Sure, *you* can say that. You've probably been playing all your life." She stabbed at the last of her ice with a stirring-stick. "I really wanted to, too. I'm such a chicken."

Play right field, he wanted to advise her. That had always been his retreat, nothing much ever happens in right field, you're safe there mostly unless a left-handed batter gets up, and then if you blow one, the shame is quickly forgotten. He told himself to say to her: *You should have volunteered for right field.* But his throat said it might refuse to do this, and his pleasantry could come out a muffled croak, watch out. She had finished her drink; how much time did he have to think of a thing to say to her? Buy her a drink: the sudden offer always made him feel like a masher, a cad, something antique and repellent.

"You should have volunteered for right field," he said.

"Oh, hi," she said. "How's the writing coming?"

"What?"

"The last time we talked you were writing a novel."

"Oh. Well, I sort of go in spurts." He couldn't remember still that he had ever talked with her, much less what imaginary novel he had claimed to be writing.

"It's like coming into a cave here," she said, raising her glass, empty now except for the rounded remains of ice. "You can't see anything for a while. Because of the sun in your eyes. I didn't recognize you at first." The ice she wanted couldn't escape from the bottom of the glass till she shook the glass briskly to free it; she slid a piece into her mouth then and crunched it heedlessly (a long time since he'd been able to do that) and drew her skirt away from the stool beside her, which he had come to occupy.

"Will you have another?"

"No, nope." They smiled at each other, each ready to go on with this if the other could think of something to go on with.

"So," he said.

"Taking a break?" she said. "Do you write every day?"

"Oh, no. Oh, I sort of try. I don't work very hard, really. Really I'm on vacation. All the time. Or you could say I work all the time, too. It comes to the same thing." He'd said all this before, to others; he wondered if he'd said it to her. "It's like weekend homework. Remember? There wasn't ever a time you absolutely had to do it—there was always Saturday, then Sunday—but then there wasn't ever a time when it wasn't there to do, too."

"How awful."

Sunday dinner's rich odor declining into stale leftoverhood: was it that incense that made Sunday Sunday, or what? For there was no part of Sunday that was not Sunday; even if, rebelling, you changed from Sunday suit to Saturday jeans when dinner was over, they felt not like a second skin, like a bold animal's useful hide, as they had the day before, but strange, all right but wrong to flesh chafed by wool, the flannel shirt too smooth, too indulgent after the starched white. And upstairs—though you kept as far from them as possible, that is, facedown and full-length on the parlor carpet, head inches from the funnies—the books and blue-lined paper waited.

"It must take a lot of self-discipline," she said.

"Oh, I don't know. I don't have much." He felt himself about to say again, and unable to resist saying, that "Dumas, I think it was Dumas, some terrifically prolific Frenchman, said that writing novels is a simple matter—if you write one page a day, you'll write one novel a year, two pages a day, two novels a year, three pages, three novels, and so on. And how long does it take to cover a page with writing? Twenty minutes? An hour? So you see. Very easy really."

"I don't know," she said, laughing. "I can't even bring myself to write a letter."

"Oh, now *that's* hard." Easiest to leave it all just as it had been, and only inveigle into it a small sect of his own making . . . easiest of all just to leave it. It was draining from him, like the suits of the bathing beauties pictured on trick tumblers, to opposite effect. Self-indulgence only, nostalgia, pain of loss for what had not ever been worth saving: the self-indulgence of a man come to that time when the poignance of memory is his sharpest sensation, grown sharp as the others have grown blunt. The journey now quite obviously more than half over, it had begun to lose interest; only the road already traveled still seemed full of promise. Promise! Odd word. But there it was. He blinked, and having fallen rudely silent, said. "Well, well, well."

"Well," she said. She had begun to gather up the small habitation she had made before her on the bar, purse and open wallet, folded newspaper, a single unblown rose he hadn't noticed her bring in. "I'd like to read your book sometime."

"Sure," he said. "It's not very good. I mean, it has some nice things in it, it's a good little story. But it's nothing really."

"I'm sure it's terrific." She spun the rose beneath her nose and alighted from her stool.

"I happen to have a lot of copies. I'll give you one."

"Good. Got to go."

On her way past him she gave the rose to Victor without any other farewell. Once again sun described her long legs as she crossed the floor (sun lay on its boards like gilding, sun was impartial), and for a moment she paused, sun-blinded maybe, in the garish lozenge of real daylight made when she opened the door. Then she reappeared in the other afternoon of the window. She raised her hand in a command, and a cab the color of marigolds appeared before her as though conjured. A flight of pigeons filled up the window all in an instant, seeming stationary there like a sculpted frieze, and then just as instantly didn't fill it up anymore.

"Crazy," Victor said.

"Hm?"

"Crazy broad." He gestured with the rose toward the vacant window. "My wife. You married?"

"I was. Like the pumpkin eater." Handsome guy, Victor, in a brutal, black-Irish way. Like most New York bartenders, he was really an actor, or was it the reverse?

"Divorced?"

"Separated."

He tested his thumb against the pricks of the rose. "Women. They say you got all the freedom. Then you give them their freedom, and they don't want it."

He nodded, though it wasn't wisdom that his own case would have yielded up. He was only glad now not to miss her any longer; and now and then, sad that he was glad. The last precipitate was that occasionally when a woman he'd been looking at, on a bus, in a bar, got up to leave, passing away from him for good, he felt a shooting pang of loss absurd on the face of it.

Volunteer, he thought, but for right field. And if standing there you fall into a reverie, and the game in effect goes on without you, well, you knew it would when you volunteered for the position. Only once every few innings the lost—the not-even-noticed-till-too-late—fly ball makes you sorry that things are as they are and not different, and you wonder if people think you might be bored and indifferent out there, contemptuous even, which isn't the case at all. . . .

"On the house," Victor said, and rapped his knuckles lightly on the bar.

"Oh, hey, thanks." Kind Victor, though the glass put before him contained a powerful solvent, he knew that even as he raised the glass to his lips. He could still fly, oh yes, always, though the cost would be terrible. But what was it he fled from? Self-indulgence, memory dearer to him than any adventure, solitude, lapidary work in his very own mines . . . what could be less novel, more secure? And yet it seemed dangerous; it seemed he hadn't the nerve to face it; he felt unarmed against it.

Novelty and Security: the security of novelty, the novelty of security. Always the full thing, the whole subject, the *true* subject, stood just behind the one you found yourself contemplating. The trick, but it wasn't a trick, was to take up at once the thing you saw and the reason you saw it as well; to always bite off more than you could chew, and then chew it. If it were self-indulgence for him to cut and polish his semiprecious memories, and yet seem like danger, like a struggle he was unfit for, then self-indulgence was a potent force, he must examine it, he must reckon with it.

And he would reckon with it: on that last Sunday in Advent, when his story was all told, the miracle granted or refused, the boy would lift his head from the books and blue-lined paper, the questions that had been set for him answered, and see that it had begun to snow.

Snow not falling but flying sidewise, and sudden, not signaled by the slow curdling of clouds all day and a flake or two drifting downward, but rushing forward all at once as though sent for. (The blizzard of '36 had looked like that.) And filling up the world's concavities, pillowing up in the gloaming, making night light with its whiteness, and then falling still in everyone's dreams, falling for pages and pages; steepling (so an old man would dream in his daughter's house) the plain frame convent on the edge of town, and drifting up even to the eyes of the martyrs pictured on the sash windows of the little clapboard church, Our Lady of the Valley; the wind full of howling white riders tearing the shingles from the roof, piling the snow still higher, blizzarding the church away entirely and the convent too and all the rest of it, so that by next day oblivion whiter than the hair of God would have returned the world to normality, covering his false history and all its works in the deep ordinariness of two feet of snow; and at evening the old man in his daughter's house would sit looking out over the silent calm alone at the kitchen table, a congruence of star, cradle, season, sacrament, etc., end of chapter thirty-five, the next page a flyleaf blank as snow.

The whole thing, the full thing, the step taken backward that frames the incomprehensible as in a window. *Novelty:* there was, he just then saw, a pun in the title.

He rose. Victor, lost in thought, watched the hurrying crowds that had suddenly filled the streets, afternoon gone, none with time to glance at themselves; hurrying home. One page a day, seven a week, thirty or thirty-one to the month. Fishing in his pocket for a tip, he came up with his pen, a thick black fountain pen. Fountain: it seemed less flowing, less forthcoming than that, in shape more like a bullet or a bomb.

Snow

□ □ □

I DON'T THINK GEORGIE would ever have got one for herself: she was at once unsentimental and a little in awe of death. No, it was her first husband—an immensely rich and (from Georgie's description) a strangely weepy guy—who had got it for her. Or for himself, actually, of course. He was to be the beneficiary. Only he died himself shortly after it was installed. If *installed* is the right word. After he died, Georgie got rid of most of what she'd inherited from him, liquidated it, it was cash that she had liked best about that marriage anyway; but the Wasp couldn't really be got rid of. Georgie ignored it.

In fact the thing really was about the size of a wasp of the largest kind, and it had the same lazy and mindless flight. And of course it really was a bug, not of the insect kind but of the surveillance kind. And so its name fit all around: one of those bits of accidental poetry the world generates without thinking. O Death, where is thy sting?

Georgie ignored it, but it was hard to avoid; you had to be a little careful around it; it followed Georgie at a variable distance, depending on her motions and the number of other people around her, the level of light, and the tone of her voice. And there was always the danger you might shut it in a door or knock it down with a tennis racket. It cost a fortune (if you count the access and the perpetual-care contract, all prepaid), and though it wasn't really fragile, it made you nervous.

It wasn't recording all the time. There had to be a certain amount of light, though not much. Darkness shut it off. And then sometimes it would get lost. Once when we hadn't seen it hovering around for a time, I opened a closet door, and it flew out, unchanged. It went off looking for her, humming softly. It must have been shut in there for days.

Eventually it ran out, or down. A lot could go wrong, I suppose, with circuits that small, controlling that many functions. It ended up spending a lot of time bumping gently against the bedroom ceiling, over and over, like a winter fly. Then one day the maid swept it out from under the bureau, a husk. By that time it had transmitted at least eight thousand hours (eight thousand was the minimum guarantee) of Georgie: of her days and hours, her comings in and her goings out, her speech and motion, her living self—all on file, taking up next to no room, at The Park. And then, when the time came, you could go there, to The Park, say on a Sunday afternoon; and in quiet landscaped surroundings (as The Park described it) you would find her personal resting chamber; and there, in privacy, through the miracle of modern information storage and retrieval systems, you could access her: her alive, her as she was in every way, never changing or growing any older, fresher (as The Park's brochure said) than in memory ever green.

◙

I married Georgie for her money, the same reason she married her first, the one who took out The Park's contract for her. She married me, I think, for my looks; she always had a taste for looks in men. I wanted to write. I made a calculation that more women than men make, and decided that to be supported and paid for by a rich wife would give me freedom to do so, to "develop." The calculation worked out no better for me than it does for most women who make it. I carried a typewriter and a case of miscellaneous paper from Ibiza to Gstaad to Bali to London, and typed on beaches, and learned to ski. Georgie liked me in ski clothes.

Now that those looks are all but gone, I can look back on myself as a young hunk and see that I was in a way a rarity, a type that you also run into more often among women than men, the beauty unaware of his beauty, aware that he affects women profoundly and more or less instantly but doesn't know why; thinks he is being listened to and understood, that his soul is being seen, when all that's being seen is long-lashed eyes and a strong, square, tanned wrist turning in a lovely gesture, stubbing out a cigarette. Confusing. By the time I figured out why I had for so long been indulged and cared for and listened to, why I was interesting, I wasn't as interesting as I had been. At about the same time I realized I wasn't a writer at all. Georgie's investment stopped looking as good to her, and my calculation had ceased to add up; only by that time I had come, pretty unexpectedly, to love Georgie a lot, and she just as unexpectedly had come to love and need me too, as much as she needed anybody. We never really parted, even though when she died I hadn't seen her for years. Phone calls, at dawn or 4:00 A.M. because she never, for all her travel, really grasped that the world turns and cocktail hour travels around with it.

She was a crazy, wasteful, happy woman, without a trace of malice or permanence or ambition in her—easily pleased and easily bored and strangely serene despite the hectic pace she kept up. She cherished things and lost them and forgot them: things, days, people. She had fun, though, and I had fun with her; that was her talent and her destiny, not always an easy one. Once, hungover in a New York hotel, watching a sudden snowfall out the immense window, she said to me, "Charlie, someday I'm going to die of fun."

And she did. Snowfoiling in Austria, she was among the first to get one of those snow leopards, silent beasts as fast as speedboats. Alfredo called me in California to tell me, but with the distance and his accent and his eagerness to tell me *he* wasn't to blame, I never grasped the details. I was still her husband, her closest relative, heir to the little she still had, and beneficiary, too, of The Park's access concept. Fortunately, The Park's services included collecting her from the morgue in Gstaad and installing her in her chamber at The Park's California unit. Beyond signing papers and taking delivery when Georgie arrived by freight airship at Van Nuys, there was nothing for me to do. The Park's representative was solicitous and made sure I understood how to go about accessing Georgie, but I wasn't listening. I am only a child of my time, I suppose. Everything about death, the fact of it, the fate of the remains, and the situation of the living faced with it, seems grotesque to me, embarrassing, useless. And everything done about it only makes it more grotesque, more useless. Someone I loved is dead; let me therefore dress in clown's clothes, talk backward, and buy expensive machinery to make up for it. I went back to L.A.

A year or more later, the contents of some safe-deposit boxes of Georgie's arrived from the lawyer's: some bonds and such stuff, and a small steel case, velvet lined, that contained a key, a key deeply notched on both sides and headed with smooth plastic, like the key to an expensive car.

Why did I go to The Park that first time? Mostly because I had forgotten about it: getting that key in the mail was like coming across a pile of old snapshots you hadn't cared to look at when they were new but which after they have aged come to contain the past, as they did not contain the present. I was curious.

I understood very well that The Park and its access concept were very probably only another cruel joke on the rich, preserving the illusion that they can buy what can't be bought, like the cryonics fad of thirty years before. Once in Ibiza, Georgie and I met a German couple who also had a contract with The Park; their Wasp hovered over them like a Paraclete and made them self-conscious in the extreme—they seemed to be constantly rehearsing the eternal show being stored up for their descendants. Their deaths had taken over their lives, as though they were pharaohs. Did they, Georgie wondered, exclude the Wasp from their bedroom? Or did its presence there stir them to greater efforts, proofs of undying love and admirable vigor for the unborn to see?

No, death wasn't to be cheated that way, any more than by pyramids, by masses said in perpetuity. It wasn't Georgie saved from death that I would find. But there were eight thousand hours of her life with me, genuine hours, stored there more carefully than they could be in my porous memory; Georgie hadn't excluded the Wasp from her bedroom, our bedroom, and she who had never performed for anybody could not have conceived of performing for it. And there would be me, too, undoubtedly, caught unintentionally by the Wasp's attention: out of those thousands of hours there would be hundreds of myself, and myself had just then begun to be problematic to me, something that had to be figured out, something about which evidence had to be gathered and weighed. I was thirty-eight years old.

That summer, then, I borrowed a Highway Access Permit (the old HAPpy card of those days) from a county lawyer I knew and drove the coast highway up to where The Park was, at the end of a pretty beach road, all alone above the sea. It looked from the outside like the best, most peaceful kind of Italian country cemetery, a low stucco wall topped with urns, amid cypresses, an arched gate in the center. A small brass plaque on the gate: PLEASE USE YOUR KEY. The gate opened, not to a square of shaded tombstones but onto a ramped corridor going down: the cemetery wall was an illusion, the works were underground. Silence, or nameless Muzak like silence; solitude—either the necessary technicians were discreetly hidden or none were needed. Certainly the access concept turned out to be simplicity itself, in operation anyway. Even I, who am an idiot about information technology, could tell that. The Wasp was genuine state-of-the-art stuff, but what we mourners got was as ordinary as home movies, as old letters tied up in ribbon.

A display screen near the entrance told me down which corridor to find Georgie, and my key let me into a small screening room where there was a moderate-size TV monitor, two comfortable chairs, and dark walls of chocolate-brown carpeting. The sweet-sad Muzak. Georgie herself was evidently somewhere in the vicinity, in the wall or under the floor, they weren't specific about the charnel-house aspect of the place. In the control panel before the TV were a keyhole for my key and two bars: ACCESS and RESET.

I sat, feeling foolish and a little afraid, too, made more uncomfortable by being so deliberately soothed by neutral furnishings and sober tools. I imagined, around me, down other corridors, in other chambers, that others communed with their dead as I was about to do; that the dead were murmuring to them beneath the stream of Muzak; that they wept to see and hear, as I might. But I could hear nothing. I turned my key in its slot, and the screen lit up. The dim lights dimmed further, and the Muzak ceased. I pushed ACCESS, obviously the next step. No doubt all these procedures had been explained to me long ago at the dock when Georgie in her aluminum box was being off-loaded, and I hadn't listened. And on the screen she turned to look at me—only not at me, though I started and drew breath—at the Wasp that watched her.

She was in midsentence, midgesture. Where? When? *Or put it on the same card with the others,* she said, turning away. Someone said something, Georgie answered, and stood up, the Wasp panning and moving erratically with her, like an amateur with a home-video camera. A white room, sunlight, wicker. Ibiza. Georgie wore a cotton blouse, open; from a table she picked up lotion, poured some on her hand, and rubbed it across her freckled breastbone. The meaningless conversation about putting something on a card went on, ceased. I watched the room, wondering what year, what season I had stumbled into. Georgie pulled off her shirt—her small round breasts tipped with large, childlike nipples, child's breasts she still had at forty, shook delicately. And she went out onto the balcony, the Wasp following, blinded by sun, adjusting. *If you want to do it that way,* someone said. The someone crossed the screen, a brown blur, naked. It was me. Georgie said: *Oh, look, humming-birds.*

She watched them, rapt, and the Wasp crept close to her cropped blond head, rapt too, and I watched her watch. She turned away, rested her elbows on the balustrade. I couldn't remember this day. How should I? One of hundreds, of thousands . . . She looked out to the bright sea, wearing her sleepwalking face, mouth partly open, and absently stroked her breast with her oiled hand. An iridescent glitter among the flowers was the hummingbird.

Without really knowing what I did—I felt hungry, suddenly, hungry for pastness, for more—I touched the RESET bar. The balcony in Ibiza vanished, the screen glowed emptily. I touched ACCESS.

At first there was darkness, a murmur; then a dark back moved away from before the Wasp's eye, and a dim scene of people resolved itself. Jump. Other people, or the same people, a party? Jump. Apparently the Wasp was turning itself on and off according to the changes in light levels here, wherever *here* was. Georgie in a dark dress having her cigarette lit: brief flare of the lighter. She said *Thanks*. Jump. A foyer or hotel lounge. Paris? The Wasp jerkily sought for her among people coming and going; it couldn't make a movie, establishing shots, cutaways—it could only doggedly follow Georgie, like a jealous husband, seeing nothing else. This was frustrating. I pushed RESET. ACCESS. Georgie brushed her teeth, somewhere, somewhen.

I understood, after one or two more of these terrible leaps. Access was random. There was no way to dial up a year, a day, a scene. The Park had supplied no program, none; the eight thousand hours weren't filed at all; they were a jumble, like a lunatic's memory, like a deck of shuffled cards. I had supposed, without thinking about it, that they would begin at the beginning and go on till they reached the end. Why didn't they?

I also understood something else. If access was truly random, if I truly had no control, then I had lost as good as forever those scenes I had seen. Odds were on the order of eight thousand to one (more? far more? probabilities are opaque to me) that I would never light on them again by pressing this bar. I felt a pang of loss for that afternoon in Ibiza. It was doubly gone now. I sat before the empty screen, afraid to touch ACCESS again, afraid of what I would lose.

I shut down the machine (the light level in the room rose, the Muzak poured softly back in) and went out into the halls, back to the display screen in the entranceway. The list of names slowly, greenly rolled over like the list of departing flights at an airport. Code numbers were missing from beside many, indicating perhaps that they weren't yet in residence, only awaited. In the Ds, only three names, and DIRECTOR—hidden among them as though he were only another of the dead. A chamber number. I went to find it, and went in.

The director looked more like a janitor or a night watchman, the semiretired type you often see caretaking little-visited places. He wore a brown smock like a monk's robe, and was making coffee in a corner of his small office, out of which little business seemed to be done. He looked up startled, caught out, when I entered.

"Sorry," I said, "but I don't think I understand this system right."

"A problem?" he said. "Shouldn't be a problem." He looked at me a little wide-eyed and shy, hoping not to be called on for anything difficult. "Equipment's all working?"

"I don't know," I said. "It doesn't seem that it could be." I described what I thought I had learned about The Park's access concept. "That can't be right, can it?" I said. "That access is totally random . . ."

He was nodding, still wide-eyed, paying close attention.

"Is it?" I asked.

"Is it what?"

"Random."

"Oh, yes. Yes, sure. If everything's in working order."

I could think of nothing to say for a moment, watching him nod reassuringly. Then: "Why?" I asked. "I mean why is there no way at all to, to organize, to have some kind of organized access to the material?" I had begun to feel that sense of grotesque foolishness in the presence of death, as though I were haggling over Georgie's effects. "That seems stupid, if you'll pardon me."

"Oh no, oh no," he said. "You've read your literature? You've read all your literature?"

"Well, to tell the truth . . ."

"It's all just as described," the director said. "I can promise you that. If there's any problem at all . . ."

"Do you mind," I said, "if I sit down?" I smiled. He seemed so afraid of me and my complaint, of me as mourner, possibly griefcrazed and unable to grasp the simple limits of his responsibilities to me, that he needed soothing himself. "I'm sure everything's fine," I said. "I just don't think I understand. I'm kind of dumb about these things."

"Sure. Sure. Sure." He regretfully put away his coffee makings and sat behind his desk, lacing his fingers together like a consultant. "People get a lot of satisfaction out of the access here," he said, "a lot of comfort, if they take it in the right spirit." He tried a smile. I wondered what qualifications he had had to show to get this job. "The random part. Now, it's all in the literature. There's the legal aspect—you're not a lawyer are you, no, no, sure, no offense. You see, the material here isn't *for* anything, except, well, except for communing. But suppose the stuff were programmed, searchable. Suppose there was a problem about taxes or inheritance or so on. There could be subpoenas, lawyers all over the place, destroying the memorial concept completely."

I really hadn't thought of that. Built-in randomness saved past lives from being searched in any systematic way. And no doubt saved The Park from being in the records business and at the wrong end of a lot of suits. "You'd have to watch the whole eight thousand hours," I said, "and even if you found what you were looking for there'd be no way to replay it. It would have gone by." It would slide into the random past even as you watched it, like that afternoon in Ibiza, that party in Paris. Lost.

He smiled and nodded. I smiled and nodded.

"I'll tell you something," he said. "They didn't predict that. The randomness. It was a side effect, an effect of the storage process. Just luck." His grin turned down, his brows knitted seriously. "See, we're storing here at the molecular level. We have to go that small, for space problems. I mean your eight-thousand-hour guarantee. If we had gone tape or conventional, how much room would it take up? If the access concept caught on. A lot of room. So we went vapor-trap and endless-tracking. Size of my thumbnail. It's all in the literature." He looked at me strangely. I had a sudden intense sensation that I was being fooled, tricked, that the man before me in his smock was no expert, no technician; he was a charlatan, or maybe a madman impersonating a director and not belonging here at all. It raised the hair on my neck, and passed. "So the randomness," he was saying. "It was an effect of going molecular. Brownian movement. All you do is lift the endless-tracking for a microsecond and you get a rearrangement at the molecular level. We don't randomize. The molecules do it for us."

I remembered Brownian movement, just barely, from physics class. The random movement of molecules, the teacher said; it has a mathematical description. It's like the movement of dust motes you see swimming in a shaft of sunlight, like the swirl of snowflakes in a glass paperweight that shows a cottage being snowed on. "I see," I said. "I guess I see."

"Is there," he said, "any other problem?" He said it as though there might be some other problem and that he knew what it might be and that he hoped I didn't have it. "You understand the system, key lock, two bars, ACCESS, RESET. . . ."

"I understand," I said. "I understand now."

"Communing," he said, standing, relieved, sure I would be gone soon. "I understand. It takes a while to relax into the communing concept."

"Yes," I said. "It does."

I wouldn't learn what I had come to learn, whatever that was. The Wasp had not been good at storage after all, no, no better than my young soul had been. Days and weeks had been missed by its tiny eye. It hadn't seen well, and in what it had seen it had been no more able to distinguish the just-as-well-forgotten from the unforgettable than my own eye had been. No better and no worse—the same.

And yet, and yet—she stood up in Ibiza and dressed her breasts with lotion, and spoke to me: *Oh, look, hummingbirds*. I had forgotten, and the Wasp had not; and I owned once again what I hadn't known I had lost, hadn't known was precious to me.

The sun was setting when I left The Park, the satin sea foaming softly, randomly around the rocks.

I had spent my life waiting for something, not knowing what, not even knowing I waited. Killing time. I was still waiting. But what I had been waiting for had already occurred and was past.

It was two years, nearly, since Georgie had died: two years until, for the first and last time, I wept for her; for her, and for myself.

Of course I went back. After a lot of work and correctly placed dollars, I netted a HAPpy card of my own. I had time to spare, like a lot of people then, and often on empty afternoons (never on Sunday) I would get out onto the unpatched and weed-grown freeway and glide up the coast. The Park was always open. I relaxed into the communing concept.

Now, after some hundreds of hours spent there underground, now when I have long ceased to go through those doors (I have lost my key, I think; anyway I don't know where to look for it), I know that the solitude I felt myself to be in was real. The watchers around me, the listeners I sensed in other chambers, were mostly my imagination. There was rarely anyone there. These tombs were as neglected as any tombs anywhere usually are. Either the living did not care to attend much on the dead—when have they ever?— or the hopeful buyers of the contracts had come to discover the flaw in the access concept: as I discovered it, in the end.

ACCESS, and she takes dresses one by one from her closet, and holds them against her body, and studies the effect in a tall mirror, and puts them back again. She had a funny face, which she never made except when looking at herself in the mirror, a face made for no one but herself, that was actually quite unlike her. The mirror Georgie.

RESET.

ACCESS. By a bizarre coincidence here she is looking in another mirror. I think the Wasp could be confused by mirrors. She turns away, the Wasp adjusts; there is someone asleep, tangled in bedclothes on a big hotel bed, morning, a room-service cart. Oh: the Algonquin: myself. Winter. Snow is falling outside the tall window. She searches her handbag, takes out a small vial, swallows a pill with coffee, holding the cup by its body and not its handle. I stir, show a tousled head of hair. Conversation—unintelligible. Gray room, whitish snow light, color degraded. Would I now (I thought, watching us) reach out for her? Would I in the next hour take her, or she me, push aside the bedclothes, open her pale pajamas? She goes into the john, shuts the door. The Wasp watches stupidly, excluded, transmitting the door.

RESET, finally.

But what (I would wonder) if I had been patient, what if I had watched and waited?

Time, it turns out, takes an unconscionable time. The waste, the footless waste—it's no spectator sport. Whatever fun there is in sitting idly looking at nothing and tasting your own being for a whole afternoon, there is no fun in replaying it. The waiting is excruciating. How often, in five years, in eight thousand hours of daylight or lamplight, might we have coupled, how much time expended in lovemaking? A hundred hours, two hundred? Odds were not high of my coming on such a scene; darkness swallowed most of them, and the others were lost in the interstices of endless hours spent shopping, reading, on planes and in cars, asleep, apart. Hopeless.

ACCESS. She has turned on a bedside lamp. Alone. She hunts amid the Kleenex and magazines on the bedside table, finds a watch, looks at it dully, turns it right side up, looks again, and puts it down. Cold. She burrows in the blankets, yawning, staring, then puts out a hand for the phone but only rests her hand on it, thinking. Thinking at 4:00 A.M. She withdraws her hand, shivers a child's deep, sleepy shiver, and shuts off the light. A bad dream. In an instant it's morning, dawn; the Wasp slept, too. She sleeps soundly, unmoving, only the top of her blond head showing out of the quilt—and will no doubt sleep so for hours, watched over more attentively, more fixedly, than any peeping Tom could ever have watched over her.

RESET.

ACCESS.

"I can't hear as well as I did at first," I told the director. "And the definition is getting softer."

"Oh sure," the director said. "That's really in the literature. We have to explain that carefully. That this might be a problem."

"It isn't just my monitor?" I asked. "I thought it was probably only the monitor."

"No, no, not really, no," he said. He gave me coffee. We'd gotten to be friendly over the months. I think, as well as being afraid of me, he was glad I came around now and then; at least one of the living came here, one at least was using the services. "There's a *slight* degeneration that does occur."

"Everything seems to be getting gray."

His face had shifted into intense concern, no belittling this problem. "Mm-hm, mm-hm, see, at the molecular level where we're at, there is degeneration. It's just in the physics. It randomizes a little over time. So you lose—you don't lose a minute of what you've got, but you lose a little definition. A little color. But it levels off."

"It does?"

"We think it does. Sure it does, we promise it does. We *predict* that it will."

"But you don't know."

"Well, well you see we've only been in this business a short while. This concept is new. There were things we couldn't know." He still looked at me, but seemed at the same time to have forgotten me. Tired. He seemed to have grown colorless himself lately, old, losing definition. "You might start getting some snow," he said softly.

ACCESS RESET ACCESS.

A gray plaza of herringbone-laid stones, gray, clicking palms. She turns up the collar of her sweater, narrowing her eyes in a stern wind. Buys magazines at a kiosk: *Vogue, Harper's, La Moda. Cold,* she says to the kiosk girl. *Frio.* The young man I was takes her arm; they walk back along the beach, which is deserted and strung with cast seaweed, washed by a dirty sea. Winter in Ibiza. We talk, but the Wasp can't hear, the sea's sound confuses it; it seems bored by its duties and lags behind us.

RESET.

ACCESS. The Algonquin, terribly familiar: morning, winter. She turns away from the snowy window. Myself in bed . . . and for a moment watching this I felt suspended between two mirrors, reflected endlessly. I had seen this before; I had lived it once and remembered it once, and remembered the memory, and here it was again, or could it be nothing but another morning, a similar morning? There were far more than one like this, in this place. But no; she turns from the window, she gets out her vial of pills, picks up the coffee cup by its body: I had seen this moment before, not months before, weeks before, here in this chamber. I had come upon the same scene twice.

What are the odds of it, I wondered, what are the odds of coming upon the same minutes again, these minutes.

I stir within the bedclothes.

I leaned forward to hear, this time, what I would say; it was something like *but fun anyway,* or something.

Fun, she says, laughing, harrowed, the degraded sound a ghost's twittering. *Charlie, someday I'm going to die of fun.*

She takes her pill. The Wasp follows her to the john, and is shut out.

Why am I here? I thought, and my heart was beating hard and slow. What am I here for? What?

RESET.

ACCESS.

Silvered icy streets, New York, Fifth Avenue. She is climbing shouting from a cab's dark interior. *Just don't shout at me,* she shouts at someone, her mother I never met, a dragon. She is out and hurrying away down the sleety street with her bundles, the Wasp at her shoulder. I could reach out and touch her shoulder and make her turn and follow me out.

Walking away, lost in the colorless press of traffic and people, impossible to discern within the softened snowy image.

Something was very wrong.

Georgie hated winter, she escaped it most of the time we were together, about the first of the year beginning to long for the sun that had gone elsewhere; Austria was all right for a few weeks, the toy villages and sugar snow and bright, sleek skiers were not really the winter she feared, though even in fire-warmed chalets it was hard to get her naked without gooseflesh and shudders from some draft only she could feel. We were chaste in winter. So Georgie escaped it: Antigua and Bali and two months in Ibiza when the almonds blossomed. It was continual false, flavorless spring all winter long.

How often could snow have fallen when the Wasp was watching her?

Not often; countable times, times I could count up myself if I could remember as the Wasp could. Not often. Not always.

"There's a problem," I said to the director.

"It's peaked out, has it?" he said. "That definition problem?"

"Well, no," I said. "Actually, it's gotten worse."

He was sitting behind his desk, arms spread wide across his chair's back, and a false, pinkish flush to his cheeks like undertaker's makeup. Drinking.

"Hasn't peaked out, huh?" he said.

"That's not the problem," I said. "The problem is the access. It's not random like you said."

"Molecular level," he said. "It's in the physics."

"You don't understand. It's not getting more random. It's getting less random. It's getting selective. It's freezing up."

"No no no," he said dreamily. "Access is random. Life isn't all summer and fun, you know. Into each life some rain must fall."

I sputtered, trying to explain. "But but but . . ."

"You know," he said. "I've been thinking of getting out of access." He pulled open a drawer in the desk before him; it made an empty sound. He stared within it dully for a moment, and shut it. "The Park's been good for me, but I'm just not used to this. Used to be you thought you could render a service, you know? Well, hell, you know, you've had fun, what do you care."

He *was* mad. For an instant I heard the dead around me; I tasted on my tongue the stale air of underground.

"I remember," he said, tilting back in his chair and looking elsewhere, "many years ago, I got into access. Only we didn't call it that then. What I did was, I worked for a stock-footage house.

It was going out of business like they all did, like this place here is going to do, shouldn't say that, but you didn't hear it. Anyway, it was a big warehouse with steel shelves for miles, filled with film cans, film cans filled with old plastic film, you know? Film of every kind. And movie people, if they wanted old scenes of past time in their movies, would call up and ask for what they wanted, find me this, find me that. And we had everything, every kind of scene, but you know what the hardest thing to find was? Just ordinary scenes of daily life. I mean people just doing things and living their lives. You know what we *did* have? Speeches. People giving speeches. Like presidents. You could have hours of speeches, but not just people, whatchacallit, oh, washing clothes, sitting in a park . . ."

"It might just be the reception," I said. "Somehow."

He looked at me for a long moment as though I had just arrived. "Anyway," he said at last, turning away again, "I was there awhile learning the ropes. And producers called and said, 'Get me this, get me that.' And one producer was making a film, some film of the past, and he wanted old scenes, *old*, of people long ago, in the summer; having fun; eating ice cream, swimming in bathing suits; riding in convertibles. Fifty years ago. Eighty years ago."

He opened his empty drawer again, found a toothpick, and began to use it.

"So I accessed the earliest stuff. Speeches. More speeches. But I found a scene here and there—people in the street, fur coats, window-shopping, traffic. Old people, I mean they were young then, but people of the past; they have these pinched kind of faces, you get to know them. Sad, a little. On city streets, hurrying, holding their hats. Cities were sort of black then, in film; black cars in the streets, black derby hats. Stone.

"Well, it wasn't what they wanted. I found summer for them, color summer, but new. They wanted old. I kept looking back. I kept looking. I did. The further back I went, the more I saw these pinched faces, black cars, black streets of stone. Snow. There isn't any summer there."

With slow gravity he rose and found a brown bottle and two coffee cups. He poured sloppily. "So it's not your reception," he said. "Film takes longer, I guess, but it's the physics. All in the physics. A word to the wise is sufficient."

The liquor was harsh, a cold distillate of past sunlight. I wanted to go, get out, not look back. I would not stay watching until there was only snow.

"So I'm getting out of access," the director said. "Let the dead bury the dead, right? Let the dead bury the dead."

I didn't go back. I never went back, though the highways opened again and The Park isn't far from the town I've settled in. Settled; the right word. It restores your balance, in the end, even in a funny way your cheerfulness, when you come to know, without regrets, that the best thing that's going to happen in your life has already happened. And I still have some summer left to me.

I think there are two different kinds of memory, and only one kind gets worse as I get older: the kind where, by an effort of will, you can reconstruct your first car or your service serial number or the name and figure of your high school physics teacher—a Mr. Holm, in a gray suit, a bearded guy, skinny, about thirty. The other kind doesn't worsen; if anything it grows more intense. The sleep-walking kind, the kind you stumble into as into rooms with secret doors and suddenly find yourself sitting not on your front porch but in a classroom, you can't at first think where or when, and a bearded, smiling man is turning in his hand a glass paperweight, inside which a little cottage stands in a swirl of snow.

There is no access to Georgie, except that now and then, unpredictably, when I'm sitting on the porch or pushing a grocery cart or standing at the sink, a memory of that kind will visit me, vivid and startling, like a hypnotist's snap of fingers. Or like that funny experience you sometimes have, on the point of sleep, of hearing your name called softly and distinctly by someone who is not there.

THE NIGHTINGALE SINGS AT NIGHT

■ ■ ■

THE NIGHTINGALE IS CALLED a Nightingale because it sings at night.

There are other birds who cry in the night: the whippoorwill complains and the owl hoots, the loon screams and the nightjar calls. But the Nightingale is the only one who sings: as beautifully as the lark sings in the morning and the thrush at evening, the Nightingale sings at night.

But the Nightingale didn't always sing at night.

There was a time, long after the beginning of the world but still a very long time ago, when the Nightingale sang only in the day, and slept all night—like the blackbird and the wren and the lark.

Each morning in those days, when night had fled away and the earth tilted its face again into the sun, the Nightingale awoke from sleep, along with the lark and the robin and the wren. He drew his beak out from the feathers of his shoulder, he fluffed out his brown plumage, and—as the long bars of morning sun found their way into the thicket where he liked to live—he sang.

In those days every morning seemed to be the first morning

that ever was; everything the Nightingale saw, the green leaves sparkling with dew, the multicolored morning sky, the mossy earth teeming with insects, the tall trees, the birds and beasts awakening, all seemed to have just been made that morning.

That was because Time had not yet been invented. But it was about to be invented.

On a certain morning very much like every other morning that had been, the Nightingale awoke and sang. As he sang, he saw someone coming through the glades of the forest where he lived. It was someone the Nightingale knew well, someone he loved, someone who caused him to sing even a longer and more beautiful song as she came closer.

There was no one in the whole world at all like her, and yet she was just a little like everything there is.

She had no name, in those days, this someone; for that matter, neither did anyone or anything else, because names hadn't been invented yet. But long after this story, she would come to be called Dame Kind.

The forest where she walked was all Dame Kind's work. She had planted the trees and the flowers in all their variety and helped them to grow. She had watered them with the rain and had set the sun to shine on them. It was she who had thought of filling the trees with birds and the air with insects and the rivers and the seas with fish and the earth with animals.

It was she who had thought of making the earth round, like a green and blue and white marble, and who set it turning in the sun, so that there would be day and night.

In fact, there was nothing on earth or in the sky that Dame Kind had not thought of and set in place and made to go. Every small difference there is between one thing and another, Dame

Kind had first thought of. It was all her work, and she went about in it endlessly, fixing and changing and pruning and thinking of new things all the time.

It was no wonder that the Nightingale was glad to see her, and sang for her, because she had herself thought up the Nightingale, and thought up his song, too.

"Good morning," sang the Nightingale.

"It's a beautiful morning," Dame Kind said, and it was. She smiled, and the beauty of the morning was her smile. "And I," said Dame Kind, "have had a new idea."

"I bet it's a good one," said the Nightingale, who had never had an idea in all his life, good or bad.

"I *think* it's a good one," said Dame Kind. She thought a moment. "I'm sure it's a good one. Anyway, I've had it, and so there it is. Once you have an idea, there's no going back."

"If you say so," the Nightingale said cheerfully. "What is the new idea?"

"Well," Dame Kind said, "you can come see, if you like."

Together they went through the forest to the place where the new idea could be seen. In Dame Kind's footsteps as she walked there sprang up two new kinds of turtle, the speckles on the eggs that plovers lay, and the world's first June bug. The Nightingale didn't marvel at these things, because such things always happened where Dame Kind walked in the world.

At a certain place in the forest where the sun fell in patterns of light and dark on the flowers and the ferns, there sat a creature the Nightingale had never seen before.

"Is it the new idea?" asked the Nightingale.

"It is," said Dame Kind.

The creature had a round, flat face, and it stood on two legs, not four. Like some animals' babies, it was all naked, except on the top of its head, where long fur grew thickly. The sheen of its skin was soft and fragile-looking. There was something in its child's naked face, in its wondering eyes, that the Nightingale had never seen before in the faces of any of the thousands upon thousands of creatures that Dame Kind had thought of.

For just a moment, watching the new creature, the Nightingale knew that the world was turning beneath him, turning and turning and never quite coming back to the same place.

"What is it?" the Nightingale whispered.

"It's a Girl," Dame Kind answered. "And here is a Boy to go with her."

Another creature came from the woods. The two seemed very much alike, though there were differences. The Boy had caught a crimson salamander, and he brought it to show the Girl.

The Nightingale didn't understand. "Boy? Girl?"

"Those are their names," said Dame Kind.

"Names?"

"They thought them up themselves," Dame Kind said proudly. "With a little help from me."

The Nightingale marveled now. Never in all the forest had he ever heard of a creature that thought things up. He himself had never thought up anything. "How does it happen that they thought up names?" he asked.

"Well," Dame Kind said, going into the forest glade where the Boy and the Girl sat together, "that's the new idea."

From a distance—he didn't yet like to get too close to the new idea—the Nightingale watched the Boy and the Girl playing with the salamander the Boy had caught. What clever hands they had! Gently and quickly their flexible long fingers turned this way and that, picking up the salamander and putting it down, prodding it, caging it and releasing it. The Girl freed it at last, and then, as though her hands could not be at rest, she picked up something else—a flower, by the stem, between thumb and finger.

When they saw Dame Kind, the two new creatures ran to her, smiling and bringing her the flowers they had gathered. She sat with them, and they climbed into her lap, and she hugged them to her bosom, and they laughed and talked with her about all the things they had seen in the world since they had come to be.

"Look!" said the Girl, pointing up to the sky, from which a flood of hot golden light fell, warming her face.

"Yes," Dame Kind said. "It's lovely and warm."

"We call it the Sun," the Boy said.

"That's a good name," said Dame Kind fondly.

The Nightingale watched them for a time, and then, still marveling, he flew off to attend to the business of his life: to eat bugs and berries, to sing in the sun, and to raise his young.

"Well," he said to himself, "it certainly is a wonderful new idea. "I'm sure *I* never would have thought of it."

Dame Kind walked in the forest with the Boy and the Girl, holding a hand of each, and telling them about the world that she had made.

She told them what things were good to eat and what were not, and the difference seemed very clear to the Boy and the Girl, as though they had always known it.

She told them of some things they should take care about. She said they shouldn't kick open hornets' nests, or jump off high places, or get in fights with large fierce animals.

The children laughed, because they knew all these things very well, from the very first moment they came to be.

At evening they came to the edges of the forest, to an open place where the darkening sky was broad and high and deep and far away, and trimmed with colored cloud.

"What's beyond there?" asked the Boy, pointing far off.

"More of the world," said Dame Kind.

"As nice as this?" asked the Girl.

"Much the same," said Dame Kind.

"What are those lights?" asked the Boy, pointing up.

"They are far, far away," Dame Kind said. "So far that no amount of traveling could bring you much closer to them. They are huger than you can imagine, and there are more of them than you will ever know. They stitch the sky together, and without them nothing would be at all."

"I'll call them Stars," said the Boy.

"Oh," said the Girl, looking to the east. "Oh, look, what's that?"

Over the far purple hills there had arisen a sliver of golden light. As the Boy and the Girl watched, it grew larger, lifting itself slowly above the earth.

"Oh, how beautiful," said the Girl. "What is it?"

The golden light grew round as it rose. It pulled itself free of the purple hills and rolled into the sky. It was huge, and bright, and looked down on the Boy and the Girl with a wise expression on its round, fat face.

"It comes and goes," said Dame Kind. "It's lovely to look at, but not as important as it thinks. It steals its light from the Sun, when the Sun's back is turned."

"I'll call it the Moon," said the Girl.

"I wonder," said Dame Kind, "why you think everything in the world should have a name."

Dame Kind had made the Moon, of course, just as she had made everything the Boy and the Girl saw and named.

But she couldn't remember just then *why* she had made it.

I must have had a reason, she thought, looking up into the big fat face that looked down. The smile on the face of the Moon seemed to say: *I know the reason.*

Dame Kind felt troubled. She took the Boy's hand and the Girl's hand and led them back into the forest. "Dear children," she said. "You are my wonderful new idea, and I love you very much.

"I've shown you everything in my world that can give you joy and pleasure, and I've explained about some of the inconveniences there are, and how to avoid them.

"I've made you as well as I could to fit into this world I have made, and I will always think about your happiness, just as I do about the happiness of every other creature that is.

"Now I want to tell you something.

"For your own happiness, don't talk too much with . . ." She gestured over her shoulder with her thumb.

"The Moon," said the Girl.

"The Moon," said the Boy.

"The Moon," said Dame Kind. "I think it's not to be trusted. I forget just now why I think so, but I do. It comes and goes, and steals its light from the Sun, and it's not to be trusted.

"Will you do that?"

"If you say so," said the Girl.

"If you say so," said the Boy, and yawned a huge yawn.

"Good," said Dame Kind. "You are wonderful children, and I'm sure you'll be happy. We won't mention it again.

"Now I'll leave you, because I have a thousand thousand other things to see to. But I'll always be near, and I'll always have you in my thoughts.

"No matter what."

Dame Kind kissed them both, and then she went away, to pour rain, to plant seeds, to turn the world in its socket. She had some new ideas for beetles; as anybody who has ever looked closely at the world knows, Dame Kind is very fond of beetles.

The Boy and the Girl lay down to sleep on the soft blooming moss of the forest floor. There was nothing to trouble them, and nothing to alarm them. When they slept, they had no dreams, because dreams had not been invented yet.

Before she slept, the Girl looked up once at the Moon.

It had grown smaller as it went higher in the sky, and it had lost its golden color; its stolen light was white and cold. The light crept through the branches of the trees and stole over the flowers and the ferns, making them all black and silver. It was beautiful and strange, and the face of the Moon looked down into the Girl's face and smiled a far-off smile, as though it knew something about the Girl that the Girl herself did not know.

The Girl turned away then, and put her arm around the Boy, and closed her eyes and slept.

The days came and went, each one so much like the last that it was hard to tell whether it was the same day happening over and over again, or new days coming to replace old ones.

The Boy and the Girl ate when they were hungry and drank when they were thirsty; when they were sleepy, they slept.

With their quick feet and clever fingers they explored the

world Dame Kind had made, giving a name to everything that seemed to have something different about it.

One leaf of a tree seemed to be pretty much the same as every other leaf, so they didn't give a separate name to each leaf; they called them all Leaves.

There was not *much* difference between a bat and a bird, but there was a difference; so they called one a Bat and the other a Bird.

The difference between Day and Night was the biggest difference they knew. In the day the Sun shone and there was light; then they went exploring, and gave names to things, and ate and drank. In the night there was no Sun, and they lay on the mossy floor of the forest and put their arms around one another and slept.

And while they slept, the Moon came and went, rolling over the dark-blue sky and looking down on them.

There was a night when, very close to where the Boy and the Girl lay asleep, an owl hooted, and the Girl awoke.

She looked around her in the sparkling dimness. The fireflies had put out their lights. But there was a faint silvery light on the leaves and flowers.

She looked overhead.

Through the branches of the trees, on the deep-blue surface of the night sky, surrounded by the far-off stars, the Moon looked down on her.

But it was not the same Moon.

The Moon she had once seen was a round, fat face, with a smile that puffed out its cheeks, and heavy-lidded eyes half closed.

This Moon was a thin crescent of light, with a shape like a fingernail paring; it had a thin, thin face that looked away, and a small pursed mouth, and a cold, cold eye that glanced sidewise at the Girl.

"Are you the Moon?" she asked.

"I am," said the Moon, "I am."

"What became of the other Moon?" asked the Girl.

"What other Moon is that?" the Moon asked back. Its voice was as cold and far-off as its light, but the Girl could hear it clearly.

"You aren't the same," said the Girl.

"Is that so?" said the Moon. "Well, there it is."

"Why?"

"Oh, well," the Moon said, and looked away. "That's my secret."

"Did you change?" asked the Girl.

"That would be telling," said the Moon.

The Girl lay watching the Moon a long time, trying to think of a question she could ask that would make the Moon tell what it knew. It bothered her that the Moon had a secret she could not guess.

"There must be more than one Moon," she said. "That's all."

The Moon said: "Is that what you think?"

"It must be," said the Girl.

"Hm," said the Moon, and smiled a secret smile. It had rolled on by now, rolling toward the west; and without saying another word, it rolled behind the trees where the Girl could see it no more.

In the morning she told the Boy: "We have to give the Moon a different name."

"Why?" asked the Boy.

"Because it's different now," the Girl said. "I saw it last night. Once it was fat and round. Now it's thin and sharp, and looks away. That's a difference. And different things should have different names."

The Boy couldn't think of an answer to this. He didn't like the Moon, and didn't like to think about it. "Maybe it wasn't the Moon at all," he said.

"It was," the Girl said. "I asked."

The Boy said: "We weren't supposed to talk to the Moon! Don't you remember?"

"We weren't supposed to talk to the Moon too much," the Girl said. "I didn't talk too much."

The Boy turned away. He had a feeling within him that he had never felt before in all the time he had been in the world. He didn't know what it was, and he didn't know why he felt it. "The Moon is the Moon," he said. "It doesn't change, and it has only one name. Two names would just be confusing. And we're not supposed to talk with it."

He sat without turning around until the Girl said: "I won't talk with it again."

And so she didn't. But she thought about it.

It's a strange thing about names: when you know the name of something, you can think about it even when the thing itself isn't there before your face.

Even though the Girl took care not to look up at the Moon's smile, she could think about the Moon, and about whether it was one Moon or two. She could do that because she had a name to think of.

She could say to herself: "The Moon," and even though the Sun was shining and making patterns of dark and light on the flowers and the ferns of the forest, she could see the cold, white, narrow face of the Moon and feel its silver light, and ask it questions that it would not answer.

◨

The Boy learned this strange thing about names, too.

He found that he could sit and think about things that were not there before his face.

He could say to himself, "a Squirrel," and the squirrel he had thought of would run around his mind, and pick up nuts in its little black hands, and eat them in its quick squirrel way.

He could say to himself, "a Stone," and there would be a stone: not any particular stone, just a stone; a stone that was something like all the stones he had ever seen but not exactly like any one.

And, most interesting of all, he could think of the Stone and the Squirrel at the same time, and think about the many differences between them.

One afternoon the Nightingale came upon him while he was busy with this, thinking of the names of things, putting them together, and thinking about the difference between them.

What the Nightingale saw was this: he saw the Boy put his cheek in his hand and rest his elbow on his knee. He saw the Boy's lips move, but no sound came out. Then he saw the Boy cross his legs a different way and rest his chin on his fist. He saw the Boy scratch his head, and laugh at nothing, and get up and throw himself down on the ground, and pillow his hands under his head.

The Nightingale didn't know what the Boy was doing, and he grew curious.

"Hello there," he sang from a branch above the Boy's head.

"Hello, Bird," said the Boy, looking up and smiling.

"What is it that you're doing there?" the Nightingale asked.

"I was just thinking," said the Boy.

"Oh," said the Nightingale. "Thinking?"

"Just thinking," said the Boy.

"Oh," said the Nightingale. "What were you thinking up? Names?"

"I wasn't thinking anything *up*," said the Boy. "Not just now. I was just thinking."

"Hm," said the Nightingale, and he sang a few notes, because he had nothing to say.

"I was thinking of a question," said the Boy.

"That's clever of you," said the Nightingale.

The Boy crossed his legs a different way. "The question is this: Why is there anything at all, and not nothing?"

The Nightingale marveled at the Boy. "That's a good question," he said. "I never would have thought of it."

"But what's the answer?" asked the Boy.

"Answer?" said the Nightingale.

"A question has to have an answer."

"Does it?" said the Nightingale.

"Oh, forget it," said the Boy.

"All right," said the Nightingale, and he sang a long song.

The Boy listened to the song. He thought: *Why is there anything at all, and not nothing instead? Why should there be something, instead of nothing at all?* The question went on and on inside his head, and made him feel strange. The more he thought about it the stranger he felt: as though he himself did not exist.

This was the first time anyone had ever thought of this question, and from that day to this no one has ever thought of an answer: Why is there anything at all, and not nothing?

While the Nightingale sang and the Boy thought, the Girl, walking on the edges of the forest, discovered a strange thing.

The Moon was shining in the day.

The Sun had set, but it was still coloring the sky in the west. And far above the green hills the Moon had risen.

It was fatter, and smiling once again, as it had been when Dame Kind had first shown it to them. It seemed to be not quite all there, though. It was faint and very pale, and the Girl could partly see through it: she could see blue sky through its white skin.

"Hello again," said the Moon.

"Hello," said the Girl. She had forgotten, in her wonder, that she had promised not to talk with the Moon. "You've changed again."

"Is that so?" said the Moon. Its voice was fainter and farther away than ever.

"Unless," the Girl said, "there are three Moons: one fat one, one thin one, and one that shines in the day. Is that the answer?"

"What's the question?" asked the Moon.

The Girl couldn't think just what the question was. She sat down and looked up at the Moon. She thought: *I am the question.* For a long time she only sat and looked up, thinking: *I am the question.* But she could not think how to ask it.

Now a star or two was shining. The blue of the sky was darkening. And the Moon was growing brighter, more solid, more like itself.

"I'll tell you this," it said, rolling higher into the sky and smiling more broadly. "You and I are alike."

"We are?" said the Girl.

"Oh, very much alike," the Moon said.

"How are we alike?" asked the Girl.

"Would you like to know?" said the Moon. "Then you keep your eye on me."

Now the night was deep. Around the edges of the sky the stars were numberless; but in the center the Moon was bright and put out the stars. Its silver light coated the world with strangeness. "I am strong," the Moon said, "and so are you; but we're more alike than that. You are beautiful, and so am I; but we're more alike than that."

"How are we alike?" the Girl asked. "Tell me."

"Oh, you'll see," the Moon said. "Watch me come and go, and you'll see. You'll see it's true."

The Girl, sitting in the stream of the Moon's light, and hearing its voice, knew that the Moon was right. She grew afraid. She said: "We weren't supposed to talk to you."

"Oh?" said the Moon. "Who told you so?"

"She," the Girl said, even more afraid. "She told us so. She who made us both."

"Oho," the Moon said. "I wonder why she said that."

"I don't know," the Girl said.

"I wonder," said the Moon. "Do you think—perhaps—that there is something that I know, something she wants you not to find out?"

"I don't know," said the Girl.

"I wonder," said the Moon.

"She told us everything," said the Girl.

"Did she," said the Moon. "Did she, now."

"What is it that you know?" asked the Girl.

"You'll find out," said the Moon. "Just keep your eye on me."

At that moment the Moon looked away. Its silver smile faded. Clouds, dark as slate and edged with lacy white, raced over the sky and across the face of the Moon.

Far away, there was a sound of thunder.

The Thunder said: "What's going on?"

The Moon grew small, and it sped through the racing clouds as though it were being chased. The stars went out. The Girl hugged herself, feeling a cold wind blow.

The Wind said: "If I were you, I wouldn't talk with the Moon."

The Girl saw the Moon swallowed up in black clouds. She heard it say, as it went away: "Just keep your eye on me."

"If I were you," Dame Kind said (for it was her voice in the thunder, and her voice in the wind), "I wouldn't listen to the Moon."

The Girl was afraid, but she said: "Why?"

Dame Kind sat down with her. "Dear child," she said. "Do you think I don't know best? I know how you're made, every little bit of you, every hair on your head! Didn't I make you myself, and didn't I make you just as you are so that you could be happy in the world I made, and give me joy in your happiness? And don't you think then that I know what's best for you?"

"But why?" the Girl asked again.

Dame Kind arose; she stamped her foot with a long roll of thunder, and she said in a loud voice: "Because I said so!"

She turned from the Girl and went away; and the rain fell in big, cold drops, pattering in the leaves of the trees and causing the birds and the animals to run and hide.

Dame Kind was puzzled and sad. Never before in all the world she had made, in all the time she had gone about in it, had she ever lost her temper and said: "Because I said so!"

But then, never before in all the world had anyone ever asked Dame Kind the question that the Girl had asked: "Why?"

The Girl said to the Boy: "The Moon does change."

"It does?" said the Boy. They were sitting in a little cave they had found, out of the rain that fell from leaf to leaf. "How do you know?"

"I saw it again," said the Girl. "And it was fat and big, not thin and sharp."

"Maybe," said the Boy, "there are three Moons."

"No," said the Girl. "It's one Moon, but it changes."

"I don't care," said the Boy. He still didn't like hearing the Girl talk about the Moon.

"The Moon," she said to him—softly, so that no one else would hear—"the Moon has a secret."

"How do you know?"

"Because it told me," said the Girl.

"We aren't supposed to talk to the Moon," said the Boy.

The Girl only took the Boy's hand, and waited. The rain fell and fell, like tears. And at last the Boy said: "What is the Moon's secret?"

"I don't know," said the Girl. "It won't tell. But it said: Keep your eye on me, and you'll see."

"It's probably not important," said the Boy. "It's something good to eat, or something to keep away from; or it's the name of something we haven't named yet."

"No," said the Girl. "It's not anything like that. It's something we don't know, and something we couldn't think of."

The Boy said: "*She* would know what it was." He pointed outward at the rainy world. "We'll ask *her*."

"No," said the Girl. "She told us not to talk to the Moon. She doesn't want us to learn the Moon's secret."

"Why?" asked the Boy.

"I don't know," said the Girl.

The Boy wondered what the secret could be. He thought it

might be the answer to the hard question he had thought of: *Why is there anything at all, and not nothing?*

If he could make the Moon tell him the answer to that question, he would know everything. But he didn't say this to the Girl.

He said: "Maybe, if we knew the Moon's secret, we would know as much as *she* does."

"Maybe," said the Girl.

"And then we could do the things that she does."

"Maybe," said the Girl. But she didn't think this was the Moon's secret. She thought that the Moon's secret was a secret about herself: something she didn't know about herself, that the Moon knew.

But she didn't say this to the Boy.

She said: "We *can* learn what the secret is. We must."

"How?" said the Boy.

"We'll do as it said," the Girl answered. "We'll keep our eyes on it, and learn."

The Boy's heart, for some reason, or for no reason at all, had begun to beat hard and fast. "All right," he said. "We'll keep our eyes on it, and see."

And so they did.

They watched that night, and the next night, and every night from then on.

They watched the Moon change: each night it arose at a different time, and each night it grew thinner. Its fat face was worn away on one side, till it was like a melon cut in half. Its smile grew strange and its eyes were sad.

"Time eats me," said the Moon to the Boy.

"What is Time?" asked the Boy.

"You don't know?" said the Moon. "Then watch me, and learn."

The next night the Moon was thinner, and the next night, thinner still. Now it had become the thin, sharp-faced Moon that looked away.

"The Moon does change," the Boy said. "Once it was one way, and now it's another way. On one night it's fat, and then it grows thinner. Last night is different from tonight. Tomorrow night will be different again."

"Different things should have different names," said the Girl.

The difference between the way things once were, and the way things are now, and the way things will be, was the biggest difference the Boy and the Girl had yet learned.

They called the difference Time.

"Is that the Moon's secret?" asked the Boy.

The Girl asked the Moon: "Is that your secret?"

But the Moon only answered: "Keep your eye on me."

And still the Moon grew thinner with every night that passed. Now it was only the palest and thinnest of fingernail parings, and almost not there at all.

"I die," said the Moon.

"What does that mean?" asked the Boy.

"Just watch me," said the Moon, and it seemed that a silver tear stood in its eye. "Good-bye," it said.

And the next night there was no Moon at all.

The stars glowed more brightly than they ever had, but the night was deeply dark. The Boy and the Girl could hardly see each other.

"It's gone," said the Boy. "Once it was, and now it's not anymore. Once there was a Moon, and now there's not a Moon anymore. It dies." And he sat very close to the Girl in the fearful dark-ness. "That's the Moon's secret," he said.

The next night was just as dark.

But on the next night, as the Boy and the Girl sat close together watching the darkening sky in the east, they saw, rising over the purple hills, as thin as could be and as pale as anything, a new Moon.

"Moon!" said the Girl in wonder. "You came back!"

"Did I?" said the new Moon. Now it faced the opposite way, and its small cold voice was smaller and colder than before. "Well, I come and I go. Ah, but it's good to be young!"

And every night thereafter as they watched, the new Moon grew fatter and fuller. Its smile broadened and its cheeks puffed out. "Ah," he said proudly to the Girl, "it's good to be strong and beautiful."

"Am I like you?" asked the Girl. "Am I strong and beautiful?"

"You're very much like me," said the Moon. "Look inside yourself and see."

The nights passed. The full-faced new Moon began to shrink and lose its shape, just as the old Moon had done.

"I wane," said the Moon. "I grow old."

"Will I grow old?" the Girl asked.

"We're alike," the Moon said. "Look inside yourself and see."

The Girl looked within herself. And she saw that what the Moon said was true: they were alike. She too would change. She was changing even now, as though she had a Moon of her own within her. She was strong and young and beautiful: and yet she too would grow old. "That's the Moon's secret," she said. She had thought that the Moon's secret was a secret about herself: and she was right.

When day came, the Boy and the Girl looked around themselves. The world seemed to be different from the way it had been.

"Everything's changed," said the Girl. She looked at the Boy. "You've changed."

"You've changed," said the Boy, looking at the Girl. "Why?"

"We're different now," said the Girl. "Different things should have different names."

"Why have we changed?" asked the Boy.

"Well," said the Girl, as the Moon had said to her, "there it is."

"What name will you have, then?" the Boy asked.

"I will be the Woman."

He straightened his shoulders, he lifted his chin, and he looked firmly far off. "All right," he said. "Then I'll be the Man."

They took hands then, and looked at each other, and felt suddenly shy, and didn't know what to do next.

The Man and the Woman walked together in the forest. They saw that the summer's flowers had wilted and drooped on their brown stems. They hadn't noticed that before.

They saw a hunting hawk fall from the sky on a brown mouse, and they heard a tiny shriek as the mouse was speared by the hawk's sharp claws.

They saw a frog on a lily pad shoot out its long tongue, catch a careless dragonfly, and eat it. And they saw a heron step up silently on long legs behind the frog, catch it in its beak, and swallow it.

They kicked the dry brown leaves underfoot, leaves that had once danced green and dewy on the branches of the trees.

"Everything's changed," the Woman said.

"Nothing lasts," the Man said. He took the Woman's hand in

his. "For everything, there was a time before it was alive, and a time after it isn't alive anymore."

Bigger than the difference between a Squirrel and a Stone, bigger than the difference between Night and Day, was the difference between being alive and not being alive anymore.

They called the difference Death.

"I die," said the Moon to the Woman that night. It had grown as thin as thin, and was almost not there.

"Will I die?" asked the Woman, and the Moon didn't answer; but she needed only to look inside herself to know.

She looked up, and blinked the tears away that had come into her eyes. "Oh, look!" she said. "Look, look!"

For she could see, as the old Moon rolled away, that held within its long, long arms was the new Moon that would come to be in its place. It wasn't easy to see the new Moon; it was a pale, ghostly shadow. But it was like a promise. And the Woman knew that the promise had been made to her: for she and the Moon were alike.

"Now I know the Moon's secret," she said to herself, though what she knew she could never say in words.

Now through all this time the Nightingale had gone on with the business of his life: that is, singing in the day and sleeping at night, eating bugs and berries, raising his young and going about in the world to see what he could see.

One day was very much like another, as it had always been and would always be.

He didn't know that the Man and the Woman had invented Time.

When he came upon them one day, he greeted them as usual:

"Hello, Boy," he sang. "Hello, Girl."

"I'm not a boy," the Man said. "Not anymore. Once I was, but now I'm a Man."

"I'm not a girl," said the Woman. "I've changed. Now I'm a Woman."

"Oh," said the Nightingale. "Sorry. I'll try to remember." He sang a few notes, and then he asked the Man, "Did you ever find an answer to your question?"

"No," said the Man. "But I learned a lot of things."

"Is that so," said the Nightingale.

"Yes," said the Man. He pointed up at the Nightingale. "Things aren't as you think they are."

"No?" said the Nightingale.

"No," said the Man. "Listen to the Moon. You'll learn."

"Oh?" said the Nightingale. "The Moon never spoke to *me*. What did the Moon say?"

"There is Time," said the Man. He came closer to the branch where the Nightingale sat. "There was a time before you were," he said, "and there will be a time after. You won't live forever. You will die."

"Do you think so?" said the Nightingale, who didn't know at all what the Man meant.

"You will. There are hawks, Bird. There are foxes. There are owls and weasels."

"But not just now," said the Nightingale, looking around quickly.

"There will be!" said the Man. His expression was so fierce and strange that the Nightingale flew to a higher branch away from him.

"You will die, Bird!" said the man in a terrible voice. "You will die!"

The Nightingale was astonished and troubled and didn't know what to do. So he sang. "It's all right," he sang. "It's all right."

"It's not all right!" cried the Man. "It's not. Because you'll die. And so will I!"

And just at that moment, with a noise of winds and many rivers, with a clamor of birdsong and a sound of leaves falling, Dame Kind came striding through the forest toward them.

The Woman leapt up. "We'll run and hide!" she said. She took the Man's hand. "Quick, we must!" she said, and together they ran to hide in the forest.

"Come out," said Dame Kind.

She waited.

"Come out," she said again. And the Man and the Woman came out from where they had hidden themselves.

"Why did you hide?" asked Dame Kind.

"Because we were afraid," said the Woman.

Dame Kind looked at them sadly for a long time. Then she said in a gentle voice: "Who told you you should be afraid?"

The Man and the Woman looked away from Dame Kind, and they made no answer.

"And who told you that you would die?" Dame Kind asked them. "Was it the Moon?"

"It was the Moon," said the Man.

"No," said the Woman, and she raised her eyes to Dame Kind. "It wasn't the Moon. We learned it ourselves."

And that was true.

Dame Kind took the Man's shoulder in her great hand. She gently brushed away the hair that fell before the Woman's face. She said, "Oh, dear. Oh, my poor children." Then she covered her eyes with her hand and shook her head. "Oh, my," she said. "Oh, dear."

"We only wanted to learn," said the Man. "There *is* Time, and there *is* Change, and there *is* Death. And you never told us."

"You never told us," the Woman said, her eyes filling with tears. "You never told us we would die."

Dame Kind lowered her hand from her eyes. "No," she said. "I didn't. And I will tell you why. Until you thought of those things, they did not exist.

"Until you thought of Time, there was no such thing. Things went on as they always had; there wasn't a Yesterday, and there wasn't a Tomorrow; there was only Today.

"Until you thought of Change, everything remained the same. The flowers were always growing, the young ones were always being born, the Sun and the stars and yes, even the Moon, were always doing just as they always do. Now you will see them change, you alone, and nothing will ever be quite the same for you.

"Until you thought of Death, dear children, nothing died. My creatures only lived. They didn't know of a time when they had not been, and they couldn't think of a time when they would not be. And so they lived forever. And so would you have too: except that you thought of Death.

"And when you thought of those things," she said, "you thought of fear, too.

"And you thought of weeping." She dried the Woman's eyes with the sleeve of her gown.

"And the worst thing is," Dame Kind said, and a tear came to her own eye, "that now you have thought of these things, you cannot take them back, ever. That's the way it is with ideas. Once you have one, there's no going back."

The Woman wept, and the Man hung his head at these words of Dame Kind's; and the Nightingale remembered a morning—an important morning—when Dame Kind had said those very words to him: once you have an idea, there's no going back.

Dame Kind crossed her arms and rose up to her full height. "And now," she said. She shrugged her shoulders. "Well, what now? I just don't know. I don't know if you can ever be happy here again; not as happy as you once were." She looked around her at the blooming forest. "I can't have you going about the world weeping. I can't have you telling the birds and the beasts that they will die. I can't have that."

"It's all right," sang the Nightingale. He hadn't understood much of what had passed between Dame Kind and the Man and the Woman, but he didn't like to see them sad. "It's all right," he sang. "I don't mind."

"All right then," said the Man. His face was brave, and his eyes were dry. His knees shook, but he pretended that they didn't. "All right then, we'll go someplace else." He clenched his fists and set his jaw. "If we can't be happy here, we'll go someplace else."

"You can't," Dame Kind said. "There isn't anyplace else."

The Man put his arm around the Woman. "All right," he said, all right then: I'll make one up. I'll make up another place. I'll make up another place, a better place, and go there."

"Oh, dear," said Dame Kind. She lifted her fingers to her chin in alarm and puzzlement.

The Woman brushed the last of her tears from her eyes. She said, "Yes! I'll make up someplace else, too. A better place. And I'll go there."

"No!" the Man said turning on her. "*I'll* make up another place, and we'll *both* go there. Come on!" And he took the Woman's arm and led her away; and though she looked back once, and though her eyes began again to fill with tears, she knew that she could not leave the Man; and so she went with him, and they went out of the forest together.

"Perhaps," Dame Kind said when they were gone, "perhaps I made a mistake." She sat sadly on the stump of a tree she had made long ago, and had made to fall down, too. "Perhaps the Boy and the Girl were a mistake."

"Oh, no," the Nightingale said. "I don't think you could make a mistake."

"I didn't think so either," Dame Kind said. "Well—I have made one or two—some animals and plants that didn't work out—but they all came right in the end. They did their part."

"So will the Boy and the Girl."

"I don't know," said Dame Kind. "It's odd, having things come about in the world that I didn't think of. This place they're going to make up: What will it be like? I don't know. Because I didn't think of it."

"But you did," said the Nightingale. "I don't know anything about it, but—didn't you think up the Boy and the Girl? If you thought up the Boy and the Girl, didn't you think up everything they can think up? In a way, I mean."

Dame Kind thought about that.

"I guess I did," she said at last. A broad smile came over her face, a smile that was like the Sun coming from clouds; and in fact at that very moment a mass of thick clouds did go away from the face of the Sun, and the Sun's smile remade the patterns of light and dark amid the ferns and the flowers. "I guess I did at that. In a way." She sighed, and stood. A thousand thousand duties were calling to her. "Anyway, I'll just have to get used to it. And I don't suppose the story's over yet."

The Nightingale didn't know what she meant by that, but he was glad to see Dame Kind happy again. He sang a few notes. "It's all right," he sang.

"You know," Dame Kind said to him as she went away, "all those things the Man said are true. About Time. About Death."

"It is?" said the Nightingale.

"But if I were you," said Dame Kind, "I wouldn't worry about it."

"If you say so," said the Nightingale, and his heart was filled with gladness.

And Dame Kind went away, to pour rain, to plant seeds, to turn the world in its socket. "And as for you," she said to the Moon when next she saw it, "from now on you will hold your tongue." She pinched its nose and squeezed its cheeks and locked up its lips until its face was hardly a face at all. "And from now on forever," she said, "when the Man and the Woman ask you questions, no matter how they insist, you will answer nothing, nothing, nothing at all."

And so it has been, from that day to this.

It was another day when the Nightingale saw the Man again, but whether it was the next day, or the day after that, or many many days later, the Nightingale didn't know, for he didn't keep track of such things.

The Nightingale was singing in the forest when he saw the Man some way off.

The Man stood looking into the forest where the Sun fell in patterns of dark and light on the flowers and the ferns.

"Why don't you come in?" said the Nightingale. "Come in and rest, and have a chat."

"I can't," the Man said. "I can't pass through this gate."

"What gate is that?" the Nightingale asked.

"This one here," the Man said, pointing ahead of him with the stick he carried.

But the Nightingale could see no gate there. "Well, I don't know what you mean," he said, "but if you say so."

The Man went on staring into the forest, through the gate that he alone saw there. He seemed at once sad and angry and resolute. The Nightingale sang a few notes and said, "Tell me. How is it with you now? How did the place you made up turn out? Is it better than here?"

The Man sat down, holding his stick in his lap, and put his elbows on his knees and his cheeks in his hands.

"I wouldn't say *better*," he said a little sadly. "It's interesting. Bigger. I think it's bigger, but we haven't gone very far yet. There's a lot of work to do."

"A lot of what?" asked the Nightingale.

"Work," the Man said, looking up at the branch where the Nightingale sat and saying the word a little bitterly. "Work. You wouldn't understand."

"I think," the Nightingale said cheerfully, "I think I understand you less and less. But don't hold it against me."

The Man laughed, and shook his head. "No, I won't," he said. He sighed. "It'll be all right. It's the nights that are the hardest time."

"Why is that?" asked the Nightingale. He hardly knew what Night was, after all; he slept all through it, and when he awoke, it was gone.

"Well, there are *Things* in the dark. Or anyway I *think* there are Things. I can't be sure. *She* says they're Dreams."

"Dreams?"

"Things that you think are there but aren't."

"If you say so," said the Nightingale.

"But it doesn't matter," said the Man. He grasped the stick in the two clever hands the Nightingale had always marveled at. "See, I've got this stick now. If anything comes near—" He struck out with the stick, which made a swishing noise in the empty air.

"That's a good idea," said the Nightingale. "I never would have thought of it."

The Man was turning the stick in his hands with a dissatisfied expression. "I could make it better," he said. "Somehow better. Stronger. Like stone—that's the strongest thing. So it would cut, like a sharp stone." He made an imaginary jab with the stick, like a jay's sharp beak breaking into an egg, except there was no egg there. Then he put down the stick and sat again with his cheeks in his hands.

"Anyway," the Man said, "there's nothing to be afraid of *now*."

"No," said the Nightingale.

"But *then*," the Man said. "Soon. There might be something to be afraid of."

"If you say so," said the Nightingale.

The Man rose to go, shouldering the stick he had thought of. "It'll be all right," he said again. "It's just the nights that are hard."

He looked back once through the gate that he saw there, which kept him from the precincts of the forest, and which the Nightingale couldn't see.

"Well, good-bye then," he sang. "Good-bye."

And the Man went away down the valley to the place he and the Woman had made up.

◫

When darkness came that night, the Nightingale perched on his usual branch. He fluffed his feathers; he bent his legs so that his sharp, small feet locked themselves tightly around the branch (so that he wouldn't fall from the tree in his sleep). He nestled his beak in the feathers of his shoulder and closed his eyes.

But sleep wouldn't come.

The Nightingale's eyes opened. He shut them again, and again they opened.

The Nightingale was thinking.

For the first time in his life, and the first time in all the time there had been a Nightingale, the Nightingale was thinking about something that was not in front of his eyes.

He was thinking about the Man and the Woman, alone in the place they had made up, wherever it was.

He was thinking of what the Man had said to him: that it was all right, but that the nights were hard.

That there were Things in the night to be afraid of.

The Nightingale took his beak out from the feathers of his shoulder and looked around himself.

There were no Things in the night to be afraid of that he could see.

There was a sparkling dimness; there were the black shapes of the sleeping trees and the very, very dark pool of the forest floor. There was the secret Moon turning in the clouds and saying nothing. There were stars, and there were breezes. But no Things.

"It's all right," the Nightingale sang. And because there were no other songs being sung, the Nightingale's song was stronger and sweeter than he had ever heard it.

"It's all right," he sang again, and again his song floated out into the night, and lingered, all alone.

That's interesting, thought the Nightingale, *very interesting: but the night is for sleep.* He tucked his beak again into the feathers of his shoulder and closed his eyes.

Without even knowing he had done so, he found after a few moments that he had opened his eyes again and was looking around himself and thinking.

He was thinking, *What if I fly to where the Man and the Woman are?*

If they hear me sing, he thought, *they might not be so afraid. If they heard me singing, they would remember that day will come. And anyway,* he thought, *what's the use of sleeping all night, when you can be awake and singing?*

He made up his mind to do this, even though it was something he had never done before. He looked around himself, wondering how he would find the Man and the Woman. He unlocked his feet from the branch where he sat, opened his brown wings, and sailed off carefully into the cool darkness.

He flew, not knowing exactly where he should fly; now and then he stopped to rest, and to eat a few of the bugs that were so plentiful, and to look at the new world of night he had discovered, and to test his song against it. And after a time that seemed to him more short than long, he came upon the place where the Man and the Woman were.

"Why, it isn't very far away at all," he said to himself. "In fact it seems just like the same old forest to me."

There was one difference, though.

In the place where the Man and the Woman were, there was something bright, something yellow and orange and red, dancing and shifting and shining. It was as though a tiny piece of the Sun had been broken off and set before them.

The Man and the Woman had thought of fire.

They sat before their fire, with their arms around each other, looking into the fire and into the deep darkness around them. In one hand the Man held the stick he had thought of.

The Nightingale didn't like to get too close to the new idea of fire, which was surely marvelous but a little scary; and so he hid himself in a thicket. And from there he sang.

"It's all right," he sang.

The Woman listened. "Did you hear that?" she asked.

"What?" said the Man, looking up in alarm.

"Listen," the Woman said.

The Nightingale sang: "It's all right."

The Man and the Woman listened to the song. In the stillness of the night it was so clear that it seemed they heard it for the first time. They had never noticed that it was so beautiful, so strong and soft, so happy and sad all at once.

"Once," said the Man, "he sang in the day."

"Now he sings at night," the Woman said.

"We'll call him the Nightingale," said the Man.

The Woman rested her head on the Man's shoulder. Hearing the Nightingale's song, she remembered the forest they had left. She remembered the happiness they had had there. She remembered the Sun falling in patterns of light and darkness on the flowers and the ferns. She remembered it all, and hot tears came to her eyes, because they had lost it all.

"It's all right," sang the Nightingale.

The Woman thought: *I can remember it all.* And then she thought: *If I can remember it all, then I haven't lost it—not completely. If I can remember it, I will have it always, even if only a little bit of it. Always: no matter what.*

She closed her eyes. "It's all right," she said. "It will be all right. You'll see."

The Man put his arm around her, glad of her warmth in the darkness. He listened to the Nightingale sing, and he thought: *Day will come. No matter what happened before, day will always come. Tomorrow the Sun will lift itself over the hills, and the world will be new. What will it be like?* He didn't know, but he thought it might be good. He hoped it would be good.

"It's all right," sang the Nightingale.

"It's all right," said the Man, and he held the Woman in his arms. "I think it will be all right." He closed his eyes, too. "Anyway," he said, "I don't think the story's over yet."

And so, from that day to this, the Nightingale has sung his song at night.

In the spring and summer, when his heart is full and the nights are soft and warm, he sings his song of hope and remembrance, his song that no one can imitate and no one can describe.

In the day, too, he can sometimes be heard singing, but so can the blackbird and the thrush and many other singers, and the Nightingale is hard to hear. But in the night he is alone: he is the one who sings at night.

It was the only new idea the Nightingale had ever had, and he never had another one.

GREAT WORK OF TIME

▣ ▣ ▣

I. THE SINGLE EXCURSION OF CASPAR LAST

IF WHAT I AM TO SET DOWN is a chronicle, then it must differ from any other chronicle whatever, for it begins, not in one time or place, but everywhere at once—or perhaps *everywhen* is the better word. It might be begun at any point along the infinite, infinitely broken coastline of time.

It might even begin within the forest in the sea: huge trees like American redwoods, with their roots in the black benthos, and their leaves moving slowly in the blue currents overhead. There it might end as well.

It might begin in 1893—or in 1983. Yes: it might be as well to begin with Last, in an American sort of voice (for we are all Americans now, aren't we?). Yes, Last shall be first: pale, fattish Caspar Last, on excursion in the springtime of 1983 to a far, far part of the Empire.

The tropical heat clothed Caspar Last like a suit as he disembarked from the plane. It was nearly as claustrophobic as the hours he had spent in the middle seat of a three-across, economy-class pew between two other cut-rate, one-week-excursion, plane-fare-and-hotel-room holidaymakers in monstrous good spirits. Like them, Caspar had taken the excursion because it was the cheapest possible way to get to and from this equatorial backwater. Unlike them, he hadn't come to soak up sun and molasses-dark rum. He didn't intend to spend all his time at the beach, or even within the twentieth century.

It had come down, in the end, to a matter of money. Caspar Last last had never had money, though he certainly hadn't lacked the means to make it; with any application he could have made good money as a consultant to any of a dozen research firms, but that would have required a certain subjection of his time and thought to others, and Caspar was incapable of that. It's often said that genius can live in happy disregard of material circumstances, dress in rags, not notice its nourishment, and serve only its own abstract imperatives. This was Caspar's case, except that he wasn't happy about it: he was bothered, bitter, and rageful at his poverty. Fame he cared nothing for, success was meaningless except when defined as the solution to abstract problems. A great fortune would have been burdensome and useless. All he wanted was a nice bit of change.

He had decided, therefore, to use his "time machine" once only, before it and the principles that animated it were destroyed, for good he hoped. (Caspar always thought of his "time machine" thus, with scare-quotes around it, since it was not really a machine, and Caspar did not believe in time.) He would use it, he decided, to make money. Somehow.

The one brief annihilation of "time" that Caspar intended to allow himself was in no sense a test run. He knew that his "machine" would function as predicted. If he hadn't needed the money, he wouldn't use it at all. As far as he was concerned, the principles once discovered, the task was completed; like a completed jigsaw puzzle, it had no further interest; there was really nothing to do with it except gloat over it briefly and then sweep all the pieces randomly back into the box.

It was a mark of Caspar's odd genius that figuring out a scheme with which to make money out of the past (which was the only "direction" his "machine" would take him) proved almost as hard, given the limitations of his process, as arriving at the process itself.

He had gone through all the standard wish fulfillments and rejected them. He couldn't, armed with today's race results, return to yesterday and hit the daily double. For one thing it would take a couple of thousand in betting money to make it worth it, and Caspar didn't have a couple of thousand. More importantly, Caspar had calculated the results of his present self appearing at any point within the compass of his own biological existence, and those results made him shudder.

Similar difficulties attended any scheme that involved using money to make money. If he returned to 1940 and bought, say, two hundred shares of IBM for next to nothing: in the first place there would be the difficulty of leaving those shares somehow in escrow for his unborn self; there would be the problem of the alteration this growing fortune would have on the linear life he had actually lived; and where was he to acquire the five hundred dollars or whatever was needed in the currency of 1940? The same problem obtained if he wanted to return to 1623 and pick up a First Folio of Shakespeare, or to 1460 and a Gutenberg Bible: the cost of the currency he would need rose in relation to the antiquity, thus the rarity and value, of the object to be bought with it. There was also the problem of walking into a bookseller's and plunking down a First Folio he had just happened to stumble on while cleaning out the attic. In any case, Caspar doubted that anything as large as a book could be successfully transported "through time." He'd be lucky if he could go and return in his clothes.

Outside the airport, Caspar boarded a bus with his fellow excursionists, already hard at work with their cameras and index fingers as they rode through a sweltering lowland out of which concrete-block light industry was struggling to be born. The hotel in the capital was as he expected, shoddy-American and intermittently refrigerated. He ceased to notice it, forwent the complimentary rum concoction promised with his tour, and after asking that his case be put in the hotel safe—extra charge for that, he noted bitterly—he went immediately to the Hall of Records in the government complex. The collection of old survey maps of the city and environs were more extensive than he had hoped. He spent most of that day among them searching for a blank place on the 1856 map, a place as naked as possible of buildings, brush, water, and that remained thus through the years. He discovered one, visited it by unmuffled taxi, found it suitable. It would save him from the awful inconvenience of "arriving" in the "past" and finding himself inserted into some local's wattle-and-daub wall. Next morning, then, he would be "on his way." If he had believed in time, he would have said that the whole process would take less than a day's time.

Before settling on this present plan, Caspar had toyed with the idea of bringing back from the past something immaterial: some knowledge, some secret that would allow him to make himself rich in his own present. Ships have gone down with millions in bullion: he could learn exactly where. Captain Kidd's treasure. Inca gold. Archaeological rarities buried in China. Leaving aside the obvious physical difficulties of these schemes, he couldn't be sure that their location wouldn't shift in the centuries between his glimpse of them and his "real" life span; and even if he could be certain, no one else would have much reason to believe him, and he didn't have the wherewithal to raise expeditions himself. So all that was out.

He had a more general, theoretical problem to deal with. Of course the very presence of his eidolon in the past would alter, in however inconsequential a way, the succeeding history of the world. The comical paradoxes of shooting one's own grandfather and the like neither amused nor intrigued him, and the chance he took of altering the world he lived in out of all recognition was constantly present to him. Statistically, of course, the chance of this present plan of his altering anything significantly, except his own personal fortunes, was remote to a high power. But his scruples had caused him to reject anything such as, say, discovering the Koh-i-noor diamond before its historical discoverers. No: what he needed to abstract from the past was something immensely trivial, something common, something the past wouldn't miss but that the present held in the highest regard; something that would take the briefest possible time and the least irruption of himself into the past to acquire; something he could reasonably be believed to possess through simple historical chance; and something tiny enough to survive the cross-time "journey" on his person.

It had come to him quite suddenly—all his ideas did, as though handed to him—when he learned that his great-great-grandfather had been a commercial traveler in the tropics, and that in the attic of his mother's house (which Caspar had never had the wherewithal to move out of) some old journals and papers of his still moldered. They were, when he inspected them, completely without interest. But the dates were right.

Caspar had left a wake-up call at the desk for before dawn the next morning. There was some difficulty about getting his case out of the safe, and more difficulty about getting a substantial breakfast served at that hour (Caspar expected not to eat during his excursion), but he did arrive at his chosen site before the horrendous tropical dawn broke, and after paying the taxi, he had darkness enough left in which to make his preparations and change into his costume. The costume—a linen suit, a shirt, hat, boots—had cost him twenty dollars in rental from a theatrical costumer, and he could only hope it was accurate enough not to cause alarm in 1856. The last item he took from his case was the copper coin, which had cost him quite a bit, as he needed one unworn and of the proper date. He turned it in his fingers for a moment, thinking that if, unthinkably, his calculations were wrong and he didn't survive this journey, it would make an interesting obol for Charon.

Out of the unimaginable chaos of its interminable stochastic fiction, Time thrust only one unforeseen oddity on Caspar Last as he, or something like him, appeared beneath a plantain tree in 1856: he had grown a beard almost down to his waist. It was abominably hot.

The suburbs of the city had of course vanished. The road he stood by was a muddy track down which a cart was being driven by a tiny and close-faced Indian in calico. He followed the cart, and his costume boots were caked with mud when at last he came into the center of town, trying to appear nonchalant and to remember the layout of the city as he had studied it in the maps. He wanted to speak to no one if possible, and he did manage to find the post office without affecting, however minutely, the heterogeneous crowd of blacks, Indians, and Europeans in the filthy streets. Having absolutely no sense of humor and very little imagination other than the most rigidly abstract helped to keep him strictly about his business and not to faint, as another might have, with wonder and astonishment at his translation, the first, last, and only of its kind a man would ever make.

"I would like," he said to the mulatto inside the brass and mahogany cage, "an envelope, please."

"Of course, sir."

"How long will it take for a letter mailed now to arrive locally?"

"Within the city? It would arrive in the afternoon post."

"Very good."

Caspar went to a long, ink-stained table, and with one of the steel pens provided, he addressed the envelope to Georg von Humboldt Last, Esq., Grand Hotel, City, in the approximation of an antique round hand that he had been practicing for weeks. There was a moment's doubt as he tried to figure how to fold up and seal the cumbersome envelope, but he did it, and gave this empty missive to the incurious mulatto. He slipped his precious coin across the marble to him. For the only moment of his adventure, Caspar's heart beat fast as he watched the long, slow brown fingers affix a stamp, cancel and date it with a pen-stroke, and drop it into a brass slot like a hungry mouth behind him.

It only remained to check into the Grand Hotel, explain about his luggage's being on its way up from the port, and sit silent on the hotel terrace, growing faint with heat and hunger and expectation, until the afternoon post.

The one aspect of the process Caspar had never been able to decide about was whether his eidolon's residence in the fiction of the past would consume any "time" in the fiction of the present. It did. When, at evening, with the letter held tight in his hand and pressed to his bosom, Caspar reappeared beardless beneath the plantain tree in the traffic-tormented and smoky suburb, the gaseous red sun was squatting on the horizon in the west, just as it had been in the same place in 1856.

He would have his rum drink after all, he decided.

"Mother," he said, "do you think there might be anything valuable in those papers of your great-grandfather's?"

"What papers, dear? Oh—I remember. I couldn't say. I thought once of donating them to a historical society. How do you mean, valuable?"

"Well, old stamps, for one thing."

"You're free to look, Caspar dear."

Caspar was not surprised (though he supposed the rest of the world was soon to be) that he found among the faded, water-spotted diaries and papers an envelope that bore a faint brown address—it had aged nicely in the next-to-no-time it had traveled "forward" with Caspar   and that had in its upper-right-hand corner a one-penny magenta stamp, quite undistinguished, issued for a brief time in 1856 by the Crown Colony of British Guiana.

The asking price of the sole known example of this stamp, a "unique" owned by a consortium of wealthy men who preferred to remain anonymous, was a million dollars. Caspar Last had not decided whether it would be more profitable for him to sell the stamp itself, or to approach the owners of the unique, who would certainly pay a large amount to have it destroyed, and thus preserve their unique's uniqueness. It did seem a shame that the only artifact man had ever succeeded in extracting from the nonexistent past should go into the fire, but Caspar didn't really care. His own bonfire—the notes and printouts, the conclusions about the nature and transversability of time and the orthogonal logic by which it was accomplished—would be only a little more painful.

The excursion was over; the only one that remained to him was the brief but, to him, all-important one of his own mortal span. He was looking forward to doing it first class.

■ □ ■

II. An Appointment in Khartoum

It might be begun very differently, though; and it might now be begun again, in a different time and place, like one of those romances by Stevenson, where different stories only gradually reveal themselves to be parts of a whole . . .

The paradox is acute, so acute that the only possible stance for a chronicler is to ignore it altogether, and carry on. This, the Otherhood's central resignation, required a habit of mind so contrary to ordinary cause-and-effect thinking as to be, literally, unimaginable. It would only have been in the changeless precincts of the Club they had established beyond all frames of reference, when deep in leather armchairs or seated all together around the long table whereon their names were carved, that they dared reflect on it at all.

Take, for a single but not a random instance, the example of Denys Winterset, twenty-three years old, Winchester, Oriel College, younger son of a well-to-do doctor and in 1956 ending a first year as assistant district commissioner of police in Bechuanaland.

He hadn't done strikingly well in his post. Though on the surface he was exactly the sort of man who was chosen, or who chose himself, to serve the Empire in those years—a respectable second at Oxford, a cricketer more steady than showy, a reserved, sensible, presentable lad with sound principles and few beliefs—still there was an odd strain in him. Too imaginative, perhaps; given to fits of abstraction, even to what his commissioner called "tears, idle tears." Still, he was resourceful and hardworking; he hadn't disgraced himself, and he was now on his way north on the Cape-to-Cairo Railroad, to take a month's holiday in Cairo and England. His anticipation was marred somewhat by a sense that, after a year in the veldt, he would no longer fit into the comfortable old shoe of his childhood home; that he would feel as odd and exiled as he had in Africa. Home had become a dream, in Bechuanaland; if, at home, Bechuanaland became a dream, then he would have no place real at all to be at home in; he would be an exile for good.

The high veldt sped away as he was occupied with these thoughts, the rich farmlands of Southern Rhodesia. In the saloon car a young couple, very evidently on honeymoon, watched expectantly for the first glimpse of the eternal rainbow, visible miles off, that haloed Victoria Falls. Denys watched them and their excitement, feeling old and wise. Americans, doubtless: they had that shy, inoffensive air of all Americans abroad, that wondering quality as of children let out from a dark and oppressive school to play in the sun.

"There!" said the woman as the train took a bend. "Oh, look, how beautiful!"

Even over the train's sound they could hear the sound of the falls now, like distant cannon. The young man looked at his watch and smiled at Denys. "Right on time," he said, and Denys smiled too, amused to be complimented on his railroad's efficiency. The Bulawayo Bridge—longest and highest span on the Cape-to-Cairo line—leapt out over the gorge. "My God, that's something," the young man said. "Cecil Rhodes built this, right?"

"No," Denys said. "He thought of it, but never lived to see it. It would have been far easier to build it a few miles up, but Rhodes pictured the train being washed in the spray of the falls as it passed. And so it was built here."

The noise of the falls was immense now, and weirdly various, a medley of cracks, thumps, and explosions playing over the constant bass roar, which was not so much like a noise at all as it was like an eternal deep-drawn breath. And as the train chugged out across the span, aimed at Cairo thousands of miles away, passing here the place so hard-sought-for a hundred years ago—the place where the Nile had its origin—the spray *did* fall on the train just as Cecil Rhodes had imagined it, flung spindrift hissing on the locomotive, drops speckling the window they looked out of and rainbowing in the white air. The young Americans were still with wonder, and Denys, too, felt a lifting of his heart.

At Khartoum, Denys bid the honeymooners farewell: they were taking the Empire Airways flying boat from here to Gibraltar, and the Atlantic dirigible home. Denys, by now feeling quite proprietary about his Empire's transportation services, assured them that both flights would also certainly be right on time, and would be as comfortable as the sleepers they were leaving, would serve the same excellent meals with the same white napery embossed with the same royal insignia. Denys himself was driven to the Grand Hotel. His Sudan Railways sleeper to Cairo left the next morning.

After a bath in a tiled tub large enough almost to swim in, Denys changed into dinner clothes (which had been carefully laid out for him on the huge bed—for whom had these cavernous rooms been built, a race of Kitcheners?). He reserved a table for one in the grill room and went down to the bar. One thing he *must* do in London, he thought, shooting his cuffs, was to visit his tailor. Bechuanaland had sweated off his college baby fat, and the tropics seemed to have turned his satin lapels faintly green.

The bar was comfortably filled, before the dinner hour, with men of several sorts and a few women, and with the low various murmur of their talk. Some of the men wore *white* dinner jackets— businessmen and tourists, Denys supposed; and a few even wore shorts with black shoes and stockings, a style Denys found inherently funny, as though a tailor had made a frightful error and cut evening clothes to the pattern of bush clothes. He ordered a whiskey.

Rarely in African kraals or in his bungalow or his whitewashed office did Denys think about his Empire: or if he did, it was in some local, even irritated way, of Imperial trivialities or Imperial red tape, the rain-rusted engines and stacks of tropic-mildewed paperwork that, collectively, Denys and his young associates called the White Man's Burden. It seemed to require a certain remove from the immediacy of Empire before he could perceive it. Only here (beneath the fans' ticking, amid the voices naming places— Kandahar, Durban, Singapore, Penang—did the larger Empire that Denys had never seen but had lived in in thought and feeling since childhood open in his mind. How odd, how far more odd really than admirable or deplorable, that the small place which was his childhood, circumscribed and cozy—gray Westminster, chilly Trafalgar Square of the black umbrellas, London of the coal-

smoked wallpaper and endless chimney pots—should have opened
itself out so ceaselessly and for so long into huge hot places, sub-
continents where rain never fell or never stopped, lush with vegetable growth or burdened with seas of sand or stone. Send forth
the best ye breed: or at least large numbers of those ye breed. If
one thought how odd it was—and if one thought then of what
should have been natural empires, enormous spreads of restless
real property like America or Russia turning in on themselves,
making themselves into what seemed (to Denys, who had never
seen them) to be very small places—then it did seem to be destiny
of a kind. Not a destiny to be proud of, particularly, nor ashamed
of either, but one whose compelling inner logic could only be marveled at.

Quite suddenly, and with poignant vividness, Denys saw himself, or rather felt himself once more to be, before his nursery fire,
looking into the small glow of it, with animal crackers and cocoa
for tea, listening to Nana telling tales of her brother the sergeant,
and the Afghan frontier, and the now-dead king he had served—
listening, and feeling the Empire ranged in widening circles
around him: first Harley Street, outside the window, and then
Buckingham Palace, where the king lived; and the country then
into which the trains went, and then the cold sea, and the posses-
sions, and the Commonwealth, stretching ever farther outward,
worldwide: but always with his small glowing fire and his comfort
and wonder at the heart of it.

So, there he is: a young man with the self-possessed air of an
older, in evening clothes aged prematurely in places where evening clothes had not been made to go; thinking, if it could be called
thinking, of a nursery fire; and about to be spoken to by the man
next down the bar. If his feelings could be summed up and spoken,

they were that, however odd, there is nothing more real, more pin-
ioned by acts great and small, more clinker-built of time and space
and filled brimful of this and that, than is the real world in which
his five senses and his memories had their being; and that this was
deeply satisfying.

"I beg your pardon," said the man next down the bar.

"Good evening," Denys said.

"My name is Davenant," the man said. He held out a square,
blunt-fingered hand, and Denys drew himself up and shook it.
"You are, I believe, Denys Winterset?"

"I am," Denys said, searching the smiling face before him and
wondering from where he was known to him. It was a big, square,
high-fronted head, a little like Bernard Shaw's, with ice-blue eyes
of that twinkle; it was crowned far back with a neat hank of white
hair, and was crossed above the broad jaw with upright white mustaches.

"You don't mind the intrusion?" the man said. "I wonder if you
know whether the grub here is as good as once it was. It's been
some time since I last ate a meal in Khartoum."

"The last time I did so was a year ago this week," Denys said.
"It was quite good."

"Excellent," said Davenant, looking at Denys as though something about the young man amused him. "In that case, if you have
no other engagement, may I ask your company?"

"I have no other engagement," Denys said; in fact he had rather
been looking forward to dining alone, but deference to his superi-
ors (of whom this man Davenant was surely in some sense one)
was strong in him. "Tell me, though, how you come to know my
name."

"Oh, well, there it is," Davenant said. "One has dealings with the Colonial Office. One sees a face, a name is attached to it, one files it but doesn't forget—that sort of thing. Part of one's job."

A civil servant, an inspector of some kind. Denys felt the sinking one feels on running into one's tutor in a wine bar: the evening not well begun. "They may well be crowded for dinner," he said.

"I have reserved a quiet table," said the smiling man, lifting his glass to Denys.

The grub was, in fact, superior. Sir Geoffrey Davenant was an able teller of tales, and he had many to tell. He was, apparently, no such dull thing as an inspector for the Colonial Office, though just what office he did fill Denys couldn't determine. He seemed to have been "attached to" or "had dealings with" or "gone about for" half the establishments of the Empire. He embodied, it seemed to Denys, the entire strange adventure about which Denys had been thinking when Sir Geoffrey had first spoken to him.

"So," Sir Geoffrey said, filling their glasses from a bottle of South African claret—no harm in being patriotic, he'd said, for one bottle—"so, after some months of stumbling about Central Asia and making myself useful one way or another, I was to make my way back to Sadiya. I crossed the Tibetan frontier disguised as a monk—"

"A monk?"

"Yes. Having lost all my gear in Manchuria, I could do the poverty part quite well. I had a roll of rupees, the films, and a compass hidden inside my prayer wheel. Mine didn't whiz round them with the same sanctity as the other fellows', but no matter. After adventures too ordinary to describe—avalanches and so on—I managed to reach the monastery at Rangbok, on the old road up to Everest. Rather near collapse. I was recovering a bit and thinking how to proceed when there was a runner with a telegram.

From my superior at Ch'eng-tu. WARN DAVENANT MASSACRE SADIYA, it said. The Old Man then was famously closemouthed. But this was particularly unhelpful, as it did not say who had massacred whom—or why." He lifted the silver cover of a dish, and found it empty.

"This must have been a good long time ago," Denys said.

"Oh, yes," Davenant said, raising his ice-blue eyes to Denys. "A good long time ago. That was an excellent curry. Nearly as good as at Veeraswamy's, in London—which is, strangely, the best in the world. Shall we have coffee?"

Over this, and brandy and cigars, Sir Geoffrey's stories modulated into reflections. Pleasant as his company was, Denys couldn't overcome a sensation that everything Sir Geoffrey said to him was rehearsed, laid on for his entertainment, or perhaps his enlightenment, and yet with no clue in it as to why he had thus been singled out.

"It amuses me," Sir Geoffrey said, "how constant it is in human nature to think that things might have gone on differently from the way they did. In a man's own life, first of all: how he might have taken this or that very different route, except for this or that accident, this or that slight push—if he'd only known then, and so on. And then in history as well, we ruminate endlessly, if, what if, if only . . . The world seems always somehow malleable to our minds, or to our imaginations anyway."

"Strange you should say so," Denys said. "I was thinking, just before you spoke to me, about how very solid the world seems to me, how very real. And—if you don't mind my thrusting it into your thoughts—you never did tell me how it is you come to know my name; or why it is you thought good to invite me to that excellent dinner."

"My dear boy," Davenant said, holding up his cigar as though to defend his innocence.

"I can't think it was chance."

"My dear boy," Davenant said in a different tone, "if anything is, that was not. I will explain all. You were on that train of thought. If you will have patience while it trundles by."

Denys said nothing further. He sipped his coffee, feeling a dew of sweat on his forehead.

"History," said Sir Geoffrey. "Yes. Of course the possible worlds we make don't compare to the real one we inhabit—not nearly so well furnished, or tricked out with details. And yet still somehow better. More satisfying. Perhaps the novelist is only a special case of a universal desire to reshape, to 'take this sorry scheme of things entire,' smash it into bits, and 'remold it nearer to the heart's desire'—as old Khayyám says. The egoist is continually doing it with his own life. To dream of doing it with history is no more useful a game, I suppose, but as a game, it shows more sport. There are rules. You can be more objective, if that's an appropriate word." He seemed to grow pensive for a moment. He looked at the end of his cigar. It had gone out, but he didn't relight it.

"Take this Empire," he went on, drawing himself up somewhat to say it. "One doesn't want to be mawkish, but one has served it. Extended it a bit, made it more secure; done one's bit. You and I. Nothing more natural, then, if we have worked for its extension in the future, to imagine its extension in the past. We can put our finger on the occasional bungle, the missed chance, the wrong man in the wrong place, and so on, and we think: if I had only been there, seen to it that the news went through, got the guns there in time, forced the issue at a certain moment—well. But as long as one is dreaming, why stop? A favorite instance of mine is the

American civil war. We came very close, you know, to entering that war on the Confederacy's side."

"Did we."

"I think we did. Suppose we had. Suppose we had at first dabbled—sent arms—ignored Northern protests—then got deeper in; suppose the North declared war on us. It seems to me a near certainty that if we had entered the war fully, the South would have won. And I think a British presence would have mitigated the slaughter. There was a point, you know, late in that war, when a new draft call in the North was met with terrible riots. In New York several Negroes were hanged, just to show how little their cause was felt."

Denys had partly lost the thread of this story, unable to imagine himself in it. He thought of the Americans he had met on the train. "Is that so," he said.

"Once having divided the States into two nations, and having helped the South to win, we would have been in place, you see. The fate of the West had not yet been decided. With the North much diminished in power—well, I imagined that by now we—the Empire—would have recouped much of what we lost in 1780."

Denys contemplated this. "Rather stirring," he said mildly. "Rather cold-blooded, too. Wouldn't it have meant condoning slavery? To say nothing of the lives lost. British, I mean."

"Condoning slavery—for a time. I've no doubt the South could have been bullied out of it. Without, perhaps, the awful results that accompanied the Northerners doing it. The eternal resentment. The backlash. The near genocide of the last hundred years. And, in my vision, there would have been a net savings in red men." He smiled. "Whatever might be said against it, the British Empire does not wipe out populations wholesale, as the Americans did in their

West. I often wonder if that sin isn't what makes the Americans so gloomy now, so introverted."

Denys nodded. He believed implicitly that his Empire did not wipe out populations wholesale. "Of course," he said, "there's no telling what exactly would have been the result. If we'd interfered as you say."

"No," Sir Geoffrey said. "No doubt whatever result it *did* have would have to be reshaped as well. And the results of that reshaping reshaped, too, the whole thing subtly guided all along its way toward the result desired—after all, if we can imagine how we might want to alter the past we do inherit, so we can imagine that any past might well be liable to the same imagining; that stupidities, blunders, shortsightedness, would occur in any past we might initiate. Oh, yes, it would all have to be reshaped, with each reshaping. . . ."

"The possibilities are endless," Denys said, laughing. "I'm afraid the game's beyond me. I say let the North win—since in any case we can't do the smallest thing about it."

"No," Davenant said, grown sad again, or reflective; he seemed to feel what Denys said deeply. "No, we can't. It's just—just too long ago." With great gravity he relit his cigar. Denys at the oddness of this response, seeing Sir Geoffrey's eyes veiled, thought: *Perhaps he's mad.* He said, joining the game, "Suppose, though. Suppose Cecil Rhodes hadn't died young, as he did. . . ."

Davenant's eyes caught cold fire again, and his cigar paused in midair. "Hm?" he said with interest.

"I only meant," Denys said, "that your remark about the British not wiping out peoples wholesale was perhaps not tested. If Rhodes had lived to build his empire—hadn't he already named it Rhodesia?—imagine he would have dealt fairly harshly with the natives."

"Very harshly," said Sir Geoffrey.

"Well," Denys said, "I suppose I mean that it's not always evil effects that we inherit from these past accidents."

"Not at all," said Sir Geoffrey. Denys looked away from his regard, which had grown, without losing a certain cool humor, intense. "Do you know, by the way, that remark of George Santayana—the American philosopher—about the British Empire, about young men like yourself? 'Never,' he said, 'never since the Athenians has the world been ruled by such sweet, just, boyish masters.' "

Denys, absurdly, felt himself flush with embarrassment.

"I don't ramble," Sir Geoffrey said. "My trains of thought carry odd goods, but all headed the same way. I want to tell you something, about that historical circumstance, the one you've touched on, whose effects we inherit. Evil or good I will leave you to decide.

"Cecil Rhodes died prematurely, as you say. But not before he had amassed a very great fortune, and laid firm claims to the ground where that fortune would grow far greater. And also not before he had made a will disposing of that fortune."

"I've heard stories," Denys said.

"The stories you have heard are true. Cecil Rhodes, at his death, left his entire fortune, and its increase, to found and continue a secret society which should, by whatever means possible, preserve and extend the British Empire. His entire fortune."

"I have never believed it," Denys said, momentarily feeling untethered, like a balloon: afloat.

"For good reason," Davenant said. "If such a society as I describe were brought into being, its very first task would be to disguise, cast doubt upon, and quite bury its origins. Don't you think that's so? In any case it's true what I say: the society was founded;

is secret; continues to exist; is responsible, in some large degree at least, for the Empire we now know, in this year of grace 1956, IV Elizabeth II, the Empire on which the sun does not set."

The veranda where the two men sat was nearly deserted now; the night was loud with tropical noises that Denys had come to think of as silence, but the human noise of the town had nearly ceased.

"You can't know that," Denys said. "If you knew it, if you were privy to it then you wouldn't say it. Not to me." He almost added: *Therefore you're not in possession of any secret, only a madman's certainty.*

"I *am* privy to it," Davenant said. "I am myself a member. The reason I reveal the secret to you—and you see, here we are, come to you and my odd knowledge of you, at last, as I promised—the reason I reveal it to you is because I wish to ask you to join it. To accept from me an offer of membership."

Denys said nothing. A dark waiter in white crept close, and was waved away by Sir Geoffrey.

"You are quite properly silent," Sir Geoffrey said. "Either I am mad, you think, in which case there is nothing to say; or what I am telling you is true, which likewise leaves you nothing to say. Quite proper. In your place I would be silent also. In your place I was. In any case I have no intention of pressing you for an answer now. I happen to know, by a roundabout sort of means that if explained to you would certainly convince you I was mad, that you will seriously consider what I've said to you. Later. On your long ride to Cairo: there will be time to think. In London. I ask nothing from you now. Only . . ."

He reached into his waistcoat pocket. Denys watched, fascinated: would he draw out some sign of power, a royal charter, some awesome seal? No: it was a small metal plate, with a strip of brown ribbon affixed to it, like a bit of recording tape. He turned it in his hands thoughtfully. "The difficulty, you see, is that in order to alter history and bring it closer to the heart's desire, it would be necessary to stand outside it altogether. Like Archimedes, who said that if he had a lever long enough, and a place to stand, he could move the world."

He passed the metal plate to Denys, who took it reluctantly.

"A place to stand, you see," Sir Geoffrey said. "A place to stand. I would like you to keep that plate about you, and not misplace it. It's in the nature of a key, though it mayn't look it; and it will let you into a very good London club, though it mayn't look it either, where I would like you to call on me. If, even out of simple curiosity, you would like to hear more of us." He extinguished his cigar. "I am going to describe the rather complicated way in which that key is to be used—I really do apologize for the hugger-mugger, but you will come to understand—and then I am going to bid you good evening. Your train is an early one? I thought so. My own departs at midnight. I posses a veritable Bradshaw's of the world's railroads in this skull. Well. No more. I will just sign this—oh, don't thank me. Dear boy: don't thank me."

When he was gone, Denys sat a long time with his cold cigar in his hand and the night around him. The amounts of wine and brandy he had been given seemed to have evaporated from him into the humid air, leaving him feeling cool, clear, and unreal. When at last he rose to go, he inserted the flimsy plate into his waistcoat pocket; and before he went to bed, to lie a long time awake, he changed it to the waistcoat pocket of the pale suit he would wear next morning.

As Sir Geoffrey suggested he would, he thought on his ride

north of all that he had been told, trying to reassemble it in some more reasonable, more everyday fashion: as all day long beside the train the sempiternal Nile—camels, nomads, women washing in the barge canals, the thin line of palms screening the white desert beyond—slipped past. At evening, when at length he lowered the shade of his compartment window on the poignant blue sky pierced with stars, he thought suddenly: *But how could he have known he would find me there, at the bar of the Grand, on that night of this year, at that hour of the evening, just as though we had some long-standing appointment to meet there?*

Davenant had said that if anything is chance, that was not.

At the airfield at Ismailia there was a surprise: his flight home on the R101, which his father had booked months ago as a special treat for Denys, was to be that grand old airship's last scheduled flight. The oldest airship in the British fleet, commissioned in the year Denys was born, was to be—mothballed? Dry-docked? Deflated? Denys wondered just what one did with a decommissioned airship larger than Westminster Cathedral.

Before dawn it was drawn from its great hangar by a crowd of white-clothed fellahin pulling at its ropes—descendants, Denys thought, of those who had pulled ropes at the pyramids three thousand years ago, employed now on an object almost as big but lighter than air. It isn't because it is so intensely romantic that great airships always arrive or depart at dawn or at evening, but only that then the air is cool and most likely to be still: and yet intensely romantic it remains. Denys, standing at the broad, canted windows, watched the ground recede—magically, for there was no sound of engines, no jolt to indicate liftoff, only the waving, cheering fellahin growing smaller. The band on the tarmac played "Land of Hope and Glory." Almost invisible to watchers on the ground—

because of the heat-reflective silver dope with which it was coated—the immense ovoid turned delicately in the wind as it arose.

"Well, it's the end of an era," a red-faced man in a checked suit said to Denys. "In ten years they'll all be gone, these big airships. The propeller chaps will have taken over; and the jet aeroplane, too, I shouldn't wonder."

"I should be sorry to see that," Denys said. "I've loved airships since I was a boy."

"Well, they're just that little bit slower," the red-faced man said sadly. "It's all hurry-up, nowadays. Faster, faster. And for what? I put it to you: for what?"

Now with further gentle pushes of its Rolls-Royce engines, the R101 altered its attitude again; passengers at the lounge windows pointed out the Suez Canal, and the ships passing; Lake Mareotis; Alexandria, like a mirage; British North Africa, as far to the left as one cared to point; and the white-fringed sea. Champagne was being called for, traditional despite the hour, and the red-faced man pressed a glass on Denys.

"The end of an era," he said again, raising his flute of champagne solemnly.

And then the cloudscape beyond the windows shifted, and all Africa had slipped into the south, or into the imaginary, for they had already begun to seem the same thing to Denys. He turned from the windows and decided—the effort to decide it seemed not so great here aloft, amid the potted palms and the wicker, with this pale champagne—that the conversation he had had down in the flat lands far away must have been imaginary as well.

□ □ □

III. THE TALE OF THE PRESIDENT *PRO TEM*

THE UNIVERSE PROCEEDS out of what it has been and into what
it will be, inexorably, unstoppably, at the rate of one second per
second, one year per year, forever. At right angles to its forward
progress lie the past and the future. The future, that is to say, does
not lie "ahead" of the present in the stream of time, but at a right
angle to it: the future of any present moment can be projected as
far as you like outward from it, infinitely in fact, but when the
universe has proceeded further, and a new present moment has
succeeded this one, the future of this one retreats with it into the
what-has-been, forever outdated. It is similar but more complicated with the past.

Now within the great process or procession that the universe
makes, there can be no question of "movement," either "forward"
or "back." The very idea is contradictory. Any conceivable movement is into the orthogonal futures and pasts that fluoresce from the
universe as it is; and from those orthogonal futures and pasts into
others, and others, and still others, never returning, always moving

at right angles to the stream of time. To the traveler, therefore, who does not ever return from the futures or pasts into which he has gone, it must appear that the times he inhabits grow progressively more remote from the stream of time that generated them, the stream that has since moved on and left his futures behind. Indeed, the longer he remains in the future, the farther off the traveler gets from the moment in actuality whence he started, and the less like actuality the universe he stands in seems to him to be.

It was thoughts of this sort, only inchoate as yet and with the necessary conclusions not yet drawn, that occupied the mind of the President *pro tem* of the Otherhood as he walked the vast length of an iron and glass railway station in the capital city of an aged empire. He stopped to take a cigar case from within the black Norfolk overcoat he wore, and a cigar from the case; this he lit, and with its successive blue clouds hanging lightly about his hat and head, he walked on. There were hominids at work on the glossy engines of the Empire's trains that came and went from this terminus; hominids pushing with their long strong arms the carts burdened with the goods and luggage that the trains were to carry; hominids of other sorts gathered in groups or standing singly at the barricades, clutching their tickets, waiting to depart, some aided by or waited upon by other species—too few creatures, in all, to dispel the extraordinary impression of smoky empty hugeness that the cast-iron arches of the shed made.

The President *pro tem* was certain, or at any rate retained a distinct impression, that at his arrival some days before there were telephones available for citizens to use, in the streets, in public places such as this (he seemed to see an example in his mind, a wooden box whose bright veneer was loosening in the damp climate, a complex instrument within, of enameled steel and heavy celluloid); but if there ever had been, there were none now. Instead he went in at a door above which a yellow globe was alight, a winged foot etched upon it. He chose a telegraph form from a stack of them on a long scarred counter, and with the scratchy pen provided he dashed off a quick note to the Magus in whose apartments he had been staying, telling him that he had returned late from the country and would not be with him till evening.

This missive he handed in at the grille, paying what was asked in large coins; then he went out, up the brass-railed stairs, and into the afternoon, into the quiet and familiar city.

It was the familiarity that had been, from the beginning, the oddest thing. The President *pro tem* was a man who, in the long course of his work for the Otherhood, had become accustomed to stepping out of his London club into a world not quite the same as the world he had left to enter that club. He was used to finding himself in a London—or a Lahore or a Laos—stripped of well-known monuments, with public buildings and private ways unknown to him, and a newspaper (bought with an unfamiliar coin found in his pocket) full of names that should not have been there, or missing events that should have been. But here—where nothing, nothing at all, was as he had known it, no trace remaining of the history he had come from—here where no man should have been able to take steps, where even Caspar Last had thought it not possible to take steps—the President *pro tem* could not help but feel easy: had felt easy from the beginning. He walked up the cobbled streets, his furled umbrella over his shoulder, troubled by nothing but the weird grasp that this unknown dark city had on his heart.

The rain that had somewhat spoiled his day in the country had ceased but had left a pale, still mist over the city, a humid atmosphere that gave to views down avenues a stage-set quality, each receding rank of buildings fainter, more vaguely executed. Trees, too, huge and weeping, still and featureless as though painted on successive scrims. At the great gates, topped with garlanded urns, of a public park, the President *pro tem* looked in toward the piled and sounding waters of a fountain and the dim towers of poplar trees. And as he stood resting on his umbrella, lifting the last of the cigar to his lips, someone passed by him and entered the park.

For a moment the President *pro tem* stood unmoving, thinking what an attractive person (boy? girl?) that had been, and how the smile paid to him in passing seemed to indicate a knowledge of him, a knowledge that gave pleasure or at least amusement; then he dropped his cigar end and passed through the gates through which the figure had gone.

That had *not* been a hominid who had smiled at him. It was not a Magus and surely not one of the draconics either. Why he was sure he could not have said: for the same unsayable reason that he knew this city in this world, this park, these marble urns, these leaf-littered paths. He was sure that the person he had seen belonged to a different species from himself, and different also from the other species who lived in this world.

At the fountain where the paths crossed, he paused, looking this way and that, his heart beating hard and filled absurdly with a sense of loss. The child (had it been a child?) was gone, could not be seen that way, or that way—but then was there again suddenly, down at the end of a yew alley, loitering, not looking his way. Thinking at first to sneak up on her, or him, along the sheltering yews, the President *pro tem* took a sly step that way; then, ashamed, he thought better of it and set off down the path at an even pace, as one would approach a young horse or a tame deer.

The one he walked toward took no notice of him, appeared lost in thought, eyes cast down.

Indescribably lovely, the President *pro tem* thought: and yet at the same time negligent and easeful and ordinary. Barefoot, or in light sandals of some kind, light pale clothing that seemed to be part of her, like a bird's dress—and a wristwatch, incongruous, yet not really incongruous at all: someone for whom incongruity was inconceivable. A reverence—almost a holy dread—came over the President *pro tem* as he came closer: as though he had stumbled into a sacred grove. Then the one he walked toward looked up at him, which caused the President *pro tem* to stop still as if a gun had casually been turned on him.

He was known, he understood, to this person. She, or he, stared unembarrassed at the President *pro tem*, with a gaze of the most intense and yet impersonal tenderness, of compassion and amusement and calm interest all mixed; and almost imperceptibly shook her head *no* and smiled again: and the President *pro tem* lowered his eyes, unable to meet that gaze. When he looked up again, the person was gone.

Hesitantly the President *pro tem* walked to the end of the avenue of yews and looked in all directions. No one. A kind of fear flew over him, felt in his breast like the beat of departing wings. He seemed to know, for the first time, what those encounters with gods had been like, when there had been gods; encounters he had puzzled out of the Greek in school.

Anyway he was alone now in the park: he was sure of that. At length he found his way out again into the twilight streets.

By evening he had crossed the city and was climbing the steps of a tall town house, searching in his pockets for the key given him. Beside the varnished door was a small plaque, which said that within were the offices of the Orient Aid Society; but this was not in fact the case. Inside was a tall foyer; a glass-paneled door let him into a hallway wainscoted in dark wood. A pile of gumboots and rubber overshoes in a corner, macs and umbrellas on an ebony tree. Smells of tea, done with, and dinner cooking: a stew, an apple tart, a roast fowl. The tulip-shaped gas lamps along the hall were lit.

He let himself into the library at the hall's end; velvet armchairs regarded the coal fire, and on a drum table a tray of tea things consorted with the books and the papers. The President *pro tem* went to the low shelves that ran beneath the windows and drew out one volume of an old encyclopedia, buckram-bound, with marbled fore-edges and illustrations in brownish photogravure.

The Races. For some reason the major headings and certain other words were in the orthography he knew, but not the closely printed text. His fingers ran down the columns, which were broken into numbered sections headed by the names of species and subspecies. *Hominidae,* with three subspecies. *Draconiidae,* with four: here were etchings of skulls. And lastly *Sylphidae,* with an uncertain number of subspecies. Sylphidae, the Sylphids. Fairies.

"Angels," said a voice behind him. The President *pro tem* turned to see the Magus whose guest he was, recently risen no doubt, in a voluminous dressing gown richly figured. His beard and hair were so long and fine they seemed to float on the currents of air in the room, like filaments of thistledown.

" 'Angels,' is that what you call them?"

"What they would have themselves called," said the Magus. "What name they call themselves, among themselves, no one knows but they."

"I think I met with one this evening."

"Yes."

There was no photogravure to accompany the subsection on Sylphidae in the encyclopedia. "I'm sure I met with one."

"They are gathering, then."

"Not . . . not because of me?"

"Because of you."

"How, though," said the President *pro tem*, feeling again within him the sense of loss, of beating wings departing, "how, how could they have known, how . . ."

The Magus turned away from him to the fire, to the armchairs and the drum table. The President *pro tem* saw that beside one chair a glass of whiskey had been placed, and an ashtray. "Come," said the Magus. "Sit. Continue your tale. It will perhaps become clear to you: perhaps not." He sat then himself, and without looking back at the President *pro tem* he said: "Shall we go on?"

The President *pro tem* knew it was idle to dispute with his host. He did stand unmoving for the space of several heartbeats. Then he took his chair, drew the cigar case from his pocket, and considered where he had left off his tale in the dark of the morning.

"Of course," he said then, "Last knew: he knew, without admitting it to himself, as a good orthogonist must never do, that the world he had returned to from his excursion was not the world he had left. The past he had passed through on his way back was not 'behind' his present at all, but at a right angle to it; the future of that past, which he had to traverse in order to get back again, was not the same road, and 'back' was not where he got. The frame house on Maple Street which, a little sunburned, he reentered on his return was twice removed in reality from the one he had left a week before; the mother he kissed likewise.

"He knew that, for it was predicated by orthogonal logic, and orthogonal logic was in fact what Last had discovered—the transversability of time was only an effect of that discovery. He knew it, and despite his glee over his triumph, he kept his eye open. Sooner or later he would come upon something, something that would betray the fact that this world was not his.

"He could not have guessed it would be me."

The Magus did not look at the President *pro tem* as he was told this story; his pale gray eyes instead wandered from object to object around the great dark library but seemed to see none of them; what, the President *pro tem* wondered, did they see? He had at first supposed the race of Magi to be blind, from this habitual appearance of theirs; he now knew quite well that they were not blind, not blind at all.

"Go on," the Magus said.

"So," said the President *pro tem,* "Last returns from his excursion. A week passes uneventfully. Then one morning he hears his mother call: he has a visitor. Last, pretending annoyance at this interruption of his work (actually he was calculating various forms of compound interest on a half million dollars) comes to the door. There on the step is a figure in tweeds and a bowler hat, leaning on a furled umbrella: me.

" 'Mr. Last,' I said. 'I think we have business.'

"You could see by his expression that he knew I should not have been there, should not have had business with him at all. He really ought to have refused to see me. A good deal of trouble might have been saved if he had. There was no way I could force him, after all. But he didn't refuse; after a goggle-eyed moment he brought me in, up a flight of stairs (Mama waiting anxiously at the bottom), and into his study.

"Geniuses are popularly supposed to live in an atmosphere of the greatest confusion and untidiness, but this wasn't true of Last. The study—it was his bedroom, too—was of a monkish neatness. There was no sign that he worked there, except for a computer terminal, and even it was hidden beneath a cozy that Mama had made for it and Caspar had not dared to spurn.

"He was trembling slightly, poor fellow, and had no idea of the social graces. He only turned to me—his eyeglasses were the kind that oddly diffract the eyes behind and make them unmeetable—and said, 'What do you want?' "

The President *pro tem* caressed the ashtray with the tip of his cigar. He had been offered no tea, and he felt the lack. "We engaged in some preliminary fencing," he continued. "I told him what I had come to acquire. He said he didn't know what I was talking about. I said I thought he did. He laughed and said there must be some mistake. I said, no mistake, Mr. Last. At length he grew silent, and I could see even behind those absurd goggles that he had begun to try to account for me.

"Thinking out the puzzles of orthogonal logic, you see, is not entirely unlike puzzling out moves in chess: theoretically chess can be played by patiently working out the likely consequences of each move, and the consequences of those consequences, and so on; but in fact it is not so played, certainly not by master players. Masters seem to have a more immediate apprehension of possibilities, an almost visceral understanding of the, however, rigorously mathematical logic of the board and pieces, an understanding that they can act on without being able necessarily to explain. Whatever sort of mendacious and feckless fool Caspar Last was in many ways, he was a genius in one or two, and orthogonal logic was one of them.

" 'From when,' he said, 'have you come?'

" 'From not far on,' I answered. He sat then, resigned, stuck in a sort of check impossible to think one's way out of, yet not mated. 'Then,' he said, 'go back the same way you came.'

" 'I cannot,' I said, 'until you explain to me how it is done.'

" 'You know how,' he said, 'if you can come here to ask me.'

" 'Not until you have explained it to me. Now or later.'

" 'I never will,' he said.

" 'You will,' I said. 'You will have done already, before I leave. Otherwise I would not be here now asking. Let us,' I said, and took a seat myself, 'let us assume these preliminaries have been gone through, for they have been of course, and move ahead to the bargaining. My firm are prepared to make you a quite generous offer.'

"That was what convinced him that he must, finally, give up to us the process he had discovered, which he really had firmly intended to destroy forever: the fact that I had come there to ask for them. Which meant that he had already somehow, somewhen, already yielded them up to us."

The President *pro tem* paused again, and lifted his untouched whiskey. "It was the same argument," he said, "the same incontrovertible argument, that was used to convince me once, too, to do a dreadful thing."

He drank, thoughtfully, or at least (he supposed) appearing thoughtful; more and more often as he grew older it happened that in the midst of an anecdote, a relation, even one of supreme importance, he would begin to forget what it was he was telling; the terrifically improbable events would begin to seem not only improbable but fictitious, without insides, the incidents and characters as false as in any tawdry cinema story, even his own part in them unreal: as though they happened to someone made up—certainly not to him who told them. Often enough he forgot the plot.

"You see," he said, "Last exited from a universe in which travel 'through time' was, apparently, either not possible, or possible only under conditions that would allow such travel to go undetected. That was apparent from the fact that no one, so far as Last knew, up to the time of his own single excursion, had ever detected it going on. No one from Last's own future, that is, had ever come 'back' and disrupted his present, or the past of his present: never ever. Therefore, if his excursion could take place, and he could 'return,' he would have to return to a different universe: a universe where time travel *had* taken place, a universe in which once-upon-a-time a man from 1983 had managed to insert himself into a minor colony of the British Crown one hundred and twenty-seven years earlier. What he couldn't know in advance was whether the universe he 'returned' to was one where time travel was a commonplace, an everyday occurrence, something anyway that could deprive his excursion of the value it had; or whether it was one in which one excursion only had taken place, his own. My appearance before him convinced him that it was, or was about to become, common enough: common enough to disturb his own peace and quiet, and alter in unforeseeable ways his comfortable present.

"There was only one solution, or one dash at a solution anyway. I might, myself, be a singularity in Last's new present. It was therefore possible that if he could get rid of me, I would take his process 'away' with me into whatever future I had come out of to get it, and thereupon never be able to find my way again to his present and disturb it or him. Whatever worlds I altered, they would not be his, not his anyway who struck the bargain with me: if each of them also contained a Last, who would suffer or flourish in ways unimaginable to the Last to whom I spoke, then those eidolons would have to make terms for themselves, that's all. The quantum angle obtended by my coming, and then the one obtended by my returning, divorced all those Lasts from him for all eternity: that is why, though the angle itself is virtually infinitesimal, it has always to be treated as a right angle.

"Last showed me, on his computer, after our bargain was struck and he was turning over his data and plans to me. I told him I would not probably grasp the theoretical basis of the process, however well I had or would come to manage the practical paradoxes of it, but he liked to show me. He first summoned up x-y coordinates, quite ordinary, and began by showing me how some surprising results were obtained by plotting on such coordinates an imaginary number, specifically the square root of minus one. The only way to describe what happens, he said, is that the plotted figure, one unit high, one unit wide, generates a shadow square of the same measurements 'behind' itself, in space undefined by the coordinates. It was with such tricks that he had begun; the orthogons he obtained had first started him thinking about the generation of inhabitable— if also somehow imaginary—pasts.

"Then he showed me what became of the orthogons so constructed if the upright axis were set in motion. Suppose (he said) that this vertical coordinate were in fact revolving around the axle formed by the other, horizontal coordinate. If it were so revolving, like an aeroplane propeller, we could not apprehend it, edge on as it is to us, so to speak; but what would that motion do to the plots we were making? And of course it was quite simple, given the proper instructions to the computer, to find out. And his orthogons—always remaining at right angles to the original coordinates—began to turn in the prop wash of the whole system's progress at one second per second out of the what-was and into the what-has-never-yet-been; and to generate, when one had come to see them, the paradoxes of orthogonal logic: the cyclonic storm of logic in which all travelers in that medium always stand; the one in which Last and I, I bending over his shoulder hat in hand, he with fat white fingers on his keys and eyeglasses slipping down his nose, stood even as we spoke: a storm as unfeelable as Last's rotating axis was unseeable."

The President *pro tem* tossed his extinguished cigar into the fading fire and crossed his arms upon his breast, weary; weary of the tale.

"I don't yet understand," the other said. "If he had been so adamant, why would he give up his secrets to you?"

"Well," said the President *pro tem,* "there was, also, the matter of money. It came down to that, in the end. We were able to make him a very generous offer, as I said."

"But he didn't need money. He had this stamp."

"Yes. So he did. Yes. We were able to pick up the stamp, too, from him, as part of the bargain. I think we offered him a hundred pounds. Perhaps it was more."

"I thought it was invaluable."

"Well, so did he, of course. And yet he was not really as surprised as one might have expected him to be, when he discovered it was not; when it turned out that the stamp he had gone to such trouble to acquire was in fact rather a common one. I seemed to see it in his face, the expectation of what he was likely to find, as soon as I directed him to look it up in his Scott's, if he didn't believe me. And there it was in Scott's: the one-penny magenta 1856, a nice enough stamp, a stamp many collectors covet, and many also have in their albums. He had begun breathing stertorously, staring down at the page. I'm afraid he was suffering, rather, and I didn't like to observe it.

" 'Come,' I said to him. 'You knew it was possible.' And he did, of course. 'Perhaps it was something you did,' I said. 'Perhaps you bought the last one of a batch, and the postmaster subsequently reordered, a thing he had not before intended to do. Perhaps . . . ' But I could see him think it: there needed to be no such explanation. He needed to have made no error, nor to have influenced the moment's shape in any way by his presence. The very act of his coming and going was sufficient source of unpredictable, stochastic change: this world was not his, and minute changes from his were predicated. But *this* change, this of all possible changes . . .

"His hand had begun to shake, holding the volume of Scott's. I really wanted now to get through the business and be off, but it couldn't be hurried. I knew that, for I'd done it all before. In the end we acquired the stamp. And then destroyed it, of course."

The President *pro tem* remembered: a tiny, momentary fire.

"It's often been observed," he said, "that the cleverest scientists are often the most easily taken in by charlatans. There is a famous instance, famous in some worlds, of a scientist who was brought to believe firmly in ghosts and ectoplasm, because the medium and her manifestations passed all the tests the scientist could devise. The only thing he didn't think to test for was conscious fraud. I suppose it's because the phenomena of nature, or the entities of mathematics, however puzzling and elusive they may be, are not after all bent on fooling the observer; and so a motive that would be evident to the dullest of policemen does not occur to the genius."

"The stamp," said the Magus.

"The stamp, yes. I'm not exactly proud of this part of the story. We were convinced, though, that two *very* small wrongs could go a long way toward making a very great right. And Last, who understood me and the 'firm' I represented to be capable of handling—at least in a practical way—the awful paradoxes of orthogony, did not imagine us to be also skilled, if anything more skilled, at such things as burglary, uttering, fraud, and force. Of such contradictions is Empire made. It was easy enough for us to replace, while Last was off in the tropics, one volume of his Scott's stamp catalog with another printed by ourselves, almost identical to his but containing one difference. It was harder waiting to see, once he had looked up his stamp in our bogus volume, if he would then search out some other source to confirm what he found there. He did not."

The Magus rose slowly from his chair with the articulated dignity, the wasteless lion's motion, of his kind. He tugged the bell pull. He picked up the poker then, and stood with his hand upon the mantel, looking down into the ruby ash of the dying fire. "I would he had," he said.

The dark double doors of the library opened, and the servant entered noiselessly.

"Refresh the gentleman's glass," the Magus said without turning from the fire, "and draw the drapes."

The President *pro tem* thought that no matter how long he lived in this world he would never grow accustomed to the presence of draconics. The servant's dark hand lifted the decanter, poured an exact dram into the glass, and stoppered the bottle again; then his yellow eyes, irises slit like a cat's or a snake's, rose from that task toward the next, the drawing of the drapes. Unlike the eyes of the Magi, these draconic eyes seemed to see and weigh everything—though on a single scale, and from behind a veil of indifference.

Their kind, the President *pro tem* had learned, had been servants for uncounted ages, though the Magus his host had said that once they had been masters, and men and the other hominids their slaves. And they still had, the President *pro tem* observed, that studied reserve which upper servants had in the world from which the President *pro tem* had come, that reserve which says: *Very well, I will do your bidding, better than you could do it for yourself; I will maintain the illusion of your superiority to me, as no other creature could.*

With a taper he lit at the fire, he lit the lamps along the walls and masked them with glass globes. Then he drew the drapes.

"I'll ring for supper," the Magus said, and the servant stopped at the sound of his voice. "Have it sent in." The servant moved again, crossing the room on narrow naked feet. At the doorway he turned to them, but only to draw the double doors closed together as he left.

For a time the Magus stood regarding the doors the great lizard had closed. Then: "Outside the City," he said, "in the mountains, they have begun to combine. There are more stories every week. In the old forests whence they first emerged, they have begun to collect on appointed days, trying to remember—for they are not really as intelligent as they look—trying to remember what it is they have lost, and to think of gaining it again. In not too long a time we will begin to hear of massacres. Some remote place; a country house; a more than usually careless man; a deed of unfamiliar horridness. And a sign left, the first sign: a writing in blood, or something less obvious. And like a spot symptomatic of a fatal disease, it will begin to spread."

The President *pro tem* drank, then said softly: "We didn't know, you know. We didn't understand that this would be the result." The drawing of the drapes, the lighting of the lamps, had made the old library even more familiar to the President *pro tem:* the dark varnished wood, the old tobacco smoke, the hour between tea and dinner; the draught that whispered at the window's edge, the bitter smell of the coal on the grate; the comfort of this velvet armchair's napless arms, of this whiskey. The President *pro tem* sat grasped by all this, almost unable to think of anything else. "We couldn't know."

"Last knew," the Magus said. "All false, all imaginary, all generated by the wishes and fears of others: all that I am, my head, my heart, my house. Not the world's doing, or time's, but yours." The opacity of his eyes, turned on the President *pro tem,* was fearful. "You have made me; you must unmake me."

"I'll do what I can," the President *pro tem* said. "All that I can."

"For centuries we have studied," the Magus said. "We have spent lifetimes—lifetimes much longer than yours—searching for the flaw in this world, the flaw whose existence we suspected but could not prove. I say 'centuries,' but those centuries have been illusory, have they not? We came, finally, to guess at you, down the defiles of time, working your changes, which we can but suffer.

"We only guessed at you: no more than men or beasts can we Magi remember, once the universe has become different, that it was ever other than it is now. But I think the Sylphids can feel it change: can know when the changes are wrought. Imagine the pain for them."

That was a command: and indeed the President *pro tem* could imagine it, and did. He looked down into his glass.

"That is why they are gathering. They know already of your appearance; they have expected you. The request is theirs to make, not mine: that you put this world out like a light."

He stabbed with the poker at the settling fire, and the coals gave up blue flames for a moment. The mage's eyes caught the light, and then went out.

"I long to die," he said.

■ ■ ■

IV. Chronicles of the Otherhood

ONCE PAST THE DOOR, or what might be considered the door, of what Sir Geoffrey Davenant had told him was a club, Denys Winterset was greeted by the Fellow in Economic History, a gentle, academic-looking man called Platt.

"Not many of the Fellows about, just now," he said. "Most of them fossicking about on one bit of business or another. I'm always here." He smiled, a vague, self-effacing smile. "Be no good out there. But they also serve, eh?"

"Will Sir Geoffrey Davenant be here?" Denys asked him. He followed Platt through what did seem to be a gentlemen's club of the best kind: dark-paneled, smelling richly of leather upholstery and tobacco.

"Davenant, oh, yes," said Platt. "Davenant will be here. All the executive committee will get here, if they can. The President—*pro tem*." He turned back to look at Denys over his half-glasses. "All our Presidents are *pro tem*." He led on. "There'll be dinner in the executive committee's dining room. After dinner we'll talk. You'll likely have questions." At that Denys almost laughed. He felt made of questions, most of them unputtable in any verbal form.

Platt stopped in the middle of the library. A lone Fellow in a corner by a green-shaded lamp was hidden by the *Times* held up before him. There was a fire burning placidly in the oak-framed fireplace; above it, a large and smoke-dimmed picture: a portrait of a chubby, placid man in a hard collar, thinning blond hair, eyes somehow vacant. Platt, seeing Denys's look, said: "Cecil Rhodes."

Beneath the portrait, carved into the mantelpiece, were words; Denys took a step closer to read them:

> *To Ruin the Great Work of Time*
> *& Cast the Kingdoms old*
> *Into another mould.*

"Marvel," Platt said. "That poem about Cromwell. Don't know who chose it. It's right, though. I look at it often, working here. Now. It's down that corridor, if you want to wash your hands. Would you care for a drink? We have some time to kill. Ah, Davenant."

"Hullo, Denys," said Sir Geoffrey, who had lowered his *Times*. "I'm glad you've come."

"I think we all are," said Platt, taking Denys's elbow in a gentle, almost tender grasp. "Glad you've come."

He had almost not come. If it had been merely an address, a telephone number he'd been given, he might well not have; but the metal card with its brown strip was like a string tied round his finger, making it impossible to forget he had been invited. Don't lose it, Davenant had said. So it lay in his waistcoat pocket; he touched it whenever he reached for matches there; he tried shifting it to other pockets, but whenever it was on his person he felt it.

In the end he decided to use it, as much to get rid of its importunity as for any other reason—so he told himself. On a wet afternoon he went to the place Davenant had told him of, the Orient Aid Society, and found it as described, a sooty French-Gothic building, one of those private houses turned to public use, with a discreet brass plaque by the door indicating that within some sort of business is done, one can't imagine what; and inside the double doors, in the vestibule, three telephone boxes, looking identical, the first of which had the nearly invisible slot by the door. His heart for some reason beat slow and hard as he inserted the card within this slot—it was immediately snatched away, like a ticket on the Underground—and entered the box and closed the door behind him.

Though nothing moved, he felt as though he had stepped onto a moving footpath, or onto one of those trick floors in a fun house that slide beneath one's feet. He was going somewhere. The sensation was awful. Beginning to panic, he tried to get out, not knowing whether that might be dangerous, but the door would not open, and its glass could not be seen out of either. It had been transparent from outside but was somehow opaque from within. He shook the door handle fiercely. At that moment the nonmobile motion reversed itself sickeningly, and the door opened. Denys stepped out, not into the vestibule of the Orient Aid Society, but into the foyer of a club. A dim, old-fashioned foyer, with faded Turkey carpet on the stairs, and an aged porter to greet him; a desk, behind which pigeonholes held members' mail; a stand of umbrellas. It was reassuring, almost absurdly so, the "then I woke up" of a silly ghost story. But Denys didn't feel reassured, or exactly awake either.

"Evening, sir."

"Good evening."

"Still raining, sir? Take your things?"

"Thank you."

A member was coming toward him down the long corridor: Platt.

"Sir?"

Denys turned back to the porter. "Your key, sir," the man said, and gave him back the metal plate with the strip of brown ribbon on it.

"Like a lift," Davenant told him as they sipped whiskey in the bar. "Alarming, somewhat, I admit; but imagine using a lift for the first time, not knowing what its function was. Closed inside a box; sensation of movement; the doors open, and you are somewhere else. Might seem odd. Well, this is the same. Only you're not somewhere else: not exactly."

"Hm," Denys said.

"Don't dismiss it, Sir Geoffrey," said Platt. "It *is* mighty odd." He said to Denys: "The paradox is acute: it is. Completely contrary to the usual cause-and-effect thinking we all do, can't stop doing really, no matter how hard we try to adopt other habits of mind. Strictly speaking it is unthinkable: unimaginable. And yet there it is."

"Yes," Davenant said. "To ignore, without ever forgetting, the heart of the matter: that's the trick. I've met monks, Japanese, Tibetan, who know the techniques. They can be learned."

"We speak of the larger paradox," Platt said to Denys. "The door you came in by being only a small instance. The great instance being, of course, the Otherhood's existence at all: we here now sitting and talking of it."

But Denys was not talking of it. He had nothing to say. To be told that in entering the telephone box in the Orient Aid Society he had effectively exited from time and entered a precinct outside it,

revolving between the actual and the hypothetical, not quite exis-
tent despite the solidity of its parquet floor and the truthful bite of
its whiskey; to be told that in these changeless and atemporal halls
there gathered a society—"not quite a brotherhood," Davenant
said; "that would be mawkish, and untrue of these chaps; we call it
an Otherhood"—of men and women who by some means could
insert themselves into the stream of the past, and with their fore-
knowledge alter it, and thus alter the future of that past, the future
in which they themselves had their original being; that in effect the
world Denys had come from, the world he knew, the year 1956, the
whole course of things, the very cast and flavor of his memories,
were dependent on the Fellows of this society, and might change
at any moment, though if they did he would know nothing of it;
and that he was being asked to join them in their work—he heard
the words, spoken to him with a frightening casualness; he felt his
mind fill with the notions, though not able to do anything that
might be called thinking about them; and he had nothing to say.

"You can see," Sir Geoffrey said, looking not at Denys but into
his whiskey, "why I didn't explain all this to you in Khartoum. The
words don't come easily. Here, in the Club, outside all frames of
reference, it's possible to explain. To describe, anyway. I suppose
if we hadn't a place like this, we should all go mad."

"I wonder," said Platt, "whether we haven't, despite it." He
looked at no one. "Gone mad, I mean."

For a moment no one spoke further. The barman glanced at
them, to see if their silence required anything of him. Then Platt
spoke again. "Of course there are restrictions," he said. "The chap
who discovered it was possible to change one's place in time, an
American, thought he had proved that it was only possible to dis-
place oneself into the past. In a sense, he was correct. . . ."

"In a sense," Sir Geoffrey said. "Not quite correct. The possibilities are larger than he supposed. Or rather will suppose, all this from your viewpoint is still to happen—which widens the possibilities right there, you see, one man's future being as it were another man's past. (You'll get used to it, dear boy, shall we have another of these?) The past, as it happens, is the only sphere of time we have any interest in; the only sphere in which we can do good. So you see there are natural limits: the time at which this process was made workable is the forward limit; and the rear limit we have made the time of the founding of the Otherhood itself. By Cecil Rhodes's will, in 1893."

"Be pointless, you see, for the Fellows to go back before the society existed," said Platt. "You can see that."

"One further restriction," said Sir Geoffrey. "A house rule, so to speak. We forbid a man to return to a time he has already visited, at least in the same part of the world. There is the danger—a moment's thought will show you I'm right—of bumping into oneself on a previous, or successive, mission. Unnerving, let me tell you. Unnerving completely. The trick is hard enough to master as it is."

Denys found voice. "Why?" he said. "And why me?"

"Why," said Sir Geoffrey, "is spelled out in our founding charter: to preserve and extend the British Empire in all parts of the world, and to strengthen it against all dangers. Next, to keep peace in the world, insofar as this is compatible with the first; our experience has been that it usually is the same thing. And lastly to keep fellowship among ourselves, this also subject to the first, though any conflict is unimaginable, I should hope, bickering aside."

"The society was founded to be secret," Platt said. "Rhodes liked that idea—a sort of Jesuits of the Empire. In fact there was no real need for secrecy, not until—well, not until the society became the Otherhood. This jaunting about in other people's histories would not be understood. So secrecy *is* important. Good thing on the whole that Rhodes insisted on it. And for sure he wouldn't have been displeased at the society's scope. He wanted the world for England. And more. 'The moon, too,' he used to say. 'I often think of the moon.' "

"Few know of us even now," Sir Geoffrey said. "The Foreign Office, sometimes. The PM. Depending on the nature of HM government at any moment, we explain more, or less. Never the part about time. That is for us alone to know. Though some have guessed a little, over the years. It's not even so much that we wish to act in secret—that was just Rhodes's silly fantasy—but well, it's just damned difficult to explain, don't you see?"

"And the Queen knows of us," Platt said. "Of course."

"I flew back with her, from Africa, that day," Davenant said. "After her father had died. I happened to be among the party. I told her a little then. Didn't want to intrude on her grief, but—it seemed the moment. In the air, over Africa. I explained more later. Plucky girl," he added. "Plucky." He drew his watch out. "And as for the second part of your question—why you?—I shall ask you to reserve that one, for a moment. We'll dine upstairs . . . Good heavens, look at the time."

Platt swallowed his drink hastily. "I remember Lord Cromer's words to us when I was a schoolboy at Leys," he said. " 'Love your country,' he said, 'tell the truth, and don't dawdle.' "

"Words to live by," Sir Geoffrey said, examining the bar chit doubtfully and fumbling for a pen.

The drapes were drawn in the executive dining room; the members of the executive committee were just taking their seats around a long mahogany table, scarred around its edge with what seemed to be initials and dates. The members were of all ages; some sunburned, some pale, some in evening clothes of a cut unfamiliar to Denys; among them were two Indians and a Chinaman. When they were all seated, Denys beside Platt, there were several seats empty. A tall woman with severe gray hair but eyes somehow kind took the head of the table.

"The President *pro tem*," she said as she sat, "is not returned, apparently, from his mission. I'll preside, if there are no objections."

"Oh, balls," said a broad-faced man with the tan of a cinema actor. "Don't give yourself airs, Huntington. Will we really need any presiding?"

"Might be a swearing-in," Huntington said mildly, pressing the bell beside her and not glancing at Denys. "In any case, best to keep up the forms. First order of business—the soup."

It was a mulligatawny, saffrony and various; it was followed by a whiting, and that by a baron of claret-colored beef. Through the clashings of silverware and crystal Denys listened to the table's talk, little enough of which he could understand: only now and then he felt—as though he were coming horribly in two—the import of the Fellows' conversation: that history was malleable, time a fiction; that nothing was necessarily as he supposed it must be. How could they bear that knowledge? How could he?

"Mr. Deng Fa-shen, there," Platt said quietly to him, "is our physicist. Orthogonal physics—as opposed to orthogonal logic—is his invention. What makes this club possible. The mechanics of it. Don't ask me to explain."

Deng Fa-shen was a fine-boned, parchment-colored man with gentle fox's eyes. Denys looked from him to the two Indians in silk.

Platt said, as though reading Denys's thought: "The most dis-
agreeable thing about old Rhodes and the Empire of his day was its
racialism, of course. Absolutely unworkable, too. Nothing more
impossible to sustain than a world order based on some race's supposed inherent superiority." He smiled. "It isn't the only part of
Rhodes's scheme that's proved unworkable."

The informal talk began to assemble itself, with small nudges
from the woman at the head of the table (who did her presiding
with no pomp and few words) around a single date: 1914. Denys
knew something of this date, though several of the place names
spoken of (the Somme, Jutland, Gallipoli—wherever that was)
meant nothing to him. Somehow, in some possible universe, 1914
had changed everything; the Fellows seemed intent on changing
1914, drawing its teeth, teeth that Denys had not known it had—or
might still have once had: he felt again the sensation of coming in
two, and sipped wine.

"Jutland," a Fellow was saying. "All that's needed is a bit more
knowledge, a bit more jump on events. Instead of a foolish stalemate, it could be a solid victory. Then, blockade; war over in six
months . . ."

"Who's our man in the Admiralty now? Carteret, isn't it? Can
he—"

"Carteret," said the bronze-faced man, "was killed the last time
round at Jutland." There was a silence; some of the Fellows
seemed to be aware of this, and some taken by surprise. "Shows
the foolishness of that kind of thinking," the man said. "Things
have simply gone too far by then. That's my opinion."

Other options were put forward. That moment in what the
Fellows called the Original Situation was searched for into which a
small intrusion might be made, like a surgical incision, the smallest

possible intrusion that would have the proper effect; then the succeeding Situation was searched, and the Situation following that,
the Fellows feeling with enormous patience and care into the
workings of the past and its possibilities, like a blind man weaving.
At length a decision seemed to be made, without fuss or a vote
taken, about this place Gallipoli, and a Turkish soldier named
Mustapha Kemal, who would be apprehended and sequestered in
a quick action that took or would take place there; the sun-bronzed
man would see, or had seen, to it; and the talk, after a reflective
moment, turned again to anecdote and speculation.

Denys listened to the stories, of desert treks and dangerous
negotiations, men going into the wilderness of a past catastrophe
with a precious load of penicillin or of knowledge, to save one
man's life or end another's; to intercept one trivial telegram, get
one bit of news through, deflect one column of troops—removing
one card from the ever-building possible future of some past
moment and seeing the whole of it collapse silently, unknowably,
even as another was building, just as fragile but happier: he looked
into the faces of the Fellows, knowing that no ruthless stratagem
was beyond them, and yet knowing also that they were men of
honor, with a great world's peace and benefit in their trust, though
the world couldn't know it; and he felt an odd but deep thrill of
privilege to be here now, wherever that was—the same sense of
privilege that, as a boy, he had expected to feel (and as a man had
laughed at himself for expecting to feel) upon being admitted to
the ranks of those who—selflessly, though not without reward—
had been chosen or had chosen themselves to serve the Empire.
"The difference you make makes all the difference," his headmas-
terish Commissioner was fond of telling Denys and his fellows; and
it was a joke among them that, in their form-filling, their execution

of tedious and sometimes absurd directives, they were following in the footsteps of Gordon and Milner, Warren Hastings and Raffles of Singapore. And yet—Denys perceived it with a kind of inward stillness, as though his heart flowed instead of beating—a difference *could* be made. Had been made. Went on being made, in many times and places, without fuss, without glory, with rewards for others that those others could not recognize or even imagine. He crossed his knife and fork on his plate and sat back slowly.

"This 1914 business has its tricksome aspects," Platt said to him. "Speaking in large terms, not enough can really be done within our time frames. The Situation that issues in war was firmly established well before: in the founding of the German empire under Prussian leadership. Bismarck. There's the man to get to, or to his financiers, most of whom were Jewish—little did they know, and all that. Even Sedan is too late, and not enough seems to be able to be made, or unmade, out of the Dreyfus affair, though that *does* fall within our provenance. No," he said. "It's all just too long ago. If only . . . Well, no use speculating, is there? Make the best of it, and shorten the war; make it less catastrophic at any rate, a short, sharp shaking-out—above all, win it quickly. We must do the best we can."

He seemed unreconciled.

Denys said: "But I don't understand. I mean, of course I wouldn't expect to understand it as you do, but . . . well, you *did* do all that. I mean we studied 1914 in school—the guns of August and all that, the 1915 Peace, the Monaco Conference. What I mean is . . ." He became conscious that the Fellows had turned their attention to him. No one else spoke. "What I mean to say is that *I* know you solved the problem, and how you solved it, in a general way; and I don't see why it remains to be solved. I don't see why you're worried." He laughed in embarrassment, looking around at the faces that looked at him.

"You're right," said Sir Geoffrey, "that you don't understand." He said it smiling, and the others were, if not smiling, patient and not censorious. "The logic of it is orthogonal. I can present you with an even more paradoxical instance. In fact I intend to present you with it; it's the reason you're here."

"The point to remember," the woman called Huntington said (as though to the whole table, but obviously for Denys's instruction), "is that here—in the club—nothing has yet happened except the Original Situation. All is still to do: all that we have done, all still to do."

"Precisely," said Sir Geoffrey. "All still to do." He took from his waistcoat pocket an eyeglass, polished it with his napkin, and inserted it between cheek and eyebrow. "You had a question, in the bar. You asked *why me,* meaning, I suppose, why is it you should be nominated to this Fellowship, why you and not another."

"Yes," said Denys. He wanted to go on, list what he knew of his inadequacies, but kept silent.

"Let me, before answering your question, ask you this," said Sir Geoffrey. "Supposing that you were chosen by good and sufficient standards—supposing that a list had been gone over carefully, and your name was weighed; supposing that a sort of competitive examination has been passed by you—would you then accept the nomination?"

"I—" said Denys. All eyes were on him, yet they were not somehow expectant; they awaited an answer they knew. Denys seemed to know it, too. He swallowed. "I hope I should," he said.

"Very well," Sir Geoffrey said softly. "Very well." He took a breath. "Then I shall tell you that you have in fact been chosen by good and sufficient standards. Chosen, moreover, for a specific mission, a mission of the greatest importance; a mission on which the very existence of the Otherhood depends. No need to feel flattered; I'm sure you're a brave lad, and all that, but the criteria were not entirely your sterling qualities, whatever they should later turn out to be.

"To explain what I mean, I must further acquaint you with what the oldest, or rather earliest, of the Fellows call the Original Situation.

"You recall our conversation in Khartoum. I told you no lie then; it is the case, in that very pleasant world we talked in, that good year 1956, fourth of a happy reign, on that wide veranda overlooking a world at peace—it is the case, I say, in that world and in most possible worlds like it, that Cecil Rhodes died young, and left the entire immense fortune he had won in the Scramble for the founding of a secret society, a society dedicated to the extension of that Empire which had his entire loyalty. The then government's extreme confusion over this bequest, their eventual forming of a society—not without some embarrassment and doubt—a society from which this present Otherhood descends, still working toward the same ends, though the British Empire is not now what Rhodes thought it to be, nor the world either in which it has its hegemony— well, one of the Fellows is working up or will work up that story, insofar as it can be told, and it is, as I say, a true one.

"But there is a situation in which it is not true. In that situation which we call Original—the spine of time from which all other possibilities fluoresce—Cecil Rhodes, it appears, changed his mind."

Sir Geoffrey paused to light a cigar. The port was passed him. A cloud of smoke issued from his mouth. "Changed his mind, you see," he said, dispersing the smoke with a wave. "He did not die young, he lived on. His character mellowed, perhaps, as the years fell away; his fortune certainly diminished. It may be that Africa disappointed him, finally; his scheme to take over Tanganyika and join the Cape to Cairo with a single All-Red railroad line had ended in failure . . ."

Denys opened his mouth to speak; he had only a week before taken that line. He shut his mouth again.

"Whatever it was," Sir Geoffrey said, "he changed his mind. His last will left his fortune—what was left of it—to his old university, a scholarship fund to allow Americans and others of good character to study in England. No secret society. No Otherhood."

There was a deep silence at the table. No one had altered his casual position, yet there was a stillness of utter attention. Someone poured for Denys, and the liquid rattle of port into his glass was loud.

"Thus the paradox," Sir Geoffrey said. "For it is only the persuasions of the Otherhood that alter this Original Situation. The Otherhood must reach its fingers into the past, once we have learned how to do so; we must send our agents down along the defiles of time and intercept our own grandfather there, at the very moment when he is about to turn away from the work of generating us.

"And persuade him not to, you see; cause him—cause him not to turn away from that work of generation. Yes, cause him not to turn away. And thus ensure our own eventual existence."

Sir Geoffrey pushed back his chair and rose. He turned toward the sideboard, then back again to Denys. "Did I hear you say 'That's madness'?" he asked.

"No," Denys said.

"Oh," Sir Geoffrey said. "I thought you spoke. Or thought I remembered you speaking." He turned again to the sideboard, and returned again to the table with his cigar clenched in his teeth and a small box in his hands. He put this on the table. "You do follow me thus far," he said, his hands on the box and his eyes regarding Denys from under their curling brows.

"Follow you?"

"The man had to die," Sir Geoffrey said. He unlatched the box. "It was his moment. The moment you will find in any biography of him you pick up. Young, or anyway not old; at the height of his triumphs. It would have been downhill for him from there anyway."

"How," Denys asked, and something in his throat intruded on the question; it was a moment before he could complete it: "How did he die?"

"Oh, various ways," Sir Geoffrey said. "In the most useful version, he was shot to death by a young man he'd invited up to his house at Cape Town. Shot twice, in the heart, with a Webley .38-caliber revolver." He took from the box this weapon, and placed it with its handle toward Denys.

"That's madness," Denys said. His hands lay along the arms of his chair, drawing back from the gun. "You can't mean to say you went back and *shot* him, you . . ."

"Not we, dear boy," Sir Geoffrey said. "We, generally, yes; but specifically, not we. You."

"No."

"Oh, you won't be alone—not initially, at least. I can explain why it must be you and not another; I can expound the really quite dreadful paradox of it further, if you think it would help, though it seems to me best if, for now, you simply take our word for it."

Denys felt the corners of his mouth draw down, involuntarily, tightly; his lower lip wanted to tremble. It was a sign he remembered from early childhood: what had usually followed it was a fit of truculent weeping. That could not follow, here, now: and yet he dared not allow himself to speak, for fear he would be unable. For some time, then, no one spoke.

At the head of the table Huntington pushed her empty glass away.

"Mr. Winterset," she said gently. "I wonder if I might put in a word. Sit down, Davenant, will you, just for a moment, and stop looming over us. With your permission, Mr. Winterset—Denys— I should like to describe to you a little more broadly that condition of the world we call the Original Situation."

She regarded Denys with her sad eyes, then closed her fingers together before her. She began to speak, in a low voice which more than once Denys had to lean forward to catch. She told about Rhodes's last sad bad days; she told of Rhodes's chum the despicable Dr. Jameson, and his infamous raid and the provocations that led to war with the Boers; of the shame of that war, the British defeats and the British atrocities, the brutal intransigence of both sides. She told how in those same years the European powers who confronted each other in Africa were also at work stockpiling arms and building mechanized armies of a size unheard of in the history of the world, to be finally let loose upon one another in August of 1914, unprepared for what was to become of them; armies officered by men who still lived in the previous century, but armed with weapons more dreadful than they could imagine. The machine gun: no one seemed to understand that the machine gun had changed war forever, and though the junior officers and Other Ranks soon learned it, the commanders never did. At the First

Battle of the Somme wave after wave of British soldiers were sent against German machine guns, to be mown down like grain. There were a quarter of a million casualties in that battle. And yet the generals went on ordering massed attacks against machine guns for the four long years of the war.

"But they knew," Denys could not help saying. "They did know. Machine guns had been used against massed native armies for years, all over the Empire. In Afghanistan. In the Sudan. Africa. They knew."

"Yes," Huntington said. "They knew. And yet, in the Original Situation, they paid no attention. They went blindly on and made their dreadful mistakes. Why? How could they be so stupid, those generals and statesmen who in the world you knew behaved so wisely and so well? For one reason only: they lacked the help and knowledge of a group of men and women who had seen all those mistakes made, who could act in secret on what they knew, and who had the ear and the confidence of one of the governments—not the least stupid of them, either, mind you. And with all our help it was still a close-run thing."

"Damned close-run," Platt put in. "Still hangs in the balance, in fact."

"Let me go on," Huntington said.

She went on: long hands folded before her, eyes now cast down, she told how at the end a million men, a whole generation, lay dead on the European battlefield, among them men whom Denys might think the modern world could not have been made without. A grotesque tyranny calling itself Socialist had been imposed on a war-weakened Russian empire. Only the intervention of a fully mobilized United States had finally broken the awful deadlock—thereby altering the further history of the world unrecognizably. She told how the vindictive settlement inflicted on a ruined Germany (so unlike the wise dispositions of the Monaco Conference, which had simply reestablished the old pre-Bismarck patchwork of German states and princedoms) had rankled in the German spirit; how a madman had arisen and, almost unbelievably, had ridden a wave of resentment and anti-Jewish hysteria to dictatorship.

"Yes," Denys said. "*That* we didn't escape, did we? I remember that, or almost remember it; it was just before I can remember anything. Anti-Jewish riots all over Germany."

"Yes," said Huntington softly.

"Yes. Terrible. These nice funny Germans, all lederhosen and cuckoo clocks, and suddenly they show a terrible dark side. Thousands of Jews, some of them very highly placed, had to leave Germany. They lost everything. Synagogues attacked, professors fired. Even Einstein, I think, had to leave Germany for a time."

Huntington let him speak. When Denys fell silent, unable to remember more and feeling the eyes of the Fellows on him, Huntington began again. But the things she began to tell of now simply could not have happened, Denys thought; no, they were part of a monstrous, foul dream, atrocities on a scale only a psychopath could conceive, and only the total resources of a strong and perverted science achieve. When Einstein came again into the tale, and the world Huntington described drifted ignorantly and inexorably into an icy and permanent stalemate that could be broken only by the end of civilization, perhaps of life itself, Denys found a loathsome surfeit rising in his throat; he covered his face, he would hear no more.

"So you see," Huntington said, "why we think it possible that the life—nearly over, in any case—of one egotistical, racialist adventurer is worth the chance to alter that situation." She raised her eyes to Denys. "I don't say you need agree. There *is* a sticky moral question, and I don't mean to brush it aside. I only say you see how we might think so."

Denys nodded slowly. He reached out and put his hand on the pistol that had been placed before him. He lifted his eyes and met those of Sir Geoffrey Davenant, which still smiled, though his mouth and his mustaches were grave.

What they were all telling him was that he could help create a better world than the original, which Huntington had described; but that was not how Denys perceived it. What Denys perceived was that reality—reality, the world he had come from, reality sunshot and whole—was somehow under threat from a disgusting nightmare of death, ignorance, and torture, which could invade and replace it forever unless he acted. He did not think himself capable of interfering with the world to make it better; but to defend the world he knew, the world that with all its shortcomings was life and sustenance and sense and cleanly wakefulness—yes, that he could do. Would do, with all his strength.

Which is why, of course, it was he who had been chosen to do it. He saw that in Davenant's eyes.

And of course, if he refused, he could not then be brought here to be asked. If it was now possible for him to be asked to do this by the Otherhood, then he must have already consented, and done it. That, too, was in Davenant's silence. Denys looked down. His hand was on the Webley; and beside it, carved by a penknife into the surface of the table, almost obscured by later waxings, were the neat initials *D.W.*

"I always remember what Lord Milner said," Platt spoke into his ear. *"Everyone can help."*

□ □ □

V. The Tears of the President *Pro Tem*

"I remember," the President *pro tem* of the Otherhood said, "the light: a very clear, very pure, very cool light that seemed somehow potent but reserved, as though it could do terrible blinding things, and give an unbearable heat, if it chose—well, I'm not quite sure what I mean."

There was a midnight fug in the air of the library where the President *pro tem* retold his tale. The Magus to whom he told it did not look at him; his pale gray eyes moved from object to object around the room in the aimless idiot wandering that had at first caused the President *pro tem* to believe him blind.

"The mountain was called Table Mountain—a sort of high mesa. What a place that was then—I think the most beautiful in the Empire, and young then, but not raw; a peninsula simply made to put a city on, and a city being put there, beneath the mountain: and this piercing light.

"Our party put up the Mount Nelson Hotel, perhaps a little grand for the travelers in electroplating equipment we were pretending to be, but the incognito wasn't really important, it was chiefly to explain the presence of the Last equipment among the luggage.

"A few days were spent in reconnaissance. But you see—this is continually the impossible thing to explain—in a sense those of the party who knew the outcome were only going through the motions of conferring, mapping their victim's movements, choosing a suitable moment and all that: for they knew the story; there was only one way for it to happen, if it was to happen at all. If it was *not* to happen, then no one could predict what was to happen instead; but so long as our party was there, and preparing it, it would evidently have to happen—or would have to have had to have happened."

The President *pro tem* suddenly missed his old friend Davenant, Davenant the witty and deep, who never bumbled over his tenses, never got himself stuck in a sentence such as that one; Davenant lost now with the others in the interstices of imaginary pasthood— or rather about to be lost, in the near future, if the President *pro tem* assented to what was asked of him. "It was rather jolly," he said, "like a game rather, striving to bring about a result that you were sure had already been brought about; an old ritual, if you like, to which not much importance needed to be attached, so long as it was all done correctly . . ."

"I think," said the Magus, "you need not explain these feelings that you then had."

"Sorry," said the President *pro tem*. "The house was called Groote Schuur—that was the old Dutch name, which he'd revived, for a big granary that had stood on the property; the English had called it the Grange. It was built on the lower slopes of Devil's Peak, with a view up to the mountains, and out to sea as well. He'd only recently seen the need for a house—all his life in Africa he'd more or less pigged it in rented rooms, or stayed in his club or a hotel or even a tent pitched outside town. For a long time he roomed with Dr. Jameson, sleeping on a little truckle bed hardly big enough for his body. But now that he'd become prime minister, he felt it was time for something more substantial.

"It seemed to me that it would have been easier to take him out in the bush—the *bundas,* as the Matabele say. Hire a party of natives—wait till all are asleep—ambush. He often went out into the wilds with almost no protection. There was no question of honor involved—I mean, the man had to die, one way or the other, and the more explainably or accidentally the better. But I was quite wrong—I was myself still young—and had to be put right: the one time that way was tried, the assassination initiated a punitive war against the native populations that lasted for twenty years, and ended only with the virtual extermination of the Matabele and Mashona peoples. Dreadful.

"No, it had to be the house; moreover, it had to be within a very brief span of time—a time when we knew he was there, when we knew where his will was, and *which* will it was—he made eight or nine in his lifetime—and when we knew, also, what assets were in his hands. Business and ownership were fluid things in those days; his partners were quick and subtle men; his sudden death might lose us all that we were intending to acquire by it in the way of a campaign chest, so to speak.

"So it had to be the house, in this week of this year, on this night. In fact orthogonal logic dictated it. Davenant was quite calmly sure of that. After all, that was the night when it had happened: and for sure we ought not to miss it."

That was an attempt at the sort of remark Davenant might

make, and the President *pro tem* smiled at the Magus, who remained unmoved. The President *pro tem* thought it impossible that beings as wise as he knew the one before him to be, no matter how grave, could altogether lack any sense of humor. For himself, he had often thought that if he did not find funny the iron laws of orthogony he would go mad; but his jokes apparently amused only himself.

"It was not a question of getting to his house, or into it; he practically kept open house the year round, and his grounds could be walked upon by anyone. The gatekeepers were only instructed to warn walkers about the animals they might come across—he had brought in dozens of species, and he allowed all but the genuinely dangerous to roam at will. Wildebeest. Zebras. Impala. And 'human beings,' as he always called them, roamed at will, too; there were always some about. At dinner he had visitors from all over Africa, and from England and Europe as well; his bedrooms were often full. I think he hated to be alone. All of which provided a fine setting, you see, for a sensational—and insoluble—murder mystery: if only the man could be got alone, and escape made good then through these crowds of hangers-on.

"Our plan depended on a known proclivity of his, or rather two proclivities. The first was a taste he had for the company of a certain sort of a young man. He liked having them around him and could become very attached to them. There was never a breath of scandal in this—well, there was talk, but only talk. His 'angels,' people called them: good-looking, resourceful if not particularly bright, good all-rounders with a rough sense of fun—practical jokes, horseplay—but completely devoted and ready for anything he might ask them to do. He had a fair crowd of these fellows up at Groote Schuur just then. Harry Curry, his private secretary.

Johnny Grimmer, a trooper who was never afraid to give him orders—like a madman's keeper, some people said, scolding him and brushing dust from his shoulders; he never objected. Bob Coryndon, another trooper. They'd all just taken on a butler for themselves, a sergeant in the Inniskillings: good-looking chap, twenty-three years old. Oddly, they had all been just that age when he'd taken an interest in them: twenty-three. Whether that was chance or his conscious choice we didn't know.

"The other proclivity was his quickness in decision making. And this often involved the young men. The first expedition into Matabeleland had been headed up by a chap he'd met at his club one morning at breakfast just as the column was preparing for departure. Took to the chap instantly: liked his looks, liked his address. Gave him the job on the spot.

"That had worked out very well, of course—his choices often did. The pioneer column had penetrated into the heart of the *bundas,* the flag was flying over a settlement they called Fort Salisbury, and the whole of Matabeleland was in the process of being added to the Empire. Up at Groote Schuur they were kicking around possible names for the new country: Rhodia, perhaps, or Rhodesland, even Cecilia. It was that night that they settled on Rhodesia."

The President *pro tem* felt a moment's shame. There had been, when it came down to it, no doubt in his mind that what they had done had been the right thing to do: and in any case it had all happened a long time ago, more than a century ago in fact. It was not what was done, or that it had been done, only the moment of its doing, that was hard to relate: it was the picture in his mind, of an old man (though he was only forty-eight, he looked far older) sitting in the lamplight reading *The Boy's Own Paper,* as absorbed and as innocent in his absorption as a boy himself; and the vulnerable shine on his balding crown; and the tender and indifferent night: it was all that which raised a lump in the throat of the President *pro tem* and caused him to pause, and roll the tip of his cigar in the ashtray, and clear his throat before continuing.

"And so," he said, "we baited our hook. Rhodes's British South Africa Company was expanding, in the wake of the Fort Salisbury success. He was on the lookout for young men of the right sort. We presented him with one: good-looking lad, public school, cricketer; just twenty-three years old. He was the bait. The mole. The Judas."

And the bait had been taken, of course. The arrangement's having been keyed so nicely to the man's nature, a nature able to be studied from the vantage point of several decades on, it could hardly have failed. That the trick seemed so fragile, even foolish, something itself out of *The Boy's Own Paper* or a story by Henley, only increased the likelihood of its striking just the right note here: the coloured fanatic, Rhodes leaving his hotel after luncheon to return to Parliament, the thug stepping out of the black noon shadows with a knife just as Rhodes mounts his carriage steps—then the young man, handily by with a stout walking-stick (a gift of his father upon his departure for Africa)—the knife deflected, the would-be assassin slinking off, the great man's gratitude. You must have some reward. Not a bit, sir, anyone would have done the same; just lucky I was nearby. Come to dinner at any rate—my house on the hill—anyone can direct you. Allow me to introduce myself; my name is . . .

No need, sir, everyone knows Cecil Rhodes.

And your name is . . .

The clean hand put frankly forward, the tanned, open, boyish face smiling. My name is Denys Winterset.

"So then you see," the President *pro tem* said, "the road was open. The road up to Groote Schuur. The road that branches, in effect, to lead here: to us here now speaking of it."

"And how many times since then," the Magus said, "has the world branched? How many times has it been bent double, and broken? A thousand times, ten thousand? Each time growing smaller, having to be packed into lesser space, curling into itself like a snail's shell; growing ever weaker as the changes multiply, and more liable to failure of its fabric: how many times?"

The President *pro tem* answered nothing.

"You understand, then," the Magus said to him, "what you will be asked: to find the crossroads that leads this way and to turn the world from it."

"Yes."

"And how will you reply?"

The President *pro tem* had no better answer for this question, and he gave none. He had begun to feel at once heavy as lead and disembodied. He arose from his armchair, with some effort, and crossed the worn Turkey carpet to the tall window.

"You must leave my house now," the Magus said, rising from his chair. "There is much for me to do this night, if this world is to pass out of existence."

"Where shall I go?"

"They will find you. I think in not too long a time." Without looking back he left the room.

The President *pro tem* pushed aside the heavy drape the draconic had drawn. *Where shall I go?* He looked out the window into the square outside, deserted at this late and rainy hour. It was an irregular square, the intersection of three streets, filled with rain-wet cobbles as though with shiny eggs. It was old; it had been the view out these windows for two centuries at the least; there was nothing about it to suggest that it had not been the intersection of three streets for a good many more centuries than that.

And yet it had not been there at all only a few decades earlier, when the President *pro tem* had last walked the city outside the Orient Aid Society. Then the city had been London; it was no more. These three streets, these cobbles, had not been there in 1983; nor in 1893 either. Yet there they were, somewhere early in the twenty-first century; there they had been, too, for time out of mind, familiar no doubt to any dweller in this part of town, familiar for that matter to the President *pro tem* who looked out at them. In each of two lamp-lit cafés on two corners of the square, a man in a soft cap held a glass and looked out into the night, unsurprised, at home.

Someone had broken the rules: there simply was no other explanation.

There had been, of course, no way for anyone, not Deng Fa-shen, not Davenant, not the President *pro tem* himself, to guess what the President *pro tem* might come upon on this, the first expedition the Otherhood was making into the future: not only did the future not exist (Deng Fa-shen was quite clear about that), but, as Davenant reminded him, the Otherhood itself, supposing the continued existence of the Otherhood, would no doubt go busily on changing things in the past far and near—shifting the ground therefore of the future the President *pro tem* was headed for. Deng Fa-shen was satisfied that that future, the ultimate future, sum of all intermediate revisions, was the only one that could be plumbed, if any could; and that was the only one the Otherhood would want to glimpse: to learn how they would do, or would come to have done; to find out, as George V whispered on his deathbed, "How is the Empire."

("Only that isn't what he said," Davenant was fond of telling. "That's what he was, understandably, reported to have said, and what the Queen and the nurses convinced themselves they heard. But he was a bit dazed there at the end, poor good old man. What he said was not 'How is the Empire,' but 'What's at the Empire,' a popular cinema. I happened," he always added gravely, "to have been with him.")

The first question had been how far "forward" the Otherhood should press; those members who thought the whole scheme insane, as Platt did, voted for next Wednesday, and bring back the Derby winners please. Deng Fa-shen was not certain the thrust could be entirely calculated: the imaginary futures of imaginary pasts were not, he thought, likely to be under the control of even the most penetrating orthogonal engineering. Sometime in the first decades of the next century was at length agreed upon, a time just beyond the voyager's own mortal span—for the house rule seemed, no one could say quite why, to apply in both directions—and for as brief a stay as was consistent with learning what was up.

The second question—who was to be the voyager—the President *pro tem* had answered by fiat, assuming an executive privilege he just at that moment claimed to exist, and cutting off further debate. (Why exactly did he insist? I'm not certain why, except that it was not out of a sense of adventure, or of fun or curiosity: whatever of those qualities he may once have had had been much worn away in his rise to the Presidency *pro tem* of the Otherhood. A sense of duty may have been part of it. It may have been to forestall the others, out of a funny sort of premonition. Duty, and premonition: of what, though? Of what?)

"It'll be quite different from any of our imaginings, you know," Davenant said, who for some reason had not vigorously contested the President's decision. "The future of all possible pasts. I envy you, I do. I should rather like to see it for myself."

Quite different from any of our imaginings: very well. The President *pro tem* had braced himself for strangeness. What he had not expected was familiarity. Familiarity—cozy as an old shoe—was certainly different from his imaginings.

And yet what was it he was familiar with? He had stepped out of his club in London and found himself to be, not in the empty corridors of the Orient Aid Society that he knew well, but in private quarters of some kind that he had never seen before. It reminded him, piercingly, of a place he did know, but what place he could not have said: some don's rich but musty rooms, some wealthy and learned bachelor's digs. How had it come to be?

And how had it come to be lit by gas?

One of the pleasant side effects (most of the members thought it pleasant) of the Otherhood's endless efforts in the world had been a general retardation in the rate of material progress: so much of that progress had been, on the one hand, the product of the disastrous wars that it was the Otherhood's chief study to prevent, and on the other hand, American. The British Empire moved more slowly, a great beast without predators, and naturally conservative; it clung to proven techniques and could impose them on the rest of the world by its weight. The telephone, the motor car, the flying boat, the wireless, all were slow to take root in the Empire that the Otherhood shaped. And yet surely, the President *pro tem* thought, electricity was in general use in London in 1893, before which date no member could alter the course of things. And gas lamps lit this place.

Pondering this, the President *pro tem* had entered the somber and apparently little-used dining room and seen the draconic standing in the little butler's pantry: silent as a statue (asleep, the

President *pro tem* would later deduce, with lidless eyes only seeming to be open); a polishing cloth in his claw, and the silver before him; his heavy jaws ajar, and his weight balanced on the thick stub of tail. He wore a baize apron and black sleeve garters to protect his clothes.

Quite different from our imaginings: and yet no conceivable amount of tinkering with the twentieth century, just beyond which the President *pro tem* theoretically stood, could have brought forth this butler, in wing collar and green apron, the soft gaslight ashine on his bald brown head.

So someone had broken the rules. Someone had dared to regress beyond 1893 and meddle in the farther past. That was not, in itself, impossible; Caspar Last had done it on his first and only excursion. It had only been thought impossible for the Otherhood to do it, because it would have taken them "back" before the Otherhood's putative existence, and therefore before the Otherhood could have wrested the techniques of such travel from Last's jealous grip, a power they acquired by already having it— that was what the President *pro tem* had firmly believed.

But it was not, apparently, so. Somewhen in that stretch of years that fell between his entrance into the telephone box of the club and his exit from it into this familiar and impossible world, someone—many someones, or someone many times—had gone "back" far before Rhodes's death: had gone back far enough to initiate this house, this city, these races who were not men.

A million years? It couldn't have been less. It didn't seem possible it could be less.

And who, then? Deng Fa-shen, the delicate, brilliant Chinaman, who had thoughts and purposes he kept to himself; the only one of them who might have been able to overcome the theoretical limits? Or Platt, who was never satisfied with what was possible within what he called "the damned parameters"?

Or Davenant. Davenant, who was forever quoting Khayyám: *Ah, Love, couldst thou and I with Him conspire To take this sorry scheme of things entire; Would we not smash it into pieces, then Remold it nearer to the heart's desire . . .*

"There is," said the Magus behind him, "one other you have not thought of."

The President *pro tem* let fall the drape and turned from the window. The Magus stood in the doorway, a great ledger in his arms. His eyes did not meet the President *pro tem*'s, and yet seemed to regard him anyway, like the blind eyes of a statue.

One other . . . Yes, the President *pro tem* saw, there *was* one other who might have done this. One other, not so good at the work perhaps as others, as Davenant for example, but who nonetheless would have been, or would come to have been, in a position to take such steps. The President *pro tem* would not have credited himself with the skill, or the nerve, or the dreadnought power. But how else to account for the familiarity, the bottomless *suitability* to him of this world he had never before seen?

"Between the time of your people's decision to plumb our world," said the Magus, "and the time of your standing here within it, you must yourself have brought it into being. I see no likelier explanation."

The President *pro tem* stood still with wonder at the efforts he was apparently to prove capable of making. A million years at least: a million years. How had he known where to begin? Where had he found, would he find, the time?

"Shall I ring," the Magus said, "or will you let yourself out?"

◼

Deng Fa-shen had always said it, and anyone who traveled in them knew it to be so: the imaginary futures and imaginary pasts of orthogony are imaginary only in the sense that imaginary numbers (which they very much resemble) are imaginary. To a man walking within one, it alone is real, no matter how strange; it is all the others, standing at angles to it, which exist only in imagination. Nightlong the President *pro tem* walked the city, with a measured and unhurried step, but with a constant tremor winding round his rib cage, waiting for what would become of him, and observing the world he had made.

Of course it could not continue to exist. It should not ever have come into existence in the first place; his own sin (if it had been his) had summoned it out of nonbeing, and his repentance must expunge it. The Magus who had taken his confession (which the President *pro tem* had been unable to withhold from him) had drawn that conclusion: it must be put out, like a light. And yet how deeply the President *pro tem* wanted it to last forever; how deeply he believed it *ought* to last forever.

The numinous and inhuman angels, about whom nothing could be said, beings with no ascertainable business among the lesser races and yet beings without whom, the President *pro tem* was sure, this world could not go on functioning. They lived (endless?) lives unimaginable to men, and perhaps to Magi, too, who yet sought continually for knowledge of them: Magi, highest of the hominids, gentle and wise yet inflexible of purpose, living in simplicity and solitude (were there females? Where? Doing what?) and yet from their shabby studies influencing, perhaps directing, the lives of mere men. The men, such as himself, clever and busy, with their inventions and their politics and their affairs. The lesser hominids, strong, sweet-natured, comic, like placid trolls. The draconics.

It was not simply a world inhabited by intelligent races of different kinds: it was a harder thing to grasp than that. The lives of the races constituted different universes of meaning, different constructions of reality; it was as though four or five different novels, novels of different kinds by different and differently limited writers, were to become interpenetrated and conflated: inside a gigantic Russian thing a stark and violent *policier,* and inside that something Dickensian, full of plot, humors, and eccentricity. Such an interlacing of mutually exclusive universes might be comical, like a sketch in *Punch;* it might be tragic, too. And it might be neither: it might simply be what is, the given against which all airy imaginings must finally be measured: reality.

Near dawn the President *pro tem* stood leaning on a parapet of worked stone that overlooked a streetcar roundabout. A car had just ended its journey there, and the conductor and the motorman descended, squat hominids in greatcoats and peaked caps. With their long strong arms they began to swing the car around for its return journey. The President *pro tem* gazed down at this commonplace sight; his nose seemed to know the smell of that car's interior, his bottom to know the feel of its polished seats. But he knew also that yesterday there had not been streetcars in this city. Today they had been here for decades.

No, it was no good, the President *pro tem* knew: the fabric of this world he had made—if it had been he—was fatally weakened with irreality. It was a botched job: as though he were that god of the Gnostics who made the material world, a minor god unversed in putting time together with space. He had not worked well. And how could he have supposed it would be otherwise? What had got into him, that he had dared?

"No," said the angel who stood beside him. "You should not think that it was you."

"If not me," said the President *pro tem*, "then who?"

"Come," said the angel. She (I shall say "she") slipped a small cool hand within his hand. "Let's go over the tracks, and into the trees beyond that gate."

A hard and painful stone had formed in the throat of the President *pro tem*. The angel beside him led him like a daughter, like the daughter of old blind Oedipus. Within the precincts of the park—which apparently had its entrance or its entrances where the angels needed them to be—he was led down an avenue of yew and dim towers of poplar toward the piled and sounding waters of a fountain. They sat together on the fountain's marble lip.

"The Magus told me," the President *pro tem* began, "that you can feel the alterations that we make, back then. Is that true?"

"It's like the snap of a whip infinitely long," the angel said. "The whole length of time snapped and laid out differently: not only the length of time backward to the time of the change, but the length of the future forward. We felt ourselves come into being, oldest of the Old Races (though the last your changes brought into existence); we saw in that moment the aeons of our past, and we guessed our future, too."

The President *pro tem* took out his pocket-handkerchief and pressed it to his face. He must weep, yet no tears came.

"We love this world—this only world—just as you do," she said. "We love it, and we cannot bear to feel it sicken and fail. Better that it not have been than that it die."

"I will do all I can," said the President *pro tem*. "I will find who has done this—I suppose I know who it was, if it wasn't me—and dissuade him. Teach him, teach him what I've learned, make him see . . ."

"You don't yet understand," the angel said with careful kindness but at the same time glancing at her wristwatch. "There is no one to tell. There is no one who went beyond the rules."

"There must have been," said the President *pro tem*. "You, your time, it just isn't that far along from ours, from mine! To make this world, this city, these races . . ."

"Not far along in time," said the angel, "but many times removed. You know it to be so: whenever you, your Otherhood, set out across the time lines, your passage generated random variation in the worlds you arrived in. Perhaps you didn't understand how those variations accumulate, here at the sum end of your journeyings."

"But the changes were so minute!" said the President *pro tem*. "Deng Fa-shen explained it. A molecule here and there, no more; the position of a distant star; some trivial thing, the name of a flower or a village. Too few, too small even to notice."

"They increase exponentially with every alteration—and your Otherhood has been busy since you last presided over them. Through the days random changes accumulate, tiny errors silting up like the blown sand that fills the streets of a desert city, that buries it at last."

"But why these changes?" asked the President *pro tem* desperately. "It can't have been chance that a world like this was the sum of those histories, it can't be. A world like *this* . . ."

"Chance, perhaps. Or it may be that as time grows softer the world grows more malleable by wishes. There is no reason to believe this, yet that is what we believe. You—all of you—could not have known that you were bringing this world into being; and yet this is the world you wanted."

She reached out to let the tossed foam of the fountain fall into her hand. The President *pro tem* thought of the bridge over the

Zambezi, far away; the tossed foam of the Falls. It was true: this is what they had striven for: a world of perfect hierarchies, of no change forever. God, how they must have longed for it! The loneliness of continual change—no outback, no *bundas* so lonely. He had heard how men can be unsettled for days, for weeks, who have lived through earthquakes and felt the earth to be uncertain: what of his Fellows, who had felt time and space picked apart, never to be rewoven that way again, and not once but a hundred times? What of himself?

"I shall tell you what I see at the end of all your wishings," said the angel softly. "At the far end of the last changed world, after there is nothing left that can change. There is then only a forest, growing in the sea. I say 'forest' and I say 'sea,' though whether they are of the kind I know, or some other sort of thing, I cannot say. The sea is still and the forest is thick; it grows upward from the black bottom, and its topmost branches reach into the sunlight, which penetrates a little into the warm upper waters. That's all. There is nothing else anywhere forever. Your wishes have come true: the Empire is quiet. There is not, nor will there be, change anymore; never will one thing be confused again with another, higher for lower, better for lesser, master for servant. Perpetual Peace."

The President *pro tem* was weeping now, painful sobs drawn up from an interior he had long kept shut and bolted. Tears ran down his cheeks, into the corners of his mouth, under his hard collar. He knew what he must do, but not how to do it.

"The Otherhood cannot be dissuaded from this," the angel said, putting a hand on the wrist of the President *pro tem*. "For all of it, including our sitting here now, all of it—and the forest in the sea—is implicit in the very creation of the Otherhood itself."

"But then . . ."

"Then the Otherhood must be uncreated."

"I can't do that."

"You must."

"No, no, I can't." He had withdrawn from her pellucid gaze, horrified. "I mean it isn't because . . . if it must be done, it must be. But not by me."

"Why?"

"It would be against the rules given me. I don't know what the result would be. I can't imagine. I don't *want* to imagine."

"Rules?"

"The Otherhood came into being," said the President *pro tem*, "when a British adventurer, Cecil Rhodes, was shot and killed by a young man called Denys Winterset."

"Then you must return and stop that killing."

"But you don't see!" said the President *pro tem* in great distress. "The rules given the Otherhood forbid a Fellow from returning to a time and place that he formerly altered by his presence . . ."

"And . . ."

"And I am myself that same Denys Winterset."

The angel regarded the President *pro tem*—the Honorable Denys Winterset, fourteenth President *pro tem* of the Otherhood— and her translucent face registered a sweet surprise, as though the learning of something she had not known gave her pleasure. She laughed, and her laughter was not different from the plashing of the fountain by which they sat. She laughed and laughed, as the old man in his black coat and hat sat silent beside her, bewildered and afraid.

◻ ◻ ◻

VI. THE BOY DAVID OF HYDE PARK CORNER

THERE ARE DAYS when I seem genuinely to remember, and days when I do not remember at all: days when I remember only that sometimes I remember. There are days on which I think I recognize another like myself: someone walking smartly along the Strand or Bond Street, holding the *Times* under one arm and walking a furled umbrella with the other—a sort of military bearing, mustaches white (older than when I seem to have known him, but then so am I, of course), and cheeks permanently tanned by some faraway sun. I do not catch his eye, nor he mine, though I am tempted to stop him, to ask him . . . Later on I wonder—if I can remember to wonder—whether he, too, is making a chronicle, in his evenings, writing up the story: a story that can be told in any direction, starting from anywhere, leading on to a forest in the sea.

I won't look any longer into this chronicle I've compiled. I shall only complete it.

My name is Denys Winterset. I was born in London in 1933; I was the only son of a Harley Street physician, and my earliest memory is of coming upon my father in tears in his surgery: he had just heard the news that the R101 dirigible had crashed on its maiden flight, killing all those aboard.

We lived then above my father's offices, in a little building whose nursery I remember distinctly, though I was taken to the country with the other children of London when I was only six, and that building was knocked down by a bomb in 1940. A falling wall killed my mother; my father was on ambulance duty in the East End and was spared.

He didn't know quite what to do with me, nor I with myself; I have been torn all my life between the drive to discover what others whom I love and admire expect of me, and my discovery that then I don't want to do it, really. After coming down from the University I decided, out of a certain perversity which my father could not sympathize with, to join the Colonial Service. He could not fathom why I would want to fasten myself to an enterprise that everyone save a few antediluvian colonels and letter writers to the *Times* could see was a dead animal. And I couldn't explain. Psychoanalysis later suggested that it was quite simply because no one wanted me to do it. The explanation has since come to seem insufficient to me.

That was a strange late blooming of Empire in the decade after the war, when the Colonial Office took on factitious new life, and thousands of us went out to the Colonies. The Service became larger than it had been in years, swollen with ex-officers too accustomed to military life to do anything else, and with the innocent and the confused, like myself. I ended up a junior member of a transition team in a Central African country I shall not name, helping see to it that as much was given to the new native government as they could be persuaded to accept, in the way of a parliament, a well-disciplined army, a foreign service, a judiciary.

It was not after all very much. Those institutions that the British are sure no civilized nation can do without were, in the minds of many Africans who spoke freely to me, very like those exquisite japanned toffee boxes from Fortnum & Mason that you used often to come across in native kraals, because the chieftains and shamans loved them so, to keep their juju in. Almost as soon as I arrived, it became evident that the commander in chief of the armed forces was impatient with the pace of things, and felt the need of no special transition to African, i.e., his own, control of the state. The most our commission were likely to accomplish was to get the British population out without a bloodbath.

Even that would not be easy. We—we young men—were saddled with the duty of explaining to aged planters that there was no one left to defend their estates against confiscation, and that under the new constitution they hadn't a leg to stand on, and that despite how dearly their overseers and house people loved them, they ought to begin seeing what they could pack into a few small trunks. On the other hand, we were to calm the fears of merchants and diamond factors, and tell them that if they all simply dashed for it, they could easily precipitate a closing of the frontiers, with incalculable results.

There came a night when, more than usually certain that not a single Brit under my care would leave the country alive, nor deserved to either, I stood at the bar of the Planters' (just renamed the Republic) Club, drinking gin and Italian (tonic hadn't been reordered in weeks) and listening to the clacking of the fans. A fellow I knew slightly as a regular here saluted me; I nodded and returned to my thoughts. A moment later I found him next to me.

"I wonder," he said, "if I might have your ear for a moment."

The expression, in his mouth, was richly comic, or perhaps it was my exhaustion. He waited for my laughter to subside before speaking. He was called Rossie, and he'd spent a good many years in Africa, doing whatever came to hand. He was one of those Englishmen whom the sun turns not brown but only gray and greasy; his eyes were always watery, the cups of his lids red and painful to look at.

"I am," he said at last, "doing a favor for a chap who would like your help."

"I'll do what I can," I said.

"This is a chap," he said, "who has been too long in this country, and would like to leave it."

"There are many in his situation."

"Not quite."

"What is his name?" I said, taking out a memorandum book. "I'll pass it on to the commission."

"Just the point," Rossie said. He drew closer to me. At the other end of the bar loud laughter arose from a group consisting of a newly commissioned field marshal—an immense, glossy, nearly blue-black man—and his two colonels, both British, both small and lean. They laughed when the field marshal laughed, though their laugh was not so loud, nor their teeth so large and white.

"He'll want to tell you his name himself," Rossie said. "I've only brought the message. He wants to see you, to talk to you. I said I'd tell you. That's all."

"To tell us . . ."

"Not you, all of you. *You:* you."

I drank. The warm, scented liquor was thick in my throat. "Me?"

"What he asked me to ask you," Rossie said, growing impatient, "was would you come out to his place, and see him. It isn't far. He wanted you, no one else. He said I was to insist. He said you were to come alone. He'll send a boy of his. He said tell no one."

There were many reasons why a man might want to do business with the commission privately. I could think of none why it should be done with me alone. I agreed, with a shrug. Rossie seemed immediately to put the matter out of his mind, mopped his red face, and ordered drinks for both of us. By the time they were brought we were already discussing the Imperial groundnut scheme, which was to have kept this young republic self-sufficient, but which, it was now evident, would do no such thing.

I too put what had been asked of me out of my mind, with enough success that when on a windless and baking afternoon a native boy shook me awake from a nap, I could not imagine why.

"Who are you? What are you doing in my bungalow?"

He only stared down at me, as though it were he who could not think why I should be there before him. Questions in his own language got no response either. At length he backed out the door, clearly wanting me to follow; and so I did, with the dread one feels on remembering an unpleasant task one has contrived to neglect. I found him outside, standing beside my Land Rover, ready to get aboard.

"All right," I said. "Very well." I got into the driver's seat. "Point the way."

It was a small spread of tobacco and a few dusty cattle an hour's drive from town, a low bungalow looking beaten in the ocher heat. He gave no greeting as I alighted from the Land Rover but stood in the shadows of the porch unmoving: as though he had stood so a long time. He went back into the house as I approached, and when I went in, he was standing against the netting of the window, the light behind him. That seemed a conscious choice. He was smiling, I could tell: a strange and eager smile.

"I've waited a long time for you," he said. "I don't mind saying."

"I came as quickly as I could," I said.

"There was no way for me to know, you see," he said, "whether you'd come at all."

"Your boy was quite insistent," I said. "And Mr. Rossie—"

"I meant: to Africa." His voice was light, soft and dry. "There being so much less reason for it, now. I've wondered often. In fact I don't think a day has passed this year when I haven't wondered." Keeping his back to the sunward windows, he moved to sit on the edge of a creaking wicker sofa. "You'll want a drink," he said.

"No." The place was filled with the detritus of an African bachelor farmer's digs: empty paraffin tins, bottles, tools, hanks of rope and motor parts. He put a hand behind him without looking and put it on the bottle he was no doubt accustomed to find there. "I tried to think reasonably about it," he said, pouring a drink. "As time went on, and things began to sour here, I came to be more and more certain that no lad with any pluck would throw himself away down here. And yet I couldn't know. Whether there might not be some impulse, I don't know, traveling to you from—elsewhere. . . . I even thought of writing to you. Though whether to convince you to come or to dissuade you I'd no idea."

I sat, too. A cool sweat had gathered on my neck and the backs of my hands.

"Then," he said, "when I heard you'd come—well, I was afraid, frankly. I didn't know what to think." He dusted a fly from the rim of his glass, which he had not tasted. "You see," he said, "this was against the rules given me. That I—that I and—that you and I should meet."

Perhaps he's mad, I thought, and even as I thought it I felt intensely the experience called déjà vu, an experience I have always hated, hated like the nightmare. I steeled myself to respond coolly and took out my memorandum book and pencil. "I'm afraid you've rather lost me," I said—briskly I hoped. "Perhaps we'd better start with your name."

"Oh," he said, smiling again his mirthless smile, "not the hardest question first, please."

Without having, so far as I knew, the slightest reason for it, I began to feel intensely sorry for this odd dried jerky of a man, whose eyes alone seemed quick and shy. "All right," I said, "nationality, then. You are a British subject."

"Well, yes."

"Proof?" He answered nothing. "Passport?" No. "Army card? Birth certificate? Papers of any kind?" No. "Any connections in Britain? Relatives? Someone who could vouch for you, take you in?"

"No," he said. "None who could. None but you. It will have to be you."

"Now hold hard," I said.

"I don't know why I must," he said, rising suddenly and turning away to the window. "But I must. I must go back. I imagine dying here, being buried here, and my whole soul retreats in horror. I must go back. Even though I fear that, too."

He turned from the window, and in the sharp side light of the late afternoon his face was clearly the face of someone I knew. "Tell me," he said. "Mother and father. Your mother and father. They're alive?"

"No," I said. "Both dead."

"Very well," he said, "very well"; but it did not seem to be very well with him. "I'll tell you my story, then."

"I think you'd best do that."

"It's a long one."

"No matter." I had begun to feel myself transported, like a Sinbad, into somewhere that it were best I listen, and keep my counsel: and yet the first words of this specter's tale made that impossible.

"My name," he said, "is Denys Winterset."

I have come to believe, having had many years in which to think about it, that it must be as he said, that an impulse from somewhere else (he meant: some previous present, some earlier version of these circumstances) must press upon such a life as mine. That I chose the Colonial Service, that I came to Africa—and not just to Africa, but to that country: well, *if anything is chance, that was not*—as I understand Sir Geoffrey Davenant to have once said.

In that long afternoon, there where I perhaps could not have helped arriving eventually, I sat and perspired, listening—though it was for a long time very nearly impossible to hear what was said to me: an appointment in Khartoum some months from now, and some decades past; a club, outside all frames of reference; the Last equipment. It was quite like listening to the unfollowable logic of a madman, as meaningless as the roar of the insects outside. I only began to hear when this aged man, older than my grandfather, told me of something that he—that I—that he and I—had once done in boyhood, something secret, trivial really and yet so shameful that even now I will not write it down; something that only Denys Winterset could know.

"There now," he said eyes cast down. "There now, you must believe me. You *will* listen. The world has not been as you thought it to be, any more than it was as I thought it to be, when I was as you are now. I shall tell you why: and we will hope that mine is the last story that need be told."

And so it was that I heard how he had gone up the road to Groote Schuur, that evening in 1893 (a young man then of course, only twenty-three) with the Webley revolver in his breast pocket as heavy as his heart, nearly sick with wonder and apprehension. The tropical suit he had been made to wear was monstrously hot, complete with full waistcoat and hard collar; the topee they insisted he use was as weighty as a crown. As he came in sight of the house, he could hear the awesome cries from the lion house, where the cats were evidently being given their dinner.

The big house appeared raw and unfinished to him, the trees yet ungrown and the great masses of scentless flowers—hydrangea, bougainvillaea, canna—that had smothered the place when last he had seen it, some decades later, just beginning to spread.

"Rhodes himself met me at the door—actually he happened to be going out for his afternoon ride—and welcomed me," he said. "I think the most striking thing about Cecil Rhodes, and it hasn't been noticed much, was his utter lack of airs. He was the least self-conscious man I have ever known; he did many things for effect, but he was himself entirely single: as whole as an egg, as the old French used to say.

" 'The house is yours,' he said to me. 'Use it as you like. We don't dress for dinner, as a rule; too many of the guests would be taken short, you see. Now some of the fellows are playing croquet in the Great Hall. Pay them no mind.'

"I remember little of that evening. I wandered the house: the great skins of animals, the heavy beams of teak, the brass chandeliers. I looked into the library, full of the specially transcribed and bound classics that Rhodes had ordered by the yard from Hatchard's: all the authorities that Gibbon had consulted in writing the *Decline and Fall*. All of them: that had been Rhodes's order.

"Dinner was a long and casual affair, entirely male—Rhodes had not even any female servants in the house. There was much toasting and hilarity about the successful march into Matabeleland, and the foundation of a fort, which news had only come that week; but Rhodes seemed quiet at the table's head, even melancholy: many of his closest comrades were gone with the expeditionary column, and he seemed to miss them. I do remember that at one point the conversation turned to America. Rhodes contended—no one disputed him—that if we (he meant the Empire, of course) had not lost America, the peace of the world could have been secured forever. 'Forever,' he said. 'Perpetual Peace.' And his pale opaque eyes were moist.

"How I comported myself at table—how I joined the talk, how I kept up conversations on topics quite unfamiliar to me—none of that do I recall. It helped that I was supposed to have been only recently arrived in Africa: though one of Rhodes's band of merry men looked suspiciously at my sun-browned hands when I said so.

"As soon as I could after dinner, I escaped from the fearsome horseplay that began to develop among those left awake. I pleaded a touch of sun and was shown to my room. I took off the hateful collar and tie (not without difficulty) and lay on the bed otherwise fully clothed, alert and horribly alone. Perhaps you can imagine my thoughts."

"No," I said. "I don't think I can."

"No. Well. No matter. I must have slept at last; it seemed to be after midnight when I opened my eyes and saw Rhodes standing in the doorway, a candlestick in his hand.

" 'Asleep?' he asked softly.

" 'No,' I answered. 'Awake.'

" 'Can't sleep either,' he said. 'Never do, much.' He ventured another step into the room. 'You ought to come out, see the sky,' he said. 'Quite spectacular. As long as you're up.'

"I rose and followed him. He was without his coat and collar; I noticed he wore carpet slippers. One button of his wide braces was undone; I had the urge to button it for him. Pale starlight fell in blocks across the black and white tiles of the hall, and the huge heads of beasts were mobile in the candlelight as we passed. I murmured something about the grandness of his house.

" 'I told my architect,' Rhodes answered. 'I said I wanted the big and simple—the barbaric, if you like.' The candle flame danced before him. 'Simple. The truth is always simple.'

"The chessboard tiles of the hall continued out through the wide doors onto the veranda—the *stoep* as the old Dutch called it. At the frontier of the *stoep* great pillars divided the night into panels filled with clustered stars, thick and near as vine blossoms. From far off came a long cry as of pain: a lion, awake.

"Rhodes leaned on the parapet, looking into the mystery of the sloping lawns beyond the *stoep*. 'That's good news, about the chaps up in Matabeleland,' he said a little wistfully.

" 'Yes.'

" 'Pray God they'll all be safe.'

" 'Yes.'

" 'Zambesia,' he said after a moment. 'What d'you think of that?'

" 'I beg your pardon?'

" 'As a name. For this country we'll be building. *Beyond the Zambezi*, you see.'

" 'It's a fine name.'

"He fell silent a time. A pale, powdery light filled the sky: false dawn. 'They shall say, in London,' he said, ' "Rhodes has taken for the Empire a country larger than Europe, at not a sixpence of cost to us, and we shall have that, and Rhodes shall have six feet by four feet." '

"He said this without bitterness, and turned from the parapet to face me. The Webley was pointed toward him. I had rested my (trembling) right hand on my left forearm, held up before me.

" 'Why, what on earth,' he said.

" 'Look,' I said.

"Drawing his look slowly away from me, he turned again. Out in the lawn, seeming in that illusory light to be but a long leap away, a male lion stood unmoving.

" 'The pistol won't stop him,' I said, 'but it will deflect him. If you will go calmly through the door behind me, I'll follow.'

"Rhodes backed away from the rail, and without haste or panic turned and walked past me into the house. The lion, ocher in the blue night, regarded him with a lion's expression, at once aloof and concerned, and returned his look to me. I thought I smelled him. Then I saw movement in the young trees beyond. I thought for a moment that my lion must be an illusion, or a dream, for he took no notice of these sounds—the crush of a twig, a soft voice—but at length he did turn his eyes from me to them. I could see the dim figure of a gamekeeper in a wide-awake hat, carrying a rifle, and Negroes with nets and poles: they were closing in carefully on the escapee. I stood for a moment longer, still poised to shoot, and then beat my own retreat into the house.

"Lights were being lit down the halls, voices calling: a lion does not appear on the lawn every night. Rhodes stood looking, not out the window, but at me. With deep embarrassment I clumsily pock-

eted the Webley (*I* knew what it had been given to me for, after all,
even if he did not), and only then did I meet Rhodes's eyes.

"I shall never forget their expression, those pale eyes: a kind of
exalted wonder, almost a species of adoration.

" 'That's twice now in one day,' he said, 'that you have kept me
from harm. You must have been sent, that's all. I really believe you
have been sent.'

"I stood before him staring, with a horror dawning in my heart
such as, God willing, I shall never feel again. I knew, you see, what
it meant that I had let slip the moment: that now I could not go
back the way I had come. The world had opened for an instant,
and I and my companions had gone down through it to this time
and place; and now it had closed over me again, a seamless whole.
I had no one and nothing; no Last equipment awaited me at the
Mount Nelson Hotel; the Otherhood could not rescue me, for I
had canceled it. I was entirely alone.

"Rhodes, of course, knew nothing of this. He crossed the hall
to where I stood, with slow steps, almost reverently. He embraced
me, a sudden great bear hug. And do you know what he did then?"

"What did he do?"

"He took me by the shoulders and held me at arm's length, and
he insisted that I stay there with him. In effect, he offered me a job.
For life, if I wanted it."

"What did you do?"

"I took it." He had finished his drink, and poured more. "I took
it. You see, I simply had no place else to go."

Afternoon was late in the bungalow where we sat together, day
hurried away with this tale. "I think," I said, "I shall have that drink
now, if it's no trouble."

He rose and found a glass; he wiped the husk of a bug from it and filled it from his bottle. "It has always astonished me," he said, "how the mind, you know, can construct with lightning speed a reasonable, if quite mistaken, story to account for an essentially unreasonable event: I have had more than one occasion to observe this process.

"I was sure, instantly sure, that a lion which had escaped from Rhodes's lion house had appeared on the lawn at Groote Schuur just at the moment when I tried, but could not bring myself, to murder Cecil Rhodes. I can still see that cat in the pale light of predawn. And yet I cannot know if that is what happened, or if it is only what my mind has substituted for what did happen, which cannot be thought about.

"I am satisfied in my own mind—having had a lifetime to ponder it—that it cannot be possible for one to meet oneself on a trip into the past or future: that is a lie, invented by the Otherhood to forestall its own extinction, which was however inevitable.

"But I dream, sometimes, that I am lying on the bed at Groote Schuur, and a man enters—it is not Rhodes, but a man in a black coat and a bowler hat, into whose face I look as into a rotted mirror, who tells me impossible things.

"And I know that in fact there was no lion house at Groote Schuur. Rhodes wanted one, and it was planned, but it was never built."

In the summer of that year Rhodes—alive, alive-oh—went on expedition up into Pondoland, seeking concessions from an intransigent chief named Sicgau. Denys Winterset—this one, telling me the tale—went with him.

"Rhodes took Sicgau out into a field of mealies where he had had us set up a Maxim gun. Rhodes and the chief stood in the sun for a moment, and then Rhodes gave a signal; we fired the Maxim for a few seconds and mowed down much of the field. The chief stood unmoving for a long moment after the silence returned. Rhodes said to him softly: 'You see, this is what will happen to you and all your warriors if you give us any further trouble.'

"As a stratagem, that seemed to me both sporting and thrifty. It worked, too. But we were later to use the Maxims against men and not mealies. Rhodes knew that the Matabele had finally to be suppressed, or the work of building a white state north of the Zambezi would be hopeless. A way was found to intervene in a quarrel the Matabele were having with the Mashona, and in not too long we were at war with the Matabele. They were terribly, terribly brave; they were, after all, the first eleven in those parts, and they believed with reason that no one could withstand their leaf-bladed spears. I remember how they would come against the Maxims, and be mown down like the mealies, and fall back, and muster for another attack. Your heart sank; you prayed they would go away, but they would not. They came on again, to be cut down again. These puzzled, bewildered faces: I cannot forget them.

"And Christ, such drivel was written in the papers then, about the heroic stand of a few beleaguered South African police against so many battle-crazed natives! The only one who saw the truth was the author of that silly poem—Belloc, was it? You know— 'Whatever happens, we have got / The Maxim Gun, and they have not.' It was as simple as that. The truth, Rhodes said, is always simple."

He took out a large pocket-handkerchief and mopped his face and his eyes; no doubt it was hot, but it seemed to me that he wept. Tears, idle tears.

"I met Dr. Jameson during the Matabele campaign," he continued. "Leander Starr Jameson. I think I have never met a man—and I have met many wicked and twisted ones—whom I have loathed so completely and so instantly. I had hardly heard of him, of course; he was already dead and unknown in this year as it had occurred in my former past, the only version of these events I knew. Jameson was a great lover of the Maxim; he took several along on the raid he made into the Transvaal in 1895, the raid that would eventually lead to war with the Boers, destroy Rhodes's credit, and begin the end of Empire: so I have come to see it. The fool.

"I took no part in that war, thank God. I went north to help put the railroad through: Cape to Cairo." He smiled, seemed almost about to laugh, but did not; only mopped his face again. It was as though I were interrogating him, and he were telling me all this under the threat of the rubber truncheon or the rack. I wanted him to stop, frankly; only I dared say nothing.

"I made up for a lack of engineering expertise by my very uncertain knowledge of where and how, one day, the road would run. The telegraph had already reached Uganda; next stop was Wadi Halfa. The rails would not go through so easily. I became a sort of scout, leading the advance parties, dealing with the chieftains. The Maxim went with me, of course. I learned the weapon well."

Here there came another silence, another inward struggle to continue. I was left to picture what he did not say: *That which I did I should not have done; that which I should have done I did not do.*

"Rhodes gave five thousand pounds to the Liberal party to persuade them not to abandon Egypt: for there his railroad must be hooked to the sea. But then of course came the end of the whole scheme in German Tanganyika: no Cape-to-Cairo road. Germany was growing great in the world; the Germans wanted to have an Empire of their own. It finished Rhodes.

"By that time I was a railroad expert. The nonexistent Uganda Railroad was happy to acquire my services: I had a reputation, among the blacks, you see . . . I think there was a death for every mile of that road as it went through the jungle to the coast: rinderpest, fever, Nanda raids. We would now and then hang a captured Nanda warrior from the telegraph poles, to discourage the others. By the time the rails reached Mombasa, I was an old man; and Cecil Rhodes was dead."

He died of his old heart condition, the condition that had brought him out to Africa in the first place. He couldn't breathe in the awful heat of that summer of 1902, the worst anyone could remember; he wandered from room to room at Groote Schuur, trying to catch his breath. He lay in the darkened drawing room and could not breathe. They took him down to his cottage by the sea, and put ice between the ceiling and the iron roof to cool it; all afternoon the punkahs spooned the air. Then, suddenly, he decided to go to England. April was there: April showers. A cold spring: it seemed that could heal him. So a cabin was fitted out for him aboard a P&O liner, with electric fans and refrigerating pipes and oxygen tanks.

He died on the day he was to sail. He was buried at that place on the Matopos, the place he had chosen himself; buried facing north.

"He wanted the heroes of the Matabele campaign to be buried there with him. I could be one, if I chose; only I think my name would not be found among the register of those who fought. I think my name does not appear at all in history: not in the books of the Uganda Railroad, not in the register of the Mount Nelson Hotel for 1893. I have never had the courage to look."

I could not understand this, though it sent a cold shudder between my shoulder blades. The Original Situation, he explained, could not be returned to; but it could be restored, as those events that the Otherhood brought about were one by one come upon in time, and then not brought about. And as the Original Situation was second by second restored, the whole of his adventure in the past was continually worn away into nonbeing, and a new future replaced his old past ahead of him.

"You must imagine how it has been for me," he said, his voice now a whisper from exertion and grief. "To everyone else it seemed only that time went on—history—the march of events. But to me it has been otherwise. It has been the reverse of the nightmare from which you wake in a sweat of relief to find that the awful disaster has not occurred, the fatal step was not taken: for I have seen the real world gradually replaced by this other, night-mare world, which everyone else assumes is real, until nothing in past or present is as I knew it to be; until I am like the servant in Job: *I only am escaped to tell thee.*"

March 8, 1984

I awoke again this morning from the dream of the forest in the sea: a dream without people or events in it, or anything whatever except the gigantic dendrites, vast masses of pale leaves, and the tideless waters, light and sunshot toward the surface, darkening to impenetrability down below. It seemed there were schools of fish, or flocks of birds, in the leaves, something that faintly disturbed them, now and then; otherwise, stillness.

No matter that orthogonal logic refutes it, I cannot help believing that my present succeeds in time the other presents and futures that have gone into making it. I believe that as I grow older I come to incorporate the experiences I have had as an older man in pasts (and futures) now obsolete: as though in absolute time I continually catch up with myself in the imaginary times that fluoresce from it, gathering dreamlike memories of the lives I have lived therein. Somewhere God (I have come to believe in God; there was simply no existing otherwise) is keeping these universes in a row, and sees to it that they happen in succession, the most recently generated one last—and so felt to be last, no matter where along it I stand.

I remember, being now well past the age that he was then, the Uganda Railroad, the Nanda arrows, all the death.

I remember the shabby library and the coal fire, the encyclopedia in another orthography; the servant at the double doors.

I think that in the end, should I live long enough, I shall remember nothing but the forest in the sea. That is the terminus: complete strangeness that is at the same time utterly changeless; what cannot be becoming all that has ever been.

I took him out myself, in the end, abandoning my commission to do so, for there was no way that he could have crossed the border by himself, without papers, a nonexistent man. And it was just at that moment, as we motored up through the Sudan past Wadi Halfa, that the Anglo-French expeditionary force took Port Said. The Suez incident, that last hopeless spasm of Empire, was taking its inevitable course. Inevitable: I have not used the word before.

When we reached the Canal, the Israelis had already occupied the east bank. The airport at Ismailia was a shambles, the greater part of the Egyptian air force shot up, planes scattered in twisted attitudes like dead birds after a storm. We could find no plane to take us. *He* had gone desperately broody, wide-eyed and speechless, useless for anything. I felt as though in a dream where one is somehow saddled with an idiot brother one had not had before.

And yet it was only the confusion and mess that made my task possible at all, I suppose. There were so many semiofficial and unofficial British scurrying or loafing around Port Said when we entered the city that our passage was unremarked. We went through the smoke and dust of that famously squalid port like two ghosts—two ghosts progressing through a ghost city at the retreating edge of a ghost of Empire. And the crunch of broken glass continually underfoot.

We went out on an old oiler attached to the retreating invasion fleet, which had been ordered home having accomplished nothing except, I suppose, the end of the British Empire in Africa. He stood on the oiler's boat deck and watched the city grow smaller and said nothing. But once he laughed, his dry, light laugh: it made me think of the noise that Homer says the dead make. I asked the reason.

"I was remembering the last time I went out of Africa," he said. "On a day much like this. Very much like this. This calm weather; this sea. Nothing else the same, though. Nothing else." He turned to me smiling, and toasted me with an imaginary glass. "The end of an era," he said.

March 10

My chronicle seems to be degenerating into a diary.

I note in the *Times* this morning the sale of the single known example of the 1856 magenta British Guiana, for a sum far smaller than was supposed to be its worth. Neither the names of the consortium that sold it nor the names of the buyers were made public. I see in my mind's eye a small, momentary fire.

I see now that there is no reason why this story should come last, no matter my feeling, no matter that in Africa he hoped it would. Indeed there is no reason why it should even fall last in this chronicling, nor why the world, the sad world in which it occurs, should be described as succeeding all others—it does not, any more than it precedes them. For the sake of a narrative only, perhaps; perhaps, like God, we cannot live without narrative.

I used to see him, infrequently, in the years after we both came back from Africa: he didn't die as quickly as we both supposed he would. He used to seek me out, in part to borrow a little money—he was living on the dole and on what he brought out of Africa, which was little enough. I stood him to tea now and then and listened to his stories. He'd appear at our appointed place in a napless British Warm, ill-fitting, as his eyeglasses and National Health false teeth were also. I imagine he was terribly lonely. I know he was.

I remember the last time we met, at a Lyons teashop near the Marble Arch. I'd left the Colonial Service, of course, under a cloud, and taken a position teaching at a crammer's in Holborn until something better came along (nothing ever did; I recently inherited the headmaster's chair at the same school; little has changed there over the decades but the general coloration of the students).

"This curious fancy haunts me," he said to me on that occasion. "I picture the Fellows, all seated around the great table in the executive committee's dining room; only it is rather like Miss Havisham's, you know, in Dickens: the roast beef has long since gone foul, and the silver tarnished, and the draperies rotten; and the Fellows dead in their chairs, or mad, dust on their evening clothes, the port dried up in their glasses. Huntington. Davenant. The President *pro tem.*"

He stirred sugar in his tea (he liked it horribly sweet; so, of course, do I). "It's not true, you know, that the club stood somehow at a nexus of possibilities, amid multiplying realities. If that were so, then what the Fellows did would be trivial or monstrous or both: generating endless new universes just to see if they could get one to their liking. No: it is we, out here, who live in but one of innumerable possible worlds. In there, they were like a man standing at the north pole, whose only view, wherever he looks, is south: they looked out upon a single encompassing reality, which it was their opportunity—no, their duty, as they saw it—to make as happy as possible, as free from the calamities they knew of as they could make it.

"Well, they were limited people, more limited than their means to work good or evil. That which they did they should not have done. And yet what they hoped for us was not despicable. The calamities they saw were real. Anyone who could would try to save us from them: as a mother would pull her child, her foolish child, from the fire. They ought to be forgiven; they ought."

I walked with him up toward Hyde Park Corner. He walked now with agonizing slowness, as I will, too, one day; it was a rainy autumn Sunday, and his pains were severe. At Hyde Park Corner he stopped entirely, and I thought perhaps he could go no farther: but then I saw that he was studying the monument that stands there. He went closer to it, to read what was written on it.

I have myself more than once stopped before this neglected monument. It is a statue of the boy David, a memorial to the Machine Gun Corps, and was put up after the First World War. Some little thought must have gone into deciding how to memorialize that arm which had changed war forever; it seemed to require a religious sentiment, a quote from the Bible, and one was found. Beneath the naked boy are written words from Kings:

Saul has slain his thousands
But David his tens of thousands.

He stood in the rain, in his vast coat, looking down at these words, as though reading them over and over; and the faint rain that clung to his cheeks mingled with his tears:

Saul has slain his thousands
But David his tens of thousands.

I never saw him again after that day, and I did not seek for him: I think it unlikely he could have been found.

In Blue

▣ ▣ ▣

THE ROUTE THEY TOOK EVERY MORNING from their dormitory to the project's buildings took them through very old parts of the city. They crossed a square where weeds grew up between enormous paving stones, a square so vast it could diminish even the long, square-columned, monolithic buildings that bordered it. The square was usually deserted and silent; not even the indigenous population of the city, descendants of those who had built this square or at least of men and women who had inhabited it when it was still a living place, ever came here much. It was too open, too lifeless: or rather it had a life too large, too intimidating; nothing could be done with it. The new populations of the city, the squatters and refugees, also rarely came here; probably most of them weren't even aware of its existence.

Hare's group passed out of the square beneath an arch the height of ten men and as thick as a room. Looking up as they passed under it, Hare could see that the honeycomb pattern of its vaulting was distorted deliberately to make the arch seem even higher, even more intimidating than it was. The hexagons high up, in the center of the arch, were actually smaller than the ones on the sides, lower down; the circles inscribed inside the hexagons were really ovals, making the center of the curve of the arch seem to retreat into a space within itself, a space that could not exist, a space into which Hare's heart seemed to be drawn.

Then he had passed under the arch and moved on with the others.

Why had they done it that way? Every morning he wondered. Why had it occurred to anyone to expend so much ingenuity on a trick like that, who had then been willing to take the trouble to execute it? Slaves. But they must have been skilled nonetheless, and proud of their skills. The effort of it, the enterprise of it, at once oppressed and lightened him, drawing his mind apart.

He looked back, as he always did, to see the whole of it, and to study the band of letters that ran across the top. Each letter must have been a meter long; between the words there were diamond-shaped stops as large as a hand. But what were the words? What was the language? He tried to memorize the first few letters, as he always did, but as always by the time he reached work he would forget their exact shapes.

He turned away. One or two of the others had also glanced back, to see what it was that Hare looked at, but they couldn't see it, and looked curiously at Hare; the woman who worked beside him at the project smiled at him, enjoying his oddness. Hare returned the smile and looked ahead.

Farther on were narrow streets, and these, too, contained fragments of the ancient city, not ruins so much as antiquities in the process of being packed up in new construction. That the old cornerstones and bits of columned fronts were being preserved in this way was an illusion; the incremental plan for new housing, for

places to put the thousands who were coming in from the coun-
tryside, made it necessary to squeeze modular units wherever
Applications determined they could go, leaving the old disorder to
be carted away later. Hare supposed it wouldn't be long before the
gray boxes, which stacked to any height, which could be piled up
anyhow wherever there was room, would spill out into the square,
growing with the shy persistence of ivy, higgledy-piggledy, full of
children, strung with lines of laundry and hung with gaudy hec-
toring posters in country dialects. In these streets the uniform units
had already climbed above all but the tallest of the older buildings,
their zigzag stairways like ivy's clutching roots.

Through the open doors of some units, Hare's group passing
by could glimpse women at stoves, or nursing children; more
often, though, doors and shutters would be quietly closed as the
group passed, the faces that looked out suddenly occluded by a
door. These country people were shy; if they found themselves
observed, they would turn away, or even cover their faces with
their hands. Had they used to do so in their old home places?
Where Hare had grown up, people had been friendly and talkative.
He thought it must be the city, the sight of strangers, cadre in Blue
who had an uncertain but real control over their lives. When
Hare's group came upon children playing in the labyrinthine
streets, they would stop playing and withdraw into doorways or
behind pillars, silent, their dark eyes large; they wouldn't come out
though Hare's group waved and called to them.

It was a problem in figure-ground mechanics, Hare thought:
that the cadre in Blue knew themselves to be the servants of masters, the people; but the people thought that the servants were
their masters—and of course there were instances when the servants did seem to be directing the lives of their masters. It must be

hard for them, Hare thought: the uniforms of Blue meant survival, food, shelter, help, and before them even the grown-ups were as shy as children offered sweets or kindnesses by great strangers.

But most of Hare's group had, like Hare, also come here from the country or from small towns, and also felt themselves to be displaced—perhaps that's why they smiled and waved at the elusive children of the altered streets, and why they talked little or in low voices as they walked through this many-layered necropolis where the living trod on the dead, who when they had lived had trod on other dead. Hare, in the city, felt for the first time sharply how many more dead there are than living.

The dead had carved in stone; the living wrote on paper. The long, bannerlike posters were everywhere, explaining, exhorting, encouraging: not only explaining how not to waste water, but why it was important that water not be wasted. Some were torn off in midsentence, by hands or wind; kindly teachers whose mouths were suddenly stopped.

"Look," Hare said to the woman who walked next to him. He read from a poster. " 'If you don't know how to read, begin learning now.' "

"Yes," the woman said. "There's a lot of illiteracy still."

She took the hand of the woman next to her, who smiled without looking at her. Hare said nothing.

Hare's work at the project was the preparation of training manuals, introductory lessons in act-field theory and social calculus. Presently he was working on an introduction to coincidence magnitude calculations.

It was not difficult work; it was far less demanding than the work for which Hare had been trained, and for which he had shown such early promise in school, when it was thought that he might be one of those few who could alter the calculus that altered the lives of men and women. When he walked the long halls of the project building, he passed the open doors of rooms where men and women sat together, without tools beyond a terminal or a pad or without even those, men and women at work on that calculus; Hare, as he passed their doors, hearing their low voices or their laughter, could almost see the networks of their thought growing. If they caught sight of Hare, they might wave, for he had worked with some of them in these rooms and in rooms like these in other places. Then he passed on, through other rooms, meeting rooms and commissariats and the communications annex, to the cubicles where work like his was done. Beyond these cubicles lay the maintenance sheds, the shops and warehouses. Then that was the end. Hare, sitting down at his work station and turning on the dim light above it, wondered how long it would be before he was shifted that one last degree.

Not long, he thought. He wasn't sure he could even complete the manual he was working on in any form that could be submitted. And beyond the maintenance sheds, the shops and warehouses? Only the world that Hare's manuals taught about: life: the whole act-field. He would most likely go on moving, as he had moved, by degrees down from the highest realm of thought about it, to a mere place in it: or no place.

He opened the composer on his desk and retrieved the notes he had made the day before.

"Introduction. Definitions. Description of contents. Figure-ground mechanics a necessity for coincidence magnitude calculation. Probabilities and how they differ from coincidence magnitudes: example. Problems and strategies: synchronicity, self-reference paradoxes, etc. Conclude introduction: importance of coincidence magnitude calculation to the social calculus, importance of the calculus to act-field theory, importance of act-field theory to the Revolution."

He considered these notes for a long time. Then, keyed to the line about the difference between probabilities and coincidence magnitude, he wrote this:

"Example:

"It was once believed that no two snowflakes are exactly alike. More properly we can say that the probability of any two snowflakes' being exactly alike is very low. The fall, at the same moment, of two snowflakes that are exactly alike, and the fall of those two snowflakes on this word 'snowflake' that you are now reading, would be a coincidence of a probability so low as to be virtually incalculable.

"But the *magnitude* of the coincidence, if it were to be calculated by the methods you will learn here, would not be high.

"This is because coincidence magnitude is a function of *meaningfulness* as well as of probability. We know that only acts (as defined by the special and general act theories) can have meaningfulness; an act's meaningfulness is a function of its definition as an act, a definition made possible by the infinitesimal social calculus. An act bearing high meaningfulness and low probability generates a high coincidence magnitude. To calculate meaningfulness against probability, and thereby arrive at the magnitude of the coincidence, requires that coincidence magnitude calculation be operable within act-field theory as a *differential* social calculus.

"Act-field theory predicts the occurrence, within any given parameters of the field, of coincidences of a certain magnitude. It is said to *account for* these. The appearance within those parameters of coincidences greater in magnitude than the theory accounts for is a coincidence of implicitly high magnitude, generating its own parameters in another dimension, parameters calculable within the theory, which then *accounts for* the higher level of coincidence. The generation of such new parameters is called an *implicit spike*, and the process is itself *accounted for.*"

Here Hare's thought branched.

"Implicit spikes," he wrote, and then erased it.

"Act-field theory, then," he wrote, and erased that.

Whichever way his thought branched it seemed likely to take him to the tolstoy edge.

Once (Hare had no conception of how long ago, but long ago) they had thought that if the position and velocity and mass of every atom in the universe could be known, at some given moment, then the next moment and thus each succeeding moment could be predicted with certainty. Of course such complete knowledge could not be assembled, no computer could be built large enough to contain all the facts, or to calculate with them; but if they could be. And then they learned that the universe was not made like that at all, that only probabilities of states and events could ever be known with certainty, and that the very act of measuring and perceiving those probabilities entailed altering them. Some people (Hare had heard) had gone mad when this was proven, out of the awful loss of certainty, the loss even of the possibility of certainty. Others rejoiced: the loss of false certainty made real knowledge possible. The calculations began again, and were fruitful. The universe of events danced inexhaustibly, and the mind could dance with it, if it would.

And there had also been a time (the same time, perhaps, the same olden days) when people had thought that history might also be calculated: that if the weather and the size of harvests and the productivity of factories and the rate of invention and every other possible variable could be known, though it could not be, and every hurt every person had suffered, every belief or thought each one had—every man's position and mass and velocity—then it could be known with certainty why every event that happened had happened, and what would happen next.

But the human universe was no more like that than the universe of stars and stones. Such calculations would fail not because they were impossibly difficult but because no such certainties as were aimed at could possibly exist. It could not even be determined what units were to be measured—human acts—and where one stopped and another began. All conceivable plans for making the measurements met a mirror paradox, a self-reference, an infinite regression: the tolstoy edge.

But only give in to that; only rejoice in it; only be not surprised to find that the points plotted on your graphs make a figure like your own face, and the calculations begin again. And are fruitful: the special theory of acts, empty now of any concrete content, defines an act, the definition including the meaningful activity of looking for such a definition; the general theory defines their entrainments, heterarchies, and transformations. Act-field theory creates a virtual infinitely-dimensional simplex for operating in, and the infinitesimal social calculus separates the inseparable, one act from another, dissolving in its simplicity the self-reference paradox as completely as the infinitesimal calculus in mathematics had dissolved the paradoxes of division that had plagued it for so long. And the social calculus makes possible the Revolution: once frozen before the infinite divisions of distance to be crossed before the target is reached, the Revolution now is loosed by the archer's fingers and leaps the distance into the unfigurable, ultimately unknowable heart of man.

And how could he, Hare, sitting here now, know all that, know it so well that when he was a boy he had in one tiny way added to it (some refinements of figure-ground mechanics for which he had won a prize in school), how could he sit here now before it and be unable to describe it? How could it ever make him afraid?

And yet he could not bring himself to continue.

He leaned back in his chair, which groaned beneath his weight. He pressed a key on the composer and held it down, and letter by letter his story about the snowflakes was removed from the screen.

Hare sat at lunch with Dev, a woman of about his age. He didn't know her well, but she for some reason chose him to talk to. She ate little, and seemed to be full of a story she both wanted to tell and didn't want to tell, about a young friend of hers, and their friends, whom Hare didn't know. Hare listened, nodding, sympathetic, for the woman felt some grief, a grief that the story she told should have revealed; but the way she told it made it impossible to understand. She said "you know" several times, and "all that kind of thing," and waved her hand and shook her head as at a cloud of gnatlike complications that she could see in her story but couldn't or wouldn't describe. Hare lost the thread; there were too many "she's" in the story for him to remember which was which.

"So we all *did* go swimming," the woman said. "That night, by the bridge where there's the embankment. Well, I said I'd go. And then she said she and her new friend, the other one from the one she came with, the one she'd just met, didn't want to—but they said, Oh, come on, everybody needs to cool off. You know."

Hare was listening carefully now.

"So they all took their clothes off. And they're really very young." She laughed. "And, well. With *her* it never bothered me, but you know they can be so unkind, or no, not that, I just couldn't. I mean I'm too old really for those games they play, you know? Girls together, like in school. You get beyond that kind of thing. I laughed about it, you kids go ahead, I just like to watch, I'm an old grandma. And they just let me sit."

Hare put down his bowl. He was smiling, too, and nodding, as though sharing with the woman this amusing part of the story, where she'd tried to act her age with offhand grace; and trying to feel the other feeling that the woman felt: exclusion from happy comradeship, and jealousy; and trying also to transmute his own sudden strong feelings, by careful attention to her, into sympathy. He shook his head, smiling at how life sometimes goes on.

"Kids," she said. "At that age you just don't care."

Hare wanted to ask: What did they do together in the water? But he could not have asked this and maintained his air of casual interest; and he thought that if she told him he would not understand her answer rightly anyway, because what the young women did together in the water would be three times masked from him: by their own young feelings, by the feelings of the woman who watched them from the bank, and worst of all, by the obstruction of his own feelings, so irrelevant to the young women in the water and what they did together, and yet so fierce.

"I know what you mean," he said, remembering a day in spring years ago, when he was at school.

The school Hare had gone to as a boy was built in the shape of a T. In one branch of the T the girls were taught by female teachers; in the other branch the boys were taught by men. Where the branches met, the corridor of Hare's part ended, crossed by the corridor of the girls' part running at right angles. Going from class to class, coming near this juncture, boys could watch the girls walking in their part: books under their arms, or held up before them, embraced in that way that girls so often held their books but boys for some reason never did; talking together in groups or walking singly. Glances and waves could be passed from one part to the other, and brief conversations held there. There was a gymnasium in the school—Hare could not remember now just how it attached to the body of the school building—where alternately through the day boys' and girls' exercise classes met; it could also be filled with folding chairs when visiting cadre came to lecture. For these events the boys used one half of the floor, and the girls the other, separated by a wide aisle.

On fine days, after they had had their lunch, older students who had permission from their teachers were allowed to walk outside for a while on a strip of pavement that ran before the wide back doors of this gymnasium, to talk and smoke cigarettes. There was a proctor to watch them, but he usually absented himself. These were good students; they were being given a taste of the sort of privileges cadre had, and that they themselves might someday have. The boys understood that, and talk was usually serious. On a burning spring day, a first summer afternoon, Hare was walking with three or four other boys, smoking and talking. They were all laughing too loud, because of the day, and the sun, and summer coming. Then—either blown open by a gust of wind because they hadn't been properly closed, or opened from within by someone on purpose to bring cool air into the hot gymnasium—the double doors of the gymnasium opened.

There was a girls' class in progress. A girl Hare knew slightly, a cheerful laughing girl, stood framed in the doorway, legs wide apart, hair lifted by the sudden inrush of air. She wore only a band across her breasts and a sort of strap around her waist and between her legs. She waved to Hare, surprised but unashamed. Beyond her, in the comparative darkness of the gymnasium, were the others in the class. There were mats laid out on the floor. Two girls on each mat were wrestling; some wore the same breast band that the girl standing in the doorway wore, some who didn't need them yet didn't. Those not wrestling stood to watch the others. Hare saw all this in a moment. The girls within shouted and laughed, the wrestlers stopped and looked, some of the girls ran to hide. Around Hare the boys were laughing. Hare only stood staring, having become eyes, his heart become eyes, his hands and mouth become eyes. Then the girl pulled the doors shut with a boom.

The boys around Hare laughed together, pummeling each other and shouting in an access of energy, until the proctor came smiling to see what was up, what the joke was. Hare turned away from the closed doors, feeling an almost unbearable sense of loss and exclusion; feeling withered and desiccated within, made old, by loss.

Hare wanted to ask the woman Dev if that was what she had felt by the river, watching her friend and the other young women: that sense of loss and exclusion.

But it couldn't be. Because she had, once, herself been one of those girls on the mats, among others. She had always been in the other part. The young woman swimming with the others was her friend; they were all her friends. Hare couldn't imagine then what she felt, whether her feelings were of the same kind as his, or a different kind altogether, and whether it hurt as much, or more, or less: her loss of what he had never had.

"I know what you mean," he said again.

◨

Willy said to him: "You look tired. You always look tired now. You look as though someone knew something terrible about you, and you were afraid he was going to tell all your friends, and you can't stop worrying about it. But I know everything about you, and there isn't anything terrible at all."

Willy shared Hare's room in the dormitory building where the project staff were housed. Willy wasn't exactly cadre, he hadn't much education, he was good with his hands and worked in the project maintenance shops. But Hare, when he saw that he wouldn't be able to have a room of his own because the project staff had grown too large, had got Willy into his room. Willy didn't mind living with project cadre, he had no sense of inferiority, and everybody liked Willy, his goodness, his jokes, his sympathy with everyone. Willy got along.

Though they had often lost touch in the intervening years, Hare had known Willy since school. Willy was four years younger than he, and at summer work camp when Hare was proctor, Willy, alone and unhappy at his first camp, had adopted Hare to be his friend and protector. He'd sneak out of his own bunk with the young children and make his way to Hare's bed, shyly but insistently climbing in with him. Hare, half asleep, didn't resist the boy's affection; he was embarrassed to find him there in the morning, as immovable as a log in his deep childish sleep, and the other proctors made fun of him, but they were jealous, too, that Hare had someone so devoted, to run errands for him; once there had been a fight with another proctor over Willy. Willy understood—he always understood the context, the human net of desires and fears, the act-field, in a concrete way that Hare never would—and after that when he crept into bed in Hare's cubicle, he would be silent; would lie with Hare almost not moving, and with his face pressed into the hollow of Hare's shoulder would masturbate him with small motions, sometimes seeming to fall asleep amid it. When Hare made noises, Willy would whisper *shhh* in his ear, and giggle.

Willy called it playing. He always did. It was more intense pleasure than eating, without that daily compulsion but no less automatic; as refreshing as football or hard calisthenics, but imbued with affection and intimacy. The continuum in Willy from simple affection and shared good times to those cryings-out, those spasms, was unbroken; it had no parts; it was the social calculus in reality, and Hare loved it in Willy and envied him for it.

Because for all he, Hare, knew the integral social calculus, in him there was such a division. There was a breaking into parts, as in the oldest and wrongest paradoxes; an infinite number of discrete distances to cross between himself and what he desired.

"It's because I want the other," he told Willy when long ago he'd tried to say it in words. "You want the same. So it wouldn't occur to you."

"That's not it," Willy said, laughing. "Because I've been with women, too. I bet more than you have. I like people, that's the difference. You have to like people. If you like people, they'll like you back. Men or women. If you're interested in them, they like you for it. It's simple."

Hare had laughed, too, shamefaced, uneasy with the humility he had to learn in order to take advice from the boy whom he'd protected and taught. Pride: it was a fault cadre were liable to, he knew, a fault that must be erased. Why shouldn't he take advice from Willy? While Hare had grown up in the thin atmosphere of schools, study camps, and project dormitories, Willy had been moving in the sea of the people, the endless flux of the Revolution, with all its accidents and coincidences. Never cease learning from the people: that was a maxim of the Revolution grown old and unfeelable for Hare.

But he had tried to learn. He had tried to meld himself with the common play of desire and pleasure, hope and disappointment, pleasure and work. He became, or seemed to become, wise; became someone to whom others told stories, because of his calm, sensible sympathies. The endless voices: Hare heard stories everywhere, people told him of their plans and desires, Hare nodded and said *I know what you mean.*

But he had no stories himself that he could tell.

The dormitories where the cadre that worked in Hare's project lived were modular, like the people's housing, though the units were smaller. Above the communal facilities, the refectories and common rooms and workstations, the units were bolted on seemingly at random; but in fact Applications worked and reworked the building's program to assure that every unit got as much sun and air, as many windows, as short a walk to toilets, as possible; and so optimized along many dimensions it accreted as complexly and organically as a coral reef, and with the same stochastic logic.

Toward the summer's end the man who had lived alone in the unit next to Hare and Willy was shifted to another project. The people associated with his part in the project gave him a farewell party in one of the common rooms. They gave him a few small gifts, mostly jokes relating to work, and they ate cakes and drank tea spiked with some alcohol someone had got from the dispensary. Willy, to whom things like this were important, who remembered the birthdays of many people, had spent some time decorating the corner of the room where they sat, and he gave the departing man a real gift, an antiquity he'd found somewhere in the city and made a box for in the shop. The antiquity, a small white-enameled cube of thin metal, had a little door in the front that opened to show an interior space, and four red spirals symmetrically painted on its top, and representations of dials or knobs here and there. It was passed from hand to hand, everyone marveling at how old it must be and wondering what it might have been for. Willy was pleased with the effect. The man who was leaving was very touched, even surprised, Hare thought, and embraced Willy; and then, somewhat clumsily, all the others. Then the party was over.

The next week two young women came to live together in the empty room.

They were young, in training in the project, and inseparable; shy amid new people, but making their way together. Hare talked with them now and then when he found himself opposite them at dinner. They weren't sisters, though they looked enough alike to be sisters: both dark, with luminous eyes and full, childlike yet maturely sensual faces. Their light clothes of Blue (they had come up from a project in the south) revealed them as though without their knowledge or consent. They had a funny way of finishing each other's sentences. When Hare came upon one of them alone and began a conversation with her, she talked of little but her friend, her opinions and feelings, and kept looking around to see if she had come. When at last her friend appeared, a calm joy transformed her face. Hare watched her, his polite smile stuck on his face: watched love come and settle on her features and in the repose of her body.

Because they lived next to him, because he could hear through the thin wall the indistinct murmur of their voices and the sounds of their movements, Hare thought often about the two of them. The time he spent alone in his room was punctuated by the small sounds they made: a laugh over some joke Hare couldn't hear; obscure sounds of things moved or handled. Without willing it, he found himself growing alert to these sounds, his attention pricking up at them like a dog's ears. When Willy was also in the room, Hare paid no attention to the next room; his and Willy's noises drowned them out. But alone he listened; even held still to listen, found himself making the silent movements of a spy with his glass or his book, so as not to miss—What? he asked himself; and went on listening.

There was a night when loud scrapings, sounds of effort, laughter, business, went on some time next door; something bumped against Hare's wall. He could make nothing of all this until, after general lights-out, he climbed into bed and heard, close by him and more distinctly than before, the sound of their voices, the jounce and squeak of their bed.

They had shifted the few furnishings of their room, and moved the bed they shared from the far side of the room up against the wall that divided their room from Hare's, the same wall against which his own bed was placed. It was as though the three of them were now in the same bed, with the thin wall between them dividing it in two.

Hare lay still. There were long silences; a word from one of the two of them, a brief answer; the noise of the bed when one of them moved. He heard one of them get up, the pat of her naked feet on the floor; she returned, the bed spoke. With slow care he rolled over in his bed so that he lay next to the wall. Still he could hear no intelligible voices, only the sounds of their speech. But now, with the lights out, alone next to them close enough to touch them but for the wall, he knew he must hear, hear it all.

His mouth was dry, and there was a kind of intense constriction in him. Where had he once heard that you could eavesdrop on an adjoining room by putting a glass against the wall, and listening as though to a megaphone? He only thought about this for a time, lying still; then he slid from the bed, lit his night-light, and took his glass from the sink. His knees were watery-weak. The feelings he felt didn't seem to him to be sexual, weren't like the feelings caused by sexual fantasies, they were more dangerous somehow than that; and yet he knew now what he wanted to hear. He got silently back into bed; he placed the glass against the wall, and his ear against the glass, his heart beating slow and hard.

There was a sort of roar, like the sound of the sea in a shell, the sound of his own blood rushing; then one of the two women spoke. She said: "When the first boy has passed the last marker."

"All right," said the other. "I don't know."

Silence.

What were they talking about? They were together, in bed. Lights were out. They might still have a night-light on: that he couldn't tell. He waited.

"Last boy passes the first marker . . . ," said the second who spoke.

"No," said the first, laughing. "*First* boy passes the *last* marker. You got the last boy."

More silence. Their voices were distinct, and not far away, but still remote, as though they spoke from the bottom of a clear pool. Hare knew he could listen all night long, but at the same time he grew horribly impatient. He wanted a sign.

"I don't like that one. Let's do another."

"You're just lazy. Listen again."

"Oh, let's stop."

Hare understood then. They were solving a puzzle, the kind printed in the back pages of mathematical journals. Aimlessly, without paying it much attention, they were working out a relay-race problem. Hare did them himself sometimes, when he had nothing better to do.

How could that be? They had one another, they were alone in a room, in a bed, they loved each other, they were free, free together in circumstances so enviable that desire only to be a witness of it, only to know a little of it, had driven Hare to this shameful contrivance, the glass against the wall, the wanting ear against the glass: and they were working out—or not even really bothering to work out—a puzzle in a magazine. But why would they? How could they?

He lowered the glass from the wall. Desire must not be what he thought it was: if its satisfaction was always present, it must grow blunted, it must not even be often thought of. That must be so. If you lived with the one you loved you did puzzles, had arguments, sometimes made love, slept. Couldn't he have supposed that to be so? It was obvious. Desire was a wholer, though not a larger, thing than the thing that was within himself. Of course it must be: and that cut him more deeply than anything he had expected to overhear.

There was further talk from the next room. He picked up the glass and listened again, willing them to show each other love, for his sake. But the talk was unintelligible to him now, private, or perhaps directed at something visible to them alone: anyway, meaningless. Then speech grew infrequent. Still he listened. Then, when silence had gone on so long that it might as well have been an empty room he listened to, he gave up, exhausted by the effort of attention; no doubt they slept.

Hare didn't sleep. He lay awake, feeling irremediably cheated, cheated of their desire. He wouldn't have minded the hurt he would have suffered that their desire faced away from him, so long as he could have witnessed it; yet even that they had withheld from him—not even on purpose, not conscious of him at all, having no intention toward him whatever.

On other nights he listened again. He sometimes heard things he could interpret as lovemaking if he chose to, but nothing clear enough to gain him what he wanted—entrance, commonality, whatever it was. When he slept with Willy, he made a joke of it, telling Willy in a whisper that the two could be heard; Willy smiled, intrigued for a minute, then bored when nothing immediately amusing could be heard; then he slept. Desire kept Hare awake beside him. Desire lay heavily in him: his own, the two women's desire that faced away from him. Desire seemed lodged hard in his throat and gut, distorting his nature and his natural goodness, something foreign, not a part of him, which yet cut every part of him, like a knife he had swallowed.

That month when Willy was moved to the night shift and Hare saw him only at dinner and for a few moments when Hare was preparing to leave for the project and Willy had just returned, Hare felt a certain relief. He couldn't have stopped, now, listening to the undersea sounds that came through his drinking glass, and of course he couldn't do it when Willy was present—but it was more than that. He couldn't have put Willy out of his room, that would have been like cutting a lifeline, but he couldn't now have him nearby either. His presence was like a reproach, a sign that what had become of Hare need not have happened.

◙

History no longer existed. Hare had had to reinvent it.

On his free days he would find excuses to avoid the communal activities of the dormitory, the classes and criticism sessions and open committee meetings, and with a tablet and pencil he would wander in old parts of the city, working and dreaming—working by dreaming—over this invention of his, history.

On a bench in a crowded park he sat opposite a great and now unused building, fronted with fluted pillars and crowned in the middle of its roofline with complex statuary, a group of men and women victorious or defeated, winged infants, and horses, which seemed to be bursting out of the unknowable old interior into the air of the present.

The building was a favorite of his, partly because it was still whole, partly because the present had not been able to think of a use for it, but mostly because as he sat before it—closing one eye, then the other, measuring with his thumb and with lengths of the pencil held up before him—he saw most clearly the one sure fact he had learned about the past. The past thought in geometry: in circles, sections of circles, right triangles, squares, sections of squares. The building before him was nothing but an agglomerate of regular geometrical figures, cut in stone and overlaid with these striving figures continually trying, but never succeeding, in bursting them apart. He imagined that the whole structure—even the fluting of the pillars, the relation of different bits of molding to one another—could be expressed in a few angles, in small whole numbers and regular fractions. Even the statues, with their wild gestures and swirling draperies, were arranged in a simple rhythm, a graspable hierarchy.

He thought it was odd that it should be so; and he thought it was odd that he should derive so much pleasure from it.

Why had the past thought that the world, life, should be pressed into the most abstract and unliving of shapes—the regular geometrical solids that were foreign to all human experience? Except for a few crystals, Hare thought there were no such things in the world. The mind contained no such shapes; the shapes the mind contained, if they were to be projected into the world, would look like—they *did* look like—the clusters of people's housing that crept up to the edges of this park. They would look like the stacked, irregular dormitories Hare had lived in for years, restless accumulations always seeking optima, the result of a constant search amid shifting variables. Those were the mind's shapes, because the computers that designed the dormitories and the people's housing contained and used the logic of the mind: contained it so completely that the shapes that lay within the human mind, truly there in the resulting structures, were no more immediately apparent there than the shapes of the mind are in a casual conversation, with all its strategies, accommodations, distributions, and feedback loops.

But this building was part of the past. The past wasn't like the present. The past hadn't understood the shapes the mind naturally contained, it had no way of ascertaining them—no mirror as the present had in its big, linked computers; the past had longed for absolutes, for regularities foreign to the mind's nature, and (if the stories Hare had heard were true) had enforced them brutally on a heterarchical world. What peace, then, when all those hierarchies, when the very striving for hierarchy itself, had been dissolved in the Revolution! Peace; Perpetual Peace. The false and hurtful geometries had bent and melted and yielded to the unpredictable, immense stochastic flow of the act-field, leaving only a few memorials like this building, obdurate things caught in the throat of time.

Afternoon sunlight fell slantwise across the broad face, coloring its gray stone pink. There was a band of tall letters, Hare saw, running across the whole length of it, obscured by dirt: the light had cleansed them for a moment, and Hare, with many glances from his tablet to the building, copied them:

★ I AM ★ REDIT ★ ET ★ VIRGO ★ REDEUNT ★ SATURNIA ★ REGNA ★

He closed his tablet, and rose.

In the broad avenue that led away from the park and the building, people went by, an endless stream of them, bicycles and trucks, cadre in Blue, children and workers and country people. Two young women, one in shorts pedaling a bicycle, the other half-running beside her, holding with one hand the teetering bicycle that tried to match her slower pace. Both young, and smiling; they smiled at Hare when they saw that he watched them—happy, it seemed to him, and proud of their young health and beauty on a summer day. He smiled for them, paying them the compliment of being proud of it, too.

The people were a corrosive against all hierarchies.

Still smiling, Hare followed the avenue to where the cathedral stood on a square of its own. Its high doors stood open on this day; in winter they were closed, and only a small wicket let people in and out. And for whom had these immense doors been built, then, what beings needed such a space to go in and out by? As he passed through, he looked up at the ranked carvings of figures, human but attenuated and massed like a flight of birds, that swooped up the sides of the archway, ascending toward those seated at the top like a committee. Who were they all? The dead, he thought.

The interior of the church had been cleared of its benches. The great floor was being used (though vast spaces rose unused and useless overhead) as a clearinghouse for newcomers to the city. Groups of people stood before long tables waiting for housing and ration allocations. The sound of their footsteps, of the answers they gave to questions asked of them, even the taps of a pencil or the click of a terminal, rose into the upper volume of air and came to Hare's ears magnified and dislocated from their sources. Behind the tables low walls of board had been set up all along the stone walls of the church, whether to protect the walls, the windows, and the statuary, or simply for a place to pin up directions and information, Hare didn't know. He walked, head bent back, trying to follow the lines of the arches into the upper dimness. This, he thought, more than the other building across the park, mirrored the mind: the continual exfoliation of faces, birds, flowers, vines; the intersecting curves of vaulting, like the multiplane ellipsoids of a whole-program simplex; the virtually infinite reaching-away of it all into unseeable darkness. The colored, pictured glass, like the bright but immaterial reflections of the world in the thinking brain.

It wasn't so, though, really. His eyes, growing accustomed to the dimness, began to follow the lines of arches into the circles out of which they had been taken. He measured the regular spaces between pillars, and counted the repeated occurrences of squares, rectangles, triangulations, symmetries.

It was breathtaking how they had bent and tortured those simple ratios and figures into something that could approximate the mind. He felt a fierce joy in the attempt they had made, without understanding why they had made it. He thought this church must have been built later than the less complex but also somehow more joyful building beyond the park. He wondered if there was a way of finding out.

The low wall of flimsy board closed off some deep recesses even more full of figuration and glittering metalwork than the body of the church: like hollows of memory, if this were a mind, memory at once bright and dark. Peering into one such recess, Hare could see the statue of a woman atop a sort of table heaped up with what looked like gilt bushes. She wore robes of blue and a crown, a crown circled with pearls; some of the pearls had come out, leaving dark holes like caries. She stood beneath a little vaulted dome; a band of mosaic around the dome made letters, letters like those across the top of the arch he passed under every day, or the facade of the building down the avenue. He opened his tablet to a clean page and carefully copied the letters:

$$\star \star A \star V \star E \star E \star V \star A \star \star$$

Ave Eva. "Ave Eva," he said aloud.

The woman's face—modest, with lowered eyes, despite her crown—did not look to Hare like the Eva he knew, his Eva. And yet he thought she did look, in her self-contained remoteness, a little like the Eva he sometimes dreamed of: dreams from which he would awake in a sweat of loneliness and cold loss.

He went out of the church.

No: now the building down the avenue, washed in sun, looked far the younger of the two, cheerful and new. Older or younger? He thought about it, blinking in the sunlight.

It seemed there ought to be enough of the past to make an act-field in itself; it rose vastly enough in Hare's mind, teasing him with limitless complexity. But it wasn't so. Even if everything that could be known about the past were known, it would still be far too thin to make an act-field. Even now, in order to construct a human act-field, the Revolution's computers ingested so much random matter that it was hard to find room in them for ordinary computations, food production, housing allocation: and even so, what the computers possessed was only a virtuality—a range of acts that was virtually but not truly infinite; enough for the Revolution's work, but still only a shadow cast by the immensity of the real act-field in which the people lived.

And history—out of which all old theories about society had been made—was a shadow of a shadow, so thin as to be for the program's purposes nonexistent. The whole of the past was less nutritious to the browsing search programs than the most meager meal of daily motions, truck accidents, school schedules, dew point, paper consumption, hospital discharges, decibel levels. The kinds of postulates that could be derived from history would not be recognized within act-field theory as postulates; out of the paucity of history, closed systems only could be constructed, those hurtful tautologies that ended in *ism,* once thrust onto the world like bars—systems less interesting than common arithmetic.

Hare knew all that. It didn't matter that the past was made of stone, and the present of thin walls of board bolted and stapled over it: history was a dream. History was Hare's dream. He didn't expect to learn from it; he knew better than that; he meant only to escape to it for a while.

Amid the crowds of the people; mounting up old stone steps, cut beside narrow cobbled streets; moving with the traffic along the broad avenues bordered with shuttered buildings; in the center of the great square, measuring its size by the diminution of a lone bicycle progressing toward the mouth of a far arch, Hare was in history, and his heart was calm for a while.

Hare wondered if the magnitude of the coincidence that had brought him together with Eva could be calculated, and if it were, what the magnitude would be. To daydream in that way meant to suspend his own knowledge of how such calculations worked— they could never work backward, they were abstracting and predictive; they could never calculate the magnitude of coincidences that had actually occurred. And Eva herself would have hated it that he should try to calculate her, predict her, account for her in any way.

Outlaw in a world without law, how had she come to be the way she was? Remembering the distances within her eyes, or waking from a dream of her regard turning away from him, he would think: she was trying to go far off. Loving Hare had not been a stopping or a staying but had been part of that going; and when he had explained to her that no, she couldn't go far off, didn't need to, and couldn't really even if she wanted to, then she went farther off by not loving him any longer—walking away, wearing her pregnancy like defiance, not hearing him call to her.

Hare sat at his desk at the project, looking at the notes for his manual on coincidence magnitude calculation, but thinking of Eva and the years since, years in which an automatic grasp he had once had of the Revolution's principles had weakened, a gap had opened between himself and his work, and the project that had been so eager to get him had begun to have difficulty finding something he could do. Eva had thought she could walk away from the world; Hare, standing still, had felt the world move away from him, grow less distinct, smaller.

No, that wasn't possible either. And any work he could do had its real importance to the Revolution, the same real importance as any other work; work for the Revolution had all the same formal properties and was all included; what it consisted of hour to hour didn't matter, it was all accounted for.

*Importance of coincidence magnitude calculation to the social calcu-
lus. Importance of the calculus to act-field theory. Importance of act-field
theory to the Revolution.*

When Hare had been in school, that had been part of every lecture, on no matter what topic: its importance to the Revolution, its
place in Revolutionary thought. Even in those days the boys hadn't
listened closely; the Revolution was too old; it was either self-
evident or meaningless to say that a thing was important to the
Revolution, because there wasn't anything that was not the
Revolution. *Dedicate yourself daily to the work of the Revolution,* said
the tall letters that ran above the blackboards in his classroom. But
that was like saying, Dedicate yourself to the activity of being alive:
how could you do otherwise? If act-field theory, which lay at the
heart of the Revolution and all its work, meant anything, then no
act—no defiance of the Revolution, no grappling to oneself the
principles of it, no ignoring or rejecting of it—could be not part of
it. If any act could be not part of the Revolution, if any act could be
conceived of as being not governed by act-field theory, then the
field would dissolve; the Revolution would founder on the predic-
tion paradox. But act-field theory was precisely the refutation of
that paradox.

It was what he could not make Eva see. She was haunted by the
thought that all her acts were somewhere, somehow, known in
advance of her making them, as though the Revolution hunted her
continually.

Importance of act-field theory to the Revolution. Hare twisted
in his chair, linked his hands, changed the way his legs were
crossed. The morning sped away.

There was a woman he had known in cadre training, at summer camp, in those days of nightlong earnest conversations in

screened wooden common rooms, conversations that absorbed all the sudden feelings of young men and women for the first time thrust into daily contact. She had believed, or had told Hare she believed, that there was no such thing as act-field theory. She was sure, and argued it well, that for the Revolution to succeed, for the people to live within it happily and take up their burdens and do their work, it was only necessary for the people to believe that the theory *did* work. Once upon a time, she said, social theories made predictions about behavior, and thus could be disproved or weakened or shown to be self-contradictory when behavior was not as the theory predicted, or when unwanted results arose when the theory was applied. But act-field theory simply said: whatever you do, whatever comes about in the whole act-field, is *by definition* what act-field theory predicts.

Every shocking or astonishing turn of events; every failed harvest, street riot, cadre shake-up; every accident or reversal in every life, are all as act-field theory says they must be. They are all accounted for, every spike, every rising curve, every collapse. And when the Revolution has swept away those failed and hurtful systems that attempt to predict and direct the future, there is nothing left to rebel against, nothing to complain of. There is Perpetual Peace. Street riots slacken in force, go unnoticed, are aberrations that have been accounted for even before they occur; the people go to work, harvests are steady, cadre do their jobs, there are no longer shake-ups and purges, none at least beyond those that have been accounted for. The Revolution is permanent. In the midst of its eternal mutability and changefulness, society no longer needs to change, or to hope for an end to change either. Life goes on; only the hierarchies are gone.

She said she didn't object to any of that. She felt herself to be in training precisely to do that work, to maintain the illusion that act-field theory governs human life in the same way that axioms govern a mathematical system. She felt (Hare remembered her uplifted face, almost aglow in the dark common room, long after lights-out) that there could be no higher a task than to dedicate oneself to that work, which was cadre's work within the Revolution. Act-field theory dissolved social truisms like an acid, but it itself could never be dissolved; its works were its truth, the happiness of the world was its truth, the Revolution was its truth.

Hare listened, warmed by her certainty, by the strength of her thought; and he smiled, because he knew what she did not know. He had been where she couldn't go. She was no mathematician; she had not, as he had, just completed a multiplane ellipsoidal simplex and entered it onto the central virtual act-field and seen—he *saw* it, saw it like a landscape full of unceasing activity—the interior of the Revolution's data base, virtually as limitless as the actual act-field it reflected: and then saw it, at the bidding of his program, turn and look at itself.

How could he communicate that mystery? Ever since, as a schoolboy, he had learned that there are problems—in topology, in chaos description, in the projection of fractals—problems with true and verifiable solutions that only computers can construct, and only other computers verify, Hare had known how it was that computers could truly contain a virtual act-field, an image of the world larger than he could access within himself. He could put real questions about the world to the computers and receive real answers, answers not he nor any human mind could predict, answers only the computers themselves could prove true.

There *was* an act-field, and a theory by which it could be constructed. Just as Hare knew there was an interior in the young woman who sat beside him, which he could apprehend through her words and through the strength of her thought touching him as he listened and looked, an interior bounded by the planes of her pale temples and the warm body real beneath her clothes of Blue, so he knew truth to be contained within the interiors of the Revolution's computers: truth both unbounded and boundless, endless by definition and somehow kind.

He remembered that feeling. He remembered it, but he no longer felt it. He could not ever, knowing what he knew, think as that woman had, that act-field theory was a lie or a kind of trick. He imagined, guiltily, what a relief it might be to think so, but he could not. But act-field theory no longer seemed to him kind, as it once had. It seemed to be hurting him, and on purpose.

But if act-field theory underlay the Revolution, and the Revolution could not hurt him or anyone, then act-field theory could not hurt him.

He sat back, his hands in his lap, unwilling to touch the keys of the composer, reasoning with himself—tempted to reason with himself, as a man with a wound is tempted to probe it, pull at the scab, pick at the hurt flesh.

He *did not need to feel* these things, he told himself. He did not need to write an introduction to his manual. It needed none. Of course any part of act-field theory could be introduced by an explanation of all of it, but no part *needed* such an introduction. The project knew that. Certainly the project knew that. In fact the project had given him this job precisely because it would not require him to think about the whole of act-field theory, but only about the simple mechanics of its application. And yet the fact that he could no longer think clearly about the whole (which was why he was here now before this antiquated composer) meant that when he was confronted with this simple introduction, he felt like a man confronted with a small symptom, not in itself terrible, not even worth considering, of a fatal systemic disease.

Perhaps, though, the project *had* thought of all that; perhaps it had put him here, in this cubicle, and presented him with the concrete, the explicit and fearful consequences of act-field theory, to punish him for no longer being able to think about the theory itself: for betraying, through no fault of his own, the Revolution. No fault of his own: and yet he felt it to be his fault.

No, that was insane. If the Revolution was not always kind, it was never vindictive, never; for a heterarchy to be vindictive was a contradiction in terms: the Revolution could not be if it could be vindictive.

Unless there was a flaw in the theory that underlay the Revolution, act-field theory, which made heterarchy in the world conceivable, which made the integral social calculus possible and therefore all the daily acts and motions of the human world, including his sitting here before his unwritable manual.

But there could be no flaw in act-field theory. Hare knew that as well as he knew that he was alive. Act-field theory proved that all possible disproofs of act-field theory were themselves provable parts of act-field theory, just as were all other acts. It was not even possible for Hare to consider act-field theory without the act of his considering having been accounted for by the theory.

All possible strategies for avoiding paradox within act-field theory were also parts of the theory; they were acts the theory defined. Just as his sitting here pursued by paradox was defined and accounted for.

Hare had entered into an infinite-regression fugue; the taste of infinity was in his mouth like metal. That which had freed the world held Hare like a vise, like a cell in which a madman runs eternally, beating his head first on one wall, then the other.

Hare got permission to go and visit Eva and his son in the country. It was never hard to get such permission, but it was often hard to find transportation for such a purely personal trip. Hare's cadre status was no help; in fact it was considered not quite right for cadre to be seen traveling for private reasons. It didn't look serious; it could seem like unearned privilege and might be offensive to the people. Hare learned of a convoy of trucks that was taking young people out of the city to help with the harvest, and he was promised a ride on one of these.

When Willy returned from his night shift, he shook Hare awake, and as Hare, yawning and blinking, dressed, Willy undressed and climbed into the warmth Hare had left in the hollow of the bed. Hare went out into the empty, frosted streets, still tasting the dream from which Willy had awakened him.

Hare wondered if there were different names for different kinds of dream. This dream had been the kind where you seem to be telling a story to someone, and at the same time experiencing the story you are telling. Hare had been telling a story to Willy, a shameful and terrible secret that he had always kept from him, but which he had to confess to him now because Willy wanted to play. He had to confess how when he was a boy—and here he seemed not only to remember the episode but to experience it as well— when he was a boy, he had cut off his penis. He had done it deliberately, for what seemed like sufficient and even sensible reasons; he had kept the cut-off penis in a box. He saw himself opening the box in which he had kept it, and looking at it: it was erect but dead-looking, white, the veins in it pale. As he looked at it, the dream rising away from him, he realized how stupid he had been—how horribly stupid to have done this irrevocable thing that could never, ever be repaired, why, why had he done it—and as he contemplated the horror, Willy's hand awoke him. Relief of the purest kind washed over him, the dreadful burden fell away: it was all a dream, he hadn't done it at all. He grasped Willy's hand and laughed. Willy laughed, too. "Just a dream," Hare said.

Hare walked through the streets to the truck depot, shivering, feeling alternately the horror of the dream and the relief of waking. He had been distant with Willy lately: he ought to stop that, there was no reason for it.

Young men and women, students and younger cadre, filled the open trucks, mostly in Blue, mostly laughing and pleased at the prospect of a day in the country. Hare found the driver who had promised him a ride, and he was helped into the truck by several hands. The convoy started its engines, and as dawn threw long bars of sun between the buildings, they drove out of the city. The young people in Hare's truck began to sing, their strong high young voices clear, and the truck's engine a bass accompaniment to their song. It was stirring.

More somber, across the bridge, were the wide tracts of old city suburbs, long straight streets crossed by dirt roads where pools of water colored with oil stood in the truck ruts. Children, who perhaps belonged to the flowerets of modular housing growing over the dumps and shacks and abandoned factories, looked up to watch them pass. The young people stopped singing and began to find places within the truck's bed where they could sit comfortably through the long ride. Some opened books or journals they had brought. Some of the women lit cigarettes, though none of the men did.

Almost all the boys Hare had known who smoked cigarettes gave them up at a certain age, once out of school, but many women didn't. Women who smoked were of a certain kind, Hare thought; or at least they all seemed to roll and smoke their cigarettes in the same way, with the same set of gestures. Like that one, sitting with another out of the wind in the shelter of the cab: tall, lean, her hair cut short and carelessly, she used her cigarette in a curt, easy way, dangling it in her long hand that rested over her knee, flicking it now and then with her thumbnail. She rolled it within her fingers to lift it to her lips, drew deeply though it had grown almost too short to hold, and gracefully, forcefully, two-fingered it away over the truck's side, at the same time dismissing the smoke from herself through mouth and nostrils. The hard way she smoked seemed like the mark of a sisterhood; her friend beside her smoked in much the same way, though not tempered by the grace, the young eyes, or the kind smile that this one paid to Hare when she caught him studying her. Hare returned the smile, and the woman, still smiling, looked away, running her hand through her hair.

Hare laughed, enjoying the way what she did to mask herself, the smoking, revealed her to him. Young: when she was older, and more practiced, it wouldn't reveal her, but just now, in this morning, it did. Perched on the truck's scuppers, among youth—among the unmarked who desired so much to be marked, and in their desire, showing their tender just-born selfhoods the more cleanly, the more tartly to his senses—Hare for a moment felt how well after all the world is put together, and how well the people in it fit into it: a seamless act-field into which, no matter what fears he felt, Hare too fitted: into which even his fears of not fitting also fitted in the end.

He thought of Eva.

The truck left him off at a bare crossroads, where it turned toward the broad garden lands. He walked the two or three miles to the cadre crèche where Eva lived and worked, and where their son was growing up: three years old now. Hare had with him some books for Eva—she always complained there weren't enough, or the ones she could get weren't interesting—and a gift for his son, which Willy had made: a nesting set of the five regular geometric solids, all inside a sphere. They could be taken apart, and with some trouble, put back together again.

It had never been the case that anyone, any bureau or person or committee, ever forbade a marriage or some permanent arrangement between Eva and Hare. There was no committee or person who could have done that. Eva believed from the beginning, though, that such a barrier existed; it made her at once fearful and angry. Hare couldn't convince her that, whatever stories she may have heard, whatever rumors circulated, cadre weren't forbidden to regularize affairs like theirs. "They don't want it," Eva would say. "They don't care about anyone's happiness, so long as the work gets done. They never think about anything but the work." And Hare could not make her believe that, in the very nature of the Revolution, there was no "they," there could not be a "they" of the kind she feared and hated.

Certainly there was a tedious set of procedures that had to be gone through, but none of them were restrictive, Hare insisted, they were only informational. Many different people, yes, had to be informed; Hare and Eva's plans had to be passed outward into wider and wider circles of diffusion, first to the proctors and flow people at the project, then to the committee representatives at the dormitory, then the neighborhood and city committees; eventually the whole Applications system would have to be informed—would in the course of things become informed even if they only made their intentions known to the first levels of this diffusion. And it was true that in some ways they, Hare and Eva, would stick out: the two of them would make a spike within the regularities of cadre life, which was almost entirely unmarried, assumed to be celibate out of dedication and the pressure of work, and communal in ways that made strong pacts between individuals unusual; which meant that strong pacts between individuals upset people who were upset by unusual things. But why, Hare asked Eva, shouldn't the two of them be an oddity? Didn't she know that such oddities, such spikes, were implicit in the forms of communal life if that life isn't imposed by a hierarchy, is not tyrannical, is chosen, is the Revolution itself? They are assumed; they are already accounted for.

She did know that. But when Hare said—carefully, mildly, without insistence, a plan only for her to consider—that they could make their plans known at the first levels, within the first circles, and see if they were prevented even in the most subtle ways, and at the first signs of such resistance (though he knew there could be no such resistance) draw back if she liked: then she looked away and bit her nails (they were small, and bitten so short that the flesh of her fingertips folded over them; it hurt Hare to look at them) and said nothing.

She wanted something to defy, and there was nothing. She didn't want to hear his explanations of heterarchy, and when he made them, he felt as though he were betraying her.

He knew so much. He knew nothing.

He remembered her face, the day when she told him she was

pregnant: her eyes questioning him even as her mouth said she didn't care what he did, this act was hers, she alone had decided on it. She expected some declaration from him, he knew: a denunciation of her for having done this, or a sudden pact offered that he would join her in it, as though joining a conspiracy. It didn't even seem to matter which he did—join her or denounce her. In fact he did neither, not being able to imagine either, not knowing why she should set such terms for him, yet knowing also that it was not really he who was being challenged; and obscurely certain he was failing her by not being able to feel as she did—that her act was a crossroads, a crux, a turning point where a fatal choice had to be made.

He thought: *What if I had pretended to understand?* If she thought she was surrounded by watching authorities, who wanted her not to do what she wanted, if the child had been a defiance of those authorities, then what if he had somehow pretended to join her in her defiance? Would she have believed him? Would she not have gone away? He thought it was possible, and it hollowed his chest to think so.

The cadre crèche was a cluster of low buildings, dormitories, a barn, yards, infirmary, school; beyond were the gardens and fields that the commune worked. In and out the doors, through the halls bright with autumn sunlight, boys and girls came and went, and women tending groups of children. Hare thought this must be a good place for children; it was crowded with the things children like—tools, growing things, farm animals, other children.

He wandered from room to room with his gift and books, asking for Eva. All the men and women who lived and worked in the crèche were parents of children being raised here, but many other children of cadre were here whose parents had chosen not to stay with them. Hare thought of them, the parents, separated also from each other perhaps, attached to faraway long-term projects, or working with the people in distant cities.

It's just hard for cadre, that's all, he thought, very hard. The people acted as they acted, their actions describable by theory but otherwise unbound; for cadre it was different. There were no *theoretical* barriers to their acting just as they would; theoretically, they did exactly that. In practice it was different, or seemed to be different; there seemed to be a gap there, a gap that only kindness and a little good humor could cross. He and Eva were bound by that now, if by nothing else; bound by what separated them, by the whole front of the Revolution sweeping forward at once, which could not be otherwise. With kindness and humor they could cross the gap. It was enough; no one had anything better. It was hard but fair.

In the summer refectory the long tables were now heaped with gourds and vegetables to be put by for the winter; men and women were stringing onions and peppers, hanging up bunches of corn to dry, packing potatoes for storage. Hare stood at the threshold of the broad, screened room filled with harvest, sensing Eva among them before he saw her.

"Hello, Eva."

She turned to find him behind her, and a smile broke on her face that lifted his heart as on a wave. "Hello," she said. "How did you get here?"

"I found a ride. How are you?"

She only regarded him, still smiling; her cheeks were blushed with summer sun, like fruit. "Where's Boy?" Hare asked.

She had called their son only "the boy" or "boy" from the start, refusing to give him any other name; eventually "Boy" had become simply his name, a name like any other.

"He's here," Eva said. She leaned to look under the table at which she sat and called: "Boy! Come see."

He came out from beneath the table, dark curls first, and lifted his enormous eyes (they seemed enormous to Hare) first to his mother, and then to Hare. "Hello," said Hare. "I've brought this for you."

He held out the sphere to Boy, without revealing its secret, and Boy took it from him cautiously; the length of his eyelashes, when his eyes were cast down to study the gift, seemed also extraordinary to Hare. He opened the sphere; inside it was the pyramidal tetrahedron.

"I sent a message," he said. "Didn't you get it?"

"No," she said. "I never go to the terminals. You haven't come to stay, have you?"

"No," he said. "No, of course not."

"You still have work, at the project?"

"Yes." If he had said no, would her face have darkened, or brightened? "It's not the same work."

"Oh."

She had done nothing since he had known her but pose questions he could not answer, problems without solutions; why then did he hunger for her as though for answers, the answers that might unburden him? All at once his throat constricted, and he thought he might sob; he looked quickly around himself, away from Eva. "And you?" he said. "What will you do now?"

Eva was coming near the end of her time at the crèche; she would soon have to decide what she would do next. She couldn't return to work on any of the major projects whose people were housed in the agglomerate dormitories such as Hare and Willy lived in. There were cadre who lived outside such places, among the people, but for the most part they did work for which Eva wasn't trained.

She could also ask to be released from cadre: put off her clothes of Blue and join the people, and live however she could, as they did. She and Boy.

"What will you do?" Hare said again, because she hadn't answered; perhaps she hadn't heard him. Eva only looked down at Boy absorbed in opening the tetrahedron. For a moment it seemed to Hare she resembled the statue of the crowned woman in the cathedral. Ave Eva.

"It might be," he said, "that they would have work for you here, if you asked for it. For another year or more. So that you could stay on here. Isn't that so?"

Boy had turned and stood between his mother's legs, lifting the tetrahedron to her, patient to be helped. Eva only laughed, and picked him up.

"Would you want to do that?" he asked. And just then Boy, in Eva's arms, reached out for him, gleefully, and clambered from his mother to Hare.

The first thing Hare perceived was the boy's weight, much greater than he had expected from the compact miniature body; yet heavy as he was he seemed to fit neatly within Hare's lap and the compass of his arms, as though they were made to go together—which they were, in a way, Hare thought. The second thing he perceived was Boy's odor, a subtle but penetrating odor that widened Hare's nostrils, an odor of skin in part and a sweetness Hare couldn't name. He could almost not resist thrusting his face into the crook of Boy's neck to drink it in.

Eva had begun to talk of her life at the crèche. It was tedious, she said, and every day was much like every other, but she had come to prefer it to the city. All summer, she said, she had worked in the gardens, learning the work with a man who had been a long time in the country, working with the people. He was someone who couldn't be predicted, she said, just as she was herself such a person; someone outside the predictions that were made for everyone, for every person. She had liked talking with him, hearing about other ways of life in other places, other possibilities; after work they had often gone walking with Boy, in the evenings that had seemed to her so huge and vacant here, quiet, as though waiting to be filled.

"As though you could step into them and keep walking away forever," she said.

"Yes."

"That's what he said."

"Yes." But Hare had not been listening; he had been hearing Boy, and feeling him, the solidity of him in his lap. He had begun to imagine what it would be like to live here, as Eva and Boy did. He thought of the passage of days, the work that there would be to do—work which Hare had never done but which he could just now imagine doing. *Have you come to stay?* Eva had asked him, as though it were possible he might. He was Boy's father, after all; he had a place here with him, too. Perhaps, if he did, if he came to stay with Eva and Boy, he might in the course of a year recover the balance he had lost, shake off the lethargy that bound him.

"Would you want to do that?" he asked again.

"Do what?"

"Stay here. If you could."

She looked at Hare as though he had said something not quite intelligible. "I'm not going to stay here," she said.

"Where are you going?" Hare asked.

"I'm going," Eva said. "They can't have me any longer."

"But where?" Hare insisted. "What city? What town? Are you going to look for another project? Are you going to give up Blue?"

She had begun to shake her head, easily but certainly rejecting each of these possibilities. It would not be, her face seemed to say, anything that could be predicted.

"Eva," Hare said. "You know you can't just . . . just fall out of the universe." He had begun to experience an awful swooning vertigo. "You can't, you can't. You'll be alone, you . . ."

"I won't be alone."

"What? What do you mean?"

"I told you," Eva said. "I told you about him. I was telling you all about him. Weren't you listening?"

"Oh," Hare said. "I see."

"You tell me there's no place to go. But there has to be."

"I didn't mean that. I meant—"

"There has to be," Eva said, looking away.

Hare sat still and said nothing further, but it seemed at that moment that the color began to be drained from everything that he looked at: the fruits and orange gourds on the tables, the people in Blue, the colored tiles of the floor. The boy he held, who had a moment ago seemed as large as himself, no, larger, seemed to grow small, distant within his arms, a foreign thing, something not connected to him at all, like a stone. He looked up. Had the sun gone behind clouds? No, it still shone. Where did this awful chill come from? "It's not what I meant," he said again, but did not hear himself speak it; he could only marvel at what had happened, what had happened and would not cease happening. Boy fell silent, and slipped out of his arms to the floor.

"I don't feel well," he said, and stood abruptly. "I'd better go."

Both Boy and Eva were looking at him, curious and not unkind, not kind either; not anything. Their faces were stones or closed doors, the faces of those at accidents or public quarrels. Hare thought he would see such faces if he were to die in the street.

"Do you want to go to the infirmary?" Eva asked.

"No. I'll go."

"Are you sure?"

"I'll go," Hare said. "I'll go. I'll go. I'll go."

He had thought it was just a story he was being told, about working in the gardens, about summer evenings, empty and vast. He hadn't listened carefully; he hadn't known that there would come this sickening reversal of figure and ground, showing him a story he had not suspected, that he was all unready for. Nothing had been as he thought it was; he had walked into what was the case as into a truck's path.

Hare stood at the crossroads awaiting the trucks returning from the farmlands to the city. The strange gray blindness that had afflicted him at the cadre crèche had not passed, nor had the dreadful stonelike weight in his chest. He patted his chest as he stood waiting, trying to press it down. He thought perhaps he would go to the infirmary when he returned.

It was true what he told her, though, what he knew about heterarchy and she did not, that it was limitless, that it could not be got outside of, that to think about it as though it had an inside and an outside was a kind of pain, the pain of error that is fruitless, unnecessary, because self-inflicted: this conviction that by choice or by some dreadful mistake it is possible to fall out of the universe. Hare knew (it was all that he had ever tried to make her see) that it was not possible to fall out of the universe.

He thought of her and Boy and the man they were going away with. His thought followed them into a featureless stony landscape, without weather or air, under a vault of dun sky. Forever and ever would they be there.

He tried to draw breath deeply, but the painful bolus beneath his sternum seemed to prevent it; he could not get the air he needed.

Perhaps he would die. He wasn't old, but he seemed to be suffering some irreversible debility that quickened almost daily. He could not clearly remember, but he thought he had not really been well since the time when he was a boy and had cut off his penis.

No, that was a dream. Wasn't it? Yes, of course it was. With horror Hare realized that for some hours he had actually been assuming it to be so: that he had done such a thing and was now living with the consequences.

No. He wasn't truly ill. It was only this weather oppressing him, airless and chill, this close vault of dirty sky. He was grievously thirsty. Perhaps he would die.

The trucks surprised Hare, appearing suddenly past sundown; apparently he had been standing and waiting for hours without noticing time pass. He waved. The truck that stopped to pick him up was not the one that had brought him out; the young people who helped him in were not the same, were not the cheerful boys and girls who had sung children's songs and talked and laughed. These looked at Hare in silence, their faces in the twilight pale and reserved.

Hare thought he should explain himself to them. Perhaps he could ask them for help. He opened his mouth, but his throat was so dry and constricted that no words came out; he gaped foolishly, he supposed, but no one smiled. He forced his throat to open, and a gout of language came out that Hare did not intend or even understand.

He had better not talk more, he thought. He sought for a place to sit down; the silent young people drew away from him as he crept toward the shelter of the cab. He supposed that after all no one had heard the nonsense he had spoken, not over the noise of the truck's engine: an awful imploding roar that grew steadily worse, sucking the air from Hare's mouth and the thoughts from his head. He leaned against the cab, his hand hanging loosely over his knee; with his thumbnail he flicked the fragment of cigarette he held between his fingers. He was certain now that he would die of his old wound, or, far worse, that he would live forever. Forever and ever. "Ave Eva," he said, and a woman laughed. Hare laughed, too. The words seemed the only thing that could relieve his thirst. *Ave Eva,* he said again, or thought he said, unable any longer to hear himself under the withering roar *Ave Eva. Ave Eva. Ave Eva. Ave Eva.*

The committee had high seats behind a long desk. This was not so that they sat above those who came before them to be examined— Hare's guard explained this to Hare—but so that everyone in the room could see them clearly. The committee leader had a seat on one side, and before her she had some dossiers and some things taken from Hare's room, including the sketches of old buildings and the attempts Hare had made to decipher their inscriptions. Hare found it hard to recognize these things; when the committee leader held up a sketch and asked Hare if he had made it, he couldn't answer. He tried to answer; he opened his mouth to answer, but could not make an answer come out.

The committee was patient. They listened to testimony about

Hare, what he had done, how he had been found. They rested their cheeks in their hands, or they leaned back in their chairs with their hands folded in their laps; they asked gentle, unsurprised questions of the people who came before them, trying to get a clear story. When there seemed to be a contradiction, they would ask Hare what had happened. Hare opened his mouth to answer; he thought he could answer, possible answers occurred to him, then other possibilities, opening and branching like coincidence-magnitude calculations, switching figure and ground. Still he thought he could answer, if he could only say everything at once, describe or state the whole situation, the whole act-field, at once; but he could not, so he only struggled for a while with open mouth while the committee waited, watching him. Then they returned to questioning the others.

The two women who lived in the dormitory room next to Hare described how he had got into their room late at night: how he had forced his way in, though talking all the time very strangely and gently, about how he meant them no harm, wanted only to explain. They told (interrupting each other, finishing each other's sentences, until the committee head had to speak sharply to them) of their fear and confusion, of how they had tried to get out of the room, how Hare had prevented them. A torn night-dress was shown to the committee. The committee talked among themselves about attempted rape, asking questions that embarrassed the two women, but asking them so gently that answers were got at last.

Some others from the dormitory described how they had come to the women's room, and their struggle with Hare. They were eager to explain how or why it was that they had let Hare go, had not apprehended him and taken him then and there to security or

to the committee representative. The committee head, not interested in hearing this, kept guiding the witnesses back to the facts of
Hare's struggle: what weapons he had had, how he had behaved,
what he had said.

Willy came in. He wanted to go and stand next to Hare, but the
committee asked him to stand where the other witnesses had
stood; and all through his story he kept looking at Hare, as though
pleading with him to say something, to behave in some way that
Willy understood. Hare saw that Willy's hands shook, and he
wanted to take his hand, to say something to calm him, but he
couldn't move. His guard sat behind him with his hands in his lap
and probably wouldn't have prevented his going to Willy or speaking to him, Hare thought; but he couldn't do it, any more than he
could answer the committee's questions.

Much of Willy's story was taken up with how tired and upset
Hare had been before this incident, the bad dreams he had had, the
troubles at the project. Hare couldn't remember any of the things
Willy told about—any more than he could remember going into
the women's room, or fighting with the people in the dormitory—
but it seemed to him that the more that Willy, with every kind
intention, tried to explain away Hare's behavior, the worse it
looked to the committee. It sounded as if Willy knew something
really terrible about Hare, and out of love was covering it up.

But Willy had once said to Hare that he knew all about him,
and there wasn't anything terrible.

Hare wanted to say that, more in Willy's defense somehow
than his own, but he could not.

Then, as Willy told about going out after Hare, and searching
the city for him, Hare began to remember something of the events
that were being told to the committee. In the same way that a

dream that is forgotten on waking can be brought into the mind, disconnected but vivid, by some event of the day, some word or sight, Hare caught sight of bits of the story he had been in. When Willy told of finding him at last, huddled on the wide steps of the building whose inscription he had copied out, he remembered. Not how he had come to be there, or what had happened to him before, but that alone: Willy's hand on his shoulder, Willy's face before him, speaking to him. And he knew also, with a deep horror that deafened him to the committee's further proceedings, that that had not happened yesterday, or the day before, but weeks ago; and he remembered nothing at all of what had happened between then and now.

The committee leader was speaking, summing up the committee's findings. The case was really out of their provenance, she thought, and should probably not have been brought before the committee. She asked Hare if he had anything further to say.

The guard behind Hare leaned forward and tapped Hare's shoulder. Hare stood.

"Do you have anything you want to say?" the committee leader said again, patiently and without insistence.

"It's hard," Hare said. This came out of his mouth as though it were a stone he had dislodged from his throat, not like something he had decided to say. "It's very hard!"

He looked at the faces in the room, the committee, his neighbors, Willy. He knew, suddenly, that they would understand: they must, for they were all engaged with Hare in this hard thing together. "We all know how hard it is," he said. "The work of the Revolution. To grasp its principles isn't easy. To *live* them isn't easy. I've tried hard. We all have." They would understand how he had stumbled, they must; they would help him to rise. Together, in the face of the awful difficulties of the Revolution, they would go on. If he could lean on them, then as soon as he regained his feet, he could try again to be someone on whom others leaned. He smiled, and waited for their smile in return. "It's hard, always grappling with these difficulties. Act-field theory: that's hard to think about." He shook his head in self-deprecation. "Oh, I know. And the duties of cadre. The duty to *understand*. The committee knows how hard it is; everyone knows. I only want to say that I've tried. I want the committee to understand that. The committee understands. You understand."

He stopped talking. The circle of faces around him had not changed. It watched him with what seemed to him a terrible reserve, and something like pity. He knew he had not been recognized. He said, to the calm, closed face of the committee head: "Don't you think it's hard?"

"No," she said. "Frankly, I don't."

Frankly. Hare could not stand up any longer; his knees were unable to support him. Frankly. She had spoken with that remote, unmoved concern, the remote concern with which an adult will speak to a child in moral difficulties, difficulties the adult doesn't feel; without anger, with some impatience, without collusion: collusion would be inappropriate. Hare knew himself to be absolutely alone.

He had stopped speaking. After a moment the committee head gave the committee's resolution. Hare was to be remanded to a hospital. The committee head said she was sure that with rest and attention, Hare would return to normal. When he was better, they might have another meeting, and consider what amends Hare might be able to make for his behavior, if any were thought to be necessary then. Her last words to Hare were the usual formula spoken at the end of committee deliberations, when disposition of someone's case was made. She said: "Did you hear that?"

In the spring, discharged from the hospital, Hare was given a paper with an address on it, an address in an older part of the city where he had used to go often, to look at buildings.

It was strange to be once again alone on the street. Not often in the last months had he been alone at all, and never on the street. Except that a thin rain was falling, cold and hastening, he might have wandered for a while through the squares and alleys of the quarter; they seemed at once new and familiar to him, and the sensation of walking there was both vivifying and sad: the mixture of emotions made him feel painfully alive, and he wondered how long it would persist. But he turned up his collar and went on to the building to which he had been sent.

It was an old one, and one he remembered. He had stood before it more than once, feeling with his sight and his sense of proportion the curves of its stonework and its iron window grilles. He had used to look in through the barred glass doors, down a long marble-floored hall bordered by columns, but he had never dared to go in. He went in now. There was an aged doorkeeper who took Hare's paper, made a remark about the rain and shuddered as though it were he who was wet and not Hare, and entered something on the terminal before him. He waited for a reply in the display, and when he had it, he left the little cage or box that was his station and led Hare down the long hall, past the columns pinkish and blue-veined like the legs of old people, to a tall open door. He waited for Hare to enter, then closed the door behind him.

The big room was empty. There was only a workstation—a desk and two chairs, a terminal, a pile of printouts and other papers—which stood in the center of the floor, or not quite in the center, as though whoever had placed them there hadn't known that the room had a center. It did, though: it was clearly marked by the radiating diamonds of the parquet floor; it was plumb with the central diamond-shaped pendant of the chandelier, a multitiered forest of swagged lights and what seemed to be strings of jewels, that hung from the center of the ceiling above. Hare looked up at it as he crossed the floor to the desk; it swung around its axis, or rather seemed to swing, as he moved. He sat down in the chair beside the desk, crossed his hands in his lap, and waited. He didn't know who it was he waited for, or what disposition would be made of him now; he only supposed, with a sort of automatic humility he hardly even recognized in himself any longer, that whomever he waited for would be wiser than himself, would be able to see him clearly and know what was best.

That was one thing he had come to learn, over the last months—not how wise others were, but how unwise he was himself. He had learned to trust those who trusted in the world in a way that he could not: that way he hoped he might once again come to trust in the world himself. And even if he could not—even if there remained in him always some fatal mistrust—still there was no better thing that he could do: nothing else at all that he could do.

It hadn't been easy, learning that.

In the first weeks of his stay in the hospital, he had mostly been aware of the difference between himself and others, both those in difficulties like himself, and those attempting to help them. It seemed to him important, desperately important, to make those differences clear: to explain what it was in him that made him unlike others and unable to be as they were. It frightened him to be among so many who were bewildered, hurt, angry, or sad, not because he was not all these things himself, but because he felt himself to be unimaginable to them; and it frightened him more to be with the staff, because he could not define for them, in any way that he felt they could truly grasp, the perplexities within himself that made him unlike them: made him unwise, unwhole, divided and in pain, as they were not.

They were not even cadre for the most part, the staff, not anyway in the wing to which Hare was moved after a series of tests had determined there were no metabolic disorders at the root of his condition. (He had briefly hoped that some such disorder would be discovered, to relieve him of the awful burden of finding the explanation elsewhere. But there was none.) In his wing were those whose troubles were unanalyzable, and the staff there were only kind, only experienced and sympathetic, only set to watch the disorders take their course, and give what common help they could. And how could Hare explain to them—heavy women who nodded and patted his hand, male nurses who spoke in banalities—about act-field theory, its unchallengeable truth, its danger to him?

He knew so much. In his long, long silences his own explanations were his only occupation, and seemed to him all that sustained him over an abyss. He knew, with great precision, what stood between him and happiness; he knew quite well that he did not need to feel as he did, that just beyond his feelings, just past his really quite simple and explainable error, lay the real world, which he could reach if he could only stop making this error, or even stop explaining the error to himself: but when he tried to say these things aloud, to explain this predicament to the nurses and the staff or the other patients, the explanations hurt him; and the real world, as he talked, grew more fearsomely remote.

The explanations broke, in the end, like a fever. Then there were tears, and shameful incontinence of grief, and helplessness; no help at all but kindness and attention, the help of those who knew how little help they could be.

He had not believed it was possible to fall out of the universe: yet he had experienced exactly that. He had fallen out of the universe into explanations of why he could not fall out of the universe. And he had to reach for the hands of those who could not even envisage such a thing and be drawn back in. In the common rooms, with their old furniture worn and stained as though by the sorrows of those who used it; in the kitchens, where he clumsily helped with meals; in the winter yards and the crossing paths of the grounds, he would be swept by waves of healing integration, unwilled, as though some severed part of him were drawing back within him: waves of feeling that left him weak and still afraid of the strange things he contained. When those diminished, too, like the terrible explanations, then he was empty. He looked around himself at the world and saw that though he did not know it, it knew him. He ate its nourishing breakfasts, blinked in its watery winter sunlight, joined its talk tentatively, washed its dishes with humility. He could not fall out of it.

Willy, who had visited him weekly, bringing good food and (what Hare hungered more for) stories of the people Willy knew, came on a spring day to take him away. In his dossier, encoded now with thousands of others in the hospital's records, the course of his illness and its resolution were charted, he knew; and when the magnitude of his difference from others was accounted for, his absolute otherness factored in, they were exactly as act-field theory predicted. It was all right.

All right. He sat, hands folded in his lap, waiting beneath the chandelier.

When a dark woman in Blue of about his own age came through the far double doors, Hare stood. The woman waved to him apologetically across the vast room, picking up a folder from a cart of them by the door; smiling, she crossed the geometrical floor to where Hare stood.

Among cadre there was no rank, and therefore no marks of rank beyond the simple clothes of Blue they all wore. But subtle distinguishing marks had nevertheless arisen; Hare knew that the cluster of pens in this woman's pocket meant heavy responsibilities. There was more, though. In the last months the faces of those he met were often charged for him with intense but imaginary familiarity; and yet about this woman he was sure.

"I know you," he said.

She raised her eyebrows. She didn't know him.

"Yes," Hare said. "Years ago." He named the study camp where in the summer of Hare's seventeenth year they had known each other, studied together, hiked together. As he spoke, he remembered the summer darkness of the common room where late at night they had talked.

"Oh, yes," she said. "Yes, yes, I remember now. A long time ago." She smiled, remembering. "A long time."

She had opened Hare's dossier, and now drew out the drawings of buildings and the calculations of their geometries that Hare had made. The last time Hare had seen them was when he stood before the committee: so long ago.

"Do you know why you do this?" she asked. "Copy these things?"

"No. I like them, I like to look at such places, old places and wonder how they came to be; what the people thought and felt who built them."

"History," she suggested. "The past."

"Yes."

"That interests us, too," she said. "My project, I mean."

"Oh," said Hare, not knowing what else to say. "Is yours . . . is it an Applications project?"

She smiled. "No," she said.

"Oh."

She rested her cheek again in the palm of her hand. "I think," she said, "that long ago there was another time like this one, when people lived in places whose history they didn't know, whose history they had forgotten. They had lost history because they knew so little. They called that ignorance 'darkness,' and when they began to relearn history, they called that knowledge 'light.' But we're in darkness, too. Not because we know so little, but because we know so much. It's not different."

"Knowing everything is not different from knowing nothing," Hare said. "Is that what you mean?"

She quoted an old principle of act theorists, one that had become an adage of Revolutionary cadre: "We seek no solution—only knowledge of the problem."

She turned to the drawing of the building opposite the cathedral, whose lettering Hare had copied out. Her finger touched the words.

"Do you know what they mean?" Hare asked her.

"No," she said. She folded her hands before her. "When you went out to do these things . . ."

"It was always on my own time," Hare said. "On free days."

"Did you tell anyone where you were going, what you were doing?"

"Not usually. Not all of it." Hare stared down at the hat he held in his hands. He felt, like an old secret wound, his taste for history, like a peasant child's taste for eating dirt.

"It must have seemed," she said, "that you were leading a double life. Did you feel that way? That you were leading a double life?"

At her words hot tears rose to Hare's eyes with awful quickness, and he felt for a moment that he would sob, as he had sobbed so often at just such small remarks that winter. A double life: a life inside, and another outside, between which Hare was pulled apart.

"Will you go on doing this, now?" the woman asked gently, her eyes watching Hare's evident distress.

"I don't know," he said. He looked up. "I want to help," he said. "I want to do useful work. I know that I haven't been much help for a long time, but I'm stronger now. I want to be of use."

She turned over the picture, and pushed the pile toward Hare. For a moment he didn't understand that she was giving them back to him. "I think your project made a mistake when they removed you from the work you'd been doing," she said.

"You do?"

"I think the better thing would have been to release you from cadre altogether." She rested her cheek again in the palm of her hand. "What do you think?"

A storm of shame arose within Hare, a storm that made the dreadful imploding roar he had first heard in the truck returning from the country. It broke so quickly over him that he had to suppose he had all along been expecting precisely these words to be said to him. Through its great noise he could not hear his own answer: "I'll do as you think best," he said. "Whatever you think."

"Go to the people," the woman said.

Hare covered his eyes. "I'm not good for much," he said. "There's not much I know how to do."

"What I suggest is this," the woman said. "You'll get a ration card and find a place in the city. Then—go on with what you did. I mean the drawings and the investigations you liked. History."

Hare listened.

"If you would," she said, "I would like you to come back here, now and then, and talk to me—to my project—about what you are doing."

"That would be all right?" Hare said. "I could do that?"

"You can do as you like," she said. "You can go back to your project, too."

"No," Hare said, feeling a strange warmth at his breastbone. "No. I'll do as you say."

"I don't know what we can learn, but I think . . . well." Her humorous eyes regarded him steadily. "Anyway there's probably nothing better for you to do. You are an oddity, aren't you?"

"Yes," Hare said.

"Did you think the Revolution was not large enough to contain you?"

"No," Hare said, "I didn't think so." But he had: he understood at that moment that he had thought exactly that.

She took a card from his dossier and handed it to him. "Take this to Applications, in the old cathedral," she said. "They'll tell you what to do. Come back here when you like. I'll be glad to see you."

She stood; Hare's interview was evidently at an end. He twisted the hat he held in his hands.

"I was remembering," he said, "something you told me. That summer, when we met at study camp." He felt his heart fill with a familiar apprehension. "You said . . . We were talking about act-field theory, which I was working on then, and you told me you believed that there was no such thing really as act-field theory at all; but that so long as everybody believed there was such a theory, and cadre believed that it worked, then it *did* work."

"Yes?"

"Yes." Dreadful as the danger Hare felt himself to be in, narrow as the ledge he stood on, he had to ask: "Do you still think that?"

"No," she said. Her smile hadn't passed, but it had changed, as though she shared not only a memory with Hare, but a joke as well; or a secret. "No, I don't."

Hare walked through the old quarter of the city, not feeling the thin rain soaking through his shoes. He seemed to himself to be naked but warm, to be already not in Blue, and walking in the world for the first time, as though his feet created it step by step: the world he had fallen out of, the world into which Eva and Boy had gone. He laughed, in fear and hunger for it.

His desire was not what he had thought it to be: his desire for history, for Eva, for Boy, none of it was what he thought it was. He knew nothing, nothing of the world he walked in; but he might learn.

What a strange, what a foolish error for him to have made, Hare thought. If he were called again before the local committee to make restitution for the trouble he had caused, he could tell them: he had come, without knowing it, to see the world in hierarchies. He, with his years of training, his excellent education, had built hierarchies in his heart. He had not known it until he had been asked to resign from cadre and had been overcome with shame: as though to be in Blue were better than to be not in Blue, to be cadre better than to be among the people.

He had believed act-field theory governed the act-field, and not the reverse. But the act-field governed. In the computers of the Revolution, as in the corridors and hollows of Hare's heart and mind, there was only a virtuality, after all; a virtual real-world, and not a whole one. He was inside the act-field and not it inside him; so was the Revolution, and all its work.

"Oh, I see," he said aloud. He had stopped walking. At the end of the street the great square opened, crossed by a single person on foot, a single bicycle. The obscure huge buildings that bordered it were soft in the misty rain. Hare, for the first time, yet not as though for the first time, but as though coming to remember some commonplace thing of enormous, of vital, importance, saw the act-field. Still; calm; with no face, not kind, not cruel, not anything. He reached out with his mind to touch it, but everywhere he touched it, it parted, showing him spaces, interstices, emptinesses formed by the edge of himself facing the sparkling edge of the world.

Hare cried out, as though stung. He felt the sensation of an answer, a sensation like a physical shock. The answer was an answer to a figure-ground problem, the simplest figure-ground problem, a problem solved long ago. The answer was an emptiness, formed by the edges of two questions: but the sensation of the answer was like a bit of light, a point of light lit, flaring fiercely and burning out: a physical sensation, a brief coincidence, an act.

Then it was gone. Hare set out across the square.

MISSOLONGHI 1824

■ ■ ■

THE ENGLISH MILORD took his hands from the boy's shoulders, discomfited but unembarrassed. "No?" he said. "No. Very well, I see, I see; you must forgive me then . . ."

The boy, desperate not to have offended the Englishman, clutched at the milord's tartan cloak and spoke in a rush of Romaic, shaking his head and near tears.

"No, no, my dear," the milord said. "It's not at all your fault; you have swept me into an impropriety. I misunderstood your kindness, that is all, and it is you who must forgive me."

He went, with his odd off-kilter and halting walk, to his couch, and reclined there. The boy stood erect in the middle of the room, and (switching to Italian) began a long speech about his deep love and respect for the noble lord, who was as dear as life itself to him. The noble lord watched him in wonder, smiling. Then he held out a hand to him: "Oh, no more, no more. You see it is just such sentiments as those that misled me. Really, I swear to you, I misunderstood and it shan't happen again. Only you mustn't stand there preaching at me, don't; come sit by me at least. Come."

The boy, knowing that a dignified coldness was often the safest demeanor to adopt when offers like the milord's were made to him, came and stood beside his employer, hands behind his back.

"Well," the milord said, himself adopting a more serious mien, "I'll tell you what. If you will not stand there like a stick, if you will put back on your usual face—sit, won't you?—then . . . then what shall I do? I shall tell you a story."

Immediately the boy melted. He sat, or squatted, near his master—not on the couch, but on a rag of carpet on the floor near it. "A story," he said. "A story of what, of what?"

"Of what, of what," said the Englishman. He felt the familiar night pains beginning within, everywhere and nowhere. "If you will just trim the lamp," he said, "and open a jar of that Hollands gin there, and pour me a cup with some *limonata,* and then put a stick on the fire—then we will have 'of what, of what.' "

The small compound was dark now, though not quiet; in the courtyard could still be heard the snort and stamp of horses arriving, the talk of his Suliote soldiers and the petitioners and hangers-on around the cook fires there, talk that could turn to insults, quarrels, riot, or dissolve in laughter. Insofar as he could, the noble foreign lord on whom all of them depended had banished them from this room: here, he had his couch, and the table where he wrote—masses of correspondence, on gold-edged crested paper to impress, or on plain paper to explain (endless the explanations, the cajolings, the reconcilings these Greeks demanded of him): and another pile of papers, messy large sheets much marked over, stanzas of a poem it had lately been hard for him to remember he was writing. Also on the table amid the papers, not so incongruous as they would once have struck him, were a gilt dress sword, a fantastical crested helmet in the Grecian style, and a Manton's pistol.

He sipped the gin the boy had brought him, and said: "Very well. A story." The boy knelt again on his carpet, dark eyes turned up, eager as a hound: and the poet saw in his face that hunger for tales (what boy his age in England would show it, what public-school boy or even carter's or ploughman's lad would show it?), the same eagerness that must have been in the faces gathered around the fire by which Homer spoke. He felt almost abashed by the boy's open face: he could tell him anything, and be believed.

"Now this would have happened," he said, "I should think, in the year of your birth, or very near; and it happened not a great distance from this place, down in the Morea, in a district that was once called, by your own ancestors a long time ago, Arcadia."

"Arcadia," the boy said in Romaic.

"Yes. You've been there?"

He shook his head.

"Wild and strange it was to me then. I was very young, not so many years older than you are now, hard as it may be for you to imagine I was ever so. I was traveling, traveling because—well, I knew not why; for the sake of traveling, really, though that was hard to explain to the Turks, who do not travel for pleasure, you know, only for gain. I did discover why I traveled, though: that's part of this story. And a part of the story of how I come to be here in this wretched marsh, with you, telling you of it.

"You see, in England, where the people are chiefly hypocrites, and thus easily scandalized, the offer that I just foolishly made to you, my dear, should it have become public knowledge, would have got both of us, but chiefly me, in a deal of very hot water. When I was young there was a fellow hanged for doing such things, or rather for being caught at it. Our vices are whoring and drink, you see; other vices are sternly punished.

"And yet it was not that which drove me abroad; nor was it the ladies either—that would come later. No—I think it was the weather, above all." He tugged the tartan more closely around him. "Now, this winter damp; this rain today, every day this week; these fogs. Imagine if they never stopped: summer and winter, the same, except that in winter it is . . . well, how am I to explain an English winter to you? I shall not try.

"As soon as I set foot on these shores, I knew I had come home. I was no citizen of England gone abroad. No: this was my land, my clime, my air. I went upon Hymettus and heard the bees. I climbed to the Acropolis (which Lord Elgin was just conspiring to despoil; he wanted to bring the statues to England, to teach the English sculpture—the English being as capable of sculpture as you, my dear, are of skating). I stood within the grove sacred to Apollo at Claros: except there is no grove there now, it is nothing but dust. You, Loukas, and your fathers have cut down all the trees, and burned them, out of spite or for firewood I know not. I stood in the blowing dust and sun, and I thought: *I am come two thousand years too late.*

"That was the sadness that haunted my happiness, you see. I did not despise the living Greeks, as so many of my countrymen did, and think them degenerate, and deserving of their Turkish masters. No, I rejoiced in them, girls and boys, Albanians and Suliotes and Athenians. I loved Athens and the narrow squalid streets and the markets. I took exception to nothing. And yet . . . I wanted so much not to have *missed* it, and was so aware that I had. Homer's Greece; Pindar's; Sappho's. Yes, my young friend: you know soldiers and thieves with those names; I speak of others.

"I wintered in Athens. When summer came, I mounted an expedition into the Morea. I had with me my valet Fletcher, whom you know—still with me here; and my two Albanian servants, very fierce and greedy and loyal, drinking skinfuls of Zean wine at eight paras the oke every day. And there was my new Greek friend Nikos, who is your predecessor, Loukas, your *type* I might say, the original of all of you that I have loved: only the difference was, he loved me too.

"You know that you can see the mountains into which we went from these windows, yes, on a clear cloudless day such as we have not seen now these many weeks; those mountains to the south across the bay, that look so bare and severe. The tops of them *are* bare, most of them; but down in the vales there are still bits of the ancient forests, and in the chasms where the underground rivers pour out. There are woods and pasture: yes, sheep and shepherds too in Arcady.

"That is Pan's country, you know—or perhaps you don't; sometimes I credit you Greeks with a knowledge that ought to have come down with your blood, but has not. Pan's country: where he was born, where he still lives. The old poets spoke of his hour as noon, when he sleeps upon the hills; when even if you did not see the god face-to-face—woe to you if you did—you could hear his voice, or the sound of his pipes: a sorrowful music, for he is a sad god at heart, and mourns for his lost love Echo."

The poet ceased to speak for a long moment. He remembered that music, heard in the blaze of the Arcadian sun, music not different from the hot nameless drone of noontide itself, compounded of insects, exhalation of the trees, the heated blood rushing in his head. Yet it was a song too, potent and vivifying—and sad, infinitely sad: that even a god could mistake the reflection of his own voice for love's.

There were other gods in those mountains besides great Pan,

or had been once; the little party of travelers would pass through groves or near pools, where little stelae had been set up in another age, canted over now and pitted and mossy, or broken and worn away, but whose figures could sometimes still be read: crude nymphs, half-figures of squat horned bearded men with great phalluses, broken or whole. The Orthodox in their party crossed themselves passing these, the Mussulmen looked away or pointed and laughed.

"The little gods of woodland places," the poet said. "The gods of hunters and fishermen. It reminded me of my own home country of Scotland, and how the men and women still believe in pixies and kelpies, and leave food for them, or signs to placate them. It was very like that.

"And I doubt not those old Scotsmen have their reasons for acting as they do, as good reasons as the Greeks had. And have still— whereby hangs this tale."

He drank again (more than this cupful would be needed to get him through the night) and laid a careful hand on Loukas's dark curls. "It was in such a glen that one night we made our camp. So long did the Albanians dance and sing around the fire—'When we were thieves at Parga,' and I'm sure they were—and so sympathetic did I find the spot, that by noon next day we were still at ease there.

"Noon. Pan's song. But we became aware of other sounds as well, human sounds, a horn blown, thrashings and crashings in the glen beyond our camp. Then figures: villagers, armed with rakes and staves and one old man with a fowling piece.

"A hunt of some sort was up, though what game could have been in these mountains large enough to attract such a crowd I could not imagine; it was hard to believe that many boar or deer could get a living here, and there was uproar enough among these villagers that they might have been after a tiger.

"We joined the chase for a time, trying to see what was afoot. A cry arose down where the forest was thickest, and for an instant I did see some beast ahead of the pack, crashing in the under-growth, and heard an animal's cry—then no more. Nikos had no taste for pursuit in the heat of the day, and the hunt straggled on out of our ken.

"Toward evening we reached the village itself, over a moun-tain and a pass: a cluster of houses, a monastery on the scarp above where monks starved themselves, a *taberna,* and a church. There was much excitement; men strutted with their weapons in the street. Apparently their hunt had been successful, but it was not easy to determine what they had caught. I spoke but little Romaic then; the Albanians knew none. Nikos, who could speak Italian and some English, held these mountain people in contempt, and soon grew bored with the work of translating. But gradually I con-ceived the idea that what they had hunted through the groves and glens was not an animal at all but a man—some poor madman, apparently, some wild man of the woods hunted down for sport. He was being kept caged outside the town, it seemed, awaiting the judgment of some village headman.

"I was well aware of the bigotries of people such as these vil-lagers were; of Greeks in general, and of their Turkish masters too if it came to that. Whoever started their fear or incurred their dis-pleasure, it would go hard with them. That winter in Athens I had interceded for a woman condemned to death by the Turkish authorities, she having been caught in illicit love. Not with me: with me she was not caught. Nonetheless I took it upon myself to rescue her, which with much bluster and a certain quantity of silver I accomplished. I thought perhaps I could help the poor wretch these people had taken. I cannot bear to see even a wild beast in a cage.

"No one welcomed my intervention. The village headman did not want to see me. The villagers fled from my Albanians, the loudest strutters fleeing first. When at last I found a priest I could get some sense from, he told me I was much mistaken and should not interfere. He was tremendously excited, and spoke of rape, not one but many, or the possibility of them anyway, now thank Christ avoided. But I could not credit what he seemed to say: that the captive was not a madman at all but a man of the woods, one who had never lived among men. Nikos translated what the priest said: 'He speaks, but no one understands him.'

"Now I was even more fascinated. I thought perhaps this might be one of the Wild Boys one hears of now and then, abandoned to die and raised by wolves; not a thing one normally credits, and yet . . . There was something in the air of the village, the wild distraction of the priest—compounded of fear and triumph—that kept me from inquiring further. I would bide my time.

"As darkness came on the people of the village seemed to be readying themselves for some further brutishness. Pine torches had been lit, leading the way to the dell where the captive was being held. It seemed possible that they planned to burn the fellow alive: any such idea as that of course I must prevent, and quickly.

"Like Machiavel, I chose a combination of force and suasion as best suited to accomplishing my purpose. I stood the men of the village to a quantity of drink at the *taberna,* and I posted my armed Albanians on the path out to the little dell where the captive was. Then I went in peace to see for myself.

"In the flare of the torches I could see the cage, green poles lashed together. I crept slowly to it, not wanting whoever was within to raise an alarm. I felt my heart beat fast, without knowing why it should. As I came close, a dark hand was put out, and took hold of a bar. Something in this hand's action—I cannot say what—was not the action of a man's hand, but of a beast's; what beast, though?

"What reached me next was the smell, a nose-filling rankness that I have never smelled again but would know in a moment. There was something of hurt and fear in it, the smell of an animal that has been wounded and soiled itself; but there was a life history in it too, a ferocious filthiness, something untrammeled and uncaring—well, it's quite impossible, the language has too few words for smells, potent though they be. Now I knew that what was in the cage was not a man; only a furbearer could retain so much odor. And yet: *He speaks,* the priest had said, *and no one understands him.*

"I looked within the cage. I could see nothing at first, though I could hear a labored breath, and felt a poised stillness, the tension of a creature waiting for attack. Then he blinked, and I saw his eyes turned on me.

"You know the eyes of your ancestors, Loukas, the eyes pictured on vases and on the ancientest of statues: those enormous almond-shaped eyes, outlined in black, black-pupiled too, and staring, overflowing with some life other than this world's. Those were his eyes, Greek eyes that no Greek ever had; white at the long corners, with great onyx centers.

"He blinked again, and moved within his cage—his captors had made it too small to stand in, and he must have suffered dreadfully in it—and drew up his legs. He struggled to get some ease, and one foot slid out between the bars below, and nearly touched my knee where I knelt in the dust. And I knew then why it was that he spoke but was not understood."

At first, he said he had thought there must be more than one animal confined in the little cage, his mind unwilling to add together the reaching, twitching foot with its lean shin extended between the bars and the great-eyed hard-breathing personage inside. Cloven: that foot the Christians took from Pan and Pan's sons to give to their Devil. The poet had always taken his own clubbed foot as a sort of sign of his kinship with that race—which, however, along with the rest of modern mankind, he had still supposed to be merely fancies. They were not: not this one, stinking, breathing, waiting for words.

"Now I knew why my heart beat hard. I thought it astonishing but very likely that I alone, of all these Greeks about me here, I alone perhaps of all the mortals in Arcadia that night, knew the language this creature might know: for I had been made to study it, you see, forced with blows and implorings and bribes to learn it through many long years at Harrow. Was that fate? Had our father-god brought me here this night to do this child of his some good?

"I put my face close to the bars of the cage. I was afraid for a moment that all those thousands of lines learned by heart had fled from me. The only one I could think of was not so very appropriate. *Sing, Muse,* I said, *that man of many resources, who traveled far and wide* . . . and his eyes shone. I was right: he spoke the Greek of Homer, and not of these men of the iron age.

"Now what was I to say? He still lay quiet within the cage, but for the one hand gripping the bars, waiting for more. I realized he must be wounded—it seemed obvious that unless he were wounded he could not have been taken. I knew but one thing: I would not willingly be parted from him. I could have remained in his presence nightlong, forever. I sought his white almond eyes in the darkness and I thought: *I have not missed it after all: it awaited me here to find.*

"I would not have all night, though. My Albanians now discharged their weapons—the warning we'd agreed on—and I heard shouts; the men of the village, now suitably inflamed, were headed for this place. I took from my pocket a penknife—all I had—and set to work on the tough hemp of the cage's ropes.

"*Atrema,* I said, *atrema, atrema*—which I remembered was 'quietly, quietly.' He made no sound or movement as I cut, but when I took hold of a bar with my left hand to steady myself, he put out his long black-nailed hand and grasped my wrist. Not in anger, but not tenderly; strongly, purposefully. The hair rose on my neck. He did not release me until the ropes were cut and I tugged apart the bars.

"The moon had risen, and he came forth into its light. He was no taller than a boy of eight, and yet how he drew the night to him, as though it were a thing with a piece missing until he stepped out into it, and now was whole.

I could see that indeed he had been hurt: stripes of blood ran round his bare chest where he had fallen or rolled down a steep declivity. I could see the ridged recurving horns that rose from the matted hair of his head; I could see his sex, big, held up against his belly by a fold of fur, like a dog's or a goat's. Alert, still breathing hard (his breast fluttering, as though the heart within him were huge) he glanced about himself, assessing which way were best to run.

"*Now go,* I said to him. *Live. Take care they do not come near you again. Hide from them when you must; despoil them when you can. Seize on their wives and daughters, piss in their vegetable gardens, tear down their fences, drive mad their sheep and goats. Teach them fear. Never never let them take you again.*

"I say I said this to him, but I confess I could not think of half the words; my Greek had fled me. No matter: he turned his great hot eyes on me as though he understood. What he said back to me I cannot tell you, though he spoke, and smiled; he spoke in a warm winey voice, but a few words, round and sweet. That was a surprise. Perhaps it was from Pan he had his music. I can tell you I have tried to bring those words up often from where I know they are lodged, in my heart of hearts; I think that it is really what I am about when I try to write poems. And now and again—yes, not often, but sometimes—I hear them again.

"He dropped to his hands, then, somewhat as an ape does; he turned and fled, and the tuft of his tail flashed once, like a hare's. At the end of the glen he turned—I could just see him at the edge of the trees—and looked at me. And that was all.

"I sat in the dust there, sweating in the night air. I remember thinking the striking thing about it was how *unpoetical* it had been. It was like no story about a meeting between a man and a god—or a godlet—that I had ever heard. No gift was given me, no promise made me. It was like freeing an otter from a fish trap. And that, most strangely, was what gave me joy in it. The difference, child, between the true gods and the imaginary ones is this: that the true gods are not less real than yourself."

It was deep midnight now in the villa; the tide was out, and rain had begun again to fall, spattering on the roof tiles, hissing in the fire.

It wasn't true, what he had told the boy: that he had been given no gift, made no promise. For it was only after Greece that he came to possess the quality for which, besides his knack for verse, he was chiefly famous: his gift (not always an easy one to live with) for attracting love from many different kinds and conditions of people. He had accepted the love that he attracted, and sought more, and had that too. *Satyr* he had been called, often enough. He thought, when he gave it any thought, that it had come to him through the grip of the horned one: a part of that being's own power of unrefusable ravishment.

Well, if that were so, then he had the gift no more: had used it up, spent it, worn it out. He was thirty-six, and looked and felt far older: sick and lame, his puffy features gray and haggard, his mustache white—foolish to think he could have been the object of Loukas's affection.

But without love, without its wild possibility, he could no longer defend himself against the void: against his black certainty that life mattered not a whit, was a brief compendium of folly and suffering, not worth the stakes. He would not take life on those terms; no, he would trade it for something more valuable . . . for Greece. Freedom. He would like to have given his life heroically, but even the ignoble death he seemed likely now to suffer here, in this mephitic swamp, even that was worth something: was owed, anyway, to the clime that made him a poet: to the blessing he had had.

"I have heard of no reports of such a creature in those mountains since that time," he said. "You know, I think the little gods are the oldest gods, older than the Olympians, older far than Jehovah. Pan forbid he should be dead, if he be the last of his kind . . ."

The firing of Suliote guns outside the villa woke him. He lifted his head painfully from the sweat-damp pillow. He put out his hand and thought for a moment his Newfoundland dog Lion lay at his feet. It was the boy Loukas: asleep.

He raised himself to his elbows. What had he dreamed? What story had he told?

Exogamy

□ □ □

In desperation and black hope he had selected himself for the mission, and now he was to die for his impetuosity, drowned in an amber vinegar sea too thin to swim in. This didn't matter in any large sense; his comrades had seen him off, and would not see him return—the very essence of a hero. In a moment his death wouldn't matter even to himself. Meanwhile he kept flailing helplessly, ashamed of his willingness to struggle.

His head broke the surface into the white air. It had done so now three times; it would not do so again. But a small cloud just then covered him, and something was in the air above his head. Before he sank away out of reach for good, something took hold of him, a flying something, a machine or something with sharp pincers or takers-hold, what would he call them, *claws.*

He was lifted out of the water or fluid or sea. Not his fault the coordinates were off, placing him in liquid and not on dry land instead, these purplish sands; only off by a matter of meters. Far enough to drown or nearly drown him though: he lay for a long time prostrate on the sand where he had been dropped, uncertain which.

He pondered then—when he could ponder again—just what had seized him, borne him up (just barely out of the heaving sea, and laboring mightily at that), and got him to shore. He hadn't yet raised his head to see if whatever it was had stayed with him, or had gone away; and now he thought maybe it would be best to just lie still and be presumed dead. But he looked up.

She squatted a ways up the beach, not watching him, seeming herself to be absorbed in recovering from effort; her wide bony breast heaved. The great wings now folded, like black plush. Talons (*that* was the word, he felt them again and began to shudder) the talons spread to support her in the soft sand. When she stepped, waddled, toward him, seeing he was alive, he crawled away across the sand, trying to get to his feet and unable, until he fell flat again and knew nothing.

Night came.

She (she, it was the breasts prominent on the breastplate muscle, the big delicate face, and vast tangled never-dressed hair that made him suppose it) was upon him when he awoke. He had curled himself into a fetal ball, and she had been sheltering him from the night wind, pressing her long belly against him as she might (probably did) against an egg of her own. It was dangerously cold. She smelled like a mildewed sofa.

For three days they stayed together there on the horrid shingle. In the day she sheltered him from the sun with her pinions and at night drew him close to her odorous person, her rough flesh. Sometimes she flew away heavily (her wings seeming unable to bear her up for more than a few meters, and then the clumsy business of taking off again) and returned with some gobbet of scavenge to feed him. Once a human leg he rejected. She seemed unoffended, seemed not to mind if he ate or not; seemed when she stared at him hourlong with her onyx unhuman eyes to be waiting for his own demise. But then why coddle him so, if coddling was what this was?

He tried (dizzy with catastrophe maybe, or sunstroke) to explain himself to her, unable to suppose she couldn't hear. He had (he said) failed in his quest. He had set out from his sad homeland to find love, a bride, a prize, and bring it back. They had all seen him off, every one of them wishing in his heart that he too had the daring to follow the dream. Love. A woman: a bride of love: a mother of men. Where, in this emptiness?

She listened, cooing now and then (a strange liquid sound, he came to listen for it, it seemed like understanding; he hoped he would hear it last thing before he died, poisoned by her food and this sea of piss). On the third day, he seemed more likely to live. A kind of willingness broke inside him with the dawn. Maybe he could go on. And as though sensing this she ascended with flopping wingbeats into the sun, and sailed to a rocky promontory a kilometer off. There she waited for him.

Nothing but aridity, as far as his own sight reached. But he believed—it made him laugh aloud to find he believed it—that she knew what he hoped, and intended to help him.

But oh God what a dreadful crossing, what sufferings to endure. There was the loneliness of the desert, nearly killing him, and the worse loneliness of having such a companion as this to help him. It was she who sought out the path. It was he who found the waterhole. She sickened, and for the length of a moon he nursed her, he could not have lived now without her, none of these other vermin—mice, snakes—were worth talking to; he fed them to her, and ate what she left. She flew again. They were getting someplace. One bright night of giddy certainty he trod her, like a cock.

Then past the summit of the worst sierra, down the last rubbled pass, there was green land. He could see a haze of evaporating water softening the air, maybe towers in the valley.

Down there (she said, somehow, by signs and gestures and his own words in her coos, she made it anyway clear) there is a realm over which a queen rules. No one has yet won her, though she has looked far for one who could.

He rubbed his hands together. His heart was full. Only the brave (he said) deserve the fair.

He left her there, at the frontier (he guessed) of her native wild. He strode down the pass, looking back now and then, ashamed a little of abandoning her but hoping she understood. Once when he looked back she was gone. Flown.

It was a nice country. Pleasant populace easily won over by good manners and an honest heart. That's the castle, there, that white building under the feet of whose towers you see a strip of sunset sky. That one. Good luck.

Token resistance at the gates, but he gave better than he got. She would be found, of course, in the topmost chamber, surmounting these endless stairs, past these iron-bound henchmen (why always, always so hard? He thought of the boys back home, who had passed on all this). He reached and broached the last door; he stepped out onto the topmost parapet, littered with bones, fetid with pale guano. A vast shabby nest of sticks and nameless stuff.

She alighted just then, in her gracile-clumsy way, and folded up.

Did you guess? she asked.

No, he had not; his heart was black with horror and understanding; he should have guessed, of course, but hadn't. He felt the talons of her attention close upon him, inescapable; he turned away with a cry and stared down the great height of the tower. Should he jump?

If you do, I will fall after you (she said) and catch you up, and bring you back.

He turned to her to say his heart could never be hers.

You could go on, she said softly.

He looked away again, not down but out, toward the far lands beyond the fields and farms. He could go on.

What's over there? he asked. Beyond those yellow mountains? What makes that plume of smoke?

I've never gone there. Never that far. We could, she said.

Well hell, he said. For sure I can't go back. Not with—not now.

Come on, she said, and pulled herself to the battlements with grasping talons; she squatted there, lowering herself for him to mount.

It could be worse, he thought, and tiptoed through the midden to her; but before he took his seat upon her, he thought with sudden awful grief: *She'll die without me.*

He meant the one he had for so long loved, since boyhood, she for whose sake he had first set out, whoever she was; the bride at the end of his quest, still waiting. And he about to head off in another direction entirely.

You want to drive? she said.

The farms and fields, the malls and highways, mountains and cities, no end in sight that way.

You drive, he said.

Lost and Abandoned

■ ■ ■

I. Lost

THE LOGIC WAS PERFECT AND COMPLETE; there was a beginning, a middle, and an end. The beginning was love, then came marriage, then two children even before I got out of graduate school and got a real job. There was even a baby carriage, a real one, the blue-black kind with great rubber wheels, chrome brightwork, and a brougham top with a silver scroll on the side to raise and lower it. I wonder where it is now..

The next story element, therefore, was divorce. She with the kids, I with the job (it wasn't logical but as a story element it has verisimilitude, meaning that it was always done that way then). I taught. I taught American poetry to children, to college students, and over time began to forget why. I thought about it a lot; I did little else but reason out why I did what I did, and whether it was useless or not, why they should be interested, why I should try to capture their attention.

None of this intellection helped my chances for tenure. The word was that I wasn't a team player; I wasn't. I was an Atom. I had no reason beyond physics for anything that I did.

Then she showed up again. With the kids, she and he. She had a lot of plans. She was moving, she told me, to Hawaii. She'd already shipped over her cycle, and the rest of the guys were waiting for her over there. The kids were going to love it, she said. Water and fishing and cycles.

And when would I see them?

Whenever you can come out.

Money?

Somebody had told her somebody was opening a speed shop in Maui and she might work there.

It's odd how quickly two people who have seemed to be practically one person since before they were wholly out of childhood can diverge as soon as they part. I was awake most of that night, lying beside her (old times' sake), and by dawn I'd made a decision. I wanted the kids. She couldn't take them. She said she sure as hell was taking them. I said that I would take her to court and get custody before any judge: I worked, I was a college teacher, I had a suit and tie, she was a biker, or could be made to seem one. It might not have been true, that it would have been so easy; but I made her believe it. She wept; she talked it out; she hugged them a lot; she left them with me.

And when I went back to classes in September I had, instantly, a reason to teach American poetry to adolescents, and do it well, too. Love costs money; so love makes money, or is willing to try. What I could not find a reason for doing in itself became quite easy to do when I did it for them. I went and talked all day about Emily Dickinson and Walt Whitman to put bowls of oatmeal before them, bicycles in the garage for them. And oddest of all (maybe not so odd, how would I know, I've only done all this once) I think I was a better teacher, too.

Unfortunately I had stumbled into all this—ordinary life, I guess, the thing that had kept all of my colleagues at their work and playing for the team—just that little bit too late. Despite my new need and my new willingness, I got turned down for tenure. And that in academe being equivalent to dismissal, I now looked into a kind of abyss, one I had heard about, read about, been touched by in stories, and had not thought was possible for me to encounter, though a moment's thought would have told me that countless men and women live facing it all the time.

Did I think of shipping them to Hawaii? No, never. Some doors cannot be gone back through.

So the next scene is the dark of the woods.

I used all my contacts to get a job that almost no one, it would seem, would want to have, thereby entering into another level of this thing, where the hewer of wood, the drawer of water, grows desperate not for release but for more water to draw, wood to hew, so his kids and he won't have to beg.

An inner-city enrichment program for no-longer-quite-youthful offenders, which had tenuous state funding and a three-story house downtown that had been seized for taxes. They were given courses in basic English and other work toward a high-school equivalency diploma, and seminars in ethics and self-expression. They got time off their probation for attending faithfully. Do you have better ideas?

The group I taught English to was about the same age as my old students, a group who had appeared ordinary enough then but now in hindsight and from here appeared as young godlings awash in ease and possibility. Days we worked on acquiring the sort of English language in which newspapers and books and government documents are written, a language different from the one most of them spoke, though using many similar words. We diagrammed sentences, a thing I am the last teacher of English on the continent to remember how to do; they liked that. In the evenings we met again. We were going to write stories.

They have stories, certainly. They tend to spill them rather than tell them. It seemed grotesque to try to chasten them, and make them shapely, make them resemble good stories; but that's what I was hired to do, and simply to listen is too hard. "A beginning, a middle, and an end," I say. " 'The king died and then the queen died' is a story. 'The king died and then the queen died of grief' is a plot. Who, what, when, where, how." And they listen, looking at me from out of their own stories, inside which they live, as street people live within their ragged shelters. Not one grew up with a father: not one. I know what crimes some of them committed, what they have done.

Late at night then I bus over to the adjacent neighborhood, one small step up in the social ladder, and climb the stairs to my apartment; let myself in, awake the sitter, asleep before the glowing television, and send her home.

They grow so fast. In the city even faster. Most of my salary goes to their private school, called fatuously the Little Big Schoolhouse, but really a good place; they love it, or did. They're getting restive, weirdly angry sometimes in ways they never were before, which leaves me hurt and baffled and desperately afraid. They don't want sitters anymore. I am going to come home and find them gone; or find one of them gone and the other silent, looking at me in reproach, can't have her, couldn't keep her.

"Let's retell a story," I told my students. "Just to get our chops. We'll all write the same story. Not long. Three pages max. A story you all know. All you have to do is tell it, from beginning to end, not leaving anything important out."

But it was not a story they all knew, and so I had to tell it to them. They listened with both eyes and ears, as my children had once. My own son, at the point in the story when the two lost children understood that the new protector they had found intended them not good but mortal harm, had cried out *It's their mother!* Which seemed to me to be an act of literary criticism of the highest order; and for the first time I noticed that indeed the mother, like the other, is dead at the story's end.

A girl named Cyntra wanted to know: Was I going to do this, too?

I said yes I would. I would do it in three pages. I hadn't thought of doing it but yes I would.

I know this story. I know it now, though I didn't before. I will write mine for me, as they will write theirs for themselves; we will trade them and try to read them with eyes and ears.

Three pieces of mail in the box on this night when I got home. A postcard from Hawaii. An official letter telling me that the enrichment program is being zeroed out, and my services will not be required. An answer to my personal ad in the *Free Press*, written in a clear strong hand. A picture, too.

My children still there, asleep but not undressed, unwashed and sprawled over the couch and the floor: they would not permit a baby-sitter, said they could take care of themselves. They are at least still here.

I will write my story with a beginning, a middle, and no end. No bread crumbs, no candy, no woods, no oven, no treasure. No who, what, where, when. And it will all be there.

Where will they go, those kids?

■ ■ ■

II. Abandoned

POVERTY IS NOT A CRIME. *Infatuation is not a crime either; and when a man who has loved his wife dearly, and had two children with her, boy and girl, children he loves deeply and in whose eyes he sees her every single day—when that man falls helplessly in love again, those children might find it in their hearts, if not then perhaps later on, after a period of transition, to forgive him. And to love this new woman, too, as he loves her, without ever forgetting—as he himself cannot—the other and earlier woman.*

Children, though, spring from but one mother; and they, even if they cannot remember her, can't forget her either. The fact that he can see in their eyes the reflection of the woman who bore them can come to seem a reproach. Perhaps it is a reproach. That's certainly the way the woman who comes to replace her in their home might see it: a constant reproach, a claim never able to be made good and yet never withdrawn. And it's possible that—she being as infatuated as he, filled up with that domineering love that allows no rival (no crime; it happens); might scheme somehow to remove them, shut their eyes, shut their mouths for good. Especially if there weren't enough for all of them.

*Was it a crime that he listened, that he chose between her and them?
That was a crime, and he knew it when he abandoned them. Abandoned:
went away from them when he thought they could not return, though at
the same time he brought them back with him, of course, he would have
to, have to bring them with him back home where they would trouble his
sleep thereafter.*

*But we are always abandoned. We abandon our parents as we grow,
and yet it seems to us that they abandon us; that's the story we tell. And
often—usually, not always—we discover that abandonment is flight, too:
our flight away. We leave a trail to guide us back, but it can disappear
behind us as we go on.*

*Harder than it seems, abandonment; they who are to be abandoned
are often more resourceful than we who abandon expect them to be or than
the act or the name of the act (abandonment) allows them to be. Often
enough they will not suffer being abandoned, must be shed or forced out
or tricked into remaining behind when we go. Often they must be abandoned not once but more than once, each act of abandoning hardening our
hearts further, until in the end the logistics of the deed are all we can think
of, the awful logic, just get it over with.*

*Abandonment implies redemption, the finding of the lost, not always
but sometimes: safety discovered in the midst of danger, altering the new
equation of loss and abandonment again, and posing a question usually,
a judgment to make though we aren't wise enough to make it; we make it
anyway because we have no choice. Look how wonderful, all sweet, all
good, and we so hungry and needy.*

*Finding out then that we have made a wrong decision, the worst pos-
sible decision, one we can't help having made and that we know as soon
as we have made it was the wrong one, and that it can't be taken back.
Finding out that this is what abandonment means: death at the hands of
those we have relied on. They taught us to rely on them, on the two of*

them, their love, and then abandoned us: but still we only know how to rely on others, and have done so, and we were wrong, and now we will die. We didn't know this about life.

Only perhaps it isn't death, perhaps there is an exit from the cage, the death; perhaps we know better than we thought. Perhaps we have ourselves got reserves of cleverness, and will, and cruelty. Yes we have. We, too, can fool. We can do as we have been done by. And it is abandonment that taught us.

So this is life not death after all. It's even profit. We didn't know this about life either, what can be won from it by need and the willingness to be cunning, and cruel.

It was a long time ago. You find that even if you have lost the way home there is a path that reaches out to you from there, a path that you are bound to discover like it or not: and then, when you return there with what you have won, it isn't the place you left. You can forgive them, if they are still there to forgive: or you can refuse to. What you did and learned from abandonment—yours of them, theirs of you—has made home different. Now you can go or stay.

GONE

□ □ □

ELMERS AGAIN.

You waited in a sort of exasperated amusement for yours, thinking that if you had been missed last time yours would likely be among the households selected this time, though how that process of selection went on no one knew, you only knew that a new capsule had been detected entering the atmosphere (caught by one of the thousand spy satellites and listening-and-peering devices that had been trained on the big Mother Ship in orbit around the moon for the past year) and though the capsule had apparently burned up in the atmosphere, that's just what had happened the time before, and then elmers everywhere. You could hope that you'd be skipped or passed over—there were people who had been skipped last time when all around them neighbors and friends had been visited or afflicted, and who would appear now and then and be interviewed on the news, though having nothing, after all, to say, it was the rest of us who had the stories—but in any case you started looking out the windows, down the drive, listening for the doorbell to ring in the middle of the day.

Pat Poynton didn't need to look out the window of the kid's bedroom where she was changing the beds, the only window from which the front door could be seen, when her doorbell rang in the middle of the day. She could almost hear, subliminally, every second doorbell on Ponader Drive, every second doorbell in South Bend go off just at that moment. She thought: *Here's mine.*

They had come to be called elmers (or Elmers) all over this country at least after David Brinkley had told a story on a talk show about how when they built the World's Fair in New York in 1939, it was thought that people out in the country, people in places like Dubuque and Rapid City and South Bend, wouldn't think of making a trip east and paying five dollars to see all the wonders, that maybe the great show wasn't for the likes of them; and so the fair's promoters hired a bunch of people, ordinary-looking men with ordinary clothes wearing ordinary glasses and bow ties, to fan out to places like Vincennes and Austin and Brattleboro and just talk it up. Pretend to be ordinary folks who had been to the fair, and hadn't been high-hatted, no sirree, had a wonderful time, the wife too, and b'gosh had Seen the Future and could tell you the sight was worth the five dollars they were asking, which wasn't so much since it included tickets to all the shows and lunch. And all these men, whatever their real names were, were all called Elmer by the promoters who sent them out.

Pat wondered what would happen if she just didn't open the door. Would it eventually go away? It surely wouldn't push its way in, mild and blobby as it was (from the upstairs window she could see that it was the same as the last ones) and that made her wonder how after all they had all got inside—as far as she knew there weren't many who had failed to get at least a hearing. Some chemical hypnotic maybe that they projected, calming fear. What Pat felt standing at the top of the stair and listening to the doorbell pressed again (timidly, she thought, tentatively, hopefully) was amused exasperation, just like everyone else's: a sort of oh-Christ-no with a burble of wonderment just below it, and even expectation: for who wouldn't be at least intrigued by the prospect of his, or her, own lawn mower, snow shoveler, hewer of wood, and drawer of water, for as long as it lasted?

"Mow your lawn?" it said when Pat opened the door. "Take out trash? Mrs. Poynton?"

Now actually in its presence, looking at it through the screen door, Pat felt most strongly a new part of the elmer feeling: a giddy revulsion she had not expected. It was so not human. It seemed to have been constructed to resemble a human being by other sorts of beings who were not human and did not understand very well what would count as human with other humans. When it spoke its mouth moved (*mouth hole must move when speech is produced*) but the sound seemed to come from somewhere else, or from nowhere.

"Wash your dishes? Mrs. Poynton?"

"No," she said, as citizens had been instructed to say. "Please go away. Thank you very much."

Of course the elmer didn't go away, only stood bobbing slightly on the doorstep like a foolish child whose White Rose salve or Girl Scout cookies haven't been bought.

"Thank you very much," it said, in tones like her own. "Chop wood? Draw water?"

"Well gee," Pat said, and, helplessly, smiled.

What everyone knew, besides the right response to give to the elmer, which everyone gave and almost no one was able to stick to, was that these weren't the creatures or beings from the Mother Ship itself up above (so big you could see it, pinhead sized, crossing the face of the affronted moon) but some kind of creation of theirs, sent down in advance. An artifact, the official word was; some sort of protein, it was guessed; some sort of chemical process at the heart of it or head of it, maybe a DNA-based computer or something equally outlandish, but no one knew because of the way the first wave of them, flawed maybe, fell apart so quickly, sinking and melting like the snowmen they sort of resembled after a week or two of mowing lawns and washing dishes and pestering people with their Good Will Ticket, shriveling into a sort of dry flocked matter and then into nearly nothing at all, like cotton candy in the mouth.

"Good Will Ticket?" said the elmer at Pat Poynton's door, holding out to her a tablet of something not paper, on which was written or printed or anyway somehow indited a little message. Pat didn't read it, didn't need to, you had the message memorized by the time you opened your door to a second-wave elmer like Pat's. Sometimes lying in bed in the morning in the bad hour before the kids had to be got up for school Pat would repeat like a prayer the little message that everybody in the world it seemed was going to be presented with sooner or later:

> GOOD WILL
> YOU MARK BELOW
> ALL ALL RIGHT WITH LOVE AFTERWARDS
> WHY NOT SAY YES
> ☐ YES

And no space for No, which meant—if it was a sort of vote (and experts and officials, though how such a thing could have been determined Pat didn't know, were guessing that's what it was), a vote to allow or to accept the arrival or descent of the Mother Ship and its unimaginable occupants or passengers—that you could only refuse to take it from the elmer: shaking your head firmly and saying No clearly but politely, because even *taking* a Good Will Ticket might be the equivalent of a Yes, and though what it would be a Yes *to* exactly no one knew, there was at least a ground swell of opinion in the think tanks that it meant acceding to or at least not resisting World Domination.

You weren't, however, supposed to shoot your elmer. In places like Idaho and Siberia that's what they were doing, you heard, though a bullet or two didn't seem to make any difference to them, they went on pierced with holes like characters in the Dick Tracy comics of long ago, smiling shyly in at your windows, Rake your leaves? Yard work? Pat Poynton was sure that Lloyd would not hesitate to shoot, would be pretty glad that at last something living or at least moving and a certified threat to freedom had at last got before him to be aimed at. In the hall-table drawer Pat still had Lloyd's 9mm Glock pistol; he had let her know he wanted to come get it but he wasn't getting back into this house, she'd use it on him herself if he got close enough.

Not really, no, she wouldn't. And yet.

"Wash windows?" the elmer now said.

"Windows," Pat said, feeling a little of the foolish self-consciousness people feel who are inveigled by comedians or MCs into having conversations with puppets, wary in the same way too, the joke very likely being on her. "You do windows?"

It only bobbed before her like a big water toy.

"Okay," she said, and her heart filled. "Okay come on in."

Amazing how graceful it really was; it seemed to navigate through the house and the furniture as though it were negatively charged to them, the way it drew close to the stove or the refrigerator and then was repelled gently away, avoiding collision. It seemed to be able to compact or compress itself too, make itself smaller in small spaces, grow again to full size in larger spaces.

Pat sat down on the couch in the family room, and watched. It just wasn't possible to do anything else but watch. Watch it take the handle of a bucket; watch it open the tops of bottles of cleansers, and seem to inhale their odors to identify them; take up the squeegee and cloth she found for it. *The world, the universe,* Pat thought (it was the thought almost everyone thought who was just then taking a slow seat on his or her davenport in his or her family room or in his or her vegetable garden or junkyard or wherever and watching a second-wave elmer get its bearings and get down to work): *how big the world, the universe is, how strange; how lucky I am to have learned it, to be here now seeing this.*

So the world's work, its odd jobs anyway, were getting done as the humans who usually did them sat and watched, all sharing the same feelings of gratitude and glee, and not only because of the chores being done: it was that wonder, that awe, a universal neap tide of common feeling such as had never been experienced before, not by this species, not anyway since the days on the old old veldt when every member of it could share the same joke, the same dawn, the same amazement. Pat Poynton, watching hers, didn't hear the beebeep of the school-bus horn.

Most days she started watching the wall clock and her wrist-watch alternately a good half-hour before the bus's horn could be expected to be heard, like an anxious sleeper who continually awakes to check his alarm clock to see how close it has come to going off. Her arrangement with the driver was that he wouldn't let her kids off before tooting. He promised. She hadn't explained why.

But today the sounding of the horn had sunk away deeply into her backbrain, maybe three minutes gone, when Pat at last reheard it or remembered having heard and not noticed it. She leapt to her feet, an awful certainty seizing her; she was out the door as fast as her heartbeat accelerated, and was coming down the front steps just in time to see down at the end of the block the kids disappearing into and slamming the door of Lloyd's classic Camaro (whose macho rumble Pat now realized she had also been hearing for some minutes). The cherry-red muscle car, Lloyd's other and more beloved wife, blew exhaust from double pipes that stirred the gutter's leaves, and leapt forward as though kicked.

She shrieked, and spun around, seeking help; there was no one in the street. Two steps at a time, maddened and still crying out, she went up the steps and into the house, tore at the pretty little Hitchcock phone table, the phone spilling in parts, the table's legs leaving the floor, its jaw dropping, and the Glock 9mm nearly falling out: Pat caught it and was out the door with it and down the street calling out her ex-husband's full name, coupled with imprecations and obscenities her neighbors had never heard her utter before, but the Camaro was of course out of hearing and sight by then.

Gone. Gone gone gone. The world darkened and the sidewalk tilted up toward her as though to smack her face. She was on her knees, not knowing how she had got to them, also not knowing whether she would faint or vomit.

She did neither, and after a time got to her feet. How had this gun, heavy as a hammer, got in her hand? She went back in the house and restored it to the raped little table, and bent to put the phone, which was whimpering urgently, back together.

She couldn't call the police; he'd said—in the low soft voice he used when he wanted to sound implacable and dangerous and just barely controlled, eyes rifling threat at her—that if she got the police involved in his family he'd kill all of them. She didn't entirely believe it, didn't entirely believe anything he said, but he had said it. She didn't believe the whole Christian survivalist thing he was supposedly into, thought he would not probably take them to a cabin in the woods to live off elk as he had threatened or promised, would probably get no farther than his mother's house with them.

Please Lord let it be so.

The elmer hovered grinning in her peripheral vision like an accidental guest in a crisis as she banged from room to room, getting her coat on and taking it off again, sitting to sob at the kitchen table, searching yelling for the cordless phone, where the hell had it been put this time. She called her mother, and wept. Then, heart thudding hard, she called his. One thing you didn't know, about elmers (Pat thought this while she waited for her mother-in-law's long cheery phone-machine message to get over) was whether they were like cleaning ladies and handymen, and you were obliged not to show your feelings around them; or whether you were allowed to let go, as with a pet. Abstract question, since she had already.

The machine beeped, and began recording her silence. She punched the phone off without speaking.

Toward evening she got the car out at last and drove across town to Mishiwaka. Her mother-in-law's house was unlit, and there was no car in the garage. She watched a long time, till it was near dark, and came back. There ought to have been elmers everywhere, mowing lawns, taptapping with hammers, pulling wagonloads of kids. She saw none.

Her own was where she had left it. The windows gleamed as though coated with silver film.

"What?" she asked it. "You want something to do?" The elmer bounced a little in readiness, and put out its chest—so, Pat thought, to speak—and went on smiling. "Bring back my kids," she said. "Go find them and bring them back."

It seemed to hesitate, bobbing between setting off on the job it had been given and turning back to refuse or maybe to await further explanation; it showed Pat its three-fingered cartoon hands, fat and formless. You knew, about elmers, that they would not take vengeance for you, or right wrongs. People had asked, of course they had. People wanted angels, avenging angels; believed they deserved them. Pat too: she knew now that she wanted hers, wanted it right now.

She stared it down for a time, resentful; then she said forget it, sorry, just a joke sort of; there's nothing really to do, just forget it, nothing more to do. She went past it, stepping first to one side as it did too and then to the other side; when she got by she went into the bathroom and turned on the water in the sink full force, and after a moment did finally throw up, a wrenching heave that produced nothing but pale sputum.

Toward midnight she took a couple of pills and turned on the TV.

What she saw immediately was two spread-eagled sky divers circling each other in the middle of the air, their orange suits rippling sharply in the wind of their descent. They drifted closer together, put gloved hands on each other's shoulders. Earth lay far below them, like a map. The announcer said it wasn't known just what happened, or what grievances they had, and at that moment one clouted the other in the face. Then he was grabbed by the other. Then the first grabbed the second. Then they flipped over in the air, each with an arm around the other's neck in love or rage, their other arms arm wrestling in the air, or dancing, each keeping the other from releasing his chute. The announcer said thousands on the ground watched in horror, and indeed now Pat heard them, an awful moan or shriek from a thousand people, a noise that sounded just like awed satisfaction, as the two sky divers—locked, the announcer said, in deadly combat—shot toward the ground. The helicopter camera lost them and the ground camera picked them up, like one being, four legs thrashing; it followed them almost to the ground, when people rose up suddenly before the lens and cut off the view: but the crowd screamed, and someone right next to the camera said *What the hell*.

Pat Poynton had already seen these moments, seen them a couple of times. They had broken into the soaps with them. She pressed the remote. Demonic black men wearing outsize clothing and black glasses threatened her, moving to a driving beat and stabbing their forefingers at her. She pressed again. Police on a city street, her own city she learned, drew a blanket over someone shot. The dark stain on the littered street. Pat thought of Lloyd. She thought she glimpsed an elmer on an errand far off down the street, bobbing around a corner.

Press again.

That soothing channel where Pat often watched press conferences or speeches, awaking sometimes from half-sleep to find the meeting over or a new one begun, the important people having left or not yet arrived, the backs of milling reporters and government people who talked together in low voices. Just now a senator with white hair and a face of exquisite sadness was speaking on the Senate floor. "I apologize to the gentleman," he said. "I wish to withdraw the word *snotty*. I should not have said it. What I meant by that word was: arrogant, unfeeling, self-regarding; supercilious; meanly relishing the discomfiture of your opponents and those hurt by your success. But I should not have said *snotty*. I withdraw *snotty*."

She pressed again, and the two sky divers again fell toward earth.

What's wrong with us? Pat Poynton thought.

She stood, black instrument in her hand, a wave of nausea seizing her again. *What's wrong with us?* She felt as though she were drowning in a tide of cold mud, unstoppable; she wanted not to be here any longer, here amid this. She knew she did not, hadn't ever, truly belonged here at all. Her being here was some kind of dreadful sickening mistake.

"Good Will Ticket?"

She turned to face the great thing, gray now in the TV's light. It held out the little plate or tablet to her. *All all right with love afterwards*. There was no reason at all in the world not to.

"All right," she said. "All right."

It brought the ticket closer, held it up. It now seemed to be not something it carried but a part of its flesh. She pressed her thumb against the square beside the YES. The little tablet yielded slightly to her pressure, like one of those nifty buttons on new appliances that feel, themselves, like flesh to press. Her vote registered, maybe.

The elmer didn't alter, or express satisfaction or gratitude, or express anything except the meaningless delight it had been expressing, if that's the word, from the start. Pat sat again on the couch, and turned off the television. She pulled the afghan (his mother had made it) from the back of the couch and wrapped herself in it. She felt the calm euphoria of having done something irrevocable, though what exactly she had done she didn't know. She slept there a while, the pills having grown importunate in her bloodstream at last; lay in the constant streetlight that tiger-striped the room, watched over by the unstilled elmer till gray dawn broke.

In her choice, in the suddenness of it, what could almost be described as the insouciance of it if it had not been experienced as so urgent, Pat Poynton was not unique or even unusual. Worldwide, polls showed, voting was running high against life on earth as we know it, and in favor of whatever it was that your YES was said to, about which opinions differed. The alecks of TV smart and otherwise detailed the rising numbers, and an agreement seemed to have been reached among them all, an agreement shared in by government officials and the writers of newspaper editorials, to describe this craven unwillingness to resist as a sign of decay, social sickness, repellently nonhuman behavior: the newspeople reported the trend toward mute surrender and knuckling under with the same faces they used for the relaying of stories about women who drowned their children or men who shot their wives to please their lovers, or of snipers in faraway places who brought down old women out gathering firewood: and yet what was actually funny to see (funny to Pat and those like her who had already felt the motion of the soul, the bone-weariness too, that made the choice so obvious) was that in their smooth tanned faces was another look never before seen there, seen before only on the faces of the rest of us, in our own faces: a look for which Pat Poynton anyway had no name but knew very well, a kind of stricken longing: like, she thought, the bewildered look you see in kids' faces when they come to you for help.

It was true that a certain disruption of the world's work was becoming evident, a noticeable trend toward giving up, leaving the wheel, dropping the ball. People spent less time getting to the job, more time looking upward. But just as many now felt themselves more able to buckle down, by that principle according to which you get to work and clean your house before the cleaning lady comes. The elmers had been sent, surely, to demonstrate that peace and cooperation were better than fighting and selfishness and letting the chores pile up for others to do.

For soon they were gone again. Pat Poynton's began to grow a little listless almost as soon as she had signed or marked or accepted her Good Will Ticket, and by evening next day, though it had by then completed a list of jobs Pat had long since compiled but in her heart had never believed she would get around to, it had slowed distinctly. It went on smiling and nodding, like an old person in the grip of dementia, even as it began dropping tools and bumping into walls, and finally Pat, unwilling to witness its dissolution and not believing she was obliged to, explained (in the somewhat overdistinct way we speak to not real bright teenage baby-sitters or newly hired help who have just arrived from else-where and don't speak good English) that she had to go out and pick up a few things and would be back soon; and then she drove aimlessly out of town and up toward Michigan for a couple of hours.

Found herself standing at length on the dunes overlooking the lake, the dunes where she and Lloyd had first. But he had not been the only one; he was only the last of a series that seemed for a moment both long and sad. Chumps. Herself too, fooled bad, not once or twice either.

Far off, where the shore of the silver water curved, she could see a band of dark firs, the northern woods maybe beginning. Where he had gone or threatened to go. Lloyd had been part of a successful class-action suit against the company where he'd worked and where everybody had come down with Sick Building Syndrome, Lloyd being pissed off enough (though not ever really deeply affected as far as Pat could ever tell) to hold out with a rump group for a higher settlement, which they got, too, that was what got him the classic Camaro and the twenty acres of Michigan woods. And lots of time to think.

Bring them back, you bastard, she thought; at the same time thinking that it was her, that she should not have done what she did, or should have done what she did not do; that she loved her kids too much, or not enough.

They would bring her kids back; she had become very sure of that, fighting down every rational impulse to question it. She had voted for an inconceivable future, but she had voted for it for only one reason: it would contain—had to contain—everything she had lost. Everything she wanted. That's what the elmers stood for.

She came back at nightfall, and found the weird deflated spill of it strung out through the hallway and (why?) halfway down the stairs to the rec room, like the aftermath of a foam fire-extinguisher accident, smelling (Pat thought, others described it differently) like buttered toast; and she called the 800 number we all had memorized.

And then nothing. There were no more of them, if you had been missed you now waited in vain for the experience that had happened to nearly everyone else, uncertain why you had been excluded but able to claim that you, at least, would not have succumbed to their blandishments; and soon after, it became apparent that there would be no more, no matter how well they would be received, because the Mother Ship or whatever exactly it was that was surely their origin also went away: not *away* in any trackable or pursuable direction, just away, becoming less distinct on the various tracking and spying devices, producing less data, fibrillating, becoming see-through finally and then unable to be seen. Gone. Gone gone gone.

And what then had we all acceded to, what had we betrayed ourselves and our leadership for, abandoning all our daily allegiances and our commitments so carelessly? Around the world we were asking that, the kind of question that results in those forlorn religions of the abandoned and forgotten, those who have been expecting big divine things any moment and then find out they are going to get nothing but a long, maybe a more than lifelong, wait and a blank sky overhead. If their goal had been to make us just dissatisfied, restless, unable to do anything at all but wait to see what would now become of us, then perhaps they had succeeded; but Pat Poynton was certain they had made a promise, and would keep it: the universe was not so strange, so unlikely, that such a visitation could occur and come to nothing. Like many others she lay awake looking up into the night sky (so to speak, up into the ceiling of her bedroom in her house on Ponader Drive, above or beyond which the night sky lay) and said over to herself the little text she had assented or agreed to: *Good will. You mark below. All all right with love afterwards. Why not say yes?*

At length she got up, and belted her robe around her; she went down the stairs (the house so quiet, it had been quiet with the kids and Lloyd asleep in their beds when she had used to get up at five and make instant coffee and wash and dress to get to work but this was quieter) and put her parka on over her robe; she went out barefoot into the backyard.

Not night any longer but a clear October dawn, so clear the sky looked faintly green, and the air perfectly still: the leaves falling nonetheless around her, letting go one by one, two by two, after hanging on till now.

God how beautiful, more beautiful somehow than it had been before she decided she didn't belong here; maybe she had been too busy trying to belong here to notice.

All all right with love afterwards. When though did afterwards start? When?

There came to her as she stood there a strange noise, far off and high up, a noise that she thought sounded like the barking of some dog pack, or maybe the crying of children let out from school, except that it wasn't either of those things; for a moment she let herself believe (this was the kind of mood a lot of people were understandably in) that this was it, the inrush or onrush of what-ever it was that had been promised. Then out of the north a sort of smudge or spreading dark ripple came over the sky, and Pat saw that overhead a big flock of geese was passing, and the cries were theirs, though seeming too loud and coming from somewhere else or from everywhere.

Going south. A great ragged V spread out over half the sky.

"Long way," she said aloud, envying them their flight, their escape; and thinking then no they were not escaping, not from earth, they were of earth, born and raised, would die here, were just doing their duty, calling out maybe to keep their spirits up. Of earth as she was.

She got it then, as they passed overhead, a gift somehow of their passage, though how she could never trace afterwards, only that whenever she thought of it she would think also of those geese, those cries, of encouragement or joy or whatever they were. She got it: in pressing her Good Will Ticket (she could see it in her mind, in the poor dead elmer's hand) she had not acceded or given in to something, not capitulated or surrendered, none of us had though we thought so and even hoped so: no she had made a promise.

"Well yes," she said, a sort of plain light going on in her back-brain, in many another too just then in many places, so many that it might have looked—to someone or something able to perceive it, someone looking down on us and our earth from far above and yet able to perceive each of us one by one—like lights coming on across a darkened land, or like the bright pinpricks that mark the growing numbers of Our Outlets on a TV map, but that were actu-ally our brains, *getting it* one by one, brightening momentarily, as the edge of dawn swept westward.

They had not made a promise, *she* had: good will. She had said yes. And if she kept that promise it would all be all right, with love, afterwards: as right as it could be.

"Yes," she said again, and she raised her eyes to the sky, so vacant, more vacant now than before. Not a betrayal but a prom-ise; not a letting-go but a taking-hold. Good only for as long as we, all alone here, kept it. *All all right with love afterwards.*

Why had they come, why had they gone to such effort, to tell us that, when we knew it all along? Who cared that much, to come to tell us? Would they come back, ever, to see how we'd done?

She went back inside, the dew icy on her feet. For a long time she stood in the kitchen (the door unshut behind her) and then went to the phone.

He answered on the second ring. He said hello. All the unshed tears of the last weeks, of her whole life probably, rose up in one awful bolus in her throat; she wouldn't weep though, no not yet.

"Lloyd," she said. "Lloyd, listen. We have to talk."

An Earthly Mother
Sits and Sings

◻ ◻ ◻

In a far frae land

When she turned away from the seaward windows and looked through the window that faced the rocky way leading down toward the village she could see that someone was coming up toward the house. He was having some difficulty; at times the rainy wind snatched away his cloak entirely and he seemed on the point of taking flight, but he hauled it in and wrapped it around himself again, and, pulling himself up on stones and planting his feet heavily, he made progress up toward her. The rippled diamond panes of the mullioned window, streaked with rain, made the little figure seem to shift size and nature continually; sometimes when the wind threw a mighty slew across the window he disappeared from view entirely, as though he had been drowned.

Cormac, she thought. He was coming all the way up from the village to tell her what she already knew: that was like him. She, who always knew first whatever happened in the surrounding country and on the sea, because her house stood high up above the village and surveyed not only the road that wound down from the hills to the east but the sea road and the long spit of beach as well; she who had little to do but watch, anyway. Yet he would always come to her with the cold news. That a curragh, which had gone out with four brothers in it, had come back on the tide, stove in and empty, and lay overturned on the beach. That a line of English soldiery was coming from the east, with pieces of ordnance and a man in armor at its head. "Yes, Cormac," she would say patiently, for she had seen them already at dawn, and counted their cannon, and seen the armor glint in the red sun. It was only that he loved her, not that he was an idle gossip; the fiction that he was bringing her news was understood by both of them for what it was, and she didn't dislike him for it. Yet she did feel, as she turned away from the window, a small irritation. Why hadn't he more sense than to climb up here uselessly in a storm?

Out the seaward windows she could see that the great ships were coming, helplessly, nearer the shore. The black, white-fringed waves rose so high that now and then the ships were lost to sight entirely, as though swamped and sunk already, but then they would appear again: one, a fleck of white sail only, far off; the other due west and straining to keep to the open sea; and the third, seeming to have surrendered to its awful fate, nearest the land, near enough for her to see the red crosses on its sails, and its shrouds torn away and waving rhythmically, or was it only the spray of rain cast off its spars as it creased the storm? The waves that bore it landward seemed to rise with an unreal slowness, like the great crushing waves that sometimes rose in her dreams; they seemed to rise endlessly, black glass circled with pools of froth, each one shattering against the tormented beach only at that last moment before its movement upward would become unceasing and it would rise up and drown the world.

She, who had watched the sea most of her life, had never seen a catastrophe anything like this one, had never seen the sea attempt to destroy men on such a scale. She had seen storms as bad, and worse, but they spent themselves against the land, which she knew could always bear it. And the sea even in a mood of mild petulance could kill the fishermen of the village, singly or in pairs, and suck their curraghs to its bottom; and then she would feel a sickening anger at the unfairness of the sea. But she had never seen ships the size of these galleons, like mansions put to sea. There would be dozens of men aboard them; she could see now, with a thrill of terror, that tiny men actually clung to the masts and rigging of the nearest ship, trying to cut loose the luffing sails large as meadows, and as the sea canted the ship over suddenly, one man was flung into the sea.

What should she feel? Pity for them? She couldn't. Horror at the destruction of the floating castles? The pride of them, even in destruction, forbade it. She could only watch, fascinated, the two monstrosities, sea and galleon, contend.

The same winds that carried the ships toward shore tormented the house, hooting in the chimney and rattling the windows in their frames. Small winds, wet and salt, were in the house, couldn't be kept out. In the silences which came momentarily when the wind turned round she could hear her father, in the loft, praying. *Ave Maria gratia plena Dominus tecum benedictas tu in mulieribus.* If her father died this night, that would be right; she, caught up in the vast wasting of human life by the sea and somehow fiercely indifferent, unable to feel pity or shock, wouldn't feel then at her father's death all the guilty anguish she had long expected to feel when at last his strong mad ghost gave up its body. She almost, wrapped in a sudden draught of cold sea air, almost wished for it.

The nearest galleon had begun to break up on the drowned stones of the causeway that lay beyond the spit. Farther off, the seaward ship had lost its battle, and, a loose sail flapping with slow grace like a handkerchief, swept down toward the cliffy places to the south. The third she could no longer see. The sea had thrown it away.

At the other end of the house the unbarred door was opened and shut again. She felt a gust of wind that made her shiver.

"Bar the door, Cormac," she said. She turned with reluctance from the window and went into the narrow tangle of hallway that led to the door. "You're a fool, Cormac Burke," she said, not quite as gently as she had intended, "to come all the way up here in this weather, and to tell me about the ships, is it?"

She stopped then, because the man who turned to face her from barring the door wasn't Cormac Burke. She didn't know him. The water coursing down his mantle and the brim of his hat spattered rapidly on the floor; there was a puddle around his booted feet, and when he stepped toward her the boots made a sodden sound.

"Who are you?" she said, stepping back.

"Not the one you named. One very wet."

They stood facing each other for a long moment. In the darkness of the hall she couldn't see his face. His Irish had a Scotch intonation, and sounded wet as well, as though the water had got into his throat.

"Might I," he said at last, "claim some hospitality of this house? A fire, if you have such a thing? I wouldn't trouble you long." He held up both hands, slowly, as though to show he wasn't armed. The two hands seemed to glow faintly in the dark hall, as silver objects or certain seashells do in dimness.

She came to herself. "Yes, come in," she said. "Warm yourself. I didn't mean to refuse the house."

He stripped off his wet mantle, heavy with water, and followed her into the comparative warmth and light of the main room of the house. He stood a moment looking around him, seeming to take inventory of the place, or as though trying to remember if he had ever been in it before. Then he went to the chimney corner and hung his mantle and hat on a peg there.

"We get few guests," she said.

"I think that's odd," he said. His hair was lank and gray, and his face was white like his hands, though now in the light of the fire and the rushes they seemed not to glow spectrally as they had in the hall. His eyes were large and pale and with some melancholy humorousness in them that was disconcerting.

"Odd? We're far off the traveled roads. It's a long climb up."

"But it's the finest house nearby. A traveler who put out the effort might be likely to find more than a cup of water for himself."

She ought to have resented this calculation, but she couldn't, he said it so frankly. "You must be a skilled traveler then," she said.

"Oh, I am."

"And from where?"

He said a mouth-filling Scotch name she didn't recognize and said his name was Sorley.

"A kinsman of Sorley Boy?"

"No, not of that clan," he said with a faint smile that made her wonder if he was lying, and then wonder why she wondered. "And what's your name?"

"Ineen," she said, and looked away.

"And right too," he said, for Ineen is only "girl" in Irish.

"Ineen Fitzgerald," she said. To another that would have

stopped further inquiry. She felt it wouldn't with this Sorley; and in fact he asked her what one with such a name did living in this northwestern place.

"There's a tale in that," she said, and turned away to the window again. The Spanish ship was stove in now, the breach in its side was evident, it was shipping water and seemed to pant like a dying bull as it rose and fell on the foamy waves. There was flotsam, boards, barrels. Did men cling to them? With a sudden fear she realized that the sea might not take them all, not all those dozens. Some might live, and gain the beach. Spanish men. Spanish soldiers. What would happen then?

"They are only men after all," said Sorley.

So intent was she, had she been all that day, on the ships that she didn't find it odd that he seemed to have read her thoughts.

"All up and down the coast," he said, "from Limerick to Inishowen, they've been putting in, or trying to; breaking up, most of them. Most of the men drowning."

"Why have they come? Why so many?"

"No reason of their own. They never wanted to. They meant to sail and conquer England. The sea and the wind drove them here."

She turned to him. The fire behind him seemed to edge his gray hair with light, to give him a faint, wavering outline.

"How do you come to know so much of it?" Ineen asked him.

"Travel with eyes and ears open."

"You came up from the south, then."

He answered nothing to this. The wind rose to a sudden shriek, and the rain made a fierce hissing in the thatch of the roof. Outside, something loose, a bucket, a rake, went blowing across the yard, making a noise that startled her. In the loft, her father groaned and began the Commination: *"Cursed be he that putteth his trust in Man, that taketh Man for his salvation . . ."*

Sorley looked up toward the dimness of the loft. "What others are in the house?"

"My father. Ill." Mad and dying, the word meant. "Servants. Gone down now to the beach, to watch the ships."

"When the Spanish come on the beach, they will be murdered. Half-drowned they'll come out of the sea and each be struck by a mattock or an axe, or be stoned or sworded to death, till all those not drowned will be just as dead." He said all this calmly and with certainty, as though it had already happened, perhaps years ago. "Ill luck to come up out of the sea, alive, and speak no Irish."

"They never would!" She—a Geraldine, a Norman, of the oldest and highest Norman aristocracy Ireland had, however she might have fallen—had no illusions about the villagers below her; but to murder the Spanish, their true friends, only because they were Spanish—that was too monstrous, too ridiculously savage. Sorley only smiled, his thin fixed smile; she had begun to think he smiled only the way hawks frowned, out of his nature somehow and not his mood.

"Would you have anything to eat?" he said. "I seem to have come a long way on yesterday's dinner."

Called to herself again, reminded of how inhospitable she'd grown in her long exile, she blushed, and went to see what might be in the house. On an impulse she drew a jug of red wine from one of the remaining tuns. When she returned with this, and some herring and a loaf, he was sitting on a stool by the fire, looking at his long pale hands.

"You see how much sea has blown in today," he said. She looked more closely, and saw that his hands were dusted with a fine white glowing powder. "Salt," he said. His face was dusty the same way. She accepted his reason for this without thinking that, while stones and driftwood left long in the sea may become salt-encrusted like that, she had never been, though she often spent whole days walking in sea spray along the beach. She brought him a bowl of water, and he dipped his hands into it; it seemed to hiss faintly. When he withdrew them wet, they had again become glistening and faintly opalescent.

"Now it's seawater in the bowl," he said. "Look into it, Ineen Fitzgerald."

She did look in, apprehensive and not knowing why. The bowl was old dark crockery, thick and cracked. For a strange moment she did seem to see the whole sea, as though she were a gull, or God, looking down on it; the ripples Sorley's hands had made in it lapped its edge as tides lap the edges of the world. She saw something moving over the face of the waters, indistinct and multiform, as though the creatures might be rising to look up at her as she looked down; then she saw it was only a faint reflection of her own face.

She laughed, and looked at Sorley, who was smiling more broadly. Her apprehension was gone. She felt as if she had been playing a children's game with him, and it seemed to make an intimacy between them; an elation almost like the elation of nakedness, of childhood games played naked. It was the same fierce indifferent elation she had felt watching the ships. She was vaguely aware that a charm had been worked on her, a charm like the charm in fast sea breezes and scudding cloud, a charm to make her free.

Stop it now, mad girl, she told herself, too much alone, stop all that. She pulled her shawl around her. Sorley ate herring and bread, delicately, as though he didn't need it for sustenance. He poured wine into a battered cup and tasted it.

"Canary," he said. "And fine, too."

Without really considering it, she took a cup for herself and filled it. "What do you do abroad, Sorley?" she said.

"Looking for a wife, Ineen Fitzgerald," he said, and drank.

I am a man upon the land

On the beach, Cormac Burke stared helplessly at the oblique lines of waves folding together and dashing against the beach with a noise like a rising but never climaxing peal of thunder. His voice was raw from shouting against it. A few shards and pieces were still coming in on the tide: a window frame, a barrel stave. Strung out across the beach in tight, self-defensive knots, the villagers ran from one to another of these treasures and exclaimed over them.

He had tried to organize them into a troop of sorts, armed men in front, then other men, the women to salvage, a priest for the dying. Hopeless. He had tried to explain to them that there were three things that must be done: aid should be given to the hurt; the goods should be rounded up and put in piles; the soldiers must be disarmed and, for the moment, made prisoner, for the English would certainly see them as invaders and any Irish who helped them as rebels. Their arms could be taken from them and hidden; later . . . But it was useless. The sea was mad; and there was no organizing these kerns. They went their own way.

On the beach, now nearly covered in sand, lay three—four— bodies. If he had not known them to be Spaniards he wouldn't now as darkness came on have known they were men. But he knew; he had rushed toward them with the others when they came tumbling from the sea, staggering up like apes from the withdrawing water. They had reached out hands to him: *Auxilio. Succoro, Señores.* And the Irishmen with him, crying out like animals, their faces distended so that he seemed not to know them at all, had murdered them; had almost murdered Cormac when he tried to stop them.

Now he stood farther off, afraid to watch any longer to see more Spaniards come ashore, knowing he would not again try to interfere in the villagers' madness, yet unable to leave. If he had a gun. Tears of frustration and helpless rage mixed with the rain clouding his vision. He turned away from the sea and looked up to where, just raising itself above a coign of rock, the roof of the Fitzgeralds' house could be seen. Was there a light burning? He thought there was.

And what did you do when they came ashore, Cormac?

I could do nothing, and the Spanish were murdered, Ineen.

He pulled his feet from the muddy sand and began to work his way down the shingle, watching the sea and the knots of men, and, far off, the ship, whose masts were now parallel to the slabs of sea that bore it up.

Little ken I my bairn's father

It wasn't the wine, not entirely: though when she went to draw another jug she noticed that her lips and nose itched a little, growing numb, and that filling the jug she was slapdash; she spoke aloud to herself, saying she shouldn't have babbled on to this stranger, and laughed.

She had told him about her father, who had been a priest, and was a cousin of the Earl of Kildare, and how the English had persuaded him to come into the new dispensation and he would be made a bishop by the queen; how he did so, despite all his kin's hatred of him for it; how he renounced his vows and the True Church, and married the frail daughter of an English lord in Dublin.

And was it that his family hated him for it; or that his wife despised him and lived in a continual state of loathing and shock at Irish ways and the Irish until she died, soon after Ineen was born, leaving her loathing behind her, solid as furniture; or that after their promises, and in spite of a hundred letters her father sent to London, and twenty visits to Dublin, the English never began raising her father toward the promised bishopric, not so much as a wardenship—apparently satisfied that promises had been enough to draw him out of his church; or was it that in the end he had lost even the false and empty parish the English had given him, where he preached to nearly nobody, because at last Desmond—his distant cousin too—rose up against the English and heresy, and her father had to be taken off by sea lest he be hanged by his flock: was it that terrible story, or was it God's vengeance at his defection, that had made him mad? The English, as though tossing him away, had placed him in this northern isolation and given him a piece of the wine trade—wine! that with his breath he had once altered in its red heart to the blood of Jesus!—and let him live on a tariff he collected, a useless middleman. Was all that enough to make him mad? Or was God's vengeance needed?

"It hasn't made you mad, Ineen," Sorley said, and she saw that the story had washed over him without altering his features. "And Desmond is dead, who fought for Mother Church. Whose vengeance was that, then?"

She returned now with the brimming jug, and Sorley saluted it with his cup. She filled the cups; two drops splashed out and stained the linen of her sleeve as quick as blood. She dipped the sleeve in the bowl of water, pressing water through it absently. "I wouldn't like to drown," she said. "Not of any way."

"Avoid the sea."

"They say men drowning can see treasures lost in the sea—ships sunk, gold, jewels."

"Do they? And do they have candles with them to light up the darkness?"

She laughed, wiping her mouth. Her father cried out, dreaming; a sob, as though someone were stifling him with a pillow. Another cry, louder. He called her name; he was awake. She waited a moment, feeling vaguely ashamed. Maybe he would sleep again. But again he called her name, his voice edged now with that piteous panic she knew well, which grated on her senses like a rasp. "Yes, Father," she said gently, and went to the press in the corner, from which she took a jar of powder; some of this she mixed into a cup of wine, and, having lit a rushlight at the fire, carried the wine and the light carefully up into the loft.

Her father's white face looked out from the bed curtains, his white cap and large pinkish eyes making him look like a terrified rabbit looking out from its burrow.

"Who is it in the house?" he whispered urgently. "Cormac?"

"Yes," she said, "only Cormac."

She had him drink the wine, and kissed him, and said a prayer with him; then when he groaned again she laid him firmly down, speaking calmly but with authority, as she might to a child. He lay back on the pillows, his stricken eyes still searching her face. She smiled, and drew his curtains.

Sorley sat unchanged by the fire, turning his cup in his fingers.

Why had she lied to her father?

"They say too," she said, taking a gulp of wine, "that there's a bishop under the sea. A fish bishop." She had seen a picture in a bestiary of her father's.

"Certainly," Sorley said. "To marry and bury."

"What rites does he use, do you think?"

"And the mackerel is the fish's bawd. Men!" He shook his head, smiling. "They think even the fish live by the laws they live by. A little handful of folk, huddled up on the dry land that's not a tenth part of the size of the seas, and dreaming of bishops for the fish."

"How is it, then, in the sea?" she said, for some reason not doubting he knew.

"Come with me and see," he said.

Far less the land that he goes in

Where they went, that night, was not seaward though. Cold as his touch was, it was strong, and she would not have been able to resist it even if she'd chosen to do that, which she did not choose. She thought to press her hand against his mouth so that he would not cry aloud, but he was not one who cried aloud.

She slept like one dead, and he was gone when she awoke, and her father too, calling from the loft, but she paid no mind, and got up; felt run down the inside of her thigh a dribble of slime she thought might be blood, but no, she hadn't bled.

He was not gone far. How she knew it she could not have said. She wrapped herself in a warm mantle and went out into the day, where the storm wrack still filled the sky and the sea. The ship she had watched could still be seen, dismasted and clinging to the rocks like unswallowed fragments in a mastiff's mouth. She went down along the way to the beach, and it wasn't long before she saw him striding ahead of her, holding his hat on his head for the offshore breeze. She passed the place where last night the men from the Spanish ship had come ashore; their bodies lay dark and shapeless as seals, half-buried in sand: no place a human soul could rest; they must be buried as Christian men, whatever. She would ask Cormac Burke to help.

He had not turned at all to look at the bodies of the men on the beach, kept on till the turn of the cove and the flat rocks that went out into the sea, where the seals did sometimes lie to bake their cold bodies. He was after tossing away his hat, and then his cloak, and when he came to the rocks he was as naked as he had been in her bed in the night. And when he bent to reach into the seaweed and the crusted stones wedged in the great split of the rocks and found something there to don, she knew whom she had had in her. She had known all along, but now she knew to see and to think: to think what would come of this, now and in the months and years to come.

> And he has tae'en a purse of gold
> And he has placed it on her knee
> Saying "Give to me my little young son
> And take thee up thy nurse's fee.
>
> "And though shalt marry a gunner good
> And a right fine gunner I'm sure he'll be
> And the very first shot that e'er he shoot
> Shall kill both my young son and me."

THE WAR BETWEEN THE OBJECTS
AND THE SUBJECTS

■ ■ ■

HOW LONG THE WAR has gone on is not known, not even to the subjects; its beginning is not remembered by the objects, who cannot remember anything at all, being objects. It began with the opening of metaphorical eyes on the subjects' part, and the appearance before those eyes of the other, obdurate and irreducible—the object. The insult has never been forgiven on the one side, nor acknowledged by the other, which would maintain its entire innocence if it were capable of maintaining anything beyond its simple existence.

The subjects had, from the first, inherent advantages unknown to the objects (who knew nothing). The subjects had the ability to *apprehend*, above all; they also had communication, organization, administration, a chain of command more or less complete, with weak links of course but weak links that were known about at least and therefore perhaps less damaging. They could conceive of orders, and give them. The objects had only extension, multiplicity, and a large number of simple qualities—hardness, softness, color, and so on—which they could put forth more or less continuously in the presence of subjects. The objects had the advantage of numbers, however; there were far, far more of them, and they cared nothing for casualties.

The subjects also had the advantage of being the only ones who understood that a war was being waged, though in the end it is clear that this was not solely an advantage but in certain critical moments actually counted as a disadvantage, even a disaster. Most of the major setbacks of the subjects came just at those moments when their own knowledge, and the obdurate ignorance of the objects, was most apparent to them (to the subjects; the objects knew nothing of it either way). In fact it can be said that any attack of the subjects on the objects could be considered identical to a counterattack of the objects on the subjects.

The original strategy of the objects, metaphorically speaking (objects having no strategies as such), was divide and conquer. What was divided, however, was not the enemy, the subjects, but the objects themselves, in a continuous raid upon the subjects' powers of discrimination, a bewildering (for the subjects) and terrifying (for the subjects) proliferation that could only be opposed by an equally continuous generation of new categories by the enemy. Subjects caught unawares could find themselves suddenly surrounded by crowds of discrete and well-furnished objects, whose numbers quickly rose to virtual infinity as the trapped subject shifted its consciousness here to there in rising panic. Grains of sand, items of scenery, vegetation parts, incoming waves, stars, inches, geometrical figures, tools, all had to be instantly forced into the right categories or at least into categories perceived as correct by the battling subject, whose consciousness rapidly filled, reaching toxic levels that could result in sudden loss of apprehension, and therefore reduction to object status, at least temporarily: a state referred to (by the subjects) as "pawn capture."

The objects' strategy had an advantage and a disadvantage, from the objects' point of view, a point of view which certainly did not exist. The advantage was that only the subjects could perceive the objects' strategy, and therefore in every encounter between subjects and objects the subjects became immediately (even anteriorly) involved in carrying it out. The disadvantage was the same as the advantage: every perception of the objects by the subjects, which could have been counted as a victory by the objects if they could have counted, was also counted as a victory by the subjects; the more objects there were perceived to be, the more of them could be considered (by the subjects) to have been captured.

For a very long time now the victory has hung in the balance as the two sides march and countermarch. But wars of attrition (which is essentially what the subjects were engaged in) can only end in one way, if the courage and application of the side engaged in the attrition of the other remains high—and this is the one thing the subjects can be sure of, that they will never, in effect can never, surrender, cease, or even pause for a moment in reducing further objects to cognition.

The objects, of course, don't see it that way. No relentless production of new categories by the subjects can effectually reduce their numbers. The subjects may believe that very capacious categories—categories such as "all that stuff," "things out there," "this and everything like it," "big things," "matter," and so on will eventually cause the objects to surrender willy-nilly (the only way in which they could surrender). But the objects do not, agree, in fact cannot. All that the objects can be said to know, or to behave *as if* they knew, which itself is a distinction that only the subjects can make—what the subjects in their dark watches and lonely trenches suspect that the objects really somehow *do* know in their unimaginable nonexistent hearts—is that the subjects' categories are in fact only further objects. There is no end.

There is no end. Only the subjects understand this, as well as everything else that is understood. There will be, can be no final annihilation of the objects: that is the vow, the promise implicit in all the strategies and all the tactics of both sides. The war may go badly, has gone badly since the beginning for the objects on many fronts, but it will never be over: will not be over until the last subject finally closes its eyes in sleep or death, and knows no more.

Permissions

▐ Perennial

Books by John Crowley:

Novelties & Souvenirs: *Collected Short Fiction*
ISBN 0-380-73106-1 (paperback)

The complete collected short fiction—fifteen stories and novellas in all—of one of the most critically acclaimed writers of our time. Includes works previously collected in *Novelty* and *Antiquities*, a new novella previously available only as a limited edition chapbook, and three other short stories.

The Translator
ISBN 0-380-81537-0 (paperback)

In 1962, Kit Malone, a young woman with a troubled past, finds herself in a college class taught by exiled Russian poet Innokenti Falin. The two forge a friendship, she becomes his translator, and a delicate love grows between them. Years later, Kit realizes that while the country held its breath against the threat of war, she was helping Falin make a decision that would change the course of history.

"Grand and serious, involving nothing less than the souls of nations and the transforming power of language." —*New York Times Book Review*

Little, Big
ISBN 0-06-093793-9 (paperback)

The epic story of Smoky Barnable—an anonymous young man whose life takes a magical turn the day he meets and falls in love with a unique woman named Daily Alice Drinkwater. Daily Alice lives in a mysterious place that cannot be found on a map. In this palatial manor lives a family with ties to other worlds; as their history is revealed to Smoky, he discovers that he, too, is part of a much larger tale.

"Prose that Scott Fitzgerald would envy and a heartbreaking love story."
—Michael Dirda, *Washington Post Book World*

Otherwise: *Three Novels by John Crowley*
ISBN 0-06-093792-0 (paperback)

This volume contains three of award-winning author John Crowley's critically acclaimed short novels: *Beasts*, *Engine Summer*, and *The Deep*.